The stirring story of the life and times of Richard Bolitho is told in Alexander Kent's bestselling novels.

1756   Born Falmouth, son of James Bolitho

1768   Entered the King's service as a Midshipman on *Manxman*

1772   Midshipman, *Gorgon* (*Midshipman Bolitho*)

1774   Promoted Lieutenant, *Destiny*: Rio and the Caribbean (*Stand into Danger*)

1775–7   Lieutenant, *Trojan*, during the American Revolution. Later appointed prizemaster (*In Gallant Company*)

1778   Promoted Commander, *Sparrow*. Battle of the Chesapeake (*Sloop of War*)

1780   Birth of Adam, illegitimate son of Hugh Bolitho and Karenza Pascoe

1782   Promoted Captain, *Phalarope*; West Indies: Battle of Saints (*To Glory We Steer*)

1784   Captain, *Undine*; India and East Indies (*Command a King's Ship*)

1787   Captain, *Tempest*; Great South Sea; Tahiti; suffered serious fever (*Passage to Mutiny*)

1792   Captain, the *Nore*; Recruiting (*With All Despatch*)

1793   Captain, *Hyperion*; Mediterranean; Bay of Biscay; West Indies. Adam Pascoe, later Bolitho, enters the King's service as a midshipman aboard *Hyperion* (*Form Line of Battle!* And *Enemy in Sight*)

1795   Promoted Flag Captain, *Euryalus*; involved in the Great Mutiny; Mediterranean; Promoted Commodore (*The Flag Captain*)

1798   Battle of the Nile (*Signal – Close Action!*)

1800   Promoted Rear-Admiral; Baltic; (*The Inshore Squadron*)

1801   Biscay. Prisoner of war (*A Tradition of Victory*)

1802   Promoted Vice-Admiral; West Indies (*Success to the Brave*)

1803   Mediterranean (*Colours Aloft!*)

1805   Battle of Trafalgar (*Honour This Day*)

1806–7   Good Hope and the second battle of Copenhagen (*The Only Victor*)

1808   Shipwrecked off Africa (*Beyond the Reef*)

1809–10   Mauritius campaign (*The Darkening Sea*)

1812   Promoted Admiral; Second American War (*For My Country's Freedom*)

1814   Defence of Canada (*Cross of St. George*)

1815   Richard Bolitho killed in action (*Sword of Honour*) Adam Bolitho, Captain, *Unrivalled*. Mediterranean (*Second to None*)

1816   Anti-slavery patrols, Sierra Leone. Battle of Algiers (*Relentless Pursuit*)

1817   Flag Captain, *Athena*; Antigua and Caribbean (*Man of War*)

1818   Captain, *Onward*; Mediterranean (*Heart of Oak*)

Also by Alexander Kent

Midshipman Bolitho
Stand Into Danger
In Gallant Company
Sloop of War
To Glory We Steer
Command a King's Ship
Passage to Mutiny
With All Despatch
Form Line of Battle!
Enemy in Sight
The Flag Captain
Signal – Close Action!
The Inshore Squadron
A Tradition of Victory
Success to the Brave
Colours Aloft!
Honour This Day
The Only Victor
Beyond the Reef
The Darkening Sea
Cross of St George
Sword of Honour
Second to None
Relentless Pursuit
Man of War
Band of Brothers

For My Country's Freedom

Alexander Kent

arrow books

Reissued in the United Kingdom by Arrow Books in 2007

1 3 5 7 9 10 8 6 4 2

First published in the United Kingdom in 1995 by William Heinemann
First published in paperback in 1996 by Pan Books

Arrow Books
The Random House Group Limited
20 Vauxhall Bridge Road, London SW1V 2SA

Addresses for companies within The Random House Group Limited
can be found at:
www.randomhouse.co.uk

The Random House Group Limited Reg. No. 954009

A CIP catalogue record for this book
is available from the British Library

ISBN 9780099502296

The Random House Group Limited makes every effort to ensure
that the papers used in its books are made from trees that have been
legally sourced from well-managed and credibly certified forests.
Our paper procurement policy can be found at:
www.randomhouse.co.uk/paper.htm

Printed and bound in Great Britain by
Cox & Wyman Ltd, Reading, Berkshire

For Kim
With my love.
The World is ours.

Yet, Freedom! yet thy banner, torn but flying,
Still streams like the thunderstorm against the wind.

– Byron, 1812

Contents

PART I: 1811

PART II: 1812

PART I: 1811

1

Regrets

Lady Catherine Somervell reined in the big mare and patted her neck with a gloved hand.

'Not long now, Tamara. We'll soon be home.'

Then she sat very still and upright in the saddle, her dark eyes looking out across the sea. It was close to noon on this first day of March 1811, and a strange misty vapour had already covered the track she had taken to visit John Allday and his new wife Unis. She could not believe that they had all been left alone for so long, untroubled by the Admiralty in London. Two and a half months, the longest time she and Richard Bolitho had ever spent together in their own home in Cornwall.

She tossed the fur-lined hood from her head and the damp air brought more colour to her face. When she looked directly south Rosemullion Head, which guarded the mouth of the Helford River, was also lost in mist, and it was only three miles distant. She was on the upper coastal track, much of the lower one having crumbled into the sea in the January storms.

And yet there were signs of spring. Wagtails darting

3

along the bank of the Helford River in their quaint diving, haphazard flight; jackdaws too, like companionable clerics on the stone walls. The ragged trees that crested the nearest hill were still leafless, their stooping branches shining from a sudden fall of rain. Nevertheless there were tiny brush strokes of yellow to mark the early daffodils that flourished there, despite the salt spray from the Channel and the Western Approaches.

Catherine urged the mare forward again, her mind lingering on the past, clinging to the weeks of freedom they had enjoyed without restraint. After the first embrace, when Bolitho had returned from the Mauritius campaign and the destruction of Baratte's privateers, she had worried that he might become restless because he was not involved with his ships and men, secretly troubled that the navy for which he had done and given so much was neglecting him.

But the love they had reawakened upon their reunion was stronger than ever, if such things were possible. Walking and riding together in spite of the inclement weather, visiting the families on the estate and, when it could not be avoided, attending more splendid occasions at the grand house of Lewis Roxby, Richard's brother-in-law and aptly nicknamed the King of Cornwall. The celebrations had marked Roxby's unexpected acquisition of a knighthood. She smiled. There would be no holding him now . . .

And what of worldly events? She had watched Richard for the usual signs of uneasiness, but there had been none. She thought of the passion and the delicate touches of love they had shared. There was nothing she did not know about her man any more.

4

And much had changed. Sir Paul Sillitoe's prediction had come true just a month ago. King George III had been declared insane and separated from all power and authority, and the Prince of Wales had become Regent until the day he would be crowned King. Some people had hinted uncharitably it was because of the Prince Regent's influence that Roxby had been knighted. Although his new title had supposedly been bestowed in recognition of his patriotic work as a magistrate and as the founder of a local militia at the time of a feared French invasion, some claimed it was because the Regent was also the Duke of Cornwall, and he would be quick to perceive Roxby's usefulness as an ally.

She looked at the sea, no longer a rival as she had once feared. Her shoulder was still burned from the sun in the longboat after the loss of the *Golden Plover* on the hundred-mile reef. Could it be two years ago? She had suffered alongside the other survivors. But she and Richard had been together, and had shared it even to the threshold of death.

There was no sun visible in the pale clouds, but the sea managed to hold its reflection, so that the undulating swell appeared to be lit from below as if by a giant lantern.

She had left Richard in the house to complete some letters for the afternoon mail coach that left from the square in Falmouth. She knew that one was for the Admiralty: there were no secrets between them now. She had even explained her own visit to Whitechapel, and the aid she had accepted from Sillitoe.

Bolitho had said quietly, 'I never thought I would trust that man.'

5

She had held him in her arms in their bed and whispered, 'He helped me when there was no one else. But a rabbit should never turn its back on a fox.'

Of the Admiralty letter he had said only, 'Someone must have read my report on the Mauritius campaign, and the need for more frigates. But I can scarce believe that a wind of change has blown through those dusty corridors!'

Another day he had been standing with her on the headland below Pendennis Castle, his eyes the same colour as the grey waters that moved endlessly, even to the horizon.

She had asked, 'Would you never accept high office at the Admiralty?'

He had turned to look at her, his voice determined and compelling. 'When it is time for me to quit the sea, Kate, it will be time to leave the navy, for good.' He had given his boyish smile, and the lines of strain had vanished. 'Not that they would ask me, of all people.'

She had heard herself say quietly, 'Because of me, because of us – that is the real truth.'

'It is not a price, Kate my darling, but a reward.'

She thought, too, of young Adam Bolitho. His frigate *Anemone* was lying at Plymouth, in the dockyard after her long voyage from Mauritius by way of the Cape and Gibraltar. She had been so savaged in her final embrace with Baratte's privateers that her pumps had been worked for every mile she was homeward bound.

Adam was coming to Falmouth today. She heard the clock chime from the church of King Charles the Martyr, where Bolithos had been christened, married

6

and laid to rest for generations. It would be good for Richard to have some time with his nephew. She doubted if he would raise the matter of Valentine Keen's wife. Confrontation was not the way to deal with it.

She considered Allday, when she had called at the little inn at Fallowfield, the Old Hyperion. A local painter had done the inn sign – *the old lady down to the last gun-port*, as Allday had proclaimed proudly after his marriage, the week before Christmas. But his fresh-faced little wife Unis, herself no stranger to the *Hyperion*, in which her previous husband had died, had confided that Allday was deeply troubled, and fretting that Sir Richard might leave him ashore when he accepted his next appointment.

She had spoken out of great affection for this big shambling sailor, not from jealousy that the navy would come between them. And she had shown pride too, acceptance of the rare bond that held vice-admiral and coxswain firmly together.

Catherine had said, 'I know. I must face it as you do. It is for our sakes that our men are out there, in constant risk from sea and cannon alike. *For us*.' She was not sure she had convinced her.

She smiled and tasted salt on her lips. *Or myself either*.

The mare quickened her pace as she reached the new road which had been laid by some of Roxby's French prisoners-of-war. Catherine suspected that it was due to their efforts that Roxby's own house and gardens were always so immaculate. Like most other estates in the county, the Bolitho land was tended mostly by old men and cripples thrown on the beach by the navy they had served. Without an authorised protection any younger man would be snatched up by the ever-greedy press-gangs. Even the protection might not help on a dark night with a man-of-war tugging at her cable, and her captain not too eager to question his returning press.

She saw the roof of the old grey house showing above the last fold in the hillside. Would Adam have any news? He would certainly notice how well his uncle looked. Exercise, good food and rest . . . Her mouth twitched. And love, which had left them breathless.

She had often wondered if Adam resembled his father in any way. There was no portrait of Hugh in the house; and she guessed that Bolitho's father had made certain of that after Hugh had disgraced himself and the family name. Not because of his gambling, the resulting debts from which had almost crippled the estate until Richard's success as a frigate captain had brought prize money to clear them. Hugh had even killed a fellow officer in a duel related to gambling.

All that, their father could possibly have forgiven. But to desert the navy and fight on the side of the Americans in their war of independence: that had been beyond everything. She thought of all the grave-eyed portraits that lined the walls and the landing. They seemed to watch and assess her whenever she climbed the stairs. Surely *they* had not all been saints?

A stable-lad took the bridle and Catherine said, 'A good rub down, eh?' She saw another horse munching busily in the stables, and a blue and gold saddle-cloth. Adam was already here.

8

She tossed her head and allowed her long dark hair to fall free on her shoulders.

As she opened the double doors she saw them standing by the great log fire. They could have been brothers, black hair and the Bolitho features she saw repeated in the portraits, the faces she had studied while this house had become a home around her. Her eyes settled only briefly on the table, and the canvas envelope which bore the Admiralty's fouled-anchor cipher. She had somehow known it would be there. It was a shock, nonetheless.

She smiled and held out her arms as Adam came to greet her. Richard would have seen her glance and her momentary dismay.

There was the true enemy.

Lieutenant George Avery stood at the window of his room and watched the bustling throngs of people and vehicles. It was market day in Dorchester: haggling over prices, country people coming in from the farms and villages to sell and buy. The taverns would be full by now.

He walked to a plain looking-glass and studied his reflection as he might examine a fledgling midshipman.

He was still surprised that he had decided to accept Sir Richard Bolitho's invitation to remain as his flag-lieutenant. He had sworn often enough that if the offer of a command were made, no matter how small or lowly, he would snatch it. He was old for his rank; he would not see thirty again. He stared critically at the well-fitting uniform, with the twist of gold lace on the left shoulder to denote his appointment as Sir Richard Bolitho's aide. Avery would never forget the day he had first met the famous admiral at his house in Falmouth. He had not expected Bolitho to accept him in the appointment, even though he was Sir Paul Sillitoe's nephew, for he hardly knew his uncle and could not imagine why he had put forth his name for consideration.

He still had nightmares about the experience which had almost cost him his life. As second-in-command of a small schooner, *Jolie*, formerly a French prize, he had been content, and excited by the dashing encounters with enemy traders. But his youthful captain, also a lieutenant, had become too confident, and taken too many risks. He could almost hear himself describing him to Bolitho during that first interview. *I thought him reckless, Sir Richard.* They had been surprised by a French corvette, which had swept around a headland and had raked them before they could stand away. The young captain had been cut in half in the first broadside, and moments later Avery had been struck down, badly wounded. Helplessly he had seen his men hauling down the ensign, the fight gone out of them in the overwhelming ferocity of the attack.

As a prisoner-of-war Avery had endured agony and despair at the hands of the French surgeons. It was not that they had not cared or been indifferent to his suffering. Their lack of resources had been a direct result of the English blockade, an irony he often remembered.

The brief Peace of Amiens, which had served only to allow the old enemies to lick their wounds and restore their ships and defences, had led to Avery's early discharge, an exchange with one of the French prisoners. On his return to England there had been no congratulations, or rewards for his past bravery. Instead he had faced a court-martial. Eventually he had been found not guilty of cowardice or of hazarding the ship. But the little *Jolie* had struck her colours to the enemy so, wounded or not, he was reprimanded, and would have remained a lieutenant for the rest of his service.

Until that day some eighteen months ago when Bolitho had given him the post of flag-lieutenant. It had been a new door opening for Avery, a new life, which he had learned to share with one of England's heroes: a man whose deeds and courage had stirred the heart of a nation.

He smiled at himself in the glass and saw the younger man appear. For only a moment his habitual expression of wariness vanished, as did the lines around his mouth. But the streaks of grey in his dark brown hair and the stiff way he held his shoulder, as the result of his wound and its treatment, gave the lie to what he saw.

He heard someone at the front door and glanced around his room: a bare, simple place without personality. Like the house itself, the vicarage where his father, a strict but kindly man, had brought him up. Avery's sister Ethel, who herself had married a clergyman when their father had been killed by a runaway horse in the street, still lived here with her husband.

He clipped on his sword and reached for his cocked hat, the gold lace still as bright as the day eighteen

11

months ago when he had gone to Joshua Miller, the tailor in Falmouth. For two generations the Miller family had been making uniform clothing for the Bolitho family although few could remember how it had all begun. Bolitho had outfitted him on his appointment as flag-lieutenant. That too had been another kindness, characteristic of the man he had come to know so well, even if he still did not fully understand him. His charisma, which he himself did not seem to know that he possessed; the way in which those closest to him were ever protective. His *little crew* as he called them: his burly coxswain Allday, his round-shouldered Devonian secretary Yovell, and not least his personal servant Ozzard, a man without a past.

He put some money on the table for his sister. She would get precious little from her miserly husband. Avery had heard him leave the vicarage very early on some mission of mercy, or to murmur a few words before a local felon was dropped from the gallows. He smiled to himself. If he was really a man of God, the Lord should be warned to begin recruiting his own little crew!

The door opened and his sister stood in the passageway, watching him as though unwilling for him to leave.

She had the same dark hair as Avery and her eyes, like her brother's, were tawny, like a cat's. Apart from that, there was little resemblance. He found it hard to accept that she was only twenty-six, her body worn out by child-bearing. She had four children but had lost two others along the way. It was harder still to recall her as a girl. She had been lovely then.

12

She said, 'The carter's here, George. He'll take your chest to the stage at the King's Arms.' She stared at him as he took her and held her closely. 'I *know* you must go, George, but it's been so lovely to have you here. To talk, and that . . .' When she was distressed, her Dorset accent was more pronounced.

Downstairs two of the children were screaming, but she did not seem to notice. She said suddenly, 'I wish I'd seen Lady Somervell, like you have.'

Avery held her more tightly. She had often asked him about Catherine, what she did, how she spoke with him, how she dressed. He stroked the drab clothing his sister had worn throughout his visit.

Once he had mentioned Catherine when Ethel's husband had been in the room. He had snapped in his reedy voice, 'A godless woman! I'll not hear her name in my house!'

Avery had retorted, 'I thought this was one of God's houses, sir.'

They had not spoken since. That was why he had quit the vicarage early, he supposed, so that they would not have to lie to one another with brotherly farewells.

All at once Avery needed to leave. 'I'll tell the carter to go now. I shall walk to the stage.' Once he would have avoided walking in the streets. Although a county town, it was usually sprinkled with sea officers. Dorchester was a popular place for naval families to buy houses, being within easy reach of Weymouth Bay, Portland and Lyme. He had seen too many such officers cross the road to avoid him when he had been recovering from his wound and awaiting a court-martial.

13

Being with Bolitho had changed all that. *But it will never change my feelings towards them*.

He embraced her again and felt her tired body against his. Where had the young girl gone?

'I'll send money, Ethel.' He felt her nod, too choked by tears to speak. 'The war will be over soon. I'll be on the beach then.' He thought of Bolitho's calm acceptance of his situation, what Allday had told him about his damaged eye, what the confidence had cost him. *At least I could be in no better company*.

Down those so-familiar stairs, bare-boarded to avoid waste, as the vicar had put it. Avery had noticed, however, that he kept a very good cellar. Past the room where his father had begun his education. At any other time the reminiscence would have made him smile. How Yovell had immediately accepted him in their *little crew* because he could speak and write Latin. Strange how, indirectly, that ability had saved the life of Rear-Admiral Herrick, Bolitho's friend.

He said, 'The roads should be better now. I'll be in Falmouth the day after tomorrow.'

She looked up at him and he thought he saw the young girl watching him through the mask.

'I'm so proud of you, George.' She wiped her face with her apron. 'You'll never know how much!'

Out on the street the carter took his money and touched his hat to the vicar's wife.

Then they kissed. Afterwards as he walked through the market Avery recalled it with distress. She had kissed him like a woman, perhaps one who had only just remembered how it could have been.

At the corner of the street he saw the coach with its

14

Royal Mail insignia standing by the inn. Its shafts were empty of horses but servants were already making luggage fast on the roof.

He turned and looked back at the street where he had grown up, but she had disappeared.

Two midshipmen on some mission or other passed him, doffing their hats in salute. Avery did not even notice them.

The knowledge hit him like a blow. He was never going to see her again.

John Allday paused in tamping tobacco into one of his long pipes, and, without lighting it, walked to the inn door.

For a long moment he looked up at the bright new sign, swinging now in the breeze. Although he could not see the Channel from here, he could picture it without effort. The wind had backed a piece since morning, and the tide would be on the ebb. He could see Falmouth, too, in his thoughts: ships shortening their cables, waiting to weigh and take advantage of wind and tide. Men-of-war, although not too many of them; the famous Falmouth packets; fishermen and lobster boats. He would get used to it. I *must*. He heard the solitary chime of the tiny parish church. His eyes softened. Where he and Unis had been wed just over two months back. He had never known such warmth, such unexpected love. He had always had an eye for 'a pretty craft', as he had put it on occasions, but Unis had surpassed them all.

The men would be leaving the fields soon; it was still dark too early to work long hours.

He heard Unis's brother, another John, preparing tankards and moving benches, the thud of his wooden leg marking his progress around the parlour. A fine man, an ex-soldier from the old 31st Foot, the Huntingdonshires. It was good to know he had his cottage next door to the inn, and would be able to help Unis when he was back at sea.

Her ladyship had ridden all the way over to Fallowfield, and had tried to reassure him. But one of the coachmen who had been here for some ale and a pasty or two had told him about the letter for Sir Richard from the Admiralty, and Allday could think of nothing else.

He heard Unis's light step come in the other door, and turned to see her watching him, a basket of freshly-gathered eggs in her arms.

'You still worrying, my dear?'

Allday re-entered the parlour and tried to laugh it off.

'It's all new to me, y'see?'

She looked around the room, at the four-and-a-half-gallon pins of ale on their trestles. Clean cloths fresh today, new bread to tempt any hardworking farm labourer on his way home. A place that offered a welcome: it looked pleased with itself.

'New to me too, now that I've got my man with me.' She smiled gently: 'Don't you worry about it. You've got my heart, and I daresay I'll take it badly when you go, and *go you will*. I shall be safe enough. Just you promise to come back to me.' She turned away towards the kitchen so that he should not see the making of a tear in her eye. 'I'll fetch you a wet, John.'

Her brother straightened his back from putting more logs on the fire and looked at Allday gravely.

'Soon, you reckon?'

Allday nodded. 'He'll be off to London first. I should be with him.'

'Not this time, John. You've Unis now. I was lucky – I lost a leg for King an' Country, though I didn't think so at the time. A cannon don't *care*. So make the most of what you have.'

Allday picked up his unlit pipe and smiled as his new wife entered with a tankard of rum.

He said, 'You knows what a man needs, my love!'

She wagged her finger and chuckled. 'You're a bad lad, John Allday!'

Across the parlour her brother relaxed, and Allday was glad. But how could he really understand? He had only been a soldier, so why should he?

Lady Catherine Somervell paused at the turn of the stairway and pulled her gown more tightly about her body. After the warmth of the great four-poster bed and the fire in the room, the air was cold around her bare feet and ankles.

She had gone to bed earlier than usual to give Richard the opportunity to speak with his nephew alone. Later they had come upstairs together, and she thought she had heard Adam stagger when he reached the door of his room.

Throughout the evening meal he had been strained and unusually subdued. They had talked of his homeward journey, and of *Anemone*, docked to replace some of the copper damaged when she had been hulled by crossfire from Baratte's privateers. Adam had looked up from his plate and for those few seconds she had seen the familiar animation, the pride in his *Anemone*.

'She took a beating, but by God, beneath the copper her timbers are as sound as a bell!'

He had mentioned that the brig *Larne* was also in Plymouth. She had brought despatches from Good Hope, but she was to remain in Plymouth to undergo an overhaul to spars and rigging. It was hardly surprising. *Larne* had been continuously at sea for nearly four years, in everything from blazing heat to screaming gales.

Watching Richard, she thought he had somehow expected it. Another twist of fate, perhaps, that would bring James Tyacke back to England: that brave, proud man, *the devil with half a face* as the Arab slavers had dubbed him. How he would loathe Plymouth, the pitiless and horrified stares each time he showed his terrible scars to the busy world of that naval port.

Adam had confirmed that Tyacke had sent his first lieutenant to London with the despatches, although a captain would normally be expected to pay homage in person to the Admiralty.

Catherine saw a candle flickering on the small table where the stairs turned down into semi-darkness. She must have fallen asleep again after hearing them come up. When she had reached out for her man she had found his place empty.

She felt herself shiver, as though someone were watching her. She looked up at the nearest portrait,

18

Rear-Admiral Denziel Bolitho, perhaps more like Richard than any of the others. He was his grandfather, and the likeness was very strong: the same eyes, and hair as black as a raven. Denziel was the only other Bolitho to have reached flag rank, and now Richard had risen higher than them all, the youngest vice-admiral on the Navy List since Nelson's death. She shivered again, but not from the cold night air. Richard had told her he would give it all away – for her, for them.

Richard had often spoken about his grandfather but had admitted he could not really remember him. He had created his impressions from what his father Captain James had told him, and of course from the portrait. With the smoke of battle in the background, Denziel was depicted at Quebec supporting Wolfe. The painter had caught the other man, the man behind the uniform. There was humour in his eyes and mouth. Had he had a mistress, as his grandson did?

Now that her eyes had become accustomed to the gloom she could see a faint glow from the great fire, then she saw Bolitho. He was sitting on the rug with one arm supporting himself against a chair, the chair where his father had used to sit and read to him. As if he could not bear to look beyond the window, to be reminded that the sea was out there. Waiting, always waiting for the next Bolitho. A goblet of brandy stood by the hearth, catching the dying embers like a magnifying glass.

Bolitho opened his eyes and stared at her, and she imagined he thought he was caught in a dream.

He made to rise but she slipped down to his side

19

and raked the embers until there was a lively flicker again.

Bolitho dragged off his coat and threw it over her shoulders. 'Forgive me, Kate, I fell asleep! I had no idea . . .'

She touched his mouth with her fingers. 'It is nothing. I'm glad I woke.'

Catherine watched his profile, his emotions clear in spite of the shadows. So many times they had sat here like this, talking, listening, needing one another. He was never impatient with her, even when they had discussed her purchase of the collier brig, *Maria José*. Another man, another sailor might have thought it rash. He had merely said, 'We shall have to see when the season begins. It is a bold venture but, even if we fail, the vessel will increase in value.' Always *we*. Even when they were parted, they were always together.

He said suddenly, 'Adam told me.'

She waited, feeling his pain like her own, but she said nothing.

Bolitho continued, 'He is in hell because of it, and because of what he believes it may do to me.'

'Will it?'

He held her more tightly around the shoulders. 'Who am I to rebuke him? I took you from another, as I took Cheney.' He looked at her, startled at hearing the name again from his own mouth. 'He wanted to leave immediately. In his condition he would have killed himself on those damned roads.'

'I came to you willingly. I loved you, I always did. If I have one regret, it is the waste of years before you found me.'

20

He looked into the fire. 'It happened after *Golden Plover* was reported lost. Zenoria was here and, like you, she awakened in the night. Adam was a boy again, crying his heart out because he thought you and I were dead. Val was thought missing as well.' He shook his head. 'What a lot that damnable vessel has to answer for!'

'We were *together*, dearest of men . . .'

'I know. I think of it often.'

She asked, 'Did he tell you everything?'

Bolitho nodded slowly. 'They were lovers, perhaps even in love. But when the news broke that we had been rescued by *Larne* the deed was already done. I do not know how Zenoria feels about it – she has a good husband and a child now. It was an act of need, not madness or deceit.' He looked at her squarely and touched her hair with great care. 'But Adam is in love with her. It is a secret he must keep, and so must she.'

'I am so glad he told you. You of all people mean so much to him.'

'There is a letter.'

She tensed as he continued. 'In despair he wrote to her. Last year sometime. That will be the test. We must wait and hope.'

Catherine picked up the goblet. It was quite hot from the fire. She felt him watching her as she swallowed some cognac. 'When will you know, Richard, about London?'

He sounded almost relieved to change the subject. 'Their lordships seem very considerate about it.'

Catherine drank more cognac and felt it burning on her lips. There was more to come.

She asked, 'Sir James Hamett-Parker has gone, I believe?'

He nodded. 'Oblivion. There is another in his place. Admiral Sir Graham Bethune. He should do well.'

She turned to face him. 'You have often said that the navy is like a family. But you have not mentioned him before.'

'It was a long time ago. I lost account of him. A good deal younger than Hamett-Parker, which will be a change for the better.'

She asked softly, 'Younger than *you*, Richard?'

Bolitho replied, 'He was a midshipman when I got my first command, in *Sparrow*, as a matter of fact.' He seemed to consider her question. 'Yes, he is younger. About four years, I would think.' He looked at her steadily and she guessed if it were light enough he would have the same expression as Adam when he spoke of his *Anemone*, the defiance and the pride. 'I was only twenty-two when I took command. That was in Antigua as well.'

'It does not seem right that he should be able to give you orders.'

He smiled. 'My tiger again! The navy works in strange ways. Luck, patronage, fate determine seniority, not always ability. Remember that Our Nel was ten years younger than Collingwood at Trafalgar, but they were still good friends.'

He took her hands and they stood up together.

Bolitho said, 'To bed now, or my girl will curse me in the morning!'

She glanced down at the rug. Where it must have

happened. It was easy to imagine Adam's feelings when he had been in this room.

She answered quietly, 'Not a girl any more, darling Richard. I am a woman now, with all a woman's passions. Hates too, when necessary.'

They walked arm-in-arm to the stairs. The solitary candle had gone out and the grey-eyed rear-admiral was in darkness.

They paused on the stairs and listened to the house, the creaks and tiny sounds which gave it life.

Bolitho said, 'They will offer me a new appointment, another flagship. I shall meet you in London. First I shall need to go to Plymouth.'

She watched him. It never failed to surprise her that he could think of so many things at once.

'I would not wish to involve you, Kate, or let anybody think he was being manipulated.'

'You are going to see James Tyacke.'

'Yes. I cannot bear to be parted from you. Every hour is precious now.'

Tyacke came to her mind as vividly as if he were in the room with them. He would be an attractive man but for the side of his face, which looked as if it had been clawed off by some terrible beast. She remembered when they had sighted *Larne* bearing down on them after the suffering and death they had witnessed; and the offer of a yellow gown, which Tyacke had kept hidden in his sea-chest, to cover her sunburned body. The gown bought for the girl who had rejected him after his injury. He was worth a better woman than she could ever have been.

Bolitho said simply, 'I want him to be my flag-captain.'

She said, 'He will never accept. I am not even certain that he should.'

Bolitho guided her to the last stairs. Then he said, 'That is the cruelty of it, Kate. I *need* him. I cannot manage without him.'

Later as they lay in the big four-poster, she considered what he had said.

And what he had not said. About his impaired vision and what might happen if the other eye was injured. He must have a captain he could trust. No wonder Richard wanted to meet Tyacke alone. He must never think that Richard was using her presence to persuade him into accepting the promotion and all it stood for. And what it would demand of him.

She pressed her body against his and murmured, 'Whatever you do, dearest of men, I shall be waiting.'

The next sound she heard was a cock crowing, and she had not been dreaming.

2

More Than Loyalty

The small unmarked carriage, its windows and doors streaked with mud from the rutted roads, paused only briefly at the gates to Plymouth dockyard in order to allow the passengers to be identified. As the wheels clanged over the cobbles Bolitho guessed that the youthful Royal Marine lieutenant in charge of the guard was probably staring after them, his mouth likely still open.

His arrival at Plymouth was a private one. He tried to smile, if only for his flag-lieutenant's benefit, but the effort was too much. It would not be private for much longer. The Royal Marine was no doubt already on his way to the port admiral's house. *Sir Richard Bolitho is here, sir!*

Bolitho clung to the window-strap and peered across the cluttered dockyard, unaware of Avery's curious stare. Of all the naval ports in England, Plymouth was most familiar to him. Here he had been parted from Catherine and had left for the Mauritius campaign. Avery had been with him then, their first commission together. Avery had kept his distance, had felt his way,

25

too hurt by what had happened to him after the court-martial to trust even his own judgement. *How he has changed.* Perhaps they both had.

'We shall walk the rest of the way.'

Avery rapped on the roof and the horses stamped to a halt.

Bolitho stepped down and felt the edge of the wind on his face. The rolling hills beyond the River Tamar were lush green. Just a river, and yet it separated him from Cornwall, his home. It looked dark and muddy, hardly surprising after all the heavy rain.

'She's over yonder.' He wondered if Avery had been aware of his withdrawn silences during the uncomfortable journey. He might even resent it now that he had returned to be his aide, having probably killed all chance of promotion for himself, let alone a command.

Bolitho looked at him now, at the strong, intelligent profile, and said, 'In truth, I am bad company. So much began and ended here.'

Avery nodded. He had been thinking of that other visit when he had seen Bolitho take leave of his lovely Catherine over at the Golden Lion. And of his own emotions when the big frigate *Valkyrie* had broken out Bolitho's flag at the foremast truck. It had been like being reborn, taken back again by the navy which had been ready to reject him.

Bolitho fell in step beside him and together they walked along the wall, their boat-cloaks hiding their uniforms and rank from any zealous onlookers aboard the many ships undergoing repair.

Avery recalled very clearly how they had stopped at

26

another dock in this same yard, and Bolitho had told him about his old seventy-four, *Hyperion*, when she had lain here, little more than a shattered hulk after surviving the greatest battle of her career up to that time. But *Hyperion* had lived again, had become a legend, and was still remembered in ballads around the taverns, songs about her last fight, when she had gone down with Bolitho's flag still flying. It was likely flying yet in the depths where she lay, her people only shadows now, where they had fallen. But they lived still in the minds of men like Sir Richard Bolitho and his faithful coxswain John Allday. They had been there. They would never forget.

Bolitho halted and looked down at the brig *Larne* of fourteen guns. How small she seemed, too small for the great oceans; but when Tyacke had gone against all reason and experience and had persisted in looking for their tiny longboat after *Golden Plover* had gone down, *Larne* had burst out of the spray like a giant.

Bolitho saw a marine picket on the jetty. To ensure that nobody deserted, even men who had been away from home for many months or years. It was an insult. James Tyacke was one captain who would never have to mark *run* against a seaman's name.

Bolitho said, 'You know what to do.' He spoke more sharply than he intended, but Avery barely noticed.

Avery could feel the written instructions, which Bolitho had dictated to his secretary Yovell. Even that was like a secret, as if Bolitho were not prepared to make up his mind. Perhaps he was unsure, then.

Avery glanced at him. Not unsure of himself? After all that he had done, that would be impossible.

27

Bolitho was saying, 'Make arrangements for an early start tomorrow. We will stay overnight.'

'The Golden Lion, Sir Richard?'

Bolitho's eyes were searching, the reflected colour of Plymouth Sound, and he imagined that he had offended him.

'I-I only meant . . .'

Surprisingly Bolitho smiled, and seized his arm through his damp cloak.

'I know. I am all aback today.' He looked towards the town. 'But some other place, I think.'

He pictured Catherine suddenly. How they had held one another before he had left for Plymouth. She would be on her way to London by now, to Chelsea. She had shared her London with him. Like all she had given him, all they would have to relinquish when he sailed again.

He had rarely felt like this before. Every day had been like a bright dawn, and even though each had known they must soon be separated it was hard even to contemplate.

He saw Avery walking away, back to the waiting carriage. His uneven shoulder, the stiff manner in which he held it, moved him deeply. *What are these men, Kate? If only all England could see her sons.* And above the fresh breeze which rattled *Larne*'s halliards and incompleted rigging he heard her voice in his mind. *Don't leave me!*

There were shouts, and Bolitho realised that the marine picket was watching him nervously. A burly figure in lieutenant's uniform but without a hat had appeared on deck, pushing seamen and dockyard workers aside as he roared, 'Man the side, you damned hawbucks! Why was I not told?'

Bolitho put one foot on the brow and raised his hat to the small quarterdeck.

'It is good to see you again, Mr Ozanne! And in fine voice, too!' Then he tossed a fold of the cloak over one shoulder to reveal an epaulette with its bright pair of silver stars.

The dockyard workers gaped with amazement, but some of the seamen gave a lively cheer. Like a meeting of old friends.

Ozanne was a Channel Islander who had originally been a merchant sailor. An excellent officer despite his earthy manner, he was old for his rank, and five years or more older than his captain.

Bolitho shook his hand. 'How was London?'

Ozanne beamed, but his eyes were wary. 'I was forgettin', Sir Richard. Captain Adam was here. *Anemone* is lyin' over there.' He considered the question. 'I didn't take to it much. But they seemed pleased to have the despatches.' He shook his big head. 'Do they always rush about like chickens at th'Admiralty, Sir Richard?'

Bolitho smiled. *The family.* 'It's quite usual, I understand!' He became serious. 'Is the captain aboard?'

'I'll call him . . .'

'No, Mr Ozanne. I know my way.' He thought, James Tyacke will know I am here. He glanced along the slender hull with its black gun-barrels, their buff-painted carriages at rest beneath canvas to protect them from the indignities of a refit. *Larne. Tyacke's ship. At my command.* He clambered down the

29

companion ladder, ducking his head beneath the beams as he walked towards the stern cabin.

Familiar smells here, which even the dockyard could not quench. Paint and tar, hemp and close humanity. Not just another overworked brig. Tyacke had overcome his terrible disfigurement to weld her into what she was, and what she had achieved. *The devil with half a face.*

Would he do it all over again? Could he even consider asking him?

Tyacke was standing framed against the sloping stern windows, his shoulders bowed between the deckhead beams in the small cabin, which nevertheless stretched the whole breadth of the stern. His face was in shadow. He said, 'Welcome aboard, sir.' He reached for his coat with the single epaulette on its left shoulder, but Bolitho said, 'No, I am here uninvited.' He dropped his boat-cloak and then hung his heavy dress coat over a chair. 'Let us be just two men for a while.'

Tyacke reached into a cupboard and produced a bottle and two goblets.

'Took this off a smuggler, sir. Seems like good stuff.'

As he turned the reflected glare from the water lit up the left side of his face. Like Avery's it was strong, with deep crow's-feet around the eye to mark the years at sea on so many oceans.

The other side of his face had been so burned that it was barely human. Only the eye had survived there, blue like Herrick's. Even his unruly hair had not escaped. Once it had been almost as dark as Bolitho's but now it was smudged with grey, whilst directly above the burns the hair had turned pure white, like the lock covering Bolitho's own scar, which he hated so much.

It had happened aboard the *Majestic* at the Battle of the Nile, as it was now called. Tyacke had been on the lower gundeck when that burning hell had exploded around him. He had never discovered what had caused the explosion, as all the gun crews of his division had been killed. Even brave Westcott, *Majestic*'s captain, had died on that terrible day.

The brandy was strong and fiery. They clinked goblets and Tyacke said, 'A willing foe and sea-room, sir! It's all I ask!'

It was strange to be drinking the familiar toast here in the dockyard. Feet thudded across the quarterdeck only inches away, and great coils of cordage were being dragged over the planking and hoisted aloft to the rigger's crew.

Tyacke regarded him steadily. Then he made up his mind, with a determination that was like something physical.

'They're taking my ship – is that it, sir?'

So easily said, but it was breaking his heart. Even now he was looking around in the shadows as if to avoid the frail sunshine falling through the skylight. So many things must have happened here. So many decisions, overwhelming to some, perhaps, with only themselves against a whole ocean. But not to this man.

Bolitho said, 'I am instructed that *Larne* will return to the African squadron and the anti-slavery patrol ... eventually. I have been assured that there are no intentions to remove any of your company for service in other hulls. I can obtain it in writing from the port admiral, if you wish.'

Tyacke was staring at his big sea-chest. Bolitho wondered if the gown was still hidden there, the one he had offered to Catherine after their rescue, to cover her nakedness from the staring sailors.

'I'd like that, sir. I've had no cause to trust a port admiral.' He looked up, momentarily confused. 'That was a stupid thing to say. I beg your pardon, sir!'

'I was once a frigate captain.' How strange that it should still hurt, after all these years. *Once* a frigate captain. 'I can recall only too well the constant poaching of good men, and their replacement with gallows-bait.'

Tyacke poured some more brandy and waited.

Bolitho said, 'I have no right to ask you, but . . .' He broke off as something heavy fell on to the deck above, followed instantly by Ozanne's furious outburst, and laughter for good measure. Laughter in a King's ship was too often a rare sound. *How can I ask him?*

Tyacke was an unmoving silhouette against the thick glass.

'But you *will*, sir.' He leaned forward, so that his face hovered in the sunshine. 'Rank has no part in this.'

Bolitho said, 'No, none. We have done too much together. And when you took us from the sea I was already far too deeply in your debt.' He thought of her in the tossing longboat, her sailor's garb plastered to her body while they had fought the ocean and the nearness of death together.

He heard himself say quietly, 'I want you to take promotion . . .' He hesitated. It was slipping away. 'And

32

be my flag-captain. There is none other I want.' *Need, need. Tell him* ... The words seemed to fill the cabin. 'That is what I came to ask.'

Tyacke stared at him. 'There is no one I would rather serve, sir. But ...' He appeared to shake his head. 'Aye, that one word *but* says it all. Without your trust in me I would have given in to self-pity. But without the freedom of this vessel – without *Larne* – I find it too hard a choice.'

Bolitho reached for his coat. Avery would be looking for him. His involvement could do nothing but harm.

He stood up and held out his hand. 'I must see the port admiral.' He looked at him steadily, knowing he would never forget this moment. 'You are my friend, Lady Catherine's too, and so shall it remain. I will request that your ship's company be allowed ashore watch-by-watch.'

He felt the hard firmness of their handshake, was aware of the emotion in Tyacke's voice. Then it was over.

Lieutenant George Avery climbed from the carriage and felt the fine drizzle falling past the coach-lamps and into his face.

'Wait here – I'll only be a moment. Then you can take us to the Boar's Head.'

It had taken longer than he had expected, or else it had got dark earlier than usual. He tugged his hat more tightly down on his forehead and turned up the collar of his boat-cloak. His stomach was making its emptiness felt, and he realised that he had not eaten since a hasty breakfast at some inn along the way.

The water of the Hamoaze beyond the dockyard was alive with riding-lights, like fireflies above their reflections. Small craft made dark shadows around them, officers coming and going, the watchful guard-boat, the unending life of a busy harbour.

Here along the wall other lanterns shone by brows and entry ports, where any novice, the unwary or a man who had taken too much to drink could easily trip over a ringbolt or some dockyard material and pitch over the edge.

He saw the brig's two bare masts, higher than before on an incoming tide. Figures by an entry port, a lieutenant's white-lapelled coat: probably the side-party assembled to see the vice-admiral ashore.

What had they been discussing, he wondered. Old times perhaps, the rescue after the shipwreck of which Allday had told him. Poor Allday; he would be beside himself with worry over this journey. Not being in his proper place, as he would put it.

Avery recognised the thickset officer as Paul Ozanne, *Larne*'s second-in-command.

'I was delayed, Mr Ozanne. I hope Sir Richard is not too displeased.'

Ozanne took his arm and guided him aft. He glanced at the cabin skylight, in darkness except for a solitary candle.

He said bluntly, 'Sir Richard left long ago. He said to tell you he would be at the port admiral's house.'

Avery tensed. Something was wrong. Badly wrong. Otherwise . . .

'What has happened?' Ozanne would know. Better than anyone, he would understand his captain and companion, and his friend, too.

'He's down there now, drinking. Worse than I ever seen him. Can't make no sense out of him. I'm fair troubled.'

Avery thought of Bolitho's expression when he had gone to board this ship. Anxious, despairing, a different man from the one he had known at sea, or at the house in Falmouth.

'Shall I have a word?' He expected a blunt rebuff.

Instead Ozanne said roughly, 'I'd be obliged, but watch your step. There might be a squall or two.'

Avery nodded in acknowledgement. It was something Allday had once said to him as a warning.

It was so dark between decks that he almost fell. *Larne* was small and cramped after a frigate, especially after the old *Canopus* in which he had been serving when Sillitoe had written to him about the possibility of an appointment to flag-lieutenant.

'Who is that out there? Lay aft if you must!'

He called, 'Avery, sir. Flag-lieutenant!' He saw the flickering candle and Tyacke's disfigured face turning away as he groped for a bottle.

'Send you, did he?'

He sounded angry, even dangerous. Avery replied, 'I thought Sir Richard was aboard, sir.'

'Well, you can see that he's bloody well not, so you can leave!' Just as suddenly, his voice changed. 'Not your fault. It's nobody's damned fault. It's this bloody war, what it's done to us.' He was muttering to himself as he opened the bottle and slopped something into

35

another glass. Some of it splashed unheeded on to the table. Avery could smell it, and thought of his empty stomach.

''Fraid it's only Geneva. I've seen off the cognac.' He gestured vaguely. 'Shift yourself. Can't see you well enough from here.'

Avery stood up, ducking to avoid the beams. *The poor bastard. He doesn't want me to see that side of his face.*

Tyacke said thickly, 'You limped. Of course, I'd forgotten. You were wounded, weren't you? And then there was the court-martial.' He repeated, 'Not your fault.'

'Anything I can do, sir?'

Tyacke did not seem to hear. 'What a lot we are, eh? I've seen his coxswain – Allday, right?'

Avery nodded, afraid to break the spell.

'I've seen him often enough, when he thinks Sir Richard isn't looking, holding his chest sometimes, hardly able to draw breath 'cause of what the Dons did to him.' His voice was louder, and Avery imagined Ozanne by the skylight, listening, hoping.

'Then there's his *old friend*, Rear-Admiral Herrick.' He spoke with unexpected bitterness. 'Now he's lost a bloody arm for his troubles!' He downed a full glass and almost choked. 'Sir Richard must enjoy helping lame ducks.'

'He's a fine man, sir. I'll not stand by and hear him slandered!'

Tyacke was on his feet in a flash. He seized Avery's lapels and dragged him across the table so that they were inches apart.

36

'Of course he's a fine man! Don't you damned well tell me what to say or think!'

Avery did not try to move or release himself. He could see Tyacke's wounded face, the blue eye bright in the candlelight, isolated by pain. But almost worse, there were tears running across the melted skin.

Tyacke was shaking him with gentle firmness. 'Look at me. *Look . . . at . . . me.*'

Avery said quietly, 'Tell me, sir.' At any moment Ozanne would come aft. Then it would be too late.

Tyacke released his grip and patted his arm, then he sat down heavily again. In a flat, toneless voice he said, 'He asked me to be his flag-captain.' He shook with silent laughter. 'Can you imagine that, man? How could I accept?'

'You think he asked you out of pity? He would never put his people at risk for that, even for a dear friend's sake.' He waited, anticipating another outburst. But Tyacke was very still, except for the painful breathing and the play of shadows across his face.

Avery remembered what had driven Allday to confide so desperately in him about Bolitho's injured eye, and how privileged he had felt to be entrusted with the secret. To share it with another now seemed tantamount to a betrayal.

But the cold grip around his heart would not release him. There was so much at stake. Too much.

He said, 'You spoke of our misfortunes just now . . .'

Tyacke shook himself. 'I meant no disrespect to you.'

'None taken.' He swallowed the raw gin and said, 'We are not the only ones.'

37

'Damn me, I know that.'

When Avery remained silent he leaned towards him again, and for a moment the flag-lieutenant believed he had gone too far.

Then he said, almost inaudibly, 'Not Sir Richard. Surely you don't mean him?'

Avery stood up very carefully. 'He is losing the sight of one eye.'

Tyacke's hand went up to his face, as it must have done when the bandages had been finally removed. It must have seemed a miracle that he had not lost his eye.

'He said nothing to me about it.'

Avery wanted to stay but knew he must leave. 'He's very like you, sir. A proud man above all else. So it was not pity, you see.' He heard Ozanne breathing heavily in the passageway. 'He needs you, now more than ever. Would you have him beg?'

He could feel Ozanne's relief as he brushed past him, afraid that Tyacke would summon him back and begin all over again. Also, he knew he was going to be sick.

He reached the carriage and managed to gasp, 'Port admiral's house, if you please!'

In the tiny cabin Lieutenant Ozanne was watching Tyacke, who was trying to refill his glass.

He asked wearily, 'What happened?'

Tyacke peered at him and wiped his eyes with his sleeve.

'Secret, Paul. If I tell you, then it's not.' His voice was very slurred.

The bottle rolled unheeded on to the deck, and

Tyacke would have followed it but for his powerful first lieutenant.

'I don't know who said what, James Tyacke, but I was a mite worried about *you*!'

He gave a great sigh and snuffed out the candle.

Then, with Tyacke's coat over one arm, he stepped outside and heard the rain on the companion ladder.

For a while longer Ozanne, who had been at sea since his boyhood, looked around and listened to the watch below crowding into their messes for their evening meal. There would be much discussion below deck about the proposed shore leave. Such generosity was unheard of.

He touched the solitary gold epaulette on Tyacke's coat and said quietly, 'I think we're losing you, James, and we'll be the poorer for it.'

Afterwards he knew he had been speaking to – and for – the whole ship.

Vice-Admiral Sir Graham Bethune strode across the thick carpet, his face alight with a warm smile as he seized Bolitho's hand.

'My God, Sir Richard, you make my heart sing to see you so well and rested! I have to admit to a certain nervousness at the prospect of meeting you for the first time since my appointment. Those far-off days when you were my captain and I was a bumbling midshipman are hard to shake off!'

The handshake, like the smile, was genuine, Bolitho thought. Bethune was not quite what he had expected, and it was true that they had not met since his first command, the sloop-of-war *Sparrow* in '82. A lifetime ago.

The round-faced midshipman with the dark freckles was no more. Instead here was a flag-officer who must be in his forties, but who looked years younger. Bright-eyed, lean and confident, a far cry from many senior officers who had languished in the halls of Admiralty. He had the same infectious smile, but there was an air of confidence and authority about him which Bolitho guessed would be a great attraction to ladies of the Court, or at the many receptions he would have to attend in his new capacity.

Bolitho felt a touch of envy and cursed himself for his own vanity. He had followed Bethune's progress to fame in the *Gazette* from time to time. The turning point had come when he had been in command of a small twenty-six-gun sixth-rate. Sailing alone, he had fallen in with two big Spanish frigates, either of which should have been able to force him to submit. Instead, after a spirited engagement, Bethune had run one enemy ashore and captured the other with hardly a man lost.

Bethune said, 'If it suits I will call a full meeting on the day after next. I think it would be foolish to delay further.' He waved Bolitho to a chair. 'But I wanted to see you first. To prepare myself. There are many changes here – of necessity. But I am sure you are well aware of that.'

A servant entered with some wine and glasses. He, too, was a different one from Godschale's or Hamett-Parker's.

Bethune toyed with his buttons. 'How is her lady-ship? Well, I trust?'

Bolitho relaxed slightly. A test, perhaps, like a ranging shot to decide on the next move.

'Lady Catherine is in good health, thank you. I will be joining her shortly in Chelsea.'

Just the merest flicker. Nothing more.

Bethune nodded. 'I would greatly like to meet her.'

Bolitho thought of Godschale sitting at the same table, complaining of the weight of his responsibilities and probably planning his next liaison with the young wife of some subordinate at the same time. His appetites had done for him in the end.

He studied his one-time midshipman with new eyes. Handsome, with the touch of recklessness some women admired. He was married, but perhaps he had a mistress somewhere.

The servant brought the glasses. It was cold hock, very refreshing after all the miles, all the changes of horses at inns which had all begun to look very much like one another. He wondered if the wine had come from the shop in St James's Street where Catherine had taken him.

Bethune said, 'I have read all your letters and despatches, particularly your views on blockade and the protection of trade routes. You are correct, of course, Sir Richard.' Again the infectious smile, a lieutenant posing as a vice-admiral. 'But it will be up to you to convince their lordships.'

Bolitho thought of Tyacke, and remembered Catherine's words when he had told her what he intended. It was still heavy on his heart. She had been right.

'There is some good news about your friend and former flag-captain, Valentine Keen.'

Bolitho hoped that Bethune had not seen his surprise. It was as though he had been reading his thoughts.

'He is to be promoted to rear-admiral, and deservedly so, as you made very clear in your original report.'

Bolitho looked away. He recalled Hamett-Parker's hostility at the suggestion, but now that Keen was secure as a flag-officer in his own right he could only recall Adam's despairing confession by the fire in Falmouth. Zenoria as the wife of a flag-officer? It was beyond imagination. The girl with the moonlit eyes would be swamped, destroyed even, by a world she would never be able to share or understand. It must not destroy Adam also.

Bethune took another tall glass of wine. 'I appreciate your convictions concerning the United States. By the way, your recent adversary Captain Nathan Beer is promoted commodore, I hear.'

Bolitho remembered the moment of fear, the splinters like barbs in his face, Herrick lurching on deck, his amputated stump bleeding as he dismissed the *Valkyrie*'s captain and took charge to fight the ship.

He said sharply, 'The next time we meet I shall make him an admiral!'

He saw the satisfaction in Bethune's eyes.

Bethune said quietly, 'You think there will be war?'

'I do. If I can explain . . .'

Bethune smiled. 'Not to me, Sir Richard. I am convinced. The others will be more concerned with expense than expediency.'

Bolitho thought of Catherine. She would be at

Chelsea, or very close to it by now. Just before he had left for Plymouth she had mentioned the surgeon in London.

'It can do no harm. Perhaps he may even be able to help.'

Bethune asked suddenly, 'Does your eye trouble you?'

He realised he had been rubbing it.

'A chill, I expect.'

Bethune said airily, 'Well, you have been in Cornwall. It is possible.'

He was a Cornishman himself. Bolitho recalled that he had made a point of mentioning it when he had taken command of *Sparrow*. He could not imagine him in Cornwall now.

But he was shrewd, very shrewd. It would not do to let him know about the injury.

Bethune was saying, 'Your choice of flagship, the *Indomitable*, did surprise me a little, although I can fathom your reasons. But some of our betters may suggest otherwise, or say perhaps that you have a penchant for elderly vessels.'

Bolitho sensed the contempt he held for his 'betters'.

Bethune added, 'I shall give you my support, but I hope you knew that. I will suggest that two other elderly vessels, *Victory* and *Hyperion*, have made milestones in history!'

A servant entered and looked at Bethune nervously. 'Sir Richard Bolitho's flag-lieutenant is in attendance, Sir Graham . . .'

Bethune smiled calmly. 'A brave man to venture

43

amongst senior officers.' He shot Bolitho a quick glance, 'And friends.'

Bolitho got to his feet as Avery entered the big room, his cocked hat crushed beneath his arm.

Was something wrong? Had Avery found the Chelsea house empty?

Avery nodded to Bethune, but Bolitho saw the quick appraisal, the sharp curiosity. Unlike poor Jenour, this man took nothing for granted.

He said, 'Letter by fast courier, Sir Richard.' Their eyes met. 'From Plymouth.'

Bolitho took it, aware that Bethune was watching him.

It was short and to the point, in Tyacke's sloping hand.

Mine is the honour. It is more than loyalty.
I shall await your orders.

His signature was scrawled across the bottom, barely legible.

Bolitho glanced at Avery, but the flag-lieutenant's expression remained inscrutable. Then he raised the letter to his nose, and saw that small cabin in his mind as he had left it in Plymouth only days ago.

Bethune smiled. 'Perfume, Sir Richard? Dare I ask?'

Bolitho shook his head. It was cognac. 'With your permission, Sir Graham, I would give you a sentiment.'

The glasses had been refilled, and another had appeared for Avery. Bethune remarked, 'I am *all* curiosity!'

Bolitho felt his eye pricking, not injury now, but for a different reason.

'To the most courageous man I have ever known.'

Avery watched him as they touched their glasses. Another secret.

Then Bolitho smiled for the first time since he had arrived. They were ready.

'So let's be about it!'

3

The Ocean is Always There

Lieutenant George Avery handed his hat to an Admiralty porter and hurried across the marble hall to where Bolitho was sitting in a high-backed chair.

'I apologise for my lateness, Sir Richard.'

Bolitho held out his hands to a well-banked fire and said, 'You are not late. They are still rewriting naval history in that room.' It was spoken without impatience or bitterness. Perhaps he had seen too much of it, Avery thought.

Bolitho wondered if his flag-lieutenant had kept exactly to the arranged time in order to avoid questions about Tyacke, and his inexplicable change of heart regarding the appointment.

Bolitho thought of Catherine that morning, the concern in her eyes while he finished dressing, his coffee untouched on the table.

He had shown her Tyacke's note. She had said, 'Let him decide, Richard. I think you should wait for Avery to tell you himself. It is what you wanted ... I know how much you need James Tyacke, but I do not envy him what he must do.'

They had stood side by side on the iron balcony of the Chelsea house and watched the misty first light across the Thames. London came alive long before dawn, but it was a leisurely awakening here. A man with his little cart and tubs of fresh oysters, setting up his stall for the various cooks and housekeepers to sample his wares. Hay for the stables, a loud-voiced knife-grinder, then a small troop of cavalry horses being taken on morning exercise to the park, looking strangely bare without their saddles and bright accoutrements. She had been wearing her heavy robe, but even so it had been chilly so close to the slow-moving river. He had held her and felt her shiver, but not only from the air.

It would soon be a time for parting. Days or weeks: after the freedom they had longed for and shared since Bolitho's return to England, it would be all the harder to accept.

He heard Avery say, 'I was so glad to learn of Commodore Keen's promotion. Well earned, from what I have heard and read of him.'

Bolitho looked up at him sharply, but it was only an innocent comment. He wondered what Zenoria would be thinking about it, Adam too. Thank God he would be sailing soon despite his shortage of men and officers.

Of one company. How many times had he heard it thus described. He recalled the big frigate *Valkyrie*, aboard which he had been rendered completely helpless by tiny splinters in his uninjured eye. Command of her had gone to Adam's contemporary Captain Peter Dawes, the son of an admiral, whose frigate *Laertes*

47

had been so badly battered by Baratte's crossfire that it was unlikely she would ever fight again.

Many people would be surprised that such a prestigious command had not been given to Adam. No doubt some of them in the room beyond were also thinking as much. But Dawes had proved his worth; he would give *Valkyrie* fair and proper leadership, unlike the brutal punishments which had been a regular occurrence under Captain Trevenen, who had vanished overboard without trace. Murder, an accident, or had he committed suicide to save himself from a charge of cowardice when Herrick had seized command?

He considered it, and knew that Adam would not wish to leave his beloved *Anemone*, even though there would hardly be a familiar face left now in her whole company.

He heard Avery breathe in as footsteps clicked across the marble floor like distant slate-hammers.

Awhite-faced clerk said, 'If you would please come this way, Sir Richard.' He glanced nervously at Avery. 'I have been told nothing about . . .'

'Then you will have no objection if my flag-lieutenant remains with me.'

Avery almost felt sorry for the clerk. Almost.

The big room was full of distinguished people, senior officers, the Lords of Admiralty, and civilians who looked more like lawyers at the Old Bailey than the planners of strategy.

Bolitho sat down and heard Avery move into a chair at his elbow. There was no sunlight through the great windows, nor were there any glittering chandeliers to dazzle his injured eye. One or two of the officers nodded to him, pleased to see him safe and apparently in excellent health. Others would welcome him for different reasons. It was common enough for a clash of personalities to cause an uproar in this powerful place. Clerks, a secretary or two and somebody's flag-lieutenant hovered beside a pillar, attempting to remain unnoticed.

Avery whispered, 'My uncle is here, Sir Richard . . .'

At that moment Sir Graham Bethune rose to his feet and rested one palm on his table. Even that looked elegant, but Bolitho wondered if he was as confident as he appeared.

'Sir Richard Bolitho is no stranger to most of you, and his name is known to many more . . .' He gave a gentle smile. 'Not least to Napoleon!' There was laughter and Bethune's eyes responded as he glanced at Bolitho.

A heavily-built admiral, whom Bolitho recognised as the Controller, said bluntly, 'We are here to discuss future tactics, if – and for my own part it is a very doubtful *if* – the Americans show intentions of war against our King.' He glared furiously at two post-captains who were whispering together, enjoying the fact that there was no longer a King to govern them. 'The United States would be insane to declare war on such a powerful navy!'

The word *insane* brought more gleeful whispers from the two captains.

Bethune said smoothly, 'Sir Paul Sillitoe is come amongst us to explain more clearly what we are about.'

Sillitoe stood up lightly, his hooded eyes scanning the gathering like a man who has something better to do.

'The situation is simple enough. Between Napoleon's land blockade and his very real threats against those of his neighbours who might dare to allow our ships to enter their ports for the purposes of trade, and our own sea blockade, we have divided the peoples of Europe into friends and foes.'

Bolitho watched him, thinking of him with Catherine when he had escorted her to Whitechapel. A man who could be an enemy, but one who was obviously so secure in his position as adviser to the Prince Regent that he spoke almost with disdain.

'It has also divided the United States into opposing parties. The War Party – let us call it – is in favour of Napoleon; the other party wants only peace. The War Party hate us and covet Canada, and also wish to continue to make money from the conflict. The United States government insists that British deserters should be safe under the American flag, and is doing all it can to weaken our fleet by encouraging many, many seamen to take advantage of their offer, *dollars for shillings*, a bribe they can well afford.' His eyes flashed. '*Yes?*'

All heads turned towards a small, dark-clad clerk at the end table. 'With respect, Sir Paul, I cannot keep up with you!'

Sillitoe almost smiled. 'Something I have thought characteristic of this edifice on many occasions!'

There was laughter and hand-clapping. In a lull Bethune leaned over and whispered, '*Convince them.*'

Bolitho stood up as the noise died away. He felt out of place here, the scene of so many disappointments. After he had been so ill with fever in the Great South Sea, war had broken out, and he could recall himself pleading for another ship, a frigate, three of which he had already commanded by that time. And the admiral's cold response. *Were a frigate captain, Bolitho.* Where plots had been made against him to force him back to Belinda's side, and where he had broken with Herrick in that very corridor outside.

He heard himself speaking, his voice carrying without effort.

'We need more frigates. It is always the way, but this time the need is all the more urgent. I am certain that the Americans will force a war. Napoleon cannot hold out much longer unless he receives their support to stretch our fleet's resources still further. Likewise, the Americans will have left it too late if they drag their feet.'

The Controller held up a quill pen. 'I must protest, Sir Richard. Nobody would dispute your gallantry and many successes at sea, but *planning* is the key to victory, not necessarily the broadside!'

A voice called, 'Hear – hear!'

Encouraged, the Controller said, 'We have many fine ships-of-the-line on the stocks or completing every week of the year.' He paused and raised his eyebrows. 'Frigates *before* the line of battle, is *that* what you advocate? For if so . . .'

Bolitho answered quietly, 'The Americans laid down seventy-fours but quickly saw the folly of it. All were converted to big frigates, and carry forty-four guns, but

51

are said to be pierced for ten additional heavy guns.' There was not a sound now. He continued, 'We crossed swords last year with one of their largest, the U.S.S. *Unity*. I can vouch for her fire power,' his voice was suddenly hard and bitter, 'as can many of our brave fellows!'

A voice called, 'What *about* the line-of-battle, Sir Richard?'

Bolitho knew it was Sillitoe, conducting the scene like a puppet-master.

He said, flatly, 'It is finished. The day of the leviathans sailing slowly to a costly and terrible embrace is over. We'll not see another Trafalgar, I am certain of it.'

He looked around at their intent faces. To some the truth of what he had said would seem like blasphemy. To those who had faced the murder of close-action it was something no one dared to admit.

Bolitho said, 'Think of it. The ship's company of one first-rate could crew four fast and powerful frigates. Ships which can move from area to area with haste and without waiting for some far-off flagship to guess what is happening. I have been offered a command which reaches from Halifax and the forty-ninth parallel south to the Leeward Islands and Jamaica. In any week of any year there are ships, convoys with rich cargoes, making their way back to this country. Without ready protection and the ability to hit back in their defence, we will stand no chance.'

Bethune asked, 'Is that why you want *Indomitable* for your flagship?'

Bolitho looked at him and forgot all the others. 'Yes.

She was cut down from a third-rate to carry the very artillery I would need. She is and always has been a fast sailer.'

Bethune smiled but his eyes were on the others.

'She was re-built and re-rated because of the operations at Mauritius, gentlemen. Unfortunately Sir Richard dished up the French before we could send *Indomitable* out there!'

There was a wave of cheering and stamping.

When he looked at Bethune again, Bolitho saw the triumph in his eyes. So long ago when they had boarded the enemy from his little *Sparrow*, he had seen that same expression. *All or nothing*.

The Controller held up one plump hand. 'Are they your only reasons, Sir Richard?'

'Yes, my lord.' He pictured the great fireplace at Falmouth, the family crest worn away by time and many hands. Where his father had spoken of his hopes and his fears for his youngest son, when he had first gone to sea. 'For my country's freedom.' He glanced at Avery and saw what might have been emotion. 'And *my* freedom from then on.'

Bethune smiled with relief. A near thing. He might have been unseated at the Admiralty when he had scarcely begun. And Bolitho? He would probably have refused any other appointment.

He said, 'I will give you everything I can, Sir Richard.'

Bolitho looked at him keenly, and afterwards Bethune thought he had been pierced through by those clear grey eyes.

'I have everything, Graham. *And I want it to last.*'

Bethune stared after him. *He called me by name.* As he had sometimes done in *Sparrow*.

Avery went to look for his hat and almost ran into his uncle, who was speaking with a tall and very dignified soldier. He did not introduce his nephew, but remarked noncommittally, 'It went well, I thought?'

Avery watched him. Sillitoe was not interested in his opinion. Eventually Sillitoe touched his arm, nothing more, but it was a kinder gesture than he had ever been offered before.

'I have to tell you, George.' The cold eyes searched his face. 'Your sister died in Dorchester. It was not unexpected, but still . . .' He sighed. 'I shall deal with it. I have never felt that her husband is in the right calling.' He walked away to where his tall companion was waiting impatiently by the steps.

Bolitho joined him. 'Is something wrong?'

But all Avery said was, 'It was that day. The last time I saw her.' He seemed to shake himself and said, 'I'll be glad to get back to sea, sir.' He was staring at the groups of people breaking up and heading for club or coffee-house, but all he saw was his sister Ethel in her drab clothing. Now she would never meet Lady Catherine.

He walked to the big doors and added, 'It will be cleaner.'

Lieutenant Paul Ozanne, the burly, red-faced Channel Islander, held open the cabin door and looked aft to where Tyacke was sitting at his table, exactly as he had left him. How many times had he opened this door, at sea or at anchor, to report the sighting of a suspected slaver, or perhaps an enemy sail? Tyacke always seemed to know anyway, even before the masthead lookout.

He noticed that Tyacke's brass-bound sea-chest had gone, and despite what he had been told privately, it saddened him.

Tyacke had explained that when he left the ship Ozanne was to be promoted to commander and given *Larne* in his place. Ozanne could still not believe the swiftness of events, or what it would mean to him.

Tyacke had said, 'You deserve it, I'd have no other. You ought to have been promoted long ago – I know no better seaman or navigator.' His tone had hardened. 'But there are those in authority, and my guess is that there always will be, who consider a man not fit for high rank if he has soiled his hands with honest work!'

The news had gone through the little brig like a flame. Ozanne had seen it on their faces. Surprise, but certainly relief too. *Larne* was too intimate, and her people had been together longer than most, for some new broom to come amongst them.

Tyacke looked up from the bare table, his face in shadow.

Ozanne said, 'They're waiting, sir.'

Tyacke nodded heavily. 'Your commission is here . . .'

'Will you wait, sir?' He already knew the answer.

'No. I wish you well, I daresay we shall meet again. It is the way of things.' He became impatient. 'Have them come in.'

Larne's officers filed into the cabin and found places

to sit. On chairs and on the stern bench seat: when the door was wedged shut the cabin was packed tight. *Larne* was well blessed with both officers and master's mates. She had taken many prizes, slavers and smugglers alike, and had always carried extra experienced men to sail their captures to the nearest friendly harbour.

There was plenty of cognac, and Ozanne recalled the day when Sir Richard Bolitho had come aboard, and later his flag-lieutenant. He had rarely seen his commander the worse for drink. Now he knew why it had happened, or one of the reasons, anyway.

Tyacke said, 'Help yourselves.' They had no choice in such a crowded cabin. He watched them without expression. Flemyng and Robyns the lieutenants, Manley Pitcair the sailing master and Andrew Livett the young surgeon, who accepted his miserly pay so that he could study tropical medicines and fevers. He had had plenty of experience on the slave coasts. The master's mates, bronzed and reliable. But no midshipmen. That would all change like everything else when he joined *Indomitable*, Bolitho's proposed flagship. She lay some two hundred yards distant but Tyacke, typically, had not gone to see her. He would begin after he had read himself in, and not before.

Everything would be different. *Indomitable* would carry a Royal Marine contingent like all men-of-war from sixth-rates upwards. Tyacke had not served alongside the Royals since the *Majestic*. He touched his scarred face and thought of Bolitho's eye, the way he had seen him rub it when he had been thinking of something else. *I should have guessed*. He looked round the cabin, so small and low-beamed, but after his first and only other command, the schooner *Miranda*, it had seemed like a palace. He had first met Bolitho in *Miranda*, when he had accepted all the discomfort and shared quarters without complaint. When she had been destroyed by a French frigate he had given him *Larne* without hesitation. The bond, broken only by distance and the demands of duty, had strengthened from then on. He thought of Avery's visit, his anger and despair. *I should have guessed*.

He cleared his throat and every face looked aft.

'Today I shall leave this command to Mr Ozanne. It is hard to describe my feelings.' He twisted round in his chair and glanced through the thick stern windows. So many times. The thump of the rudder-post, the frothing sea rolling away from beneath the counter. *So many times. God, I shall miss you, girl!*

But he said, 'I have requested that Robert Gallaway be promoted to acting-lieutenant until it can be confirmed.' He saw the master's mate staring round with surprise and pleasure while his friends thumped him on the back. He would leave Ozanne to select a replacement for Gallaway. It would probably be his first duty. A pleasant way to begin a commission. The others were not even troubled by meeting his gaze. That, too, would be different in another ship. What had he expected? That he would be permitted to keep sailing the deep-water trade routes like a phantom? Now he would be out in the open for all to see.

He took a swallow from his goblet. He would stay at

an inn Pitcair had told him about. Small, no questions asked. He smiled sadly. When he received his next allotment of prize money he could buy land of his own.

He said, 'We have done a great deal together, and we are all the better for it. The ocean is always there waiting for us, with a mood to suit every watch and occasion. But the ship . . .' Just once he reached out and touched the curved timbers. 'There is never one like the last.' He heard a boatswain's call, unusually muted in the packed cabin. 'All hands! All hands muster on deck!' Even the thudding of bare feet was subdued.

A seaman tapped the door and thrust his head inside. One of the older hands who had been allowed ashore because of Bolitho's request to the port admiral.

'Beg pardon, zur! But the carriage be alongside!'

Tyacke nodded. 'Very well, Houston. I'll come up.'

The seaman hesitated, unsure amidst all of his lieutenants and warrant officers.

'What is it?'

The man named Houston dragged a bright gold dollar on a chain from his pocket.

'For a lady, zur – took it from that brigantine! Good luck, Cap'n!' Then he fled.

Tyacke stood up slowly, glad that he must bow his head between the beams and hide his face.

Thank God he was not being pulled ashore in the gig, which was what Ozanne would have arranged had they been at anchor instead of alongside the wall. Pulled ashore by his own officers. Ozanne was that kind of man.

He was saying now to the others, 'Wait on deck, please, gentlemen.'

Then, when they had filed out, he stood by the door. 'I'll never forget what you done for me, James. Never fret, I'll take good care of her. You'll be that proud when you see her again.'

Tyacke gripped his hand. 'I know that, old friend.' What Bolitho called his coxswain. He wanted to say aloud, *I'm afraid. Maybe I can't do it.* But all he said was, 'She can still outsail the best of them!'

Then, followed by Ozanne, he climbed the companion ladder, and hesitated by the coaming.

My men. No, not any more.

They were clinging to the shrouds and ratlines, framed against a clear bright sky. There were no dockyard workers to be seen. This was *Larne*'s moment and they would share it with nobody.

The carriage with the big sea-chest on its roof waited amongst the dockyard litter. Tyacke measured the distance with his eye. It was probably the longest journey he would ever take.

He shook hands with the officers and the men of the side-party. A murmur here and there, firm, rough hands, questioning glances; he had to press his sword against his thigh with all his strength to contain himself.

Lastly Paul Ozanne, *Commander* Ozanne. Only their eyes spoke: no words would come.

Tyacke raised his hat and climbed on to the brow. The calls twittered and then someone yelled, 'Huzza for the Captain, lads! *Huzza!*'

People hurried to the sides of other vessels nearby

as the wild cheering echoed and re-echoed against the old stone walls. For such a small ship's company, the din was enough to drown every other sound. Straight-backed, his sword at his side, Tyacke walked steadily towards the carriage, the cheers washing around him like breakers on the reefs.

He climbed into the carriage and the driver flicked his whip.

He did not look back. He dared not.

Catherine was waiting at the foot of the stairs when Young Matthew drove Bolitho back from the Admiralty after yet another meeting. She watched him anxiously, looking for a sign, some hint that he was over-taxing himself.

He took her in his arms, his mouth touching her hair, her neck.

'It's settled, Kate. I am to command the new squadron.' He searched her face as she had studied his. 'We can soon return to Falmouth. It will be a while yet before my ships are ready.' He smiled. 'And Young Matthew complains that London is too noisy and dirty for his tastes.'

She linked her arm through his and turned him towards their room at the rear of the house with its tiny walled garden.

'How is George Avery?'

'Relieved, I think.'

'I have written to him about his sister. I did not even know he had a family. He said not when I first met him.'

'I know. There is another story there, I believe. By "family" I think he may have meant somebody like you.'

He saw the brandy on the table and wondered if Tyacke had left *Larne* yet. He could remember his own farewells only too vividly.

'For me, Richard, will you visit the surgeon before we leave Chelsea?'

He kissed her lightly. 'For you, anything.'

She watched him pour some brandy. He was looking better than she had expected, his face showing once again the benefit of their being together for over two months, but last night she had been unable to comfort him, and sleep had been denied to both of them.

She said, 'Perhaps there will be no war across the Atlantic?'

'Perhaps.'

She saw his fingers playing with her locket beneath his shirt. He had worn it deliberately for this latest visit to the Admiralty. His protection, he had called it.

'How was Sir Graham Bethune today?' She had felt his hurt and jealousy at the beginning, but Bethune had stood by her man against the pack. Sillitoe too, although she was doubtful if his motives were so easily defined.

'He was fair and helpful. He has given me most of what I requested. Maybe I will have the rest when the extent of my orders is realised.'

He did not mention that he would be sailing first to English Harbour in Antigua. The Leeward Squadron, as Bethune had dubbed it, would establish itself there. But he could not tell her. Not yet. There would be pain

61

enough in parting, and Antigua held so many memories. Where he had found her again, and rediscovered the love which had changed his life. His eye fell on a sealed envelope with a coat of arms adorning it.

'When did this arrive?'

'I thought I would leave it until later. A footman delivered it after you had gone this morning.'

Bolitho picked it up and stared at it. 'Will they never give up? Can they not understand that we belong to each other? Are they so hypocritical that they really expect me to go to Belinda?' He ripped it open with a knife. 'I shall see them in damnation first!'

She watched his change of expression. At a loss, astonished as if he were a small boy again.

'It is from the Prince Regent, Kate. An invitation to dine . . .'

She said, 'Then you must go, Richard. Your position demands that you . . .'

He leaned over her and pulled down the back of her gown and kissed her bare shoulder.

He said quietly, '*We* are invited, Kate.' He held out the heavily embossed card and she read aloud, '*Admiral Sir Richard Bolitho, KB, and Catherine, Lady Somervell.*' She exclaimed, 'It must be a mistake. Carlton House indeed . . . They have even given you the wrong rank.'

He said, almost shyly, 'I forgot to tell you, darling Kate. I have been promoted.'

In the kitchen Sophie, her maid, and the cook both stared at the wall as Catherine shouted, '*You forgot!*' She flung her arms around him. 'Bless you, darling – no wonder they all love you! *You forgot!*' Her fine dark eyes flashed. 'But all my clothes are in Falmouth. There is no time for . . .' She gripped his hand with both of hers. 'Except for the green silk. You remember.'

He smiled at her. 'Antigua. Oh yes, I remember.'

She could not look at him. 'Take me upstairs. I have to remind you. How it is. How it will always be. Together.'

In the kitchen they heard Catherine's familiar laughter. Then there was silence.

The cook glanced at the hob and shook one of the pots.

'They'll be supping late, in my opinion.' She looked at Sophie. 'Disgraceful, annit?' Then she smiled. 'Bless 'em!'

4

Royal Command

For most of the journey from Chelsea, along the Thames and towards Parliament, Bolitho and Catherine spoke little, each reflecting on the immediate future.

Sillitoe had sent a brief note by hand to Chelsea, intimating that the invitation to Carlton House was not a mere matter of vanity or curiosity. Bolitho guessed that he had been told to ensure that they both attended.

This was also the day when Bolitho had visited a consulting physician recommended by the great man himself, Sir Piers Blachford of the College of Surgeons. Catherine had stayed in the carriage, unwilling to wait at Chelsea until the examination was finished.

It had been very thorough, and Bolitho's eye still smarted from the probing and the stinging ointment.

When he had returned to the carriage she had known, despite his smile and his cheery wave to Young Matthew, that it had been in vain.

Even now as she gripped his hand beneath her cloak she could sense his distress, wondering perhaps if he could ever come to terms with it. It seemed that nothing could be done unless some new technique were developed. The doctor had spoken of damage to the retina and had warned that further probing could destroy the eye altogether.

He had used the terminology of his profession in an almost matter-of-fact fashion, the language of his world. It had probably meant very little to Richard except for the verdict. His eye would only get worse, but it might be a considerable time before the disability became obvious to anybody else.

Then, this evening, there had been that precious moment when she had descended the stairs in her green silk gown, and he had watched her all the way. So many memories: their hands touching briefly when Bolitho had all but fallen on the step in that house above English Harbour.

Her hair was piled on her head, *brailed up*, as Allday had once described it, to reveal the gold filigree earrings Bolitho had given her, the ones she had managed to hide in her stained clothing when her husband and Belinda Bolitho had connived to have her wrongly imprisoned for debt, with deportation an almost certain outcome.

Around her neck she wore his latest present, which he had commissioned for her as a surprise when he had returned home from the sea. It was a diamond pendant fashioned in the shape of an open fan, like the one he had brought her from Madeira.

She had watched his eyes, had felt them like warmth from the sun. The pendant rested provocatively in the shadow between her breasts. He had said quietly, 'You will be the most beautiful lady tonight.' It had touched

65

her deeply. A lady in title only, but to Richard she knew it meant far more.

A few people pointed at the crest on the carriage door, but here in the heart of London fame was commonplace and too often ephemeral.

Bolitho seemed to read her thoughts. 'I will be glad to go home, Kate.' Their hands embraced beneath the cloak, like lovers themselves. 'I do not know why we are here.' He turned and looked her full in the face. 'But I shall enjoy showing you off. I always do. Is that so childish?'

She stroked his hand. 'I would have you no other way, and I am *proud* to be at your side.'

Even if Sillitoe was wrong, and the invitation had come only out of curiosity, the love of scandal by those who had no cause to fear it, she would show only dignity.

The sky over London was unusually clear but the windows of Carlton House were ablaze with lights, as smartly liveried linkmen and boys ran to open doors and lower carriage steps. Above the bustle of horses and staring spectators they heard the sound of music, violins and a harpsichord. Bolitho felt her hand on his arm and heard her whisper, 'Like Vauxhall Pleasure Gardens. I shall take you there again.'

He nodded. He was pleased she still remembered that night when she had shown him a part of her London.

Bewigged footmen whisked away their cloaks and Bolitho's cocked hat. He watched them being carried into an ante-room and marked it carefully in case a hasty retreat should become necessary. Aware of his uncertainty, she smiled at him, her eyes flashing in the glitter of a thousand candles.

Most men in his position would be revelling in it, she thought. Here was a real hero, loved, feared, respected and envied. But she knew him so well. Could sense his wariness, his determination to protect her from any who might try to harm her.

They were ushered into a great room with a painted ceiling of water nymphs and fantastical sea-horses. The orchestra was here, although Catherine suspected there was a second playing elsewhere in this extravagant building. It appeared to have been newly decorated, and perhaps was a reflection of the Prince Regent's tastes or personality. Described behind his back as a gambler, drinker and debauchee, and to his face by his father as 'king of the damned', his blatant affair with Mrs Fitzherbert and countless mistresses who had followed her clearly demonstrated the contempt in which he held both his father and society.

There were several women present. Some were plain and seemingly ill at ease, with nothing to say, their husbands on the other hand loud-mouthed and sweating badly as the room became more crowded. There were other women less overawed by their surroundings, some vivacious, and wearing gowns cut so low it was a marvel they stayed in position. It was almost a relief to see Sir Paul Sillitoe, who was pointing them out to a footman while he himself came to greet them.

'Congratulations, Sir Richard! You are turning many heads this evening!' But his eyes were on Catherine as he raised her hand to his lips. 'Each time we see you, Lady Catherine, it is like a first meeting. You look enchanting.'

She smiled. 'You are all flattery, sir.'

Sillitoe became business-like. 'It is a small gathering by Prinny's standards. The main banquet room is partitioned off. We must accept it as an intimate affair. The Prince Regent's dislike for the prime minister has worsened, I am given to believe. He will not be missed.'

Bolitho took a tall, beautifully shaped goblet from a tray and saw the footman's eyes dart between them. Did Sillitoe obtain all his intelligence from men like this? The extent of his knowledge was uncanny, the power that that knowledge would represent almost dangerous.

Sillitoe was saying, 'About forty of us, I understand.'

Bolitho glanced at Catherine. Sillitoe would know exactly how many, and the worth and perhaps the secrets of each and every one of them.

He had returned his attention to Catherine now, his hooded eyes giving nothing away. 'There will be many wines at table . . .'

She touched the diamond fan at her breast. 'I take heed of your warning, Sir Paul. Our host gains entertainment and amusement from his guests if they imbibe too freely, is that it?'

Sillitoe bowed. 'You are perceptive as always, Lady Catherine. I knew I had no need to mention it.'

Bolitho saw faces turning away when he caught them staring. *Well, let them stare, damn them*. He could easily imagine some of these men making fools of themselves, and ladies becoming the perhaps not unwilling prey of others. He had seen it happen in army establishments often enough. Was that what they thought now, watching Catherine, seeing her defiance of convention as a threat to their own manhood, or a challenge to it?

He thought of her in those last days in the sun-blistered longboat, keeping his hopes alive when to everyone else rescue had seemed impossible, and the prospect of death their only escape. Even now, as she turned to glance around the room, the faint scars of sunburn on her bare shoulders were still visible after all the months since *Golden Plover* had smashed on to the reef. Suddenly he wanted to take her in his arms, to keep holding her until the terrible pictures in his mind were no more.

Instead, he asked, 'When I am away . . .' He saw her stiffen, and knew Sillitoe was trying not to listen. 'I would wish for nothing dearer than a portrait of you.'

She tilted her chin and he saw a pulse beating in her throat. 'I would be happy to oblige you, Richard.' She reached out and gripped his hand. It was as if the room were completely empty. 'Your thoughts are always of me, never for yourself . . .'

She turned away as the doors were flung open and an equerry called importantly, 'Pray be upstanding for His Royal Highness the Prince of Wales, Regent of all England!'

Bolitho studied him intently as he entered the colourful gathering. For one so heavy he walked with a light step; he even seemed to glide, and Bolitho was reminded suddenly of a ship-of-the-line, losing the wind even as she floated smoothly to her anchorage.

69

He was not quite certain what he had expected: something perhaps between Gillray's cruel cartoons and the paintings he had seen at the Admiralty. He was about six years younger than Bolitho but his excesses had worn badly. A devotee of fashion, he was elegantly dressed, his hair swept forward in the very latest style, while his lips remained pursed in a little amused smile.

As he moved slowly down the room women curtsied deeply while their partners bowed, flushed with pleasure if they were noticed.

But the Prince, 'Prinny' as Sillitoe had outrageously called him, looked straight at Bolitho and then, more deliberately, at Catherine. 'So *you* are my new admiral.' He bowed his head to Catherine who had subsided into a curtsy. 'Please rise, Lady Catherine.' His eyes rested on the glittering pendant and what lay beneath. 'This is an honour. You will sit with me.' He offered his hand to Bolitho. 'You have a good tailor, sir. Do I know him?'

Bolitho kept his face impassive. A courier to Falmouth and a letter of instructions to the tailor there, old Joshua Miller, who had worked on the new uniform without pause. The others would be ready when he hoisted his flag above *Indomitable*.

He replied, 'He works in Falmouth, Your Royal Highness.'

The Prince smiled. 'Then indeed I shall *not* know him.' His eyes moved to the diamond fan again. 'It must bore you, my lady, living in the country when Sir Richard is away, hmm?'

'I keep too busy to become bored, sir.'

He gently patted her wrist. 'One so beautiful should never be busy!'

They led the way into the adjoining room. Bolitho had heard that when it had been fully extended for a more lavish banquet recently, the table had been over two hundred feet long, with an artificial stream running from a silver fountain at its head.

They were not to be disappointed at this more humble gathering, it appeared. A veritable army of footmen and servants lined the walls, and music drifted gently through the far doors.

Bolitho took his place without enthusiasm. He had recognised the expression in the Prince Regent's eyes, the lewd confidence of one used to getting his own way. As a footman pulled out a chair for Catherine she glanced over the table at him, her eyes very level and compelling. *Remember me*, they seemed to say, reassuring him. *The woman in the boat. The one who loves you and no other*.

The Prince sat back in a tall chair at the head of the table. It was more like a throne, Bolitho thought, with an ornately carved back featuring the plumes of his own coat of arms and the royal crown and cipher, *G.R.* It seemed that he already imagined himself as King.

Catherine sat on his right hand, Bolitho on his left. As far as the Prince of Wales was concerned, his other guests could think what they chose.

He raised one hand and instantly, like a well-trained platoon of Royal Marines demonstrating a complicated drill, the footmen and servants moved into action.

As was customary, Bolitho had expected Grace to

be spoken; in fact he had seen a severe-looking bishop at the opposite end of the table in the act of getting to his feet. The Prince gave no sign that he had seen him, but Bolitho guessed that, like Sillitoe, His Royal Highness missed very little. Soon the table was groaning with the weight of huge platters, some of gold, some of silver. The number of staff in the kitchens must be equally large, Bolitho thought. Spring soup, then slices of salmon and caper sauce were served with fried fillet of sole. Each dish would have satisfied even the hungriest midshipman, but when he glanced along the table Bolitho saw little hesitation as silver flashed in the candlelight, and hands moved and plunged as if his fellow guests had not eaten for days.

The Prince remarked as more glasses were filled, 'This is a lighter wine, Lady Catherine, not much to my taste. I prefer something with a little more *body*.'

She met his gaze and said, 'From Madeira, I believe.' She had not reacted to the emphasis he had placed on the last word; in fact, it was even rather amusing. He was no different from other men after all. She looked across at Bolitho and raised her glass. 'To our new admiral, sir!'

A few sitting close by followed suit, but most were more concerned with emptying their plates in anticipation of the next offering.

The Prince said, 'Indeed, yes. I was impressed with your choice of words at the Admiralty, Sir Richard, although your choice of a flagship surprised me until I perceived the logic of it. The vital need for speed and gunnery to act as one ... there are still many who will not believe it. Merchants and so forth, who can see only an increase in trade and thicker linings to their purses if we slacken our pressure on the enemy. This war must be pursued. I insist on it!' He gave Catherine a wry smile. 'Forgive this talk, Lady Catherine. Doubtless you have heard enough on the subject.'

'Where Sir Richard is concerned, I am always ready to learn more, sir.'

He wagged one finger at her. 'His will be an enormous responsibility.'

She replied calmly, 'Cannot that be said of every captain who sails alone, and with only his own skills and courage to sustain him?'

He nodded, surprised perhaps by her directness. 'Ah yes, but an admiral's responsibility is *total*!'

Bolitho leaned back as white-gloved hands darted around him and plates vanished as if by magic. It gave him time to consider the Prince's remarks. He had heard that he was eager to increase pressure on the French, finish it once and for all. No wonder the prime minister was absent; Spencer Perceval leaned towards appeasement, if only to avoid war with the United States.

But the Regent's powers were severely limited for another twelve months, and no drastic actions might be commenced that could have far-reaching effects to which, after this period, the King might object if recovered from his madness.

He looked up and found Catherine watching him, thinking no doubt of the dangers inherent in this new appointment. They needed an admiral who would act without hesitation, who would not drag his feet and wait for conflicting instructions from London. That was the official position. They both knew the reality. He had often told her about the loneliness of command when sailing out of company without higher authority. If you were successful, others would take the credit. If you failed, the blame was yours alone.

He raised his glass to her.

The Prince was running his eyes over the next course, a highly decorative array of roast rack of lamb, larded capon and braised turkey, ham, tongue and several kinds of vegetables. And, of course, more wine. He said, 'I should have seated you at the other end of the table, Sir Richard. You and this lady are akin to conspirators!'

But he laughed, and Bolitho noted that several guests were nodding and laughing too, although they could not possibly have heard a word. It was just as well that the soldiers and sailors in the field or on the ocean who often paid for their service with their lives could not see those who took them so much for granted. 'I am told that you will sail first to Antigua?' He gestured to a footman, who served him a second portion of capon. It gave Bolitho time to look at her, and recognise the shadow of pain at the Prince's abrupt disclosure. *I should have told her when I knew.*

He answered, 'I shall assemble my squadron there, and I hope to gain some local knowledge as well.'

The Prince dabbed his chin and said casually, 'I knew your late husband, Lady Catherine. An eager man at the tables.' He gazed at her. 'Reckless, to a point of danger.'

'I know.'

'But we all have our weaknesses. Even I . . .' He did not elaborate, but attacked the braised turkey with renewed vigour.

Then he remarked, 'Your choice of captain, Sir Richard.' He snapped his fingers absently in the direction of a footman. 'Tyacke, isn't it? You could have had any captain. Any man would be prepared to kill for such a chance. And yet you chose him without hesitation. Why so?'

'He is an excellent seaman and an accomplished navigator.'

'But only the commander of a lowly brig?'

The Prince stared down with astonishment as Catherine laid one hand on his sleeve.

She said quietly, 'But is it not also true that Nelson chose Hardy for his flag-captain when *he* in fact commanded a lowly brig?'

He roared with laughter. '*Touché*, Lady Catherine! I am impressed!'

She started with alarm as a glass fell on the table and the wine spread towards her like blood. Bolitho said, 'Forgive me, sir.' But he was speaking to Catherine, and she knew it.

The light from one of the great chandeliers had dazzled him, and he had missed the wineglass even as he reached for it. No one else seemed to have noticed.

The Prince patted her hand, beaming genially at her. 'We will take more wine while these fellows replace the cloth.' He did not remove his hand and added, 'There are so many things I wish to know.'

'About me, sir?' She shook her head and felt the diamond pendant warm against her breast.

'You are much spoken of, Lady Catherine. Admired too, I've no doubt!'

'I am loved by but one, sir.'

Bolitho glanced at the footman who had replaced his glass. 'Thank you.' The man almost dropped his tray, and Bolitho guessed that he was rarely acknowledged, let alone addressed.

He looked down the table, and found Sillitoe watching him. Too far away to hear anything, but near enough to guess what the Prince was doing. What he did so often and so well.

'My spies tell me that you are a good horsewoman. Perhaps when Sir Richard is away you would join me for a ride. I adore horses.'

She smiled, the light and shadow on her high cheekbones making her appear even more lovely. 'I shall not come, sir.' When he leaned towards her she shook her head and laughed. 'Not even for you!'

The Prince appeared surprised and uncertain. 'We shall see!' Then he turned to Bolitho and said, 'All real men must envy you.' His irritation was plain as a woman several places away leaned forward and pitched her voice until it was audible.

'I have wondered, Lady Catherine, and others must have asked you since that terrible shipwreck . . .'

Catherine glanced at Bolitho and gave a slight shrug. This was familiar ground. His sister Felicity had put forth the very suggestion this woman was about to make.

'What have you wondered, madam?'

'All those men in one small boat.' She looked around, her eyes just a little too bright. She had obviously not been warned about the Prince's love of wine. 'And you the only *lady* amongst them?'

Catherine waited. Sophie apparently was not included in the ordeal. She was only a servant.

She said coolly, 'It is not an experience I would wish to repeat.'

On the opposite side of the table, a worried-looking man with thinning hair said in a fierce whisper, 'That is *enough*, Kathleen.'

His wife, very much younger, tossed her head. 'Things which women must do, but in front of staring eyes . . .'

Bolitho said abruptly, 'Do you never ask about the sailors who are at sea in all conditions, madam? How they live? Why they tolerate such conditions? Then I will tell you. It is out of necessity.' He turned towards Catherine. 'I shall never forget her courage, and I would suggest *you* do not, either!'

The Prince nodded and said in a stage whisper, 'I expect that Lady Kathleen would have welcomed the experience!' His eyes were hard with dislike as the insinuation reached the woman in question.

The remainder of the evening was an ordeal of endurance and discomfort. Another great course arrived, this time of guinea-fowl, oyster patties and curried lobster, with more wine to wash it down. Finally, a rhubarb tart was served with three kinds of jelly and, lastly, cheesecakes. Bolitho wanted to drag out his watch, but knew his host would see and resent it.

He looked across at Catherine and she blew out her cheeks at him. 'I shall not eat again for another month!'

Eventually it was over. After the ladies had withdrawn there was port and cognac for the gentlemen – the latter, assured the Prince, not contraband. Bolitho guessed that most of the guests were beyond caring. The Prince detained them until the last, as Bolitho had known he would. He watched a servant bringing his hat and cloak, but before he could take them the Prince said in his thick voice, 'Admiral Bolitho, may good fortune go with you.' Then he took Catherine's hand and kissed it lingeringly. He looked into her dark eyes. 'I never envied a man before, Lady Catherine, not even to be King.' Then he kissed her hand again and held her bare arm with his strong fingers. 'Sir Richard is that man.'

Finally they were in the carriage, the iron-shod wheels rattling over the cobbles and into the darkened streets.

He felt her nestle against him. 'I am sorry about Antigua.'

'I think I knew.'

'You were wonderful, Kate. I had to bite my tongue at times.'

She rubbed her head against his shoulder. 'I know. I almost told that Kathleen woman a thing or two!' She laughed bitterly. 'Are you tired, Richard?' She touched his arm. '*Too* tired?'

He slipped his hand beneath her cloak and caressed her breast.

'I will wake you when we see the Thames, Kate. Then we shall see who is tired!'

Young Matthew heard her laugh. All those carriages and famous people, but when the others heard whose

78

coachman *he* was they had treated him like a hero. Wait until they reached Falmouth again, he thought. He might even stretch the story for Ferguson and Allday's benefit and say that the Prince of Wales had spoken to *him*!

The Thames showed itself in the moonlight like blue steel and Bolitho moved slightly in his seat.

He heard her whisper, 'No, I am not asleep. Do not take your hand away. I shall be ready.'

The Crossed Keys Inn was small but commodious, and perched beside the road that ran north from Plymouth to Tavistock. It was rarely used by the coaching trade, which was hardly surprising. James Tyacke on his walks after dark had discovered that in places the track was hardly wide enough for a farm wagon, let alone a coach-and-four.

This evening he sat in a corner of the parlour and wondered how the inn paid for itself. It was run by a homely little woman named Meg, a widow like so many inn and alehouse proprietors in the West Country. Few folk from the nearby village of St Budeaux seemed to come here, and during the day most of the customers were farm workers who – thank God, he thought – kept to themselves.

He sat in the shadow of the big chimney-breast and watched the flickering flames in the hearth. It was April and the trees were in bud, the fields alive with birds. But it was still cold at night.

Soon he would eat, one of Meg's rabbit pies most likely. Then another walk maybe. He glanced around the parlour, the furniture scrubbed and clean, the walls decorated with hunting scenes and some old brasses. It was his last night here. He stared at the new uniform coat that lay on a bench seat opposite his own. The cost of gold lace had risen since his last purchase, he thought. Just as well he had received a large payment of prize money. Memories came, sudden and vivid: *Larne*'s gunner dropping a ball across the bows of some stinking slaver, terrified black faces, naked women chained together in their filth like animals. The slavers themselves, Portuguese and Arab, men prepared to bribe and barter. When they were brought to him they knew it was pointless. There were no more bargains to be made, only the rope at the end of the passage to Freetown or the Cape.

The thrill of the chase, with every spar threatening to splinter itself under a full press of canvas.

Ozanne had her now. Tyacke could think of no better man.

He stared again at his coat, a bright new epaulette on the right shoulder. It seemed somehow out of place, he thought. But he was a captain now, no matter how junior. He wondered if Avery had told Sir Richard how he had betrayed his secret in order to persuade him.

Suppose Avery had kept silent. *Would I have changed my mind? Or would I still be in the dockyard in* Larne?

Two men came in and moved to a table on the far side of the room. Meg seemed to know them and brought tankards of ale without being asked. On her way back to the kitchen she paused to poke the fire. If she had been shocked by Tyacke's face she had not shown it. Perhaps she had seen worse in her time.

'So we'm losin' yew tomorrer, Mr Tyacke.'

'Yes,' he said, turning slightly away from her.

'I've told Henry to fetch 'is cart bright 'n' early for yew.'

Tomorrow. Weeks of uncertainty. Now it was almost time.

Tyacke had not been back in England for years. On his way here from the dockyard he had watched the passing scenery like a stranger in some foreign country. Through the city itself, shop after shop. Hairdressers and hatters, painters and distillers, and more inns and lodging-houses than he could imagine. Plenty of sea-officers, and sailors who he assumed had the protection and were free to come and go as they pleased. He recalled the disbelief amongst *Larne*'s company when Bolitho had granted permission for his men to go ashore. Only one had failed to return. Drunk, he had fallen into a dock and drowned.

He had seen plenty of women, too. Some prettily dressed and decorative, the wives of army and naval officers, perhaps. Others, like Meg of the Crossed Keys, trying to do men's work, to replace those who might never come home.

He said, 'I've been very comfortable here. Maybe I'll see you again some day.'

She turned to look at him, and although he watched carefully for it, there was no abhorrence in her eyes when they rested on his face.

'I'll fetch your supper soon, zur.'

81

They both knew they would not meet again.

He sipped his brandy. Good stuff. Maybe smugglers came this way ... His thoughts returned to his new command. How different she would be. Designed originally as a small third-rate of sixty-four guns, she had been cut down to her present size by the removal of most of her upper deck and corresponding armament. But her forty twenty-four pounders remained, with an additional four eighteen-pounders for bow and stern-chasers. Tyacke had studied every detail of the ship, and her history since she had been built at the famous William Hartland yard at Rochester on the Medway.

He considered Bolitho's comments, the ship's possible use if war broke out with the United States. All the big new American frigates carried twenty-four pounders and for sheer firepower were far superior to English frigates like *Anemone*.

More to the point, perhaps, his new command had a far greater cruising range. Her original company of over six hundred had now been reduced to two hundred and seventy, which included fifty-five Royal Marines.

She was still undermanned, but then every ship was, which was in or near a naval port.

All those unknown faces. How long would it be before he came to know them, their value, their individual qualities? As a captain he could ask what he pleased of his officers. Respect, as he had seen with Bolitho, had to be earned.

He thought again of the ship herself. Thirty-four years old, built of fine Kentish oak when there had been such trees for the asking. In newer ships some of the timbers were barely seasoned, and their frames were cut by carpenters, not shaped over the years for extra strength. Some were built of teak on oak frames, like John Company's ships, which were mostly laid down in Bombay. Teak was like iron, but hated by the sailors who had to work and fight in them. Unlike oak splinters, teak could poison a man, kill him far more slowly and painfully than canister shot.

Tyacke swallowed more brandy. His new command had first tasted salt water while he had been in his mother's arms.

His face softened into a smile. *We must have grown up together*. She had even been at the Nile. He tried not to touch his scarred cheek. Other battles too. The Chesapeake and the Saintes, Copenhagen, and then because she was too small for the line of battle she had shared all the miseries of blockade and convoy duty.

There must be a lot of experienced post-captains asking why Sir Richard should hoist his flag above an old converted third-rate when he could have had anything he wanted. A full admiral now. He wondered what Catherine Somervell thought about it. He could see her as if she were beside him, first in the dirty and soaking sailor's clothing, and then in the yellow gown he had carried with him since the girl of his choice had rejected him. It was strange, but he could even think of that without the pain, as if it had happened to somebody else.

He tried to remember if he had all he needed, and his thoughts returned to Bolitho's mistress. But the term offended him. *His lady*. She would make certain that Bolitho was well provided for when *he* left home.

He thought he could smell cooking and realised how

hungry he was. It made good sense to eat well tonight. He would be too tense and anxious later on. He smiled again as he recalled that Bolitho had told him he was always nervous when he took over a new command. *But remember, they are far more worried about their new captain!*

And what about John Allday – 'his oak', as he called him – would he be so eager this time to quit the land?

One of the men at the other table put down his tankard and stared at the door. His companion almost ran through the adjoining room where some farm-hands were drinking rough cider. Then Tyacke heard it. The tramp of feet, the occasional clink of metal.

Meg bustled in, her hands full of knives and forks.

'The press, sir. They'm not usually this far from 'ome.' She smiled at him. 'Never fear. I'll see they don't disturb yew.'

He sat back in the deep shadows. Being in charge of a press-gang was a thankless task. As a junior lieuten-ant he had done it only once. Whimpering men and blaspheming women. Curiously enough, although most of the shore parties who performed that duty were themselves pressed men, they were usually the most ruthless.

There were muffled shouts from the rear of the inn and Tyacke guessed that the man who had rushed from the room had been taken. His companion came back, shaking despite the folded protection he had been fortunate enough to carry.

The door crashed open and a young lieutenant strode into the parlour.

84

He snapped, 'Stand up and be examined!' Then he seemed to realise that the man in question had already been inspected and swung towards the shadowy figure by the chimney-breast.

'And you! Did you hear me? In the King's name!'

Tyacke did not move but thrust out his foot and pushed the bench seat into the candlelight.

The lieutenant gaped at the gleaming gold lace and stammered, 'I did not know, sir! Few officers come this way.'

Tyacke said quietly, 'Which is why I came. Not to be shouted at by some arrogant puppy hiding in the King's coat!' He stood up. Meg, two armed seamen in the doorway and the man who had been examined all froze as if it were some kind of mime.

Tyacke turned very slowly. 'What is your name, lieutenant?'

But the young officer was unable to speak; he was staring at Tyacke's terrible wound as if mesmerised.

Then he muttered in a small voice, 'Laroche, s-sir.'

'May I ask what ship?'

'*Indomitable*, sir.'

'Then we shall meet tomorrow, *Mister* Laroche. I am Captain James Tyacke.'

Suddenly he had the parlour to himself.

Meg hurried in again, a steaming pot wrapped in a cloth.

'I be that sorry, zur.'

Tyacke reached out and touched her arm. 'It was nothing. We all have to begin somewhere.'

Tomorrow it would be all over the ship. He considered it. *Indomitable. My* ship.

Again he thought about Bolitho and the memory steadied him.

They will be far more worried about you.

Meg left him to his supper but paused in the door to watch him, wondering how it had happened, how such a fine-looking man could ever learn to accept it.

She quietly closed the door, and thought of him long after he had gone.

5

Indomitable

Henry the carter tugged slightly at the reins as the wheels clattered over the first of the dockyard cobbles.

He said, 'She's out at anchor, zur.' He glanced at his passenger's strong profile, unable to understand why anybody would willingly go to sea, captain or not.

Tyacke stared across the gleaming water and was surprised that he was so calm. No, that was not it. He felt no emotion whatsoever.

He glanced towards the wall and was relieved to see that *Larne* had moved her berth, doubtless to complete her re-rigging. He wondered if they knew he was here, if someone was watching him with a telescope at this very second.

He said, 'There are stairs at the end.'

'Roight, zur. I'll make sure there be a boat waitin' for 'ee.'

Oh, there will be, he thought. Even if the boat's crew had been up since before dawn. Tyacke had done it himself often enough. Waiting for the new lord and master, imagining what he would be like: the man who would rule everybody's life from senior lieutenant

87

to ship's boy; who could promote, disrate, flog and, if necessary, hang anyone who did not abide by his orders.

He shivered slightly but disdained to put on his boat-cloak. It was a fair morning and the sea was a mass of dancing white horses, but it was not the cool air that caused him to tremble. It was this moment, which he had dreaded, of this particular day.

He saw a flurry of splashes and knew it was a boat casting off from a mooring buoy. His arrival had been noted.

'Thank you, Henry.' He put some coins into the man's fist and stared at the big brass-bound chest. They had travelled a long way together since he had recovered from his injuries. His complete world was contained in it.

Recovered? Hardly that. It was impossible not to be reminded of it daily. He saw himself reflected in other people's faces, and the horror and the pity he saw there had never ceased to wound him.

All through the night he had gone over everything he had discovered about *Indomitable*, his head filled, as if it would burst if he could not rest. All the lieutenants had been aboard throughout the refit, even the luckless Laroche who had blundered into the inn parlour. The first confrontation. There would be many more.

He gazed out at the moored ship. Without her original top-hamper she looked like any other large frigate at this distance. Like the *Valkyrie*, with her main gundeck higher than fifth- and sixth-rates so that her devastating broadside could be used to maximum effect. He watched the approaching boat critically, the oars rising and falling like wings. He thought even Allday would approve.

He turned to speak once more, but the little cart had gone. Only the sea-chest remained. The gig swung in a tight arc, the bowman poised with his boathook to grip the mooring ring on the stairs.

After what seemed an eternity a young lieutenant ran up the stairs and raised his hat with a flourish.

'Protheroe, sir! At your service!'

'Ah, yes. Fourth lieutenant.' He saw the young officer's eyebrows lift with surprise, and thought for a moment that his memory had betrayed him.

'Why – yes, sir!'

Tyacke turned deliberately to reveal the burned side of his face. It had the effect he expected. When he turned back, Protheroe had gone pale. But his voice was controlled as he rapped out orders, and two seamen ran to collect the heavy chest.

Tyacke glanced at them as they hurried past with their eyes averted. Laroche had obviously told a grim story about their new captain.

Protheroe watched the chest being carried down to the gig, no doubt terrified that they would let it fall into the water. Not long out of a midshipman's berth, Tyacke thought.

'May we proceed, Mr Protheroe?'

The lieutenant stared around with dismay. 'I was looking for your coxswain, sir.'

Tyacke felt his mouth break into a smile.

'I am afraid that the commander of a brig does not run to his own cox'n!'

'I see, sir.' He stood aside and waited for Tyacke to descend the weed-lined steps.

Again the quick stares from the boat's crew, then every eye looking instantly away as his glance passed over them. Tyacke sat down in the sternsheets and held his sword against his thigh, as he had done when he left *Larne*.

'Let go! Bear off forrard! *Out oars!*'

Tyacke turned to watch the gap of lively water widening. *I am leaving. God for what?*

'Give way all!'

He asked, 'How long have you been in *Indomitable*?'

'A year, sir. I joined her while she was still laid up in ordinary and about to complete her rebuilding.' He faltered under Tyacke's eyes. 'Before that I was signals midshipman in the *Crusader*, thirty-two.'

Tyacke stared across the stroke oarsman's broad shoulder at the masts and yards rising up to greet him, as if they were lifting from the seabed. Now he could see the difference. One hundred and eighty feet overall, and of some fourteen hundred tons, her broad beam betrayed that she had been built originally for the line of battle. Her sail plan had changed little, he thought. With a wind over the quarter she would run like a deer if properly handled.

He saw the pale sunlight gleaming on several telescopes and knew the men were stampeding to their stations.

What would his first lieutenant be like? Perhaps he had expected promotion, even command of the powerful ship once her overhaul was completed. *Indomitable*'s last captain had left her months ago, leaving his senior lieutenant in charge until their lordships had decided what to do with her. They had not. He gripped his sword even tighter. Sir Richard Bolitho had made that decision. He could imagine the words. *So be it.*

'Bring her to larboard, Mr Protheroe!' There was an edge to his voice, although he had not realised it.

As he watched the long tapering jib-boom reaching out towards them like a lance, he saw the figurehead where it crouched beneath the beakhead. *Crouched* was right. It was in the form of a lion about to attack with both paws slashing at the air. A fine piece of work, Tyacke thought, but it was not the original figurehead, which would have been far too big for the rebuilt hull. Except for the bright red mouth and gleaming eyes, it shone with expensive gold paint, perhaps a gift from the builders who had converted her.

'Carry on, Mr Protheroe.' He was suddenly eager to begin, his stomach in knots as the gig veered towards the main chains and the entry port, where he had already seen the scarlet of the marines. *My marines.*

He thought of Adam Bolitho's frigate, *Anemone.* Lying alongside this ship, she would be overwhelmed.

His experienced eye took in everything, from the buff and black hull that shone like glass above the cruising white horses, to the new rigging, shrouds and stays freshly blacked-down and every sail neatly furled, probably by the petty officers themselves for this important occasion.

For all of us, a voice seemed to say.

He would find himself a personal coxswain. Another Allday, if there was such a man. He would be more than useful at times like these.

91

The gig had hooked on, the oars tossed, the seamen staring directly astern. Anywhere but at their new captain.

Tyacke rose to his feet, very aware of the lively gig's movement, waiting for the exact moment to climb up to the entry port.

'Thank you, Mr Protheroe. I am obliged.'

Then he seized the handropes and stepped quickly on to the tumblehome before the sea could drag him down.

Like the walk from *Larne* to the waiting carriage, the minutes seemed endless. As his head rose above the port, the sudden explosion of noise was deafening. The bayoneted muskets of the Royal Marines snapped in salute in time with their officer's sword, and the calls of boatswain's mates, followed by the rattle of drums, rose and then fell silent.

Tyacke removed his hat in salute to the extended quarterdeck with its neatly-packed hammock nettings. He noticed that the wheel and compass boxes were unsheltered. Builders and designers, then as now, saw only the efficiency of their work, not men being shot down by enemy sharpshooters with nothing but the stowed hammocks to protect them.

A square-faced lieutenant stepped from the ranks of blue and white, warrant officers and midshipmen, two so young that Tyacke wondered how anyone could have allowed them to leave home.

'I am Scarlett, the senior here.' He hesitated and added, 'Welcome to *Indomitable*, sir.'

A serious-looking face. Reliable . . . perhaps.

'Thank you, Mr Scarlett.' He followed the first lieutenant along the rank, all standing in order of seniority. Even Protheroe had managed to slip into the line during the brief ceremony at the entry port.

Four lieutenants, including the unfortunate Laroche. Their eyes met and Tyacke asked coldly, 'How many men did you press, Mr Laroche?'

He stammered, 'Three, sir.' He hung his head, expecting the mainmast to fall on him.

'We shall find many more. I daresay all Plymouth knew you were abroad last night.' He moved on, leaving the third lieutenant looking dazed.

Scarlett was saying, 'This is Isaac York, sir, our sailing master.'

A capable, interesting face: you would know him as a deep-water sailor even if he were disguised as a priest.

Tyacke asked, 'How long have you been sailing master, Mr York?'

He was younger than most masters he had known, the *characters* of almost every vessel.

York grinned. 'A year, sir. Afore that I was master's mate aboard this ship for four years.'

Tyacke nodded, satisfied. A man who knew how she would handle under all conditions. The face appeared about thirty, except that his neatly cut hair was slate-grey.

They turned to the quarterdeck rail. The midshipmen could wait.

Tyacke felt in his coat for his commission. As so ordered, he would read himself in.

'Have all hands lay aft, Mr Scarlett – ' He stopped, and saw the first lieutenant's instant uncertainty. 'That man, by the boat tier . . .'

Scarlett relaxed only slightly. 'That's Troughton. He serves as cook. Is something wrong, sir?'

'Have him come aft.'

A midshipman scuttled away to fetch him and most of the men already on deck turned to watch as the one-legged sailor in the long white apron clumped on to the quarterdeck.

'If you do not approve, sir?' Scarlett sounded apprehensive.

Tyacke stared at the limping figure. He had sensed somebody's eyes upon him even as he had come aboard. *Now, of all times* . . . There was utter silence as he strode over to the cook and, reaching him, put his hands on the thin shoulders.

'Dear God. I was told you were dead, Troughton.'

The man studied him feature by feature and, lastly, the scars. Then he glanced down at his wooden leg and said quietly, 'They tried to do for both of us that day, sir. I'm so glad you've come to the old *Indom*. Welcome aboard!'

Very solemnly they shook hands. So she even had a special nickname, Tyacke thought. It was like a triumph: someone had survived on that hideous day. A young seaman working with a handspike to retrain one of his guns. He should have been killed; Tyacke had imagined him being thrown outboard with all the other corpses. But he himself had been deafened and blinded, and had heard only screams. His own.

As the ship's company swarmed aft and he took out

94

his commission and unrolled it, Tyacke saw men whispering to each other, those who had seen the incident trying to describe it to their friends. The scarred captain and a one-legged cook.

Grouped behind him, most of the officers were too young to understand, but York the master and the first lieutenant knew well enough what it meant.

And when Tyacke began to read himself in they both leaned closer to hear, as if this tall straight-backed man gave the formality both significance and a new impact.

It was addressed to James Tyacke Esquire, appointing him to the *Indomitable* on this day in April 1811. Not far from the place where Drake was alleged to have kept the fleet and the Dons waiting while he finished his game of bowls.

Willing and requiring you forthwith to go on board and take upon you the charge and command of captain in her accordingly; strictly charging and commanding all the officers and company of the said Indomitable . . . At that point Tyacke looked across the mass of upturned faces. *The old Indom.* But the one-legged cook was not in sight. Perhaps he had imagined it, and Troughton had been only a lingering spectre who had come back to give him the strength he had needed.

Eventually it was all over, ending with the customary warning. Threat, as he perceived it. *Hereof nor you nor any of you may fail as will answer the contrary at your peril.*

He rolled up the commission and said, 'God Save the King!'

There was neither sound nor cheering, and the silence at any other time would have been oppressive.

He replaced his hat and gazed aloft where Sir Richard Bolitho's flag would soon be hoisted to the mainmast truck for the first time.

'You may dismiss the hands, Mr Scarlett. I will see all officers in my quarters in one hour, if you please.'

The figures crowded below the quarterdeck rail were still thinking only of their own future, and not of the ship. *Not yet.*

And yet despite the silence he could feel only a sense of elation, an emotion which was rare to him.

This was not his beloved *Larne*. It was a new beginning, for him and for the ship.

Lieutenant Matthew Scarlett strode aft, glancing this way and that to ensure that the ship was tidy, the hammock nettings empty, all spare cordage coiled or flaked down until the new day. The air that touched his face when he passed an open gun-port was cold, and the ship's motion was unsteady for so powerful a hull.

He had overheard the sailing master lecturing some of the 'young gentlemen' during the dog watches. 'When the gulls fly low over the rocks at night, it'll be bad next day, no matter what some clever Jacks tell you!' Scarlett had seen the two newest midshipmen glance doubtfully at one another. But the gulls *had* flown abeam even as the darkness of evening had started to close in around the anchored ship. Isaac York was rarely mistaken.

Past the unattended double-wheel and further aft

into the shadows, where a Royal Marine sentry stood in the light of a spiralling lantern. The *Indomitable* had been converted to contain two large cabins aft, one for her captain, and the other for use by the senior officer of a flotilla or squadron.

But for Tyacke's arrival and the vessel's selection as Sir Richard Bolitho's flagship, one of the cabins might have been his. He acknowledged the watchful sentry and reached for the screen door.

The sentry tapped the deck with his musket and bawled, 'First Lieutenant, *sir*!'

'Enter!'

Scarlett closed the door behind him, his eyes taking in several things at once.

Tyacke's supper stood on a tray untouched; the coffee he had requested must be ice-cold. The table was completely covered with books, canvas folios and pages of the captain's own notes.

Scarlett thought of the officers all packed into this cabin shortly after the captain had read himself in. Could that have been only this morning? Tyacke must have been going through the ship's affairs ever since.

'You have not eaten, sir. May I send for something?'

Tyacke looked at him for the first time. 'You were at Trafalgar, I believe?'

Scarlett nodded, taken aback by the directness.

'Aye, sir. I was in Lord Nelson's weather column, the *Spartiate*, seventy-four. Captain Sir Francis Laforey.'

'Did you ever meet Nelson?'

'No, sir. We saw him often enough aboard the flagship. Few of us ever *met* him. After he fell, many of

97

our people wept, as if they had known him all their lives.'

'I see.'

Scarlett watched Tyacke's sun-browned hands leafing through another book. 'Did *you* ever meet him, sir?'

Tyacke stared up from the table, his eyes very blue in the swaying lanterns.

'Like you, I only saw him in the far distance.' He was touching his scarred face, his eyes suddenly hard. 'At the Nile.'

Scarlett waited. So that was where it had happened.

Tyacke said abruptly, 'I understand that the purser's clerk has been doing the work of ship's clerk as well as his own?'

'Yes, sir. We have been very short-handed, so I thought . . .'

Tyacke closed the book. 'Pursers and their clerks are necessary, Mr Scarlett. But it is sometimes a risk to give them too much leeway in ship's affairs.' He pushed the book aside and opened another where he had used a quill as a marker. 'Detail one of the reliable midshipmen for the task until we are fully manned.'

'I shall ask the purser if . . .'

Tyacke regarded him. 'No, *tell* Mr Viney what you intend.' He paused. 'I have also been going through the punishment book.'

Scarlett tensed, with growing resentment at the manner in which the new captain was treating him.

'Sir?'

'This man, Fullerton. Three dozen lashes for stealing

98

some trifle or other from a messmate. Rather harsh, surely?'

'It was my decision, sir. It was harsh, but the laws of the lower deck are harder than the Articles of War. His messmates would have put him over the side.' He waited for a challenge, but surprisingly Tyacke smiled.

'I'd have offered him four dozen!' He glanced around and Scarlett studied the burned half of his face. *He looks at me as the captain, but inwardly he must bleed at every curious stare.*

Tyacke said, 'I will not tolerate unfair or brutal punishment. But I will have discipline in my ship and I will always support my officers, unless . . .' He did not finish it.

He pushed some papers along the black and white chequered deck-covering and revealed a bottle of brandy.

'Fetch two glasses.' His voice pursued the first lieutenant as he pulled open a cupboard.

Scarlett saw all the other carefully-stowed bottles. He had watched it being swayed up on a tackle just the previous day.

He said cautiously, 'Fine brandy, sir.'

'From a lady.' Who but Lady Catherine would have taken the trouble? Would even have cared?

They drank in silence, the ship groaning around them, a wet breeze rattling the halliards overhead.

Tyacke said, 'We will sail with the tide at noon. We will gain sea-room and set course for Falmouth, where Sir Richard Bolitho will hoist his flag. I have no doubt that Lady Catherine Somervell will come aboard with him.' He felt rather than saw Scarlett's surprise. 'So make certain the hands are well turned out, and that a bosun's chair is ready for her.'

Scarlett ventured, 'From what I have heard of the lady, sir . . .' He saw Tyacke tense, as if about to reprimand him. He continued, 'She could climb aboard unaided.' He saw Tyacke nod, his eyes distant, for that moment only another man entirely.

'She could indeed.' He gestured towards the bottle. 'Another thing. As of tomorrow, this ship will wear the White Ensign and masthead pendant accordingly.' He took the goblet and stared at it. 'I know that Sir Richard is now an Admiral of the Red, and to my knowledge he has always sailed under that colour. But their lordships have decreed that if we are to fight, it will be under the White Ensign.'

Scarlett looked away. 'As we did at Trafalgar, sir.'

'Yes.'

'About a coxswain, sir?'

'D'you have anyone in mind?'

'There's a gun captain named Fairbrother. A good hand. But if he doesn't suit I'll find another.'

'I'll see him after breakfast.'

Rain pattered across the tall stern windows. 'It's going to blow tomorrow, sir.'

'All the better. I went through your watch and quarter bills.' Immediately he sensed Scarlett's anxiety. One who resented criticism, or had been unfairly used in the past. 'You've done a good job. Not too many bumpkins in one watch, or too many seasoned hands in another. But once standing down-Channel I want all hands turned-to for sail and gun drill. They will be our

100

strength, as always.' He stood up and walked aft to the windows, now streaked with salt spray.

'We carry eight midshipmen. Keep them changing around – get them to work more closely with the master's mates. It is not enough to tip your hat like some half-pay admiral, or have perfect manners at the mess table. As far as the people are concerned they *are* King's officers, God help us, so they will perform accordingly. Who is in charge of signals, by the way?'

'Mr Midshipman Blythe, sir.' Scarlett was amazed at the way the captain's mind could jump so swiftly from one subject to the next. 'He will be due for examination for lieutenant shortly.'

'Is he any good?' He saw the lieutenant start at the bluntness of his question and added more gently, 'You do no wrong, Mr Scarlett. Your loyalty is to me and the ship in that order, and not to the members of your wardroom.'

Scarlett smiled. 'He attends well to his duties, sir. I must say that his head sometimes gets larger as the examination draws closer!'

'Well said. One other thing. When Sir Richard's flag breaks at the mainmast truck, remember, I am still *your* captain. Always feel free to speak with me. It is better than keeping it all sealed up like some fireship about to explode.' He watched the effect of his words on Scarlett's open, honest features. 'You can carry on now. I feel certain that the wardroom is all agog for your news.' But he said it without malice.

He realised that Scarlett was still there, his hands playing with his cocked hat.

'Is there something else, Mr Scarlett?'

'Well, sir . . .' Scarlett hesitated. 'As we are to be of one company, war or no, may I ask something?'

'If it is reasonable.'

'Sir Richard Bolitho. What is he like, sir? Truly like?'

For a moment he thought he had tested the captain's confidences too far. Tyacke's emotions were mixed, as if one were fighting the other. He strode across the spacious cabin and back again, his hair almost brushing the deckhead.

'We spoke of Lord Nelson, a leader of courage and inspiration. One I would have liked to meet. But serve under him – I think not.'

He knew Scarlett was staring at him, earnestly waiting. 'Sir Richard Bolitho, now . . .' He hesitated and thought of the brandy and wine Lady Catherine had sent aboard for him. He felt suddenly angry with himself for discussing their special relationship. *But I did invite his confidence.* He said quietly, 'Let me say this, Mr Scarlett. I would serve no other man. For that is what he is. A man.' He touched his face but did not notice it. 'He gave me back my pride. And my hope.'

'Thank you, sir.' Scarlett reached the screen door. Afterwards he guessed that the captain had not even heard him.

James Tyacke looked around the large cabin before examining his face in the mirror that hung above his sea-chest. For a second or two he touched the mirror, scratched here and there, dented around the frame. He

102

often wondered how it had survived over the years. *Or me, either*.

The ship had quietened somewhat after all the bustle and preparations to get under way. Calls twittered and voices still shouted occasional orders, but for the most part they were ready.

Tyacke walked to the stern windows and rubbed the misty glass with his sleeve.

It was blustery, the windows full of cruising white horses, the nearest land only a wedge of green.

He could faintly hear the clank, clank of pawls as the seamen threw their weight on the capstan bars. But down aft, this cabin was like a haven, a barrier between him and the ship. Unlike the little *Larne* where everybody had seemed to get under his feet.

Any minute now and Scarlett would come down and report that they were ready. He would be curious, no doubt, to see how the new captain would perform on his first day at sea.

Tyacke had already been on deck at the first suggestion of dawn, with Plymouth Sound glittering in a moving panorama of small angry waves.

He had found the master, Isaac York, by the compass boxes speaking with two of his mates; the latter had melted away when they had seen their captain up and about so early. They might think him nervous, unable to stay away from the scurrying seamen both on deck and aft.

'How is the wind, Mr York?'

York had peered aloft, his eyes crinkling into deep crow's-feet. 'Steady enough, sir. East by north. It'll be lively when we clear the land.'

Confident. A professional sailor who could still appreciate being consulted by his captain.

He had added in an almost fond tone, 'The *Indom*'s a fine sailer, sir. I've known none better. She'll hold close to the wind even under storm stays'ls. Not many frigates could boast as much.' He had squinted up at the small monkey-like figures working far above the deck. 'With her press of canvas she can shift herself!' A man proud of his ship, and of what he had achieved to become her master.

Tyacke dragged out his watch. Almost time. He listened to the clank of the capstan and could picture the straining seamen as they fought to haul the ship up to her anchor. Boots thumped overhead: the Royal Marines who were part of the afterguard preparing to free the mizzen sails and the big driver when so ordered. The seamen always claimed contemptuously that the marines were only given the task because the mizzen mast was the simplest rigged, and even they could manage it.

More feet were running over the deck. Tyacke tried to identify every sound. The boats were hoisted on their tier. The ship's launch had been landed and a new, dark green barge lashed in its place, the admiral's own boat. He thought about the colours being hoisted that morning, the White Ensign curling in the wind. Nelson at Trafalgar had been the first admiral to fight a fleet action under that flag. In the smoke and hatred of a sea-battle it was absolutely vital that every captain should know friend from foe, and the Red Ensign or even the Blue had been too dangerous at Trafalgar, where French and Spanish flags of similar colouring could easily have confused the identity of ships, and impeded the immediate response to signals.

He knew that Scarlett was coming even before the sentry yelled out the news. He compared him to the two Royal Marine officers, Captain Cedric du Cann and his lieutenant, David Merrick. Men who would never question their orders, no matter what. Perhaps it was better to be like them. Imagination could be a risky possession.

He called, 'Enter!'

Scarlett, hat tucked underneath one arm, opened the screen door, his eyes seeking out his captain. To assess his demeanour, or plumb the depths of his uncertainty?

'The anchor is all but hove short, sir.'

'I shall come up.'

Scarlett was still watching him. 'The master has laid a course to weather Nare Head, sir.'

'I know.'

Scarlett saw him glance around the cabin. He himself had gone on deck after a late night in the wardroom, fending off speculation and gossip until the others had tired of it. Except the purser, James Viney, who had repeatedly questioned him about the captain's decision regarding his clerk. Scarlett was beginning to wonder if Viney did have something to hide. It was often said that half the inns and lodging-houses in naval ports were either owned or supplied by pursers at the country's expense. But once on deck, Scarlett had seen the captain's skylight still aglow. Did he never sleep or rest? Could he not?

Tyacke led the way up the companion ladder and on to the breezy quarterdeck. A slow glance took it all in.

105

Seamen standing at braces and halliards, topmen already aloft, spread out on the yards and silhouetted against the sky like dwarfs.

Three men on the wheel; York was taking no chances. The lieutenants like little islands of blue and white at each mast, each man staring aft as Tyacke walked to the quarterdeck rail.

He listened to the capstan and heard the faint scrape of a violin, the sound of which had been inaudible in his quarters.

The signals midshipman, Blythe, was standing with his small crew of seamen, his face severe as he watched the captain.

Tyacke nodded to him. He could well imagine he would have a big head.

He glanced aft. The two marine officers with some of their men, their scarlet coats very bright in the drifting spray. York was with his mates near the wheel, but peered up at him and touched his hat.

'Standing by, sir!'

Tyacke saw a squat figure in a plain blue coat and carrying a rattan cane walking along the larboard guns. That would be Sam Hockenhull, the boatswain, seeking the new men, all of whom were probably sick with dismay at being torn from their loved ones, to go to God knew where, and for how long. Beyond Hockenhull he could see one upraised paw of the lion figurehead. Further still, the blurred outline of Plymouth and what looked like a church tower.

He walked across the deck, feeling the stares, hating them.

'There are two collier brigs, larboard quarter, Mr York.'

The master did not smile. 'Aye, sir. I've marked 'em well.'

Tyacke looked at him. 'I'm told that if you ram a fully laden collier it's like hitting the Barrier Reef.'

Then York did grin. 'I'll not be the one to find out, sir!'

'Anchor's coming home now, sir!'

Tyacke folded his arms. 'Get the ship under way, if you please.'

'Stand by the capstan.'

More calls twittered urgently. Spithead Nightingales, the sailors called them.

'Loose the heads'ls!'

Hockenhull the boatswain jabbed the air with his rattan. 'You – move yourself! Take that man's name, Mr Sloper!'

'Loose tops'ls!' That was Scarlett, his powerful voice magnified by his speaking-trumpet while he wiped the drifting spray from his eyes.

'Man the braces! Mr Laroche, put more hands on the weather side as she comes clear!'

Tyacke shaded his eyes and watched the headsails flapping and banging until brought under command. Then up to the topsail yards where the tan-coloured canvas was barely under control, the wind eagerly exploring it as if to hurl the topmen down to the deck.

Tyacke studied the great mainsail yard, its canvas still neatly lashed into place. From the quarterdeck it looked twice the length of *Larne*'s mainyard, where one or two slavers had danced their lives away.

'*Anchor's aweigh, sir!*'

Released from the land *Indomitable* heeled over to the thrust of canvas and rudder, the sea almost brushing the lee gunports while she came about, sails thundering as fore and mainsails were hauled and beaten into submission. Some men lost their footing on the deck and fell gasping until dragged back to the taut braces, helped or punched as seemed necessary.

Tyacke watched the two anchored colliers slide past, as if they and not *Indomitable* were moving.

He heard the squeak of halliards and saw a new ensign break out from the gaff, so white against the angry clouds.

'Hold her steady! Steer south-west by south!'

He walked up the tilting deck while men dashed hither and thither on the wet planking.

'Steady she goes, sir! Full an' bye!'

Tyacke called, 'Once we clear the Point we will set the driver, Mr Scarlett!' He had to shout above the violent din of rigging and canvas, the crack of halliards and shrouds as every inch of cordage took and held the strain.

Scarlett touched his hat. 'Aye, *aye*, sir!' He wiped his face and grinned. 'Someone wishes us well.'

Tyacke crossed to the nettings and stared across the choppy water. It was *Larne*. Out at an anchorage now; perhaps leaving this very day. But it was not that. Every yard was manned, with more seamen clinging to the ratlines to wave and cheer. Even *Indomitable*'s own chorus could not drown the wild cheering.

Scarlett glanced round curiously as Tyacke removed his hat, and then waved it slowly back and forth above his head.

The uninjured side of Tyacke's face was turned towards him, and he felt something like pity as he realised what he was seeing.

It was a last farewell.

6

Cross of St George

Bolitho put his arm around her shoulders and said, 'This is far enough, Kate. The path is barely safe even in such clear moonlight.'

They stood side by side on the rough track from Pendennis Point and looked out across the sea. It shone like melting silver, so brightly that the stars seemed faint and insignificant by comparison.

They had walked and ridden every day since their return from London, savouring every moment, sharing every hour, not speaking of the future.

The hillsides were covered now with bluebells and brilliant, contrasting yellow gorse.

How much longer? Three days perhaps. At the most.

As if reading his thoughts, she said quietly, 'Tomorrow your *Indomitable* will come.'

'Aye. I hope James Tyacke is settling down to the change.'

She turned lightly and he felt her looking at him, her hair shining as she pulled out the combs and let it fall across her shoulders.

'Will *we* settle down, darling Richard?' She shook

her head, angry with herself. 'Forgive me. It is not easy for either of us. But I shall miss you so.' She paused, unable to speak of what was uppermost in both their minds. 'There may be farewells, but we will never be parted!'

Tiny lights blinked on the water, like fallen stars, lost in the great full moon.

Bolitho said, 'Fishermen at their pots.' He tried to smile. 'Or revenue officers after another kind of catch.'

'You know what we promised one another?' She had been wearing a shawl but it had slipped down her arms, to leave her shoulders bare in the moonlight.

'Not to waste a minute, Kate. But that was then. This is now. I never want to be parted from you again. Once this matter is settled . . .'

She touched his mouth with her fingers, so cool in the night air. 'I am so proud of you, and you cannot even understand why. You are the *only* man who can do it. You have the experience and the success, and you will give heart to all those under your charge and command. Have their lordships given you all that you wanted?'

He caressed her shoulders, their smoothness and their strength exciting him as always.

'All that they *have* is more likely. Apart from *Indomitable* and *Valkyrie* I shall have six other frigates, as soon as *Anemone* has completed her refit at Plymouth. And there are three brigs as well. Not a fleet, but a flying squadron to be reckoned with.' Thank God *Larne* was ordered back to the anti-slavery patrols. It would have been torture for Tyacke to see her in company day after day.

111

His thoughts turned to George Avery. He was not staying at the house but had gone over to the inn at Fallowfield, where Allday would be fretting about everything as sailing time drew relentlessly closer. It might help Allday to have somebody with him to whom he could talk about the ship and the destination, just as it might help the flag-lieutenant to accept that his sister was dead. That he could have done nothing to save her.

She said suddenly, 'Richard, are you troubled about your daughter?'

Bolitho caught his shoe on some loose stones and felt her arm instantly supporting him. 'There are no secrets from you, Kate.' He hesitated. 'She will be nine years old in two months' time. But I do not know her, nor she me. Her mother has made her into a doll, not like a real child at all.'

It was always there. Guilt, a sense of responsibility. It was nothing of which she could be jealous.

He said, as though reading her thoughts, 'I love only you.'

Catherine faced him. 'I shall always remember what you gave up because of me.' She shook her head as he began to protest. 'No, hear me, Richard. Because of our love you have been abused and taken for granted, when all England should honour the bravest and the gentlest of her commanders.' She relented. 'The man who *forgot* to tell his lover he had been made an admiral!'

'I shall never be allowed to forget that!' He turned her towards the deeper shadows of the hillside. 'They

112

will have a search party out looking for us. We had best get back to the house.'

She put her arm around his waist. 'Home.' One word. It was enough.

The austere stone buildings did not soften against the perfect sky. There was a light in the adjoining cottage. Ferguson, Bolitho's steward, was still awake, doing his books or planning something to please his old friend Allday before he left.

An old dog slumbered in the yard. It was quite deaf, and was no longer much use as a guard dog. But like the crippled and injured men who worked on the estate, the harvest of the war at sea, it belonged here.

Strange not to see leaping flames in the great fireplace. Summer was almost here. Catherine tightened her grip on his arm. But they would not share it together. She glanced at the rug by the empty grate. Where two young people, believing they had lost everything dear to them, had found one another and had loved, and might still be damned for it.

She had sensed Richard's unease when he had mentioned Adam's *Anemone*, which was still lying at Plymouth. It was a heavy secret to carry.

She glanced over her shoulder and saw the sea beyond the windows shining in the moonlight. *The enemy.* She could feel the portraits watching from the stairwell. They had all left here, never to return. She thought of the painting Richard wanted done of her, and she had wondered briefly if he would also like one of his brother Hugh, but this was not the time to ask him. Her man was sailing to confront the Americans, and she sensed that in the present hostile atmosphere neither country would back down. There was too much at stake. He would not wish to be reminded of his brother's treachery. Had Hugh known of Adam's existence, perhaps things might have been different. But fate, having determined the course of lives, could not be unwritten.

Together they walked to the broad opened windows and listened to the silence. Once they heard an owl, and Bolitho remarked, 'The mice will have to take care tonight.'

Tomorrow the ship would come. He would be inextricably involved in its affairs, and haunted by the inevitability of their parting.

She said, 'Dear Bryan has left some wine for us!'

He took her in his arms and felt the tension in her body. 'He knows.'

'Knows what?'

'That I want you, dearest Kate. *Need* you.'

She let him kiss her, on the mouth, the throat, and then on her bare shoulder, watching his hands in the strange light moving over her gown until she could wait no longer.

Then she stood quite naked like a silver statue, her fine breasts uplifted, her arms stretched out to hold him away.

'Undress, Richard.' Then she lay in the moon's path before drawing him down beside her. When he reached for her she exclaimed, 'They call me a whore, dearest of men . . .'

'I will kill anyone who . . .'

She knelt beside him, tracing each scar on his body, even the deep wound in his forehead.

She kissed him, not with tenderness, but with a fierce abandon he had rarely experienced. Again he tried to embrace her, but she denied him. 'I am here to torment you, Richard. You are mine, completely, for this night!'

Bolitho felt her fingers touch and then grip him, and all the while she was kissing him, her tongue exploring his body as he had so often explored hers.

She broke away and he felt her breasts move over his skin, prolonging every sensation.

Then all at once she was above him, her legs straddling him while she gazed into his face. 'I have teased you enough. I shall give you your reward.' He moved to possess her, but she pretended to resist, her nakedness framed against the moonlight, until with a cry she felt him enter her.

As dawn laid its first brush-strokes across the sky they still slept entwined on the bed. The wine stood nearby, untouched, and the owl was long silent. She opened her eyes and turned to study his profile, youthful now in sleep.

She ran her fingers over his body, not wishing to wake him, not wanting to stop. She touched herself and smiled secretly. *Whore, lover, mistress. I am all of these things if you desire me.*

She caressed him again and waited, her heart beating, for him to respond.

It was as if she had spoken her thoughts aloud. The next instant he was holding her down like a captive.

'You are *shameless*, Kate!' Then he kissed her

passionately, stifling her gasp as he took her without restraint.

Down in the yard Ferguson looked up at the opened windows. The curtains were fluttering out over the sills, blown by some inshore breeze.

So many years since the press gang had taken him; he thought of it even now. Especially when the press still trod the streets looking for men. He thought, too, of the Battle of the Saintes where he had lost his arm, and Bolitho's coxswain had been killed trying to protect his captain's back. Somehow, since then, the *little crew* had grown around them. Allday, also a pressed man, had become Bolitho's coxswain, and he too would soon be off to sea again.

He heard Lady Catherine's quick laugh. Or were they tears? It troubled him greatly. More than he could remember.

John Allday glanced around the parlour of the Old Hyperion and said, 'So *Indomitable* anchors tomorrow.'

Lieutenant George Avery watched him thoughtfully. This was a different Allday from the one he had seen in the smoke of battle, or holding Sir Richard Bolitho in his arms when he had been struck down by splinters. Not even the same big gentle man he had watched going to his wedding, here in Fallowfield on the Helford River.

He was obviously still uneasy about his new existence, and Avery could sympathise with him. It was strangely peaceful. He could hear Allday's wife Unis speaking with some ploughman in the adjoining room,

116

and the thump of her brother John's wooden leg as he put up another cask of beer.

A friendly place, and he was glad he had stayed here after hearing about Ethel's death. He had slept and eaten better than he could remember, and Unis had been very kind to him.

He said, 'So the Coastguard say.' Again he watched the conflicting emotions in Allday's weathered face. Needing to go. Wanting to stay. He was not even concerned about sitting at the same table as an officer any more. *Any more than I am.* It was Bolitho's doing, his example. *My little crew.* Allday put out a lighted taper and laid his pipe aside, trying to explain it.

'It's all so *different*, y'see, sir? People talk about their farms and the sales of stock an' grain.' He shook his shaggy head. 'I thought I'd get used to it. Resign meself to the land.' He stared hard at the perfect model he had given Unis of the old *Hyperion*, in which her first husband had been killed. 'But not yet, see?'

Avery heard the pony and trap being brought into the yard, ready to take him to Falmouth where he might be needed at any time now. He thought of Tyacke's outburst, and wondered how he would behave when next they met.

Allday was saying, 'Then we get all the old Jacks in here, too. Not a whole man amongst 'em. But the way they talks you'd think every captain was a bloody saint, and each day afloat was a pleasure trip!' Then he grinned. 'Not what they really thought, I'll wager!'

Unis entered the parlour, and exclaimed, 'No, don't get up, Mr Avery!'

Avery remained standing. She was a pretty little

117

woman, natural and uncomplicated like the country-side, the wild flowers and the bees. She had probably never had an officer stand up for her before in her life. Or anyone else, for that matter.

He said, 'I must be leaving, Mrs Allday.' Even that sounded strange, he thought. He saw their quick exchange of glances. The big, shambling sailor and the wife he had never expected to find. The look told it all. Sudden anxiety, courage too, and full knowledge of what it would mean.

She said, 'You go with Mr Avery, John. Give my best wishes to Lady Catherine.' She looked level-eyed at Avery. 'A beautiful lady, that one. She's been good to me.'

Allday said hesitantly, 'Well, if you don't need me, Unis—'

She folded her arms and pretended to glare at him. 'You know you're anxious to see Sir Richard, so be off with you. You just come back to me tonight.' Then she kissed him, standing on tip-toe to reach his face. 'Like a bear with a sore head, you are, John Allday!'

Avery said impulsively, 'I've been so happy here.' He spoke with such sincerity that she wiped her eyes surreptitiously with her fingers.

She said, 'You'll always be welcome. Until you get settled down, like.'

'Yes. Thank you, Mrs Allday.'

He saw her hand on his sleeve and heard her say, 'You don't say much, and I've no right to pry, but you've carried a deal of worry these past years, I can tell.' She gave his arm a gentle squeeze. 'And sad though it is, it isn't the loss of your sister I'm speaking of!'

He took the work-worn hand and kissed it. It smelt of fruit and flour.

She stood beside her brother and watched Allday hoist the lieutenant's chests into the trap.

As the pony clattered across the yard, out of the inn's shadow and into the bright April sunlight, she said wretchedly, 'Oh, John, why must it be?'

Her brother, also called John, wondered if she were speaking to him.

He said quietly, 'You told him yet?'

She shook her head. 'It wouldn't be fair. It wouldn't be right.' She laid her hand across her apron. 'He'll have enough to worry about, fighting them Yankees. I won't have him fretting over me at the same time.' She smiled. ''Sides, I don't know for sure, do I? Bit late in life to have a babe of my own.'

Her brother put his arm around her. 'You'll be brave, lass.'

Unis shaded her eyes, but the trap had vanished beyond the hedgerow where some swifts were performing like darts.

She said suddenly, 'My God, John, I'll miss him so.'

He saw her sudden determination and was proud of her.

'But I'll not let on, or make a big show of it.' She thought of the grave-faced lieutenant with the tawny eyes. Allday had told her that Avery had read her letters for him. She had been deeply touched, especially

119

now that she knew the lieutenant better. There was a woman behind his sadness; she was certain of it. Perhaps when he read her letters to Allday he was pretending they had been written to him.

Someone called from the inn and she tidied her hair before going to serve him.

'I'll go, lass. You stay an' dream a while.'

She smiled. It was like the sun breaking through cloud. 'No, I'll deal with *him*! You chop some wood.' She glanced again at the empty road. 'It'll blow cold off the river tonight.'

Then she squared her shoulders and marched through the door.

The man uppermost in her thoughts sat in the back of the trap, one leg swinging above the narrow road while he watched the passing countryside. He had known leaving would be hard. Some dogs were rounding up sheep in one field and he thought of his time as a sheep-minder, when *Phalarope* had put a press gang ashore on Pendower and caught several men who were trying to keep their distance. *Including me.* Nobody had realised that the frigate's young captain was a local man, born and raised in Falmouth before being packed off to sea like all the other Bolithos. A lot of water since then. Young Adam a successful frigate captain himself now ... He sighed, remembering how his own son had quit the navy and gone to settle in the promised land of America. It still hurt him. It always would, the way his son had turned away from him, instead of continuing as Adam's coxswain.

And now Richard Bolitho was a full admiral. *An' I'm an admiral's coxswain, as I promised him.* Flag at the main. Time, he thought, troubled by its swift passage; where did it all go?

Avery was also watching the scenery. But he was thinking of Unis Allday's words. A deal of worry. How did she know?

Two farm workers plodding in the opposite direction waved and yelled, 'Yew give them buggers a quiltin'!'

Avery raised his hat to them, remembering Bolitho's bitter words when they had joined the unhappy *Valkyrie* at Plymouth.

What did men like these care who they were going to fight? Dutch, French or Dons, it was all the same to them. So long as their bellies were full and they did not have to go to sea or follow the drum, what did it signify to them? He gave a wry smile. *I am becoming cynical, like Sir Richard.* To take his mind off it, he twisted round and looked at his companion. 'You've a fine wife, Allday. I envy you.'

Allday's eyes crinkled. 'Then we'll have to do something about that, won't we, sir?'

Avery smiled easily. He would never have believed it possible for this kind of relationship to exist within the rigid strictures of the navy.

Allday asked, 'You sorry to leave, sir?'

Avery thought about it and remembered his sister's last, desperate embrace. *If only I had known.*

He shook his head. 'No. There's nobody to leave.'

Allday studied him. Most people would think Lieutenant Avery had all that a man could need. Aide to England's most famous sailor, with all the chances of rank and prize money denied to others. But, in fact, he had nothing.

121

He was both surprised and saddened by his discovery, and said awkwardly, 'Perhaps you would have the goodness to write a letter for me once we weighs anchor, sir?'

Avery's clear eyes settled on him. It was like seeing a man reaching for a lifeline.

'It would be an honour.' He almost added, *old friend*.

Catherine Somervell was crossing the yard with a sheaf of flowers over one arm when they arrived. She shaded her eyes and watched as they climbed from the trap. 'Why, Mr Avery – and John Allday! I was not expecting two such important visitors!' She held out her hand and Avery took it; not like Sillitoe, she thought, nor like the Prince Regent either. He kissed it and she sensed his hesitancy; he was still uncertain about something, perhaps herself and her relationship with Bolitho. It was possible that she would never know.

She greeted Allday with affection. 'Why, John Allday, I swear you have filled out a little! Good food and affection do wonders for a man, body and soul.'

Allday said uneasily, 'I have to get back, m'lady. But tomorrow...'

She said, 'Ah, yes, tomorrow. We shall have to make the best of it.'

From an upstairs window Bolitho watched them. His Kate walking between the two uniforms. She looked so at ease with them, so right. He thought of her in the night: the eager desperation of one for the other. Love, passion, and the unspoken dread of parting.

A shaft of sunlight pierced through the leaves in the

light offshore breeze, and he put his hand to his eye as if it had been stung. Holding one hand over it he looked again, and after a few seconds his vision seemed to clear and sharpen. It must be the effect of the drops the doctor had given him. Beneath the windows, she turned between two of the most important men in his life. She was as tall as Avery, and perhaps a little taller than Allday.

She must have felt his eyes upon her. She looked up, searching his face, perhaps sensing what had just happened.

She held up the flowers and blew him a kiss.

But all he heard was her voice on the wind. *Don't leave me.*

Captain James Tyacke stood by the quarterdeck rail and watched the throng of bustling figures, which to any ignorant landsman would seem like chaos. He laid one sunburned hand on the rail and was surprised to see it so still even though his whole body seemed to be trembling with an excitement he had rarely known.

It was not recklessness. Not exactly, but he had had to discover what his ship and his unknown company could do.

Shortly after *Indomitable* had hoisted anchor and successfully beat clear of the Sound, the wind had risen slightly, and by the time she had been laid on her new south-westerly course down-Channel spray was bursting over the beakhead, soaking even the upper yards where dazed and uncertain figures were being pushed and dragged from one task to the next.

Lieutenant Scarlett had ventured, 'We are thirty hands short, sir.'

Tyacke had given him a brief glance. 'In a sea fight we could lose that many in minutes.'

'I – I know, sir.'

Tyacke had retorted sharply, 'I *know* you know, but most of these people do not. So get the hands aloft and make all plain sail!'

As the wind and quarter-sea had mounted the *Indomitable*, big though she was, had seemed to bound from trough to trough like the lion she followed, spray and spindrift pouring from the bulging canvas like tropical rain. Tyacke had glanced at the sailing master, his slate-grey hair flapping in the wind, his arms folded as he watched his helmsmen and master's mates. He had felt his captain's scrutiny and looked up, his eyes gleaming as he had called, *'She can do it, sir!'*

Tyacke had seen Scarlett and Daubeny the second lieutenant clinging to the stays and staring at him. He said, 'Stun's'ls, Mr Scarlett!'

Like giant ears the studding sails were eventually run out from their yards, men slithering and clutching wildly for handholds.

Now, as he looked up at the squared yards and furled sails, at the gulls circling noisily around the ship hoping for scraps, he was amazed by what he had done, what they had all managed to do, one way or the other. Every spar had held, although he had seen the great mainyard bending like an archer's bow under the tremendous pressure of wind. Here and there cordage had parted, snapping above the din like musket shots, but that was not uncommon with new ropes and

124

halliards. The stretched and seasoned rigging had taken all the strain with no complaint save the clatter and bang of flapping canvas.

Tyacke walked to the taffrail and back again. That was it, why *Indomitable* was so different from any other ship. It was her power through the water even in half a gale. The noise, frightening to the untrained landmen, had been exhilarating; with each great plunge into sunburst clouds of spray it had been staggering, a sound he could liken to a great gale through a forest, menacing and then rising to a wild shriek of triumph. Isaac York the master had claimed they had logged some fifteen knots, when under those conditions most vessels would have been tempted to shorten sail – or, if undermanned, to lie to under reefed topsails until it was all over.

As they had closed with the land Tyacke had touched the first lieutenant's arm, and was certain he had started with alarm.

'Shorten sail, if you please, Mr Scarlett.'

He saw the other man's confusion, thinking perhaps he had misunderstood the order. Tyacke had pointed at the larboard battery of twenty-four pounders. 'You decide. If we fight, and I should fall, *you* will command here. Can you do it?'

Scarlett had stared at him. There had been a lot of coastal shipping moving in and out of the harbour, and the distance between the two headlands, Pendennis Point and St Anthony, had probably looked no wider than a farm gate.

But with York close by, Scarlett had not hesitated.

On the starboard tack with all sails clewed up except

125

topsails and jib, *Indomitable* must have made an impressive entrance.

But now, safely at anchor, he might well ask himself why he had done it. Even if Scarlett had collided with another vessel or put the ship aground, the responsibility would lie with her captain. As it should.

Scarlett was here again. 'All secure, sir.'

'Very well, sway out the barge and put my cox'n in charge.' He almost smiled. 'I have no doubt that Allday will bring the barge back himself.'

He saw no understanding on Scarlett's face. Like these others, the legend had passed him by. He would be part of it soon enough. He heard a yelp of pain and saw a man hurrying forward, holding his shoulder where a boatswain's mate had obviously struck him with his starter. Nearby, the junior lieutenant Philip Protheroe stood watching the land. He had ignored the incident.

Tyacke said, 'Remind that young man of what I said when I took command. An officer must be obeyed. He must also set an example.' Unwittingly his hand had gone to his disfigured face. 'Even if you have been badly used, it does not give you the right to abuse others who cannot answer back.'

Scarlett said, 'I understand, sir.'

He said curtly, 'I am glad to know it!'

He watched the new green-painted barge being hoisted and swayed over the starboard gangway, and then lowered slowly into the water alongside, and beckoned to the gun-captain who had been chosen for his coxswain. He was a short, completely square man with a puggy face and a chin so blue it must defy every razor.

'You! Over here!'

The man bounded over and knuckled his forehead.

'Aye, sir!'

'Your name is Fairbrother, right? Bit of a mouthful in times of haste!'

The man stared at him. ''Tis the only one I got, sir.'

Tyacke said, 'First name?'

'Well, Eli, sir.'

'Right then, Eli, take the barge to the stairs. Wait until they arrive, however long it takes.' From the corner of his eye he saw a boatswain's chair being lowered from the mainyard. For Lady Catherine Somervell, he had no doubt in his mind. He sensed the curiosity around him. Some of these men had not been with a woman for over a year, perhaps longer.

What would they have thought had they seen that same Catherine Somervell being hauled aboard *Larne*, wet through in her seaman's shirt? He knew he himself would never forget.

He looked around the harbour; he had not been in Falmouth for many years. It had not changed. The brooding castle on one headland and the big St Mawes battery on the opposite one. It would take a bold captain to try to cut out a sheltering merchantman here, he thought.

Tyacke beckoned to the harassed first lieutenant again. 'I want all the boats in the water. Send the purser ashore in one.' He did not miss Scarlett's sudden interest. 'As many fresh vegetables as he can find, fruit too if he can get it. It's possible, with the Dons being so friendly nowadays!' Scarlett did not miss the sarcasm. 'And I want Captain du Cann to have his marines in a guardboat, with a picket or two on the nearest land in case some poor wretch tries to run.'

He spoke without emotion, and yet Scarlett sensed that his new captain felt a certain sympathy for those who were so tempted.

'Boat approaching, sir!'

That was Lieutenant John Daubeny, officer-of-the-watch.

Tyacke called to a midshipman, his mind groping for his name.

'Over here, lad.' He took a telescope from the rack and rested it on the youth's shoulder. It came to him: his name was Essex, the one appointed to take over the duties of purser's clerk.

The boat and contents swam into focus.

He quickly recognised the round shoulders of Yovell, Sir Richard's faithful servant. The boat also contained chests and packing-cases, and the beautifully carved wine-cooler which Catherine had given to Bolitho to replace her original gift, now lying on the seabed with *Hyperion*.

Scarlett was saying as though almost to himself, 'It will be strange, not being a private ship any more.'

Tyacke closed the glass with a snap. 'Thank you, Mr Essex. You are exactly the right height.'

The youth was nervous but pleased. Tyacke saw him drop his eyes rather than look at him.

He said heavily, 'Strange for me also, Mr Scarlett.'

He watched the boat come alongside, Hockenhull,

the squat boatswain, leaping down with some of his men to unload it.

Tyacke glanced up to the top of the mainmast. An admiral's flag. *How do I feel?* But it would not come to him. Neither pride nor uncertainty. It was something already decided, like a storm at sea, or a first broadside. Only fate would determine the outcome.

'Sir! Sir! The barge is bearing off!'

Tyacke gazed along the upper deck. All the confusion had gone now. This was a ship of war.

'Not so loud, Mr Essex,' he said. 'You'll awaken the sheep.'

Some of the seamen nearby grinned. Tyacke turned aside. It was another small beginning.

'Clear lower deck, Mr Scarlett. Man the side, if you please.'

Boatswain's mates and sideboys in ill-fitting white gloves assembled, followed by the tramp of boots as the guard of honour fell in by the entry port, their lieutenant, David Merrick, looking like an actor in an unfamiliar role. Then the officers, warrant officers, and Captain du Cann standing in his perfectly-tailored scarlet coat with several marines and a squad of young fifers and drummers.

Tyacke saw a midshipman below the massive mainmast with its surrounding girdle of boarding pikes. The flag was expertly folded over the youth's shoulder, done by more experienced fingers than his own, Tyacke thought. He lifted a glass again and sensed Midshipman Essex's eagerness to assist him. But he would share none of it this time.

She was dressed in deep green as he had somehow

known she would be, with a broad straw hat tied under her chin with a matching ribbon. Beside her, Bolitho sat with his sword between his legs, one hand lying close to but not touching hers.

The flag-lieutenant was with them, and at the tiller he saw Allday's powerful figure, Tyacke's own coxswain beside him.

'Stand by with the boatswain's chair!'

One small fifer moistened his lips, and a drummer boy gripped his sticks exactly as he had been taught at the barracks.

The sideboys had gone down the side, ready to assist the lady passenger into the chair. There would be many eyes watching her today. The rumours, the gossip, the slander and the indisputable courage after the loss of the *Golden Plover*.

Tyacke heard the distant bellow, 'Oars – *up*!' Allday seemed very calm, as always. Like twin lines of bones the dripping oars rose, and steadied even as the bowman hooked on to the main chains.

The tackle squeaked, and two seamen swung the chair above the gangway.

'*Belay that!*' Tyacke knew Scarlett was watching him, his face full of questions, but he no longer cared.

She was looking up at him, her hair breaking from beneath her hat while she rested one hand on Sir Richard's shoulder. She was laughing, then she took off her shoes and handed them to Avery before reaching out for the guide-ropes and staring straight up at the gilded entry port. Allday was looking anxious, Avery too, but she waited for the right moment before

130

stepping out on to the thick, wooden stairs which curved into the ship's tumblehome, spaced apart for a seaman but hardly for a lady.

Tyacke held his breath until he saw her head and Sir Richard's cocked hat appear above the top stair.

'Royal Marines, present *arms*!' The flash of bayonets and the usual cloud of pipeclay rising from the slings, the shrill of boatswain's calls, ear-splitting at close quarters.

Bolitho raised his hat to the quarterdeck, his eyes resting only briefly on the White Ensign curling from its staff, then he turned to face forward. Then he said, 'A moment, if you please!'

In the silence he held out his hand to support her, so that Avery could kneel and replace Catherine's shoes. He saw the smudge of tar on her foot and a bad snare in her stocking.

As she straightened up their eyes met, and Tyacke saw what passed between them. The love. But above all, the triumph.

Then the fifes and drums broke into *Heart of Oak*. Only then did Bolitho look up at the mainmast as the flag was run smartly to the truck, where it broke immediately to the wind.

Somehow he knew that Catherine was near to tears. With all society against them, they had achieved this, and they were together.

He stared at the flag until his eyes watered, or was that his own emotion?

His flag. The cross of St George.

There was cheering too, but not because of the flag

or the honour of the occasion. It was because of her. The sailor's woman who had come amongst them to show that she at least cared, for them and for her man.

The din subsided and Catherine curtsied to Tyacke before saying, 'You look *very* well, James Tyacke.' Then as he reached out to take her hand, she lifted her face and kissed him on the cheek. 'You are so welcome here.' Then she looked over the rail at the silent, watching sailors and marines. 'They will not let you down.'

She could have been speaking to either of them, Tyacke thought. Or to the ship, *Indomitable*.

7

Like a Troubled Sea

Richard Bolitho sat on the long leather bench seat at the foot of the tall stern windows and watched the sea heaving and breaking astern. The ship was no longer quivering to the squeak and rumble of gun trucks, and he guessed that Lieutenant Scarlett had decided to discontinue yet another drill and await better weather while the crews recovered their strength. Sail and gun drill: Tyacke had exercised all hands within a day of leaving Falmouth. He had seen Tyacke glancing at him, as though to know his opinion, whenever he had taken a walk on the quarterdeck, but Bolitho had left him to his own devices. It was difficult enough for him as it was, without interfering or making suggestions.

He felt the timbers bite into his shoulder as the ship plunged into another long trough, every stay and spar creaking to the pressure. It was late afternoon and the watch would be changing soon. He glanced at the unfinished letter on his table, and imagined her face when she opened it, whenever that might be. Unless they met with a friendly homebound vessel, the letter was likely to be put ashore in Antigua.

He massaged his forehead and pictured her as she had gone down the side in Falmouth, that time in a boatswain's chair as he had insisted. They had cheered her again when she had been assisted into his barge, with Allday and Avery to see her safely ashore.

Only she had known the pain their parting had given him. Equally, she had realised that by coming aboard into his world, no matter how briefly, she had made such a difference for all the men who were sailing into the unknown. Six days out from Falmouth, and a thousand miles already logged. This night they would pass the Azores and cross the fortieth parallel of latitude, south-by-south-west, and further still.

He stared at the sea again, shark-blue with long ranks of yellow-toothed breakers. *Indomitable* was taking it well, and smashed over every obstacle with a kind of arrogance he had rarely seen before. Many of the new hands, raw to the navy and its brutal indifference, had either been seasick or knocked senseless when the pitching deck caught them unawares and flung them against unyielding guns or stanchions. But they would learn; they had no choice. Bolitho had noticed that Tyacke was always on deck whenever drills were being carried out, or some violent change of tack sent the topmen swarming aloft, leaving the landmen and marines to man the braces and trim the great yards while the wind roared around them.

He had heard Scarlett call after a particularly hard exercise at the larboard battery, 'Better that time, sir!'

And Tyacke's blunt reply. '*Not good enough*, Mr Scarlett! It took twelve minutes to clear for action. I want it done in eight!'

134

Six days. How different from those times when he had been so eager to get to grips with the enemy, any enemy that their lordships dictated.

He thought suddenly of the moment when *Indomitable* had weathered the headland to find open water in the Channel. Catherine had said nothing of her plans, but he had known she was watching him. He had snatched a telescope from the rack and steadied it carefully while the ship had leaned over stiffly in the offshore wind.

Below the point, where the cliffs dropped to the rocks and the tiny beaches were then covered by the tide. She had been there, her hair blowing unheeded in the wind, one hand holding Tamara's bridle while she levelled a small glass on the slow-moving ship. She would have seen *Indomitable* come to life, sails being freed from every yard and sheeted home so that they bulged like steel breastplates. She would have seen it all, would have watched the spray leaping beneath the snarling lion while *Indomitable* carried her man away, beyond touch, each denied to the other. In her own way she had given an example to Tyacke's watching sailors. Showing that she knew how they felt, and that she shared the same pain of separation.

Then the land had crept out, and Bolitho had handed the telescope to a staring midshipman.

He had seen the boy's awe and had said quietly, 'Aye, Mr Arlington, mark it well. The other price of war.'

The midshipman had not understood. But it must have made a good tale in the gunroom. *How the admiral had confided in him.*

Ozzard tapped at the door and entered silently. 'May I lay for supper at seven bells, sir?'

'Thank you. Yes.' Crossing the first bridge. He would dine with both Tyacke and Avery tonight.

He glanced around the cabin. At least here were familiar furnishings, the mahogany sideboard and dining table, tugging occasionally at their lashings whenever the tiller head gave a particularly violent jerk. Kate's fine wine-cooler; and beyond in the smaller sleeping compartment he could just see the two new dressing-chests and mirror Catherine had insisted on buying for him.

Ozzard stood in his usual stooped position, his hands held molelike in his apron. He seemed ill at ease, but these days that was nothing new. As he had with Allday, Bolitho had offered him his freedom to stay behind in safety at the house in Falmouth. But Ozzard had always refused, apparently determined to remain as his trusted servant for as long as he was needed. Not that he liked the sea; he was openly terrified whenever they had been called to battle. It was as if he served not out of duty or straightforward loyalty, but as some kind of penance.

He heard the sentry shout, 'Captain, *sir*!'

Tyacke entered, his lean body angled to the extreme slope of the deck.

'I hope I am not disturbing you, sir?'

Bolitho waved him to a chair. 'Of course not. Is something wrong?'

Tyacke glanced around the cabin as if he were seeing it for the first time. 'I can't say for certain, sir.'

Bolitho gave him time to assemble his thoughts.

'You have been on deck for most of the day, James. Will you take a glass with me?'

Tyacke seemed about to refuse, then reconsidered and nodded. Perhaps the casual use of his Christian name had taken him by surprise.

'At noon, sir, when our young gentlemen were shooting the sun, one of them, Craigie, was skylarking. The master sent him aloft to mend his manners.'

He took a glass of cognac from Ozzard and examined it thoughtfully. Bolitho watched him. Mastheading was a common enough punishment, used to curb a midshipman's high spirits. He had endured it himself. For him it had been worse than for most, as he had always hated heights. The way *Indomitable* was leaning over on the starboard tack would be enough to teach anyone a lesson, but it was hardly something to concern the captain enough to bring him aft.

Tyacke looked at him and gave a slight smile. 'I know, sir. We all went through it.' The smile vanished. 'Mr Craigie is not the brightest of stars, but he is blessed with good eyesight.' He did not see, or seem to see, the flicker of emotion on Bolitho's face. 'There is a sail to the nor'-east, sir. When he told the officer of the watch a glass was sent aloft. It was a sail right enough.' He lifted his goblet. 'And the ship is still there. Maybe a trivial matter, but I thought you should know.'

Bolitho rubbed his chin. 'And on the same tack?'

'Never changes, sir.'

'What d'*you* think, James?'

Tyacke seemed surprised that he should be asked. 'Whoever it is might take us for a liner with our rig.'

He stroked the arm of his chair. 'By God, he'd get a surprise if this lady turned on him!'

It was like hearing somebody else. The voice of pride. How Tyacke had spoken of his *Larne*.

'Could we catch him, d'you think?'

Bolitho watched Tyacke's expression. Calculating, seeking conclusions. Strange that they had already given the unknown vessel a character of its own.

'I'll need three days more, sir. Then, if the weather holds, we should be picking up the north-east trades. That'll give us power to come about and catch him.' He paused, almost hesitantly. 'I know this is faster than any brig, sir, but I've done it with *Larne* when some crafty slaver tried to spy out our intentions.'

Bolitho realised that it was the first time Tyacke had mentioned his last command since *Indomitable* had broken out his flag at the main. 'What do you think of the people, James? Are they coming together as one company?'

Instead of answering, Tyacke stood up. 'With your permission, sir?' Then he opened the big skylight, his hair ruffling in the sudden breeze. 'They're standing easy. I've worked them hard, day in day out since I took command in Plymouth. They may loathe me, fear me, I know not which, nor must I allow myself to care. Good men and scum side by side, gallows-bait and mothers' boys.' His mouth softened as he said, 'Now, sir, you listen to them.'

Bolitho joined him beneath the skylight and peered up at the straining mizzen topsail far above them.

They were singing. Men off-watch and idlers, resting on deck after a long hard day. It was one of Dibdin's songs, sometimes used by shantymen when a ship was being hauled up to her anchor in readiness to weigh.

> *'This life is like a troubled sea—*
> *Wear helm or weather all a-lee,*
> *Wear helm or weather all a-lee,*
> *The ship will neither stay nor wear,*
> *But drive of every rock in fear,*
> *Of every rock in fear.'*

It was as though Catherine were here, as she had been in the longboat when she had urged Allday to sing to raise their spirits when all had seemed lost.

Tyacke was still watching him, his eyes very blue and steady. He said, 'Your lady understood, sir.' He closed the skylight and gave the lusty voices back to the sounds of sea and wind. 'They will not let you down.'

Bolitho touched the locket, which she had fastened around his neck before they had parted.

I shall take it from you when you come to me as my lover again . . .

He made up his mind. 'So be it then, James. When the trades are good to us, we'll go and snare that cunning fox and discover what he is about.'

Tyacke picked up his hat. 'I'll see you at supper, sir. And thank you.'

'For what?'

Tyacke shrugged. 'Just – thank you, sir.' Then he was gone.

Ozzard entered the cabin and glanced around without curiosity as Bolitho returned to the skylight and opened it.

They will not let you down.
'Nor I you.' But the singing had stopped.

Captain Adam Bolitho strode through the dockyard, his hat tugged down on his forehead against the lively breeze from the Sound. He glanced past hurrying seamen and dockyard workers to the wall where *Larne* had been moored to complete her overhaul, and beyond to the glittering sea itself, now reflecting the afternoon sunlight like a million flashing mirrors.

From this place *Indomitable* had weighed anchor for Falmouth. In his heart he knew he had wanted to go aboard before she had made sail, to wish Tyacke good fortune, but convention had held him back. Although Tyacke was older than he, he was still very junior in rank.

He was also aware that Tyacke might have misconstrued his visit, or considered it patronising. It was better to leave him to find his own way, and make his own mistakes without critical eyes or well-meaning advice. Adam admired Tyacke greatly. Next to his uncle he had encountered no greater strength of character, nor higher courage in any man.

He half smiled. Bolitho must have had a quiet word with the port admiral on his behalf. *Anemone* had been desperately short-handed; after her battle with the privateers, death and mutilation had taken a heavy toll. But when she quit Plymouth this time, her company would be almost complete again. Bolitho must have asked for more men. Scum they might be; many would otherwise have been hanged or deported, but firm discipline and fair treatment would soon change that. The hard men who would never break, Adam would take on himself to train. They often proved to be the best sailors, especially those who had never known anything but poverty and oppression. He tightened his jaw. But if they did not respond to training and example he would change them in other ways.

He thought of his three lieutenants. All had seen action before, but only one had ever served in a frigate. To Adam the navy was divided down the middle. There were frigates, and then there were all the rest.

The warrant officers were experienced, prime seamen of quality. Again, he suspected his uncle had some hand in their acquisition. But he did not know any of them, as he had his other company. Perhaps it was better that way. He thought of friends he had seen fall in that last sea-fight, of the midshipman for whom he had had such hopes of early promotion. The youth had died in his arms, his eyes staring up at him until they became fixed and unmoving.

Yes, it was better not to become too close. He had seen his uncle's grief too many times when those dear friends he called his *Happy Few* had been killed, one by one.

Catherine would be alone now, waiting and wondering, not daring to hope that it might be over quickly, that his uncle might come home safely once again.

He would put into Falmouth and pay his respects to her before taking *Anemone* to join the new squadron in Antigua.

He had no doubt at all that there would be war. He

had never forgotten the American captain, Nathan Beer, now a commodore of his own squadron. An impressive man, a dangerous adversary.

He saw the port admiral's house with its tower and fine gilded weathervane. His would be a quick visit for the sake of courtesy only, although it might be difficult to escape the admiral, who was known for his bounteous hospitality to the young captains who passed through the dockyard.

A carriage was just arriving at the house, and two others were waiting nearby.

Adam frowned, trying to think of some excuse that would allow him to leave.

The carriage rolled to a halt, the horses stamping noisily on the stones as a Royal Marine ran to open the door and lower the step. Something fell on the ground, and Adam picked it up.

'Excuse me, ma'am. You dropped this.'

He stared past her at the severe-looking man who was regarding him as he would an intruder.

Zenoria looked straight into his eyes, only a pulse in her throat betraying her outward composure.

'Why, Captain Bolitho. This is a surprise.'

Adam waited for the rebuff, fearing she would turn away. He offered his hand, but she rested hers on the marine's white glove instead. 'Did you know I would be here?'

He said, 'I did not, I swear it.'

She frowned slightly, as though warning him. 'This is Mr Petrie, from London.' She turned to the sharp-faced man. 'May I introduce Captain Adam Bolitho, of His Britannic Majesty's Ship *Anemone*.'

The man attempted to smile. It obviously did not come easily to him.

Zenoria added, 'He is a lawyer, Captain, and he is under instruction to complete the purchase of a suitable house for us here in Plymouth.'

Her poise and her self-confidence impressed and surprised him, but when she turned from the others he recognised the pain in her eyes. *The girl with the moonlit eyes*, Bolitho had called her. He controlled his own emotion with an effort.

A harassed-looking lieutenant hurried down the steps. 'I see you have introduced one another...' He shook his head. 'I am all aback today, ma'am. I should have remembered your husband is a great friend of Sir Richard Bolitho.' He turned to Adam. 'I was going to send word to your ship, Captain, inviting you to sup with the admiral. But there was no time – you see, sir.'

'I understand. I was once a flag-lieutenant myself.'

Relieved, the lieutenant led the way up the steps but hesitated when he realised that Adam had not followed.

Adam said, 'I am not certain. I mean no offence to your admiral after what he has done for my ship...' He looked at her again. No contempt, no resentment. But there was something. 'I have no desire to intrude.'

She said quickly, 'For my part, there is no intrusion. Do come, Captain Bolitho. I hope to see Lady Catherine while I am in the West Country...' She hesitated, 'Again.'

Then they were in the large reception room, with its vast paintings of sea battles and memorabilia in glass cases; a great house where admirals had lived for many years, which had never become a home. The port admiral, a small, energetic man with an old-fashioned queue, bounced to greet them. There were several other officers present, and a solitary scarlet-coated marine. Women too, with the uncomplaining faces of service wives.

The admiral took Zenoria's arm and Adam heard him say, 'I hear you're buying Boscawen House, m'dear? A fine old place – the views are breathtaking. Hunting's good around there too.'

She replied, 'Rear-Admiral Keen's father suggested Mr Petrie should deal with the matter.' She glanced at the solemn Petrie. 'He knows more than I about such things.'

The admiral nodded, his eyes running over her like an invisible hand. 'Quite so, m'dear. A man of the City, he *would* know. Not something to trouble your pretty head about.'

She looked across the room until she found Adam, and her gaze seemed to say, *Help me.*

It was suddenly obvious to him. Like the house in Hampshire and the stifling kindness of Keen's family, nobody had even asked her for her opinion.

The admiral was saying to the room at large, 'I'll be hauling down my flag next year – a quieter appointment for me at the Admiralty.' He gave his short barking laugh. 'I think Boscawen House would make the perfect residence for my successor, what?'

The others laughed and raised their glasses.

Adam saw her looking nervously around, imagining how it might be when Valentine Keen came home again. His father had made no secret of his resentment that Keen should prefer the hazardous life of the navy to power and success in the City. Any more than he would want his grandson to follow Keen into the world of sea and ships.

Adam was surprised he had not heard some mention of this appointment. He glanced at her slight figure again. Like a little girl amongst all these people who knew and wanted no other life. Lost. Completely lost.

Suppose somebody knew or even suspected the truth? He strode to the admiral's side, caution gone like the wind from a shot-riddled sail.

'I beg your pardon, sir, but may I show Rear-Admiral Keen's wife the beautiful garden you have here?'

'So long as you behave yourself, m'lad! I *know* about young frigate captains!' His barking laugh followed them to the French windows that opened on to a wide terrace, which was decorated with large urns of plants.

As soon as it was possible to speak, Adam said, 'I am so sorry about this, Zenoria – I really did not know you were here.' She said nothing, and he continued more urgently, 'My ship sails in three days. You have nothing to fear from me. I wronged you . . . I will never forget. I would never have harmed you, because . . .'

Her eyes were misty. He dared not think there might be kindness in them for him. 'Because?' One word, so gently said.

'I have no right.'

She put her hand on his sleeve. 'We should walk,

but remain in view of the house. I know from Lady Catherine's experience how cruel are those who know nothing but envy.'

They walked slowly by the wall, her gown touching the salt-roughened grass, his sword slapping against his thigh.

Then she asked abruptly, 'Can *you* see me with all these clever, worldly people?' She turned to look up at him. 'In truth, Adam, *can* you?'

He placed his hand over hers and they walked on. 'You will captivate them, as you do me.' He waited, expecting her to react angrily, reject him as she had in Hampshire, the last time he had seen her.

But she said, 'When Val returns he will rightly expect me to be proud of his achievements, and I *want* to be equal to his expectations. I *am* proud of him, and I have never forgotten what I owe him.'

He said, holding her hand against his arm, 'And what about you, little mermaid, are you owed nothing? What if others care?'

She glanced up at him. 'I know you care. Of course I know. I remember . . .'

'What do you remember?' She was faltering, pulling away.

'When I found you in tears, Adam, grieving for Sir Richard. And then . . .'

'I loved you, Zenoria. I shall always love you. I want no other.'

She stared at him, her eyes frightened. '*Stop!* You must not say such things!'

They halted at the end of the wall and looked at one another for a long moment. An old gardener carrying a rake passed them; they neither saw nor heard him.

Adam said quietly, 'I am not proud of what I am, Zenoria. But if I could take you from your husband, a man I like and greatly admire, then I would do it.' He saw her agitation but did not release his grip. 'I would not hesitate.'

'Please, somebody is coming!'

It was the flag-lieutenant. 'The admiral desires you to join the others for refreshments. Afterwards, there will be a recital.' His eyes moved between them but were without curiosity.

Adam offered his arm and they walked slowly back towards the house.

'Shall I leave, Zenoria?'

She shook her head, her profile suddenly very determined. 'No. Talk to me about your ship – anything, d'you understand? But do not reveal your heart again like that.'

He said, 'I still have your glove.' Something to say, to control his need of her.

'Keep it for me.' Her voice was husky. 'Think of me sometimes, will you?'

'Always. *I love you*, Zenoria.' They re-entered the house in silence.

The admiral raised his eyebrows. 'God swamp you, Captain Bolitho, I thought you had spirited her away!'

She curtsied as if to conceal the colour in her cheeks.

'Only little mermaids can do that, sir!'

Their eyes met across the table. Nothing could ever be the same again.

147

8

Dreams

The figures standing around the quarterdeck and grouped by the big double-wheel were still only shadows, revealed, but without personality against the pale planking.

John Allday waited by the hammock nettings, and glanced at the lightening sky. It would be dawn very soon: the few stars beyond the topgallant yards were fainter than when he had last looked. Then, by daylight, they would know if the captain and sailing master had judged it correctly.

The whole ship's company had been standing-to since the early hours. Peering around in the darkness, trying to remember who was where. Seeking out friends, perhaps, or maybe looking out for a boatswain's mate, ready to use his starter on anyone who was slow to move when the orders came.

James Tyacke was pacing from one side of the broad quarterdeck to the other. Suppose daylight found *Indomitable* with the ocean to herself? It would be a bad beginning for him as captain, Allday thought.

He felt the wind against his neck and shivered. It

had shifted, as York had predicted. The ship was as close-hauled as she would bear, the canvas cracking overhead, losing the wind until the vigilant helmsmen brought her back under command again.

Allday heard someone speaking hoarsely to Eli Fairbrother, the gun-captain selected to be the captain's coxswain. He moved into the deeper shadows by the nettings. He was in no mood to chat with the man. He might prove to be a good hand, given time, but at the moment he was so overwhelmed by his unexpected promotion that he would not stop talking about it.

Allday glanced up again into the darkness. He could see some of the shrouds and ratlines now, and far above, a flapping white movement, like a seabird trapped in the rigging. The admiral's flag at the mainmast truck.

All the years, the pain and the danger. Friends and enemies wiped away, lost like smoke in the wind. To serve with Bolitho had been all he had ever wanted, needed. They had both taken a few bad knocks over their years together, and Allday had shared the best and the worst of it. His *oak*, Bolitho called him, and the name meant much to Allday. It gave him a sense of belonging that few Jacks were lucky enough to enjoy.

Now they were off again. He rubbed his chest where the Spanish blade had nearly killed him. *Always the pain*. Sir Richard with his wounded eye; he needed his oak more than ever now.

He sighed. But now there was Unis. Ever since *Indomitable* had put out from Falmouth he had thought of her. In so short a while Unis had become precious, so dear to him. Once he might have laughed at anybody

149

else who had claimed such an attachment. Not any more. Even Ozzard, who was quick to find fault with most women, had held his peace.

It had been a difficult parting. Ferguson had come over to Fallowfield with his little trap to collect him. They had agreed it would be better so, instead of saying goodbye in Falmouth. He couldn't bear the thought of leaving her like all those other women who sometimes stood for hours, days even, to stare at some man-of-war in the hope of catching a glimpse of their loved ones.

He had held her very gently. With her he was always gentle, protective, careful not to offend, and she had pressed her face into his blue coat.

'I'll not break, John. Harder, hold me harder – then kiss me and go.' Then she had looked up at his face, as if to hold every detail. '*I love 'ee*, John Allday. You've brought peace and purpose to my life.'

Allday had said awkwardly, 'I've not much to offer, my lass. But I'll be back, you see if I'm not!'

'I'll not forgive you if you stay away!' Then there had been tears on her cheeks and she had dashed them away, angry with herself. 'Now be off with you!' Then she had hesitated, as if uncertain what to do.

'What is it, lass?'

She had answered, 'I put a few things in your bag. I don't want you depending on ship's victuals.'

Then she stood on tip-toe and kissed him hard on the mouth. 'I'll pray for you, John.'

Allday had grasped the side of the trap. He knew she could not see him, even though she was smiling and waving. Her eyes were blinded by tears.

He had found himself beside Ferguson and the trap

had moved away. Once he had looked back. Unis had been staring at the road, while the Old Hyperion inn sign swung relentlessly above her head

He thought she had been going to tell him something. When Lieutenant Avery read her next letter to him, maybe she would explain what it was.

All Ferguson had said was, 'You're a lucky man, John.'

Allday heard voices nearby. The admiral was coming up.

He heard the new coxswain, Fairbrother, exclaim, 'An' not only that, but the cap'n calls me by my first name!'

Allday sighed again. *Lucky? When I could be with Unis?* He stared into the dark water alongside. But for once he could find no comfort in the familiarity of his world.

Bolitho was wearing his old sea-going coat without the proud epaulettes, and was hatless.

He saw Allday by the side and asked, 'How goes it today, old friend?'

Allday glanced towards Tyacke's coxswain. *'He calls me by my first name.' He can put that in his pipe and smoke it!* He answered, 'Well enough, Sir Richard.'

Bolitho found Tyacke by the quarterdeck rail with the first lieutenant. Allday could hide nothing from him. They had been together too long for that. He was missing Unis, the first real love he had ever known. *As I miss you, Kate.*

Tyacke remarked, 'We'll soon know, sir.' He turned to the first lieutenant. 'Check each mast, Mr Scarlett. The lieutenants must be certain of every man in their

151

divisions when we come about, even if it takes a mite longer. I don't want the ship in irons, nor do I want to see anyone lost overboard.'

Scarlett had already done it, but knew better than to argue or explain. As he moved forward along the weather gangway he glanced aloft. The flag and mast-head pendant were much lighter. He thought of Tyacke and the admiral beside him: so different, and yet not so different. He saw Avery with a telescope tucked under one arm. In the wardroom several of the others had tried to pry information out of him concerning the admiral and what he was really like. He had seen Avery's strange tawny eyes flash like a tiger's, watched him deflect each question like an experienced duellist.

Faces took on shape and identity, and then the first pale sunshine ran down the upper spars, and revealed to many that the wind had indeed shifted.

Tyacke cupped his hands. '*Ready ho!*'

Figures scampered to braces and halliards, while each lieutenant and midshipman checked his men, very aware of the two figures silhouetted against the paling sky by the quarterdeck rail.

'Put the helm down!'

Bolitho could feel the quarterdeck rail quivering under his hand as the straining seamen let go the headsail sheets, so that the sails could lose the wind and yet not prevent the ship's head from swinging.

'*Off tacks and sheets!*' Scarlett's voice boomed through his speaking-trumpet even as the shadowy bows began to stagger into the eye of the wind.

'Mains'l haul! *Haul*, lads! Put your bloody backs into it!'

152

Hockenhull, the squat boatswain, sounded fierce but was grinning as the ship around and above him fought to answer the demands of sail and rudder.

'*Mains'l haul!*'

Bolitho watched the hands hauling at the braces to swing the great yards around, the sails in wild confusion until, with something like a roar, they refilled and the ship heeled right over, canvas taut and bulging, lines being turned expertly on to belaying pins, while the landmen tried to keep out of everybody's way. Bolitho shaded his eyes and stared up again. Big though she was, and with a partly-trained company, Tyacke had brought the ship about to lay her on the opposite tack.

The helmsman yelled, 'Steady she goes, sir! West by north! By an' large!'

Even he sounded excited, and when Bolitho looked at York, the master, he was grinning hugely like a midshipman with a fresh apple pie.

'Deck, there!'

The masthead lookout, the man who saw everything before anyone else. Bolitho saw Tyacke's brown hand tighten on the rail. *If there was anything to see.*

'Sail, fine on the lee bow, sir!'

Tyacke turned to the signals midshipman. 'Aloft with you, Mr Blythe, and take a glass with you!'

Bolitho said, 'That was *well done*, Captain Tyacke.' Together they watched the spray bursting over the beakhead. Tyacke said quietly, 'Mr York was right about this ship.'

'Deck there!'

Tyacke smiled. 'Already? He must have flown up there.'

Blythe's voice reached them again. 'Barque, sir! She's all aback!'

Tyacke said contemptuously, 'Trying to make a run for it, is he?' He swung round. 'Mr Scarlett, get the t'gallants on her and set the forecourse, driver too!' When the first lieutenant hesitated, he snapped, '*Lively* it is, Mr Scarlett! I'll not lose the bugger now!'

Bolitho saw the flash of resentment in Scarlett's eyes, but this was no time to consider a man's hurt pride.

Tyacke was beckoning to another midshipman, Craigie, the one who had sighted the stranger in the first place.

'Find the gunner, Mr Craigie, and have him lay aft.' He fumbled in his coat and Bolitho saw the gleam of gold. 'You did well. Quite well.'

The midshipman stared at the coin in his grubby palm. 'Th-thank you, sir!'

Tyacke's voice pursued him forward to the main hatchway. 'But next time you skylark on duty, the prize had better be worthwhile!'

Several of the seamen who were hauling and coiling a confusion of halliards and tackles grinned.

Bolitho smiled. If the barque proved to be useless it would no longer matter.

They had just accomplished something, and they had done it as one company.

Richard Bolitho opened his eyes and stared at the deckhead, his ears and mind taking in the sounds, the angle of a small shuttered lantern telling him instantly how *Indomitable* was behaving.

But for the lantern the cabin was in complete darkness, the occasional grumbling clatter of the rudder-head the predominant sound. Not much wind then. Two or three times in the night his sailor's instinct had awakened him, and as usual he had felt a sense of loss at not being up there with the watch on deck when the ship had changed tack yet again. He had never lost that feeling, and he had often wondered if other flag-officers still yearned for the more personal command of a captain.

He lay with his hands behind his head looking into the darkness. It was hard to believe that *Indomitable* would reach Antigua tomorrow or, if the wind failed them again, the next day at the latest. Even now he knew that the small island of Barbuda was less than fifty miles to the north-west, part of the natural chain that formed the Leeward Islands.

Tyacke could be well pleased with his fast passage. Three weeks from Falmouth, England, to Falmouth and English Harbour in Antigua; and they had been uneventful after the early excitement of sighting and boarding 'Blythe's barque', as it had become known, only to discover that although she wore 'American colours she had been under charter to the British government, and had carried nothing more interesting than a mixed cargo of china clay and building materials for Port Royal in Jamaica.

Scarlett had returned fuming with his boarding party. Because of the charter he had been unable to examine the company for British deserters, let alone search the vessel. Later they had sighted and stopped several vessels of various sizes and flags, but apart from a few deserters they had found very little to their advantage. It had seemed as though the whole ocean had become a desert, and every ship going about her business had somehow avoided them.

There had been little to do but carry out regular sail and gun drills, and, as usual, inactivity had had its side-effects: outbursts of anger and violence on the lower deck, usually between the trained and experienced hands and the amateurs and landmen, whom they seemed to delight in provoking.

The punishment book had made its first appearance and several floggings had been awarded. Bolitho had known and served in ships where floggings had been too commonplace to mention, because a wrong word had been taken for insolence, or a captain had cared little for his subordinates' methods provided the end results were acceptable. But Bolitho knew Tyacke had felt it badly. After his little schooner *Miranda* and the brig *Larne*, with their tightly-knit companies, the ritual of punishment in a ship of *Indomitable*'s size had sickened him.

Not that he had lost his determination or pride, and neither his wardroom nor the midshipmen were spared the edge of his tongue. At the boarding of one schooner Avery had accompanied the first lieutenant, and afterwards there had been open hostility from Scarlett, while Avery had withdrawn into apparent indifference and been loath to discuss the subject. Tyacke, in his own forceful fashion, had uncovered the bones of the matter.

156

On board the schooner, Scarlett had admitted that it was almost impossible to discover the presence of deserters, or others taking an illegal passage to escape from the navy, as long as individual masters spoke up for them or provided false papers.

Avery, who had been told to act only as an observer and not interfere with the first lieutenant's procedures, had apparently answered that men should be stripped of their shirts for inspection without requesting permission from anybody. A sailor's back, even if he had been flogged but once, would carry the scars of the cat to the grave. Distinctive naval tattoos were another definite way to identify a deep-water sailorman as a King's seaman who had run.

Scarlett had retorted sharply, 'I'll trouble you to keep your ideas to yourself, sir!'

Avery had responded equally coldly, and when Tyacke had told him later, Bolitho had been well able to imagine him saying it.

'You can go to hell for all I care!'

Hard work, perverse winds and sometimes blistering heat, each had played a part. Men used to the English Channel and to North Sea blockade duties were resentful at being chased through every minute of a drill, while the newly-pressed hands made mistakes that brought scorn and humiliation in their wake.

He closed his eyes, but sleep defied him. It would be dawn soon, and land was in sight, from the masthead at least, exciting many of their company who had never left England before in their lives.

He thought of the dream which had pursued him, almost from the boarding of 'Blythe's barque'. He was

157

not certain how many times it had returned since then, but he knew it had never varied, and when he had woken only minutes ago, he had known somehow that the dream had awakened him. Even his heart had been pounding, something very rare for him unless the dreams had become nightmares, like the ones in which he had seen Catherine being carried away from him, her naked body and streaming hair, and her terror, making him call her name aloud before he had burst out of it.

The dream was completely different. Always the same picture, the narrow waters of Carrick Roads in Falmouth, the murky hump of Pendennis Castle lying across the starboard bow of the ship flying an admiral's flag: *his* flag – the knowledge of that had been quite definite, as it so often was in dreams. The squadron had been all around him, ready to weigh, or still shortening their cables. About to leave Falmouth, as he had done so many times.

Without realising it he was out of his cot, his bare feet on the deck's cool slope; and the sudden icy chill of recognition seemed to freeze his whole body, even though his brain told him that the cabin was as hot and humid as before.

The ships of the squadron had all been his own. *Undine, Sparrow* and *Phalarope, Black Prince* and *Hyperion*. There had even been the topsail cutter *Avenger*, in which he had served under his brother Hugh.

The realisation was unnerving, and he knew that the dream would return yet again. What did it mean? What had brought all those familiar ships to Falmouth, only to depart? And which one had he been on board at the time?

He felt *Indomitable* shiver, the awakening rattle of rigging and blocks. A freshening breeze. There was the responding slap of bare feet overhead, brief orders to send the watch to braces and halliards and re-trim the great yards and contain the wind once more.

He saw them in his mind: figures in the darkness, the helmsmen as they felt the spokes in their hands, their eyes peering aloft to seek out the shaking sail, or the small gauge nearby so that they could discover the wind's true direction.

Perhaps it would be better after Antigua, once he knew what awaited him. *The total responsibility*. For him there had been too much time to brood, to consider the various courses of action for which he would be praised or abused by the far-off Admiralty.

He even wondered if Avery regretted having accepted this appointment, or if Tyacke had only changed his mind out of sympathy.

He felt the deck lift and slide across a trough; she was moving again. He reached the main cabin and groped his way right aft to the tall windows. He managed to open one of the quarter shutters which, within hours, would be packed with blown salt-spray. No moon, but there were plenty of stars to make the ship's wake sparkle.

How would he feel at English Harbour, where he and Catherine had found each other again?

She would be remembering it too. The house above the harbour; their love, which had driven even sanity to the winds.

He felt the damp air around his body, and wondered what his seamen and marines would think if they saw him now, dressed only in a loose pair of white trousers, in case he was needed. *I am playing the captain again.*

His thoughts returned to the barque. Her name was *La Perla*, and she was registered at Boston. His mind shied away from it. *The enemy.* Her master had denied that he had been deliberately following this ship. He smiled to himself. *The old Indom*, as the one-legged cook, Troughton, had called her. The master had insisted that he had every right in the world to be where he was; but he had obviously been surprised by *Indomitable*'s speed and agility, and like some others he had mistaken her for the ship-of-the-line she had once been.

He touched the thick glass. What tales could she tell? How many hundreds of feet had trod these decks, what ambitions and failures had lived here?

He heard whispers, and then a door opened. Somehow he knew it was Ozzard before he could smell the coffee.

'Thought you were about, Sir Richard.' His small figure seemed to glide down towards him as the helm went over yet again. 'This'll do you good.'

Ozzard always knew. Perhaps he could rarely sleep himself.

The coffee was excellent. He could see her again in the shop in St James's Street, choosing the coffee with the care she showed for everything. *For me.*

He found his watch secured to his sea-going coat, and held it against the shuttered lantern. *So many memories, dearest Kate.*

There was about four hours' difference between them. A spring morning in Falmouth, the air filled with birdsong and the hum of bees, and always, the salt tang of the sea. Perhaps she was out visiting Nancy and her husband, 'the King of Cornwall'. Or perhaps she was changing after an early ride, standing by the tall cheval-glass, disrobing as he had seen her do, a prelude to love in that same room.

He put the empty coffee-cup on the deck where it would be safe from any sudden gust, and climbed once more into his cot.

He imagined that it was a little lighter in the adjoining great cabin, and recalled when she had come to him in the night on another occasion. Dazed with sleep he had gone to her, and had kissed her, but her lips had been like ice. And when he had called her name he had realised that, too, had been a dream.

But even across the ocean he had heard her cry out, '*Don't leave me.*'

He closed his eyes and felt something like peace for the first time since *Indomitable* had weighed.

The phantom squadron did not return.

The small carriage rattled along a straight, well-kept road, the Hampshire countryside laid out in fresh square fields of green and yellow like part of a giant patchwork quilt. It was early still, but when she lowered the window Zenoria could hear the trilling evensong of thrushes, interrupted occasionally by the harsh croak of crows.

They would reach Keen's family home within half

161

an hour and as always she thought with apprehension of the reception she would get from his sisters. She had visited the proposed new house at Plymouth three times, and on each occasion the lawyer Petrie had accompanied her. He was dozing now on the seat beside her; even he was finding the journeys and negotiations with the land agents in Plymouth more than tiring.

She watched the passing fields and the darker patches of trees on the edge of the New Forest. In a day or so she would go with Petrie to London. Val's father thought that a man in his position should have a town house as well. He had never meant to offend her, quite the opposite, but he made no secret of the fact that he believed women had no place in matters of property and business, and he probably thought that she had no idea at all of what might be expected of her. He had hinted of further promotion for Val, and every likelihood of a title; and once out of the navy a firm and prosperous place with him in the City.

As she had wandered through room after room in the vastness of Boscawen House in Plymouth, her mind had been unable to accept it: the entire house and spacious gardens filled with servants and workers who would watch her every move, discuss her behind her back, perhaps laugh at her attempts to entertain her betters. She had lost her temper only once when Petrie had explained that there was really no need for her to tire herself with visiting the great empty house, or looking through deeds and past amendments. She had said sharply, 'I would remind you that it will be *my* house too, Mr Petrie! I am also one of the family.'

He had studied her, not unkindly, and had replied, 'It will be a new and very different experience for you, Mrs Keen. There will be many who will envy you. If you will excuse my impertinence, you are a very fortunate young lady, married to one of England's heroes who will, I know, do all he can to make your life a happy one.'

She had felt suddenly weary of it. 'I know, Mr Petrie. He is a good man, and I owe him much.'

If Petrie knew what she meant, he had given no sign.

If only she had had time to visit Catherine at Falmouth. She felt something like a hand on her heart.

The day proposed for the London visit was the sixth of June. It was as if Adam were here with her. It had been on that day that she had kissed him, and he had given her some wild roses from beside the track. Where was Adam now? Had he joined his uncle, or would he be ordered to Val's squadron instead? The thought brought colour to her cheeks. Two who loved her, and yet neither could speak of it.

She could remember his searching gaze at the port admiral's supper in Plymouth. Could it really be two months ago?

The hand on her arm, his expression so intense but tender, in the way she had never forgotten. *I love you, Zenoria.*

The carriage slowed on the last rise before the final approach to the Keen estate and farmland. She heard the clink of metal as the guard unholstered his pistols. It was pleasant, peaceful countryside, so unlike the wild rocky coast of her Cornwall, but there were dangers here nevertheless. Deserters, living rough and stealing what they could, footpads, highwaymen; it was not a road on which to travel unprepared.

Petrie stirred and adjusted his spectacles. 'Ah, nearly home, I see.'

She had not realised he was awake. 'A tiring week, Mr Petrie, for us both.'

He nodded sagely. 'It is good of your husband's family to allow me to stay in the house, Mrs Keen. It saves a good deal of time, money too.'

'Yes.' *As I am allowed to stay here also.*

She turned to the window again so that he should not see her face. She could smell the flowers and the hedgerows, like perfume. But not Cornwall.

She tried not to think of the last time Adam had come to this house. How she had berated him, blamed him for what had happened. Then, hating herself for the things she had said, she had run to the front door to call him back. But the road, this road, had been empty. Perhaps while she was in London she might see something he would like. A small present . . . No. It would be cruel, a temptation which she could never honour.

The tall iron gates were open, and with sudden energy the two horses quickened their pace, and she saw a groom hurrying to meet them. Keen's family's country house was an awesome building, which never failed to overwhelm her.

Petrie shifted his legs and said, 'I see you have another visitor, my dear.' He did not see her sudden anxiety: he was contemplating the supper they would provide for him.

She said in a small voice, 'Not a visitor.'

Then he did look at her, the way her hand had gone to her throat.

She said, 'I recognise the carriage. It is the doctor.'

She waited for the horses to wheel round in front of the broad steps before being braked to a halt.

The big double doors opened, as if they had been waiting for this very moment. Although it was still a bright summer's evening there were chandeliers alight everywhere, and Zenoria saw Val's sister and her husband standing in the great marble hallway like players poised in the wings.

All at once she was running, heedless of one shoe which had caught in the step and fallen on the driveway.

Then she saw the doctor, a tall, grey man with an out-thrust lower lip. He seized her as she tried to pass him. He had a grip like iron.

'Be brave, Mrs Keen. I did all that I could. We all did.'

She heard a scream, her own. Calling his name, *'Perran! Perran!'*

She tore herself free and ran to the open windows, and stared out at the well-cut grass and formal flower beds, where her little son would sit and play with his nurse or Val's bereaved sister.

She peered blindly at the tall shadows which were already crossing the lawn.

'Dear God! Perran!'

But only the startled crows replied.

She heard someone cry, 'Quick! Hold her!'

Then there was nothing.

9

The Mark of Satan

Lady Catherine Somervell allowed herself to be guided to some cane chairs and a table arranged in the shadow of one of Roxby's big oaks, pleased that she had thought to bring a pair of shoes to exchange for her riding-boots. She sat down and adjusted her wide-brimmed hat to keep the sunlight from her eyes while Bolitho's sister Nancy directed a servant to bring tea.

It was a lovely summer day, the air full of birdsong and insects, and the sounds of men haying in the adjoining fields.

Nancy said, 'I'm pleased for Lewis, of course – he's such a dear, and never says a harsh word to me.' She chuckled. 'Not within earshot, in any case. But, really, can you imagine my feelings when they bow and call me m'lady?'

She reached out impulsively. 'For you it is different, Catherine. But I shall never get used to it.' She glanced across to the stone terrace where Roxby was studying some plans with two visitors. 'Lewis adores it, as you can see. He never stops. Now he's discussing the folly he wants built, can you credit it?'

Catherine let her chatter on while the table was being laid. Summer in Cornwall. How perfect it could be, if only he were here. He had been away so long, and there was still no word. She had read in the newspapers that some of the mail-packets had been attacked and plundered. Might their letters have gone astray?

She looked up and found Nancy watching her. 'What is it, my dear?'

Nancy smiled. 'I worry about you. And I miss him too – he is my brother, after all.' She sat down comfortably, spreading her skirts. 'Is something else troubling you?'

Catherine shrugged. How pretty Richard's younger sister must have been. Pretty and fair, like their mother.

'Richard spoke to me about his daughter. It is her birthday quite soon.'

'There is nothing you can do, Catherine. Belinda would never allow her to accept a gift, or anything else.'

'I know. I do not want to see her anyway. When I think of what she tried to do, how she intended to hurt Richard, I know the true meaning of hate.'

She took the cup offered to her and sipped the tea, conscious of the sun's warmth on the one shoulder turned to its light. She hoped her fatigue did not show in her eyes: she had been sleeping badly, sometimes hardly at all.

Every night she dreamed or thought of Richard, imagined him coming into the room and touching her, arousing her. And yet every day increased the distance between them, as if the ocean had swallowed the ship and all aboard her.

He was still with her, even though the seas divided them, so that she found herself unwilling to visit people, even to discuss the collier brig and the day-to-day running of the estate with Bryan Ferguson not that he needed her help.

She thought of the other faces she knew and loved. Valentine Keen, last heard of at Cape Town; Adam, who had called briefly to see her before sailing to join his uncle, Allday and Tyacke, Avery and the portly Yovell. At least they had one another to sustain them.

She heard Roxby's resonant voice bidding his visitors farewell. She watched him as he strolled across the lawn, his hands in his breeches' pockets. He loved riding and blood sports, but his fondness for good living was exacting a toll. She hoped that Nancy had noticed, and would use her influence to good effect. His face was very red, and it was all too apparent that he was breathing with difficulty. As if he had read her thoughts, he dragged out a large handkerchief and mopped his streaming face. Sir Lewis Roxby, Knight of the Hanoverian Guelphic Order, landowner and magistrate, described in London as 'a friend of the Prince of Wales'. He had come a long way for the son of a local farmer.

Roxby waved the tea aside. 'Something a bit stronger for me, m'dear!'

'Catherine's still waiting for a letter, Lewis.'

Roxby nodded gravely. 'Bad business. Understand how you feel.'

His eyes took in her sun-browned shoulder, the

168

proud or perhaps defiant manner in which she held her head. He had heard all about her boarding his brother-in-law's flagship at Falmouth. Up the side like a powder monkey, to raise cheers even from the pressed men whose fate would be in Richard's hands.

What a woman. He thought with dislike of Nancy's sister, Felicity. She would have something vicious to say about it. Mercifully she did not come to the house very often now with her stupid son, and when she did call Roxby was careful to keep away, in case he lost his temper again.

He said, 'He'll be home before you know it, m'dear.' He punched the back of his chair. 'By God, he'll soon drub those damn' Yankees as he did Baratte!'

Nancy held up one hand, something she rarely did to her husband.

'Now, Lewis. Don't agitate yourself so.'

Catherine saw the quick exchange. So she *had* noticed. It was just as well.

Roxby grinned. 'I'll go and fetch a drink for meself.' He shook his head. 'I don't know. You women . . .' He walked away heavily, and Catherine watched as Nancy gestured for fresh tea. How different her life might have been had she been allowed time to fall in love with Richard's young friend Martyn, when they had both been midshipmen together. Here, she had comfort and respect, and she did not have to lie awake at night listening to the wind or the boom of surf below the cliffs. But Nancy was a sea-officer's daughter, and the sister of England's most famous living sailor. She might still have preferred that other life.

She saw Nancy look up, surprised. Roxby was

coming back from the house, carrying a sealed envelope with a perplexed expression on his face. In those remaining seconds Catherine realised he had even neglected to bring himself the promised drink.

Nancy stood up. 'What is it?'

Roxby stared at them. 'Not sure, m'dear. It was sent to your house, Catherine. Special courier.'

Catherine felt her heart leap. Like a pain. Then she said, 'Let me see.' She took the envelope, seeing at a glance that it carried a crest which was vaguely familiar. But she did not recognise the handwriting.

Roxby had drawn close to his wife's side and had put his arm around her shoulders. He could feel the tension like something hostile. An enemy.

Catherine looked up at both of them. 'It is from Valentine Keen's father. He thought I should be told without any delay. Val and Zenoria's child is dead. It was an accident. Suffocated.' The words were falling from her lips without order or understanding. 'Zenoria was not at the house when it happened. She collapsed. Val's father has written to him. The Admiralty has been informed.' She turned away, seeing and hearing nothing, feeling only the scalding tears which would not come. How long had all this taken? To write the letters, to mourn the child, to arrange for a special courier. She almost spat out the word. *Eventually*. While the family stood together in grief, and turned their backs on the girl who had come amongst them. Was it so cruel?

She heard Ferguson's voice. So he was here too. She reached out to grip his hand, unable to see him.

Roxby asked gruffly, 'Have you heard something?'

'Yes, Sir Lewis.' But he was looking at Catherine. 'One of the stable lads thought he saw Mrs Keen in Falmouth.'

Roxby exploded. 'That's impossible! It's miles to Hampshire, man!'

Catherine said quietly, 'So they let her go. Allowed her to leave the house, after what had happened to her.' She thrust out the letter. 'I think you should read it.' She put her other hand on his arm. 'As a dear friend, and perhaps later as a magistrate.'

Roxby cleared his throat and peered at some figures beyond the trees who had paused to discover what had happened.

'You, Brooks! Ride like the devil to Truro and fetch Captain Tregear with his dragoons! Tell him I sent you!'

'*No.*' Catherine released their hands. 'I know where she is. When I rode here I knew someone was watching me. I did not know she was saying goodbye . . .'

Ferguson took her hand. 'Let me take you home, m'lady.' He was pleading, trying to help, as Allday would have done.

Roxby called, 'Carriage! Fetch some men!'

But it was already too late. They left the carriage where Catherine had waited with Tamara to watch *Indomitable* clear the harbour, all those weeks ago.

Then along the winding cliff path, which had crumbled away in so many places, dangerous even for a sure-footed Cornish girl in the dark. But it had not been in the dark, and as they scrambled up the last stretch Catherine saw the familiar landmark, like some crouching thing, known locally as Trystan's Leap.

Catherine stood motionless, her gown and hair moving slowly in the light breeze off the water. She was aware of nothing but the rise and fall of the sea's glistening face, the longboat, so tiny from up here, backing oars like a water-beetle to avoid the hissing rocks which the receding tide would soon reveal to the sun.

They were lifting a small figure from the undertow, an oar moving this way and that to maintain control of the boat.

She heard herself say, 'I am going down. I must.'

She felt a hand seize her wrist, to guide her as she began her descent. But there was nobody beside her. Aloud she said, 'Richard, it's you.'

When she reached the suddenly bare, shining crescent of beach her gown was torn, her hands cut and bleeding.

One of the coastguards stepped between her and the little bundle on the sand.

'No, my lady. You can't go no further.' It was Tom, who had so often seen and spoken with her when they had met on these same cliffs. He dropped his eyes as she stared at him. ''Er face is gone. The rocks—'

'Just for a moment – I beg you!'

Another voice called, 'I've covered she some, Tom.'

The coastguard let her pass him then, and she walked blindly to the body. She knelt down on the hard wet sand and grasped the out-thrust hand. So cold, so very still. Even the wedding ring had been battered by the rocks.

Very gently she raised the corpse, so that the bandaged head drooped against her shoulder as if she were listening.

Then she opened the neck of the torn clothing until she could see the beginning of the scar where the whip had laid open Zenoria's back on the transport, from which Val had rescued her. On their walks along this coast Zenoria had referred to it as the mark of Satan.

She could hear Roxby gasping and panting down the last part of the track, then his hands firm on her shoulders as some of the others took the girl's body from her.

'Was it her?'

'Yes. There can be no mistake.' Then she said, 'Perhaps she cried out. I might have heard, or thought it was a seabird.' Then she shook her head, rejecting it, knowing she must. 'No. She wanted to go. We who are closest to her might have helped her more. But the pain is only just beginning.'

Ferguson asked, 'What shall we do, m'lady?'

She said, 'We must do what Richard would have done, were he here. We must take her back to the sea, to Zennor, from whence she came. Perhaps her spirit will be at peace there. God knows she had little of it elsewhere.'

Afterwards, Bryan Ferguson knew it was something he would never forget. Nor want to.

Sir Richard Bolitho walked slowly across the stone-flagged terrace and felt the heat coursing up through his shoes. It was very hot, and the sun seemed to stand directly above Monk's Hill, unwavering, and appearing to discourage even the movement of small craft in the wide expanse of English Harbour. Other houses, used mostly by senior officials and dockyard officers, stood out white and stark against the lush greenery, like this building, to which he had come seven years ago, and where he had found Catherine again. Seven years. It seemed impossible. So much had happened since that time. Friends killed: fine ships lost or battered into hulks in every corner of the world and across every ocean.

He reached the stone balustrade and touched it with his fingers. Like a heated gun-barrel. Just as it must have been when she had stood here in this very place and position to watch the painful approach of his ship, *Hyperion*. The old ship's name had meant very little to her, and she had been totally unprepared for the shock when she had heard her husband mention that *Hyperion* had become a flagship. *My flagship*.

He cupped one hand over his left eye and looked at the ships anchored here. Part of his squadron sprawling untidily to their cables in the airless heat.

Beyond the larger *Indomitable*, the three frigates, *Zest*, *Virtue* and *Chivalrous*, made perfect reflections on the still water, their ensigns and pendants barely moving. The big frigate *Valkyrie*, now commanded by Captain Peter Dawes, lay at Halifax, with two sixth-rates in company. Together they and three brigs represented the Leeward Squadron. Only one was still missing, and she should arrive here very shortly. Adam's *Anemone*, fresh from her refit and manned almost completely by strangers, would complete a lively and useful force. Adam might miss the faces lost in the last fight with Baratte, but improving the performance of the new men and the ship herself would keep him too busy to brood. He loved *Anemone* more than any ship: he would not rest until she responded to his hand like the true thoroughbred she was.

Bolitho took his hand from his eye and was surprised that it gave him no pain or irritation. The air was clearer, and perhaps his freedom ashore with Catherine had helped more than he knew. He studied his ships again, each one as strong or as fragile as the man who commanded her.

So many times had Bolitho come to this small but powerful outpost in the Caribbean to stand against the American rebels, the Dutch, the Spaniards and the old enemy, France. And now the new American navy was posing a threat once again. There had still been no declaration of war, nor even a suggestion from either government that danger threatened on the horizon.

Bolitho watched a few boats weaving in and out among the moored men-of-war. Otherwise nothing stirred. In a month or so that would change with the beginning of the hurricane season. It had been that time of year when he had come here last, and found Catherine.

He thought of her letters, which had arrived only two days ago, all together in a sealed bag, having gone to Gibraltar first by accident. He smiled, hearing her voice in each written word, savouring them. Strange how, unlike letters, unpleasant and direct despatches from higher command never seemed to go astray, but found you without any apparent difficulty.

He had read through all of them twice, and he would read them again later when the ship was at rest.

Once, when he had been sitting at his table, the ship dark around him and lanterns glinting on the water like fireflies, he had heard the low murmur of a voice reading aloud close by. He understood now what it meant: his flag-lieutenant George Avery was reading a letter from home for Allday's benefit.

A small, unlikely thing perhaps, but Bolitho had been touched by it. The lieutenant, who like Tyacke never received letters from anybody; and the one who received them and could not read them. Another bond among *We Happy Few*.

Catherine's letters were written with care and with love. Their contact was so important, vital to him, and she understood exactly what he needed to know. Seemingly inconsequential details of the house, the weather, her roses and the people who were part of that other life which he had had to discard, like all those other times, and all those Bolithos before him.

She told him of the cliff walks, and the gossip in the town, of Roxby's obvious pleasure in his knighthood, of her mare Tamara. But she never wrote of the war.

Except once. She had been writing of *Indomitable*'s departure, how she had waited with Tamara to watch the powerful ship spreading sail and heading for the Channel.

It was such a proud sight, darling Richard. But I was the proudest of all. I did not cry, I could not, I could not allow tears to hide those precious moments. There goes my man. An admiral of England, the rock so many have depended on for so long. Only a man, you once

176

described yourself. So typical of you, dearest of men, but not true. You lead, they follow, so it will be until the last shot in this damnable war. Last night you came to me again darling Richard. I allowed you to touch me before you left me ... There was more, her words bringing him a poignant elation and comfort, which made other concerns unimportant.

Was that why he had stayed away from this fine house until her letters had arrived to sustain him? *Am I still so unsure, although our love has survived even the fiercest trial?*

He crossed to the nearest door and paused in the bars of dusty sunlight. Although the furniture was covered with protective sheets, and the valuable candlesticks and crystal had been removed, he could still see it as it had been. When he had stumbled, half blinded by reflected lights, and she had reached out to steady him. He had not known Catherine was here, whereas she had endured the knowledge of his arrival, and emotions and memories of their affair too powerful not to be re-awakened.

There was a gleam of scarlet from the other end of the terrace as a Royal Marine wandered past the windows. He was one of a handful who had been instructed to watch over the empty house, and to ensure that nothing went missing before the next occupant arrived from England. As Somervell had been despatched to take up residence here. A man trusted by the King, a man respected because of his lovely wife, and perhaps for little else by those who truly knew him.

Out into the impressive reception area, and beyond

177

it the big staircase where he had found her at night, when the curtains had swirled through the rooms like torn sails in a mounting wind. She had carried a loaded pistol hidden against her thigh. He would never forget the look in her fine, dark eyes when she had recognised her intruder.

She had written that she was losing her maid Sophie, who was to marry the son of a prosperous farmer over near Fallowfield. He wondered if Allday was still troubled over his separation from Unis. Love, permanent love, was so new to him, and completely unexpected.

Bolitho walked out into the glare again, glad he had come back to this place. Perhaps it would be possible to write to her about it, in a way that would not hurt her. He smiled faintly, sensing that she would already know he had made his pilgrimage here.

He descended the worn stone steps and paused to look back at the house. The windows were shuttered. Blind. And yet curiously he felt as if the place were watching him.

Allday was sitting on a bollard by the waterfront, his hat tilted over his eyes. He stood up immediately and signalled to the long, greenpainted barge idling in the shadow of a stores hulk. Bolitho wondered if the new barge crew knew how lucky they were to have him to watch over them. Other coxswains, no matter how junior, might have left them baking in the heat until they were required, but this big, shambling sailor always cared. Until somebody crossed him. Then the heavens would fall.

Allday watched the approaching barge with a critical

eye. A second coxswain had been appointed as his assistant, mostly to supervise its cleaning and general maintenance. He would be a help to Allday, who was so often troubled by his old chest wound. Bolitho looked away. Allday's expression seemed to suggest that the man in question still had a long way to go.

'A lot of memories in this place, old friend.'

Allday answered thoughtfully. 'Indeed, sir, more than a few.'

Bolitho said impulsively, 'I know how you are feeling ... about home. But I have to tell you, Lady Catherine is grateful that you came with me. And so am I.'

It was like a cloud drifting away. Allday gave a great grin, so that his troubled thoughts seemed to go with it.

'Ah, well, we just need Cap'n Adam alongside now, and we'll be ready for anything...' His eyes hardened as the barge tossed oars too soon and came against the fenders with a sickening lurch. Unabashed, Protheroe, the young fourth lieutenant, leapt ashore and removed his hat with a flourish. 'At your service, Sir Richard!'

Beyond his shoulder Bolitho heard Allday growl at the second coxswain, 'I don't care, see? Even if he is a bloody officer, *you* take charge. Don't treat the barge like a battering-ram!'

Protheroe's bright confidence had been replaced by two vivid spots of colour in his cheeks. He had heard every word, as Allday had intended.

Bolitho settled himself in the sternsheets and waited for the barge to glide away from the jetty.

He glanced at Protheroe and said quietly, 'If it is of any consolation, I once collided with my admiral's barge when I was a midshipman.'

'Oh?' The relief flooded his face. '*Oh!*'

After the din and turmoil of being piped on board, Bolitho took Allday to one side. 'Captain Tyacke and I are being entertained to dinner in the wardroom tonight. It may be the last chance we get for a while.'

'I knows about that, sir.'

Bolitho hid a smile. Like many other people Allday probably thought it was absurd that the admiral and the ship's captain had to wait for an invitation before they could enter the wardroom mess. His father had dismissed it as tradition, part of the navy's mystique. But where did all that go when the screens were torn down, and the decks were cleared from bow to stern, and such gentility was drowned and lost in the din of war?

'When it is done, and if you have a mind, lay aft and join me and Captain Tyacke for a wet, as you would call it.'

Allday grinned, and thought of the captain's new coxswain, Eli Fairbrother. *The day he gets asked for a wet will be the day.*

Bolitho saw Scarlett, the first lieutenant, waiting nearby.

'Mr Scarlett, how may I help you?'

Scarlett almost stammered. 'Tonight, Sir Richard, I . . .'

'We have not forgotten. And I intend that we should entertain all our captains who may be present as soon as *Anemone* arrives. It is always good to know the men who command the ships you may have to rely on.'

180

Scarlett came out of his troubled thoughts. 'A sail was sighted at noon, Sir Richard.'

Bolitho recalled once more *Hyperion*'s approach at snail's pace as Catherine had described it to him so many times. Today, there was even less wind at the newcomer's disposal.

Scarlett glanced at the listless masthead pendant. 'The army lookout station on Monk's Hill sent word that she may be the schooner *Kelpie*. She is apparently due.' He sensed the question in Bolitho's eyes. 'Mail-packet, Sir Richard, from the Bermudas.' An odd expression, a sadness, Bolitho thought, crossed his face. 'Before that, England.'

Bolitho turned away. Maybe another letter from Catherine? Perhaps new directions from the Admiralty?

Bethune might have changed his mind, or been ordered to change it. He had seen the doubts for himself. It was dangerous, as it was delicate. The Americans could be provoked into war, or they could be dissuaded from open conflict. Nothing would be achieved by sitting still and pretending a confrontation would go away of its own accord.

'So let's be about it then,' he said.

Scarlett was still staring after him as he strode aft to the cabin.

Lieutenant George Avery nodded to the marine sentry and waited for Ozzard to open the screen door for him.

The great cabin was lit only by two lanterns, and right aft beyond the tall stern windows he could see some scattered shore lights, and the moon's silver reflection on the gently breathing water.

He saw his admiral sitting on the bench seat, his heavy gold-laced coat draped over Ozzard's arm, his shirt open while he sipped a tall glass of hock.

Bolitho said, 'Be seated.' He saw Allday begin to rise for the lieutenant, but he changed his mind as Avery shook his head. To Bolitho he said, 'Let it be like that time in Freetown, Sir Richard. There are no officers here tonight. Only men.'

Bolitho smiled. Avery was more outspoken than usual; but there had been plenty of wine at the wardroom dinner, and so much food that, considering the temperature and the unmoving air between decks, it was a wonder some of them had not collapsed.

After the first awkward formalities between the mostly young officers and their admiral, as well as their formidable captain, things had settled down. Unlike meat from the cask, rock-hard when the cooks got their hands on it, there was a pleasant surprise on offer, an unlimited supply of fresh roast pork. The captain of the dockyard had his own pigs on the island, and had presented the meat from his own larder.

Apart from the four lieutenants and the two Royal Marine officers, the wardroom consisted of the ship's specialists. Isaac York, the sailing master, seemed to have an endless fund of stories about strange ports he had visited since going to sea at the age of eight. It was Bolitho's first real meeting with the ship's surgeon, Philip Beauclerk, young for his trade, with the palest eyes Bolitho had ever seen. Almost transparent, like sea-polished glass. An educated, quiet-spoken man, a far cry from the rough and ready surgeons, the butchers as they were called; men like George Minchin who had once served in *Hyperion*, and had been on board when the old ship had given up the fight. Wild-eyed, crude, and often half-drunk with rum, he had nevertheless saved many lives that day. And he had not quit the ship until the last of the wounded, or those who were not beyond hope, had been taken off.

Minchin would be in Halifax now, serving in the big frigate *Valkyrie*, where Bolitho had last met him.

Bolitho had caught Beauclerk watching him several times throughout the meal, the general drinking and the seemingly endless procession of toasts. It was impossible that he could know anything about his eye. Or was it? There was no more private society than the medical profession. But Beauclerk had spoken with great intelligence and interest about what might lie ahead, and was probably trying to guess what his own part might be. It was very hard to picture him like Minchin in that raging, bloody hell on the orlop deck, the wings-and-limbs tubs filled to overflowing with the gory remnants of those who had been cut down in battle.

Three midshipmen had been invited too, and one of them, Midshipman David Cleugh, had been required to call the Loyal Toast. This he did in a piping, quavery voice. He had then been sternly ordered to drink a full goblet of brandy by the captain of marines. For, by coincidence, it was the midshipman's twelfth birthday.

The quietest man in the wardroom had been James Viney, the purser. He had been unable to drag his eyes from the captain, who sat directly opposite him. Like a

183

mesmerised rabbit, Bolitho had thought. Tyacke had not come aft for a last drink, and had made his excuses as the messmen had started to clear away the table so that cards and dice could be produced. Out of politeness nobody would move until the senior guests had departed.

Tyacke, his torn face in shadow, had said only, 'I want to go through a book or two before I turn in.'

Bolitho recalled the purser's nervousness. The books might have a lot to do with that.

Bolitho had thrust out his hand, and had seen the sudden surprise in those clear blue eyes that reminded him so much of Thomas Herrick. 'Thank you, James.'

'For what, sir?' His handshake had been firm, nevertheless.

Bolitho had answered quietly, 'You know for what. As I know what this evening cost you. But believe me, you will not regret it. Nor will I.'

Ozzard brought another glass of hock and placed a goblet of rum almost within Allday's reach: his quiet, stubborn way of showing he was not *his* servant.

They sat in silence, listening to the ship's private noises and the dragging step of a watchkeeper overhead.

Avery said suddenly, 'The leaves will soon fall in England.' Then he shook his head and winced. 'God, how I shall pay for all that wine in the morning!'

Bolitho touched the locket inside his shirt and saw Avery glance as it flashed in the lantern light. Perhaps they all saw him in different ways. Few would imagine he could be as he was when he and Catherine were together.

Scarlett had also asked Yovell as a guest, but he had declined, and had spent the evening in the tiny cabin that also served him as an office and writing-space.

Allday had assured him that Yovell was quite happy to be alone. He had said with some amusement, 'He reads his Bible every night. There's still quite a lot of it to take in!'

Through the open skylight and stern windows they heard the creak of oars. It was so still that every sound seemed to carry.

Then the hail, '*Boat ahoy!*'

Avery looked surprised. 'Who is abroad at this hour?' He stood up. 'I'll go and see, sir.' He smiled suddenly, and appeared young and relaxed, as he must have been once. 'There may not be another officer sober enough to deal with it!'

The oars were louder, nearer. Then came the reply. '*Officer-of-the-Guard!*'

Bolitho massaged his eyes. He was tired, but rare moments with friends like these could not be ignored.

He thought of Scarlett, anxious and unsure of himself during the meal. Was it so important to him? He was a good officer, and watching him going about his duties Bolitho might have believed that he was completely confident, with perhaps only his next promotion uppermost in his mind. He had noticed, however, that neither he nor Avery had spoken to one another.

Avery returned, carrying a waterproof envelope.

'Would you believe, sir, the mail-schooner *Kelpie* entered harbour in pitch darkness after all. The guard-boat stood by just in case.' He held out the envelope.

'*Kelpie* met with *Anemone*. She's waiting until first light before she comes in.'

Bolitho said, 'Very wise, with the harbour full of ships, and Adam with a raw company.'

He saw Allday watching him questioningly.

Bolitho said, 'It's from Lady Catherine.'

A cold hand seemed to touch him and he could not shake it off. He recognised her handwriting instantly, and had seen an Admiralty wax seal on the envelope. *A priority*. For private correspondence?

Avery stood up. 'Then I shall leave you, sir.'

'No!' He was surprised by the sharpness of his own voice. *What is the matter with me?* 'Ozzard, recharge the glasses, if you please.' Even Ozzard was motionless, watching, listening.

'If you will excuse me.' Bolitho slit open the envelope and unfolded her letter.

He was suddenly quite alone, with only the letter, her words rising to meet him.

My darling Richard,

I would give anything not to write this letter, to send you news which will grieve you as it has me.

I have to tell you that Val's little boy is dead. It was an accident, and he suffocated in his cot before anyone could help him.

Bolitho looked away, feeling the sting in his eye and yet unable to hide it.

He heard Allday ask thickly, 'What is it, sir?'

But Bolitho shook his head and read on.

The others saw him fold the letter and then raise it to his lips. Then he became aware of his companions.

186

He felt as though he had been absent from them for a long time.

Ozzard held out a glass of brandy and bobbed nervously. 'Just a sip, sir.'

'Thank you.' He could barely taste it. As a child before entering the navy he had often walked with his mother along that path. To Trystan's Leap. It had been frightening even in daylight, full of legend and superstition. He felt the cold hand on his heart again, and in his mind's eye he saw her falling, so slowly, her long hair like weed as she came to the surface, her slender body broken on those terrible rocks. He asked, although it did not seem like his own voice, 'They sighted *Anemone*, you say?'

Avery responded crisply, 'Aye, sir. Standing about five miles to the sou'-west.'

Bolitho stood up and crossed to the two swords, which hung on their rack. *Adam*, he thought, *Adam, Adam* . . .

How could he tell him? And what of Val, so proud of his first son, who was one day to wear the King's uniform?

He touched the old family sword. What did fate intend?

He said, 'I want no talk of this.' He turned, and looked at each of them in turn. The stooping little figure by the pantry hatch; Avery, on his feet again, his eyes wary, uncertain. Lastly he looked at Allday.

'I have to tell you that Rear-Admiral Keen's child is dead.' He tried not to think of Catherine on the beach with the dead girl's body in her arms. 'Shortly afterwards . . .' There was no point in telling these honest men that the family had said and done nothing at all until Keen's father had been located in London. 'The girl we saw wed Val at Zennor killed herself.' He saw Allday's fists open and close as he added, 'At Trystan's Leap.'

Avery said, 'Rear-Admiral Keen will be desolate, sir.'

Bolitho turned to him, calm now, knowing what must be done. 'Do something for me. Go now and ensure that there is a note in the signals log for the morning watch. As soon as *Anemone* is within signals range I want *Captain repair on board* hoisted. Then hoist *Immediate* when she is anchored.'

Allday offered roughly, 'I could clear away the barge and collect him, sir.'

Bolitho stared at him. 'No, old friend. This is a private matter for as long as we may keep it so.' To Avery he said, 'Please do it. I will see you tomorrow.' He paused. 'Thank you.'

Allday made to follow but Bolitho said, 'Wait.'

Allday sat down heavily. They were alone, and they could hear Ozzard tidying up in his pantry.

'You knew . . . their feeling for one another.'

Allday sighed. 'I seen 'em together.'

'There was no intrigue, if that's what you mean?'

Allday watched him carefully. Knowing this man so well, but with no words to help him now that he needed it.

He said, 'Not in the way we means, sir. But love's new to me, and I've heard tell that it can be a blessing, then again it can be a curse.'

188

'And you knew all this.'

'*Felt* it, more like.'

'No one must suspect. Captain ... Adam means so much to me.'

'I knows it, sir. It must have been another world to that poor lass.' He shrugged. 'They looked so *right* together, I thought.'

Bolitho walked past him, but paused with his hand on his massive shoulder.

'A curse, you said?' He thought of Catherine's words, a cry from the heart. *The Mark of Satan.*

He said quietly, 'Then let them have peace now.'

He was still sitting at the open stern windows when the first pale sunlight spread across English Harbour.

In Cornwall, the passage of time would have blurred the memories of most people, while in some isolated villages there would be those still pondering on the old beliefs, curses and morals, and the torment for those who defied them.

But this morning there was still a pretence of peace. Above his head on the quarterdeck he knew Avery had not slept either, and was watching even as Adam's *Anemone* glided slowly to her anchorage. For him it would still be a puzzle, a mystery he was not privileged to share, but he must sense that the answer lay in the flags barely moving in the breeze.

Captain repair on board. Immediate.

PART II: 1812

10

Deception

Captain James Tyacke stood at the top of the companion ladder and waited for his eyes to become accustomed to the early morning darkness. It was a moment he never grew tired of. Quiet because the hands had not yet been piped to begin another day, private because of the lingering shadows. Above all, private; no easy thing in a man-of-war, not even for her captain.

In a short while the sun would change everything, reaching from horizon to horizon, all privacy gone. Water was getting short; they would have to return to Antigua in a few days' time. What would they find? Fresh orders, news from England, the war, that other world?

None of it mattered much to Tyacke. The *Indomitable* was his main concern. Week in, week out, he had drilled his company until it was almost impossible to tell the seasoned professionals from the landmen. Gunnery and sail drill, but with leisure still for the simple pleasures sailors enjoyed. Parted from their homes, it was all they had to keep them out of mischief.

Hornpipes and wrestling in the dog watches, and contests, mast against mast, to see which one could reef or make more sail in the least time.

Indomitable was now a ship of war which could give a good account of herself if so called.

But mostly she had been concerned with constant patrols, the stop-and-search procedure even of neutrals to prevent trade with French ports, and to seek out deserters from the King's navy. The Leeward Squadron had taken several prizes and recovered many such deserters, mostly sailing in American merchantmen, trying to reach a new life in what they believed to be a democratic paradise. Compared with the hardships they were forced to suffer under the British flag in this endless war, it probably was.

The first lieutenant was officer-of-the-watch and he could sense his presence on the opposite side of the quarterdeck. Scarlett had become used to Tyacke's ways, his early walks on deck when most captains would have been content to leave a morning watch to their senior lieutenants.

It was still cold, the quarterdeck rail damp with moisture. When dawn came up that would all change: the vapour would rise from the sails and rigging like steam, and the tar in the deck seams would cling to shoes and bare feet alike.

Tyacke could see it clearly in his mind's eye, as if he were a sea-eagle soaring high above the blue water with the ships like tiny models below: in a ragged, uneven line abreast, *Indomitable* in the centre and the two smaller frigates, one to starboard and one to larboard. Once they had exchanged the first signals their line would extend and take proper station. The masthead lookouts would be able to see one another, just, and together their span of vision would cover a range of some sixty miles. To the spies, and to the small trading vessels who would sell their information to anybody, the Leeward Squadron that patrolled as far north as the Canadian port of Halifax would have become well known. A protection or a threat: their presence could be interpreted either way. The big forty-two gun frigate *Valkyrie* was the senior ship at Halifax, and the rest of their vessels could operate either together or independently between the two main bases.

Tyacke thought of the wild storms they had weathered in the Caribbean. Given the choice he preferred these waters rather than endure Halifax's bitter winters, where rigging could swell in the blocks and freeze, leaving any ship barely able to tack or shorten sail.

He considered the other captains, knowing them now as individuals. The necessity of that had been taught him by Bolitho. To assume you knew a captain's mind simply because he *was* a captain could be as dangerous as any hurricane.

All the leagues they had sailed, in company or with the ocean to themselves. He imagined green fields in England. They had gone through another winter, into a new year, and now that year was half gone. It was June 1812, and if it was to be as demanding as the previous year, overhauls would have to be arranged.

English Harbour at Antigua was adequate for limited repairs, but not for an extensive campaign. And should there be a sea-fight with more destruction to hulls and rigging ... He sighed. When had the navy *ever* had enough of anything?

He stepped back from the rail and heard the first lieutenant crossing the damp planking.

'Good morning, Mr Scarlett. Is all well?'

'Aye, sir. Wind steady at nor'-east by north. Course west by north. Estimated position some one hundred and fifty miles north-east of Cape Haitien.'

Tyacke smiled grimly. 'As close to that damned country as I'd ever want to get!'

Scarlett asked, 'What orders for the forenoon, sir?' He hesitated as Tyacke turned sharply towards him. 'What is it, sir?'

Tyacke shook his head. 'Nothing.' But there *was* something. It was like a sixth sense, which he had at first refused to accept when he had been on the anti-slavery patrols, sometimes a premonition of where his prey might be found.

He felt it now. Something would happen today. He moved restlessly across the deck, telling himself he was a fool. Like the morning when Adam Bolitho had come eagerly aboard at Antigua in response to the flagship's signal. *Immediate.* When he had left *Indomitable* an hour or so later he had walked like a man face to face with some terrible fate.

Bolitho had sent for him and had broken the news about Rear-Admiral Keen's wife and her death on the Cornish cliffs. Just for a moment Tyacke had imagined that Bolitho had once felt a certain tenderness for the girl. Then he had dismissed the idea, thinking of

Catherine Somervell, how she had come aboard at Falmouth, and how the sailors had loved her for it.

What then? In his heart he knew the connection that bound them was a deeper secret than he would ever share. But why should a young woman's tragedy have the power to affect them so profoundly? It happened. Women and their children often died of fever or other causes on their way to join their husbands, in the navy, or the army with its far-flung outposts and lonely forts. Even the Caribbean possessions were described as the Islands of Death. Certainly more soldiers died of fever out here than ever fell to an enemy ball or bayonet. Death was commonplace. Perhaps it was the rumour of suicide that they could not accept.

Allday would know, he thought. But when it came to sharing secrets, Allday was like the Rock of Gibraltar.

Scarlett joined him again. 'The admiral's about early, sir.'

Tyacke nodded. He wanted to shake Scarlett. A good officer and very conscientious, and as popular with the lower deck as any first lieutenant could hope to expect.

Don't be timid with me. I told you before. My blood may be spilled before yours, and you could find yourself in command. Think of it, man. Talk to me. Share your thoughts.

He said, 'He has always been the same, I believe.' Had he, he wondered? Or was some premonition driving Bolitho also?

It was slightly brighter now. Topgallant masts

197

touched with pale light, as though they floated separately above the dark mass of spars and black rigging. Bolitho's flag rippling, as if newly awakened like the man it represented. A boatswain's mate and a handful of men checking the boats on their tier, inspecting hatch fastenings, putting fresh oil in the compass lamps. A ship coming to life.

The master's mate of the watch said softly, 'Admiral's comin' up, sir.'

'Thank you, Mr Brickwood.' Tyacke recalled the beginning, when all these men had been unfamiliar. Knowing from his own experience and later from Bolitho's example how important it was to remember each man's name as well as his face. In the navy you owned little else.

The midshipman-of-the-watch, a youth named Deane, said rather loudly, 'Half-past four, sir!'

Bolitho walked amongst them, his ruffled shirt very clear against the deck and the sea's dark backdrop beyond.

'Good morning, Sir Richard.'

Bolitho looked towards him. 'It is, too, Captain Tyacke.' He nodded to the first lieutenant. 'And you, Mr Scarlett? Are your lookouts aloft?'

'Aye, sir.' Hesitant again: it was impossible to know what he was thinking.

Bolitho rubbed his hands. 'That is a vile smell from the galley funnel. We must endeavour to take on more supplies when we return to English Harbour. Fresh fruit, with any luck.'

Tyacke hid a smile. Just for a moment Bolitho was

allowing himself to be a captain again, with a captain's concern for every man and boy aboard.

'Walk with me, James.' Together they began to pace the quarterdeck. In the dim light they could have been brothers.

Bolitho asked, 'What ails that man?'

Tyacke shrugged. 'He's an officer not lacking in some fine qualities, sir, but . . .'

'Aye, James, I have often found *but* to be the hurdle!'

He looked up as the first thin sunlight felt its way through the tarred rigging and out along the braced mainyard. Even the sea had gained colour, a rich blue which gave it an appearance of even greater depth than the thousand-odd fathoms claimed to lie beneath *Indomitable*'s keel.

Tyacke watched Bolitho's profile, the obvious pleasure it gave him to see another dawn. In spite of all his service, he could still suppress and contain his inner worries, if only for this moment of the day.

Bolitho turned aside as the usual procession of figures trooped aft to speak either with the first lieutenant or the captain. When the hands had been fed the main deck would become the market-place, where the professional men would work with their own little crews. The sailmaker and his mates, repairing and still more repairing. Nothing could be wasted with a ship so many hundreds of miles from harbour. The carpenter, too, with his team. He was Evan Brace, said to be the oldest man in the squadron. He certainly looked it. But he could still repair, and if necessary build, a boat as well as any man.

Bolitho heard a familiar Yorkshire voice. Joseph Foxhill was the cooper, up early to obtain deck space where he could scour and clean some of his empty casks before they were refilled.

A midshipman strode beneath the quarterdeck rail, the white patches on his collar showing brightly through the withdrawing shadows, and he was reminded painfully of Adam. He tended to think of him always as a midshipman, the lively colt-like boy who had joined his ship when his mother had died. He sighed. He would never forget the look on Adam's dark features when he had told him about Zenoria. It had been pitiful to see his stunned disbelief. Like the tragedy you try to pretend has not happened. You will awake, and it will have been a dream . . .

He had not resisted when Bolitho had made him sit down, and he had asked his uncle quietly to repeat what he had said. Bolitho had listened to his own voice in the sealed cabin; he had even closed the skylight in case someone overheard. Adam was a captain, perhaps one of the best frigate captains the fleet had ever known, but in those quiet, wretched, faltering moments he had seemed that same dark-haired boy, who had walked all the way from Penzance to Falmouth with only hope and Bolitho's name to sustain him.

He had said, 'May I see Lady Catherine's letter, Uncle?'

Bolitho had watched him, seen his eyes moving slowly over the letter line by line, perhaps sharing the intimacy, as if she too were speaking to him. Then he had said, 'It was all my fault.' When he had looked up from the letter Bolitho had been shocked to see the tears running down his face. 'But I could not stop. I loved her so. Now she is gone.'

Bolitho had said, 'I was a part of it, too.' Catherine's words seemed to ring in his mind. *The Mark of Satan.* Was there, *could* there be substance in the old Cornish beliefs and superstitions?

After that they had sat mostly in silence, until at last Adam had made to leave.

'I grieve for Rear-Admiral Keen. His loss is all the more tragic because . . .' He had left the rest unsaid.

He had picked up his hat and straightened his uniform. When he returned to his ship they would only see him as their captain. So it must be.

But as Bolitho had watched him climb down into his boat to the trill of calls, he had seen only the midshipman.

He stirred himself as voices pealed down from aloft.

'Deck there! *Zest* in sight to larboard!'

Like yesterday, and all the others before it. He could picture the rakish thirty-eight-gun frigate, her captain too, Paul Dampier, young, perhaps too headstrong, and very ambitious. Rather like Peter Dawes, the admiral's son who now commanded *Valkyrie* out of Halifax.

'Deck there! *Reaper* in sight to starboard!' A smaller frigate of twenty-six guns. James Hamilton, her captain, was old for his rank and had been attached to the Honourable East India Company until he had re-entered the navy at his own request.

And away to windward would be the little brig *Marvel*. Ready to run down on anything suspicious, to search coves and inlets where her larger consorts might lose their keels; to run errands, almost anything.

Bolitho had often seen Tyacke watching her whenever she was close by. Still remembering. *Marvel* was very like his *Larne*.

He saw Allday at the foot of the quarterdeck ladder. He had his head on one side, and was ignoring the rush of seamen to trim the yards again, urged on no doubt by the smell of breakfast.

Bolitho asked sharply, 'What is it?'

Allday looked at him impassively. 'Not certain, sir.'

'Deck there! Sail in sight to th' nor'-east!'

Tyacke glanced around until he found Midshipman Blythe. 'Aloft with you, my lad, and take a glass!'

There was an edge to his voice and Bolitho saw him stare at the horizon, already glassy bright and searing.

'Prepare to make more sail, Mr Scarlett!'

Blythe had reached the mainmast crosstrees. 'Sail to the nor'-east, sir!' Just the slightest hesitation. 'Schooner, sir!'

Scarlett remarked, 'Well, she's not running away.'

With *Indomitable* and the other two frigates hove-to, and the brig *Marvel* making sail to block the stranger's escape if she proved hostile, every available glass was trained despite the heavy, regular swell.

Midshipman Cleugh, Blythe's haughty assistant, called in his squeaky voice, 'She's *Reynard*, sir!'

Scarlett said, 'Courier. I wonder what she wants?'

Nobody answered.

Allday climbed silently up the ladder and stood at Bolitho's shoulder.

'I've got a feeling, sir. Something's wrong.'

It was almost an hour before the schooner was near enough to drop a boat. Her captain, a wild-eyed lieutenant named Tully, was taken down to the cabin where Bolitho was pretending to enjoy some of Ozzard's coffee.

'Well, Mr Tully, and what have you brought me?'

He watched as Avery opened the bag and then dragged out the sealed and weighted envelope.

But the schooner's young captain exclaimed, 'It's war, sir! The Americans are already at the Canadian frontier . . .'

Bolitho took the despatches from Avery's hand. 'Where are their ships?' One letter was from Captain Dawes in *Valkyrie*. He had taken his ships to sea as already arranged, and would await fresh orders as they had planned, it seemed so long ago.

He repeated, 'But where are their ships?'

Dawes had written as a postscript, *Commodore Beer's squadron quit Sandy Hook during a storm.*

He could almost hear the words. *A total responsibility*. But he felt nothing. It was what he had expected. Hoped, perhaps. To end it once and for all.

Tyacke, who had been waiting in silence, asked suddenly, 'What is the date of origin, sir?'

Avery replied, 'Ten days ago, sir.'

Bolitho stood up, aware of the silence in the ship, despite the heavy movement. Ten days, and they had been at war without knowing it.

He swung round. 'The next convoy from Jamaica?'

Tyacke said, 'Sailed. They'd not know either.'

Bolitho stared at the chair by the stern bench. Where Adam had sat with Catherine's letter. Where his heart had broken.

He asked, 'What escort?' He saw Tyacke's face. He,

too, had known that this was coming. But how could that be?

Avery said, '*Anemone*, sir. If they were not expecting . . .'

Bolitho interrupted him sharply. 'Make a signal to *Zest* and *Reaper*, repeated *Marvel*. *Close on flagship and remain in company.*' He looked directly at Tyacke, excluding everyone else. 'We shall lay a course for the Mona Passage.' He could recall it so clearly, that much disputed channel to the west of Puerto Rico, where he and so many faces now lost had fought battles now forgotten by most people.

It was the obvious route for any Jamaica convoy. Heavily laden merchantmen would stand no chance against ships like the U.S.S. *Unity*, or men like Nathan Beer.

Unless the escort saw through the deception and turned to defend the convoy against overwhelming odds, as *Seraphis* had faced John Paul Jones's *Bonhomme Richard* in that other war against the same enemy.

It was just possible. That convoy had been saved. *Seraphis* had been beaten into submission.

He looked at Tyacke but in his heart, he saw only Adam.

'All the sail she can carry, James. I think we are sorely needed.'

But a voice seemed to echo back, mocking him.

Too late. Too late.

*

Richard Hudson, first lieutenant of the thirty-eight-gun frigate *Anemone*, strode aft to the quarterdeck even as eight bells chimed out from the forecastle. He touched his forehead as a mark of respect to the second lieutenant, whom he was about to relieve. Like the other officers he wore only his shirt and breeches, and was hatless, and he could feel even the lightest garment plastered to his body like a second skin.

'The afternoon watch is aft, sir.'

The words were formal and timeless, the navy's custom from the Indian Ocean to the Arctic, if so ordered.

The other young lieutenant, the same age as himself, replied with equal precision, 'The course remains at south-east by south, the wind has backed to about north by west.'

Around and below them, midshipmen and the duty watch took their stations while others filled in their time splicing and stitching, the endless tasks of maintaining a ship-of-war.

Hudson took a telescope from its rack and winced as he held it to his eye. It was as hot as a gun-barrel. For a moment or two he moved the glass across the drifting heat haze and the dark blue water until he found the shimmering pyramids of sail, the three big merchantmen which *Anemone* had been escorting from Port Royal, and would continue to escort until they had reached the Bermudas, where they would join a larger convoy for the Atlantic crossing.

Even the thought of England made Hudson lick his lips. Summer, yes, but it might be raining. Cool breezes, wet grass under foot. But it was not to be. He realised that the second lieutenant who had been in charge of the forenoon watch was still beside him. He wanted to talk, up here where he could not be heard. It made Hudson feel both guilty and disloyal. He was the first lieutenant, responsible only to the captain for the running and organisation of the ship and her company.

How could things have changed so much in less than a year? When his uncle, a retired vice-admiral, had obtained him the appointment in *Anemone* through a friend in the Admiralty, he had been overjoyed. Like most ambitious young officers he had yearned for a frigate, and to be second-in-command to such a famous captain had been like a dream coming true.

Captain Adam Bolitho was all that a frigate commander was supposed to be: dashing and reckless, but not one to risk lives for his own ends or glory. The fact that Bolitho's uncle, who commanded their important little squadron, was as celebrated and loved in the fleet as he was notorious in society ashore, gave the appointment an added relish. Or it had, until the day Adam Bolitho had returned to *Anemone* after his summons to the flagship at English Harbour. He had always been a hard worker, and had expected others to follow his example: often he carried out tasks normally done by common seamen, if only to prove to the landmen and others pressed against their will that he was not asking the impossible of them.

Now he was driving himself to and beyond the limit. Month by month they had patrolled as near to the American mainland as possible, unless other ships were in close company. They had stopped and searched ships of every flag and taken many deserters, and on several occasions had fired on neutral vessels which had showed no inclination to heave-to for inspection. A quarter of *Anemone*'s total company were even now in captured prizes and making either for Antigua or Bermuda.

Even that seemed to give the captain no satisfaction, Hudson thought. He shunned the company of his officers, and only came on deck when required for sailing the ship, or in times of foul weather, which had been plentiful over the past months. Then, soaked to the skin, his black hair plastered to his face, looking more like a pirate than a King's officer, he had never budged until his ship was out of danger.

But he was curt, impatient now, an entirely different man from the one Hudson had first met in Plymouth.

Vicary, the second lieutenant, said, 'I'll be glad when this convoy is out of our hands. Slow to sail, slow even to co-operate – sometimes I think these damned grocery captains take a delight in ignoring signals!' Hudson watched a fish leap and fall into the heaving water. He had found himself assessing even the most commonplace remarks for some secret significance.

Captain Bolitho was never brutal with punishment; otherwise, sailing with only the elderly brig *Woodpecker* in company, he might well have expected serious trouble. Hudson had questioned some of the retaken deserters himself, and many had pleaded that they had run only because of unfair and in some cases horrific floggings for even minor offences. Now, returned to British ships but in the same war, their treatment would be gauged by their behaviour.

Hudson glanced at the men working on deck, some trying to remain in the shadows of the reefed topsails, or watching the marine sentry with his fixed bayonet on sweating guard over the fresh-water cask.

If only they could be free of the merchantmen and their painfully slow progress. Day in, day out, only the wind seemed to change: and there was precious little of that, too.

Hudson said, '*You* think that all this is a waste of time, do you, Philip?'

'Yes, as a matter of fact, I do. This is a drudge's work. Let them fend for themselves, I say! They are quick enough to squeal and appeal to higher authority if we take a few of their prime seamen to fill the gaps, but they bleat even louder when *they* are in danger themselves!'

Hudson thought of a verse he had once heard somewhere. *God and the Navy we adore, when danger threatens but not before!* Obviously nothing had changed.

Anemone had been driven hard. A proper refit was inevitable. He tried not to hope too much. One of the ships awaiting their arrival at Bermuda had been out here for less time than *Anemone*, and she was going to sail home as an additional escort. *Home.* He almost gritted his teeth. Then he lifted the telescope again and moved it deliberately towards the distant sails. Further downwind the brig *Woodpecker* stood above the thick heat haze like a pair of feathers, so white against the pitiless sky.

He said, 'Why don't you cut on down to the wardroom? It'll be a mite cooler if nothing else.' He lowered the glass and waited. *Here it comes.*

Vicary said, 'We've always got on well. I can't talk to anyone else. You know how things get twisted.'

'*Distorted*, you mean?' Vicary was twenty-four, a native of Sussex, fair-haired and blue-eyed with, Hudson thought, what his mother could have called *such an English face.* He contained a fond smile and retorted, 'You know I cannot discuss the matter.' Even that felt like disloyalty.

'I appreciate that.' Vicary plucked at his stained shirt. 'I just want to know *why.* What happened to change him? We deserve that much, surely?'

Hudson toyed with the idea of sending him below with a direct order. Instead he said, 'Something very personal, perhaps. Not a death, or we'd have heard of it. His future is assured, provided he can stay alive, and I don't just mean in the line of battle.'

Vicary nodded, perhaps from satisfaction that their friendship was not in danger. 'I did hear a few tales about a duel somewhere. Everyone knows it goes on, despite the law.'

Hudson thought of the captain's uncle as he had been when he had come aboard to meet the officers. Adam was so like him, exactly as Bolitho must have been at the same age. The hero, the man who was followed into battle with a kind of passion, as they had once followed Nelson. And yet unlike so many high-ranking and successful officers – *heroes* – Hudson had felt that Sir Richard Bolitho was a man without conceit, and one who truly cared for the men he inspired. It was more than charisma, as he had heard it described. When the admiral looked at you, *you* as an individual person, you could feel it run through your blood. And you knew in the same breath that you would follow him anywhere.

He felt suddenly troubled. Adam Bolitho had once been very like that.

He saw the master-at-arms and the boatswain standing by the weather side and its rank of long eighteen-pounders, and the sight brought him out of his thoughts with a jolt. Punishment was to be carried out at two bells, when the watch below had finished their meal. He could smell the rum on the hot breeze, which was barely enough to fill the sails.

Punishment was usually carried out in the forenoon; it gave all hands time to get over it and wash away the memory with rum. But for some reason the captain had ordered an extra gun drill today, had even been on deck to time it himself, as if he did not trust his officers to stress the importance of teamwork.

Had they been running free with all canvas filled and driving the *Anemone* until every strand of rigging was bar taut, it would have been just another punishment. Two dozen lashes: it could have been many more for the man in question. This would not be the first time he had received a striped shirt at the gangway. He was a hard man, a lower-deck lawyer, a born trouble-maker. Captain Bolitho could have awarded double that amount.

But this was different. Moving so slowly, with nothing in sight but the far-off convoy and brig, it could be like a spark in a powder keg. The nearest land was

210

Santo Domingo, some hundred miles to the north: the perverse wind made it impossible to tack any closer. But in another two days they would reach the Mona Passage where many changes of tack would be required, keeping all hands busy for days until they broke out into the Atlantic.

Hudson turned as a shadow moved across the rail. It was the captain.

Adam Bolitho gazed at them impassively. 'Nothing to do but *gossip*, Mr Vicary?' He looked at the first lieutenant. 'I would have thought you could discover something not too tiring for an officer to do, if he has no stomach for his lunch?'

Hudson said, 'We have not had too much time to talk of late, sir.'

He studied his captain as he walked to the compass and then glanced at the limply flapping masthead pendant.

The helmsman called huskily, 'Sou'-east by south, sir, steady she goes!'

Hudson noted the dark shadows beneath the captain's eyes, the restless way he moved his hands. Like the rest of them he was casually dressed, but he wore his short fighting-sword, which was unusual. The boatswain's party was preparing to rig a grating, and Hudson saw Cunningham, the surgeon, appear in the companion-way. When he realised the captain was on deck he disappeared down the ladder without another glance.

But the captain had seen him. He said, 'The surgeon has protested to me about punishment being carried out. Did you know that?'

Hudson said, 'I did not, sir.'

'He states that the seaman in question, Baldwin, whose name has repeatedly appeared in the punishment book – and not only in *Anemone*'s, I suspect – has some internal illness, too much rum and other more damaging potions. What do you say, Mr Hudson?'

'He is often in trouble, sir.'

Adam Bolitho said sharply, 'He is scum. I'll suffer no insubordination in *my ship*.'

Hudson had always been very aware of the captain's love for this ship. Such a personal attachment seemed only another aspect of the Bolitho legend. But now he thought he knew why he was so intense about it. His beloved *Anemone* was all he had in the world.

The other lieutenant had used the opportunity to go below. It was a pity, Hudson thought; had he stayed he would have seen it for himself. Or would he?

The boatswain lumbered aft and called, 'Ready, sir!'

Adam said, 'Very well, Mr M'Crea, put up the prisoner and clear lower deck.'

As if to a secret signal, the Royal Marines marched up to line the quarterdeck, their bayoneted muskets and equipment gleaming as if at their barracks, their faces as scarlet as their tunics.

George Starr, the captain's coxswain, brought the old sea-going coat and hat to cover him with a cloak of authority.

'All hands! All hands! Lay aft to witness punishment!'

The seaman named Baldwin strode aft, the master-at-arms and ship's corporal on either side of him. A big man, a bully, he ruled his own mess like a tyrant.

A boatswain's mate and another seaman took his arms as soon as they had stripped him of his chequered shirt, and seized him up to the grating by his wrists and his knees. Even from the quarterdeck, it was possible to see all the old scars on the strong back.

Adam removed his hat and took out his thumbed copy of the Articles of War. He had been aware of Hudson's scrutiny, just as he had sensed Vicary's keen resentment. Given time, both would make good officers. He felt the anger stirring. *But they did not command.*

He saw the surgeon taking his place and recalled his pleas on behalf of the prisoner. Cunningham was a whining hypocrite. He would not cross the road to help a child knocked down by a runaway horse.

From the corner of his eye he saw the boatswain drag the infamous cat-o'-nine-tails from its red baize bag.

Adam hated the use of the cat, as his uncle had always done. But if, like the line of sweating marines, it was all that stood between disobedience and order, then so be it.

He put his hand in his pocket and bunched his knuckles until the pain helped to steady him.

He could feel his coxswain Starr watching him. Worried and anxious, as he had been over the months. A good man. Not another Allday: but there was no such creature.

He loosened his fingers carefully, testing the moment as he felt her glove in his pocket. So many times he had taken it out and had stared at it, remembering her eyes when he had handed it to her. How they had walked together in the port admiral's garden: feeling her presence like a beautiful wild flower.

What can I do? Why did you leave me?

He realised with a start that he had begun to read the relevant Article, his voice level and calm. *Calm? I am destroying myself.*

He heard himself say, 'Carry on, Mr M'Crea. Two dozen!'

The drums rattled noisily and the boatswain's brawny arm went back. The lash seemed to dangle there for an eternity until it came down across the prisoner's naked back with a crack. M'Crea was a powerful man and, although a fair one, was probably enjoying this task.

He saw the red lines break into bloody droplets. But he felt no revulsion, and that alone frightened him.

'*Deck there!*'

It was as if the call had turned them all to stone. The lash dangling from the boatswain's out-thrust fist, the drumsticks suddenly still in the heavy air. The prisoner himself, face pressed against the grating, his chest heaving as he dragged in breath like a drowning man.

Hudson raised his speaking-trumpet. 'What is it, man?'

'Sail on the larboard quarter!' He hesitated. The heat haze was probably just as bad in that direction. '*Two* sail, sir!'

Hudson knew that every eye but the prisoner's was turned upon the little group of officers on the quarter-deck. But when he looked at the captain he was astonished to see Adam's expression, his utter lack of surprise. As if a question which had troubled him had suddenly been made clear.

'What do you think, sir?'

'Well, no matter who they are, they are certainly not ours. That we do know.' He was thinking aloud, as if there was nobody else near him. 'They must have used the Windward Passage, west of Port au Prince. That way they would have the wind which is eluding us.'

Hudson nodded, but did not understand.

Adam looked at the towering mainmast spars, the quivering canvas.

'I shall go aloft.'

The man at the grating tried to twist his head. 'What about me, you bastard?'

Adam handed his hat and coat to Starr and snapped, 'Be *patient*, man. And Mr M'Crea, another dozen for his damned impertinence!'

He reached the crosstrees, surprised that he was not even breathless. He acknowledged the lookout, one of the best in the squadron, a man who looked twice his real age.

'Well, Thomas, what do you make of them?'

'Men-o'-war, zur. No doubt o' that!'

Adam unslung his telescope, aware of the great trembling mast and yards, the bang and slap of canvas, the very power of the ship beneath him. He had to wait a few seconds more. Even the lookout's familiar Cornish accent caught him unawares like a trap.

Then he levelled the telescope, as he had done so many times in his *Anemone*.

The smaller of the two vessels could have been

anything in the haze. Sloop or brig, it was impossible to determine. But about the other one there was no such doubt.

It could have been yesterday: the U.S.S. *Unity*'s great cabin, and his conversation with her captain, Nathan Beer, who had known his father during the American Revolution.

'Yankee,' he said shortly.

'Thought as much, zur.'

'Well done, Thomas. I'll see you have an extra tot for this.'

The man watched him, puzzled. 'But we bain't at war with *they*, zur?'

Adam smiled and made his way down like a practised topman.

He met Hudson and the others and saw all the questions in their eyes, although nobody spoke.

He said crisply, 'One of them's the big Yankee frigate *Unity*, forty-four guns that I know of for sure, maybe more now.' He glanced at the nearest guns. *Unity* carried twenty-four pounders. He remembered the American mentioning them. Pride or threat? Probably both.

He glanced at the sky. Two hours before they were up to *Anemone*. Seven hours more before the convoy could escape in the darkness.

Hudson said carefully, 'What are their intentions, sir?'

Adam thought of the splendid sight *Unity* had made as she edged round to beat closer to the wind, the other vessel responding to a bright hoist of signal flags.

There was no need for such a manoeuvre. Her

216

captain could remain on his present course untroubled by either the convoy or her escort. Instead, he was taking the wind-gage, and would hold it until he was ready.

'I think they intend to attack, Dick. In fact, I am sure of it.'

The use of his first name surprised Hudson almost as much as the simple acceptance of something unthinkable.

'You *know* this ship, sir?'

'I have been aboard her and have met her captain. An impressive man. But *know* her? That is another matter.'

Adam stared along the deck above the mass of silent figures towards the beakhead, the perfect shoulder and gilded hair of the figurehead. *Daughter of the Wind.*

Almost to himself he said, 'We are of one company, Dick. Some good, some bad. But every so often we must forget our differences. We become an instrument, to be used rightly or wrongly as directed.'

'I see, sir.'

He touched Hudson's arm, as he had seen his uncle do on many occasions.

'I want you to make a signal to Commander Eames of the *Woodpecker*, repeated to our fat charges. *Make more sail. Disperse the convoy.*' He hesitated for only a few seconds. *Suppose I am wrong?* But his conviction to the contrary was more compelling. 'Then make *Enemy in sight to the north-west.*'

He heard men calling out as the midshipman in charge of signals and his crew ran to the halliards, while Hudson repeated the instructions behind them. He saw

Lieutenant Vicary staring at him, his face suddenly pale under the tanned skin.

He asked quietly, 'Will we be able to outreach them, sir?'

Adam turned and looked at him, and through him. 'Today we are the instrument, Mr Vicary. We fight, so that others shall survive.'

Hudson glanced at the streaming flags. 'Orders, sir?'

Adam tried to discover his innermost feelings. But there were none. Did that mean there would be no tomorrow?

'Orders? Carry on with the punishment.' He smiled and was suddenly very young. 'Then you may beat to quarters. The rest you know.'

He turned away as the drums began to roll again and the frozen images came to life.

A voice called out as the lash cracked down, '*Woodpecker*'s acknowledged, sir!'

Adam watched the punishment without emotion. They were committed. *I committed them.*

The instrument.

11

Like Father, Like Son

Adam Bolitho returned to his place by the quarterdeck rail and looked along the full length of his command. The deck had been sanded around each eighteen-pounder so that the gun-crews would not slip and fall in the heat of battle. Equally, sand soaked up the blood if the enemy's iron came crashing inboard.

Lieutenant Hudson strode aft and touched his hat. 'Ship cleared for action, sir.' His face was full of questions.

Adam said, 'Well done, Mr Hudson. Nine minutes. They are improving.'

He stared up at the clear sky and felt his heart quicken as the masthead pendant licked out in the breeze. This time it did not fall back limply to the mast. The wind was getting up. Very slightly, but if it held . . . He shut the ifs and buts from his mind.

Instead he said, 'You are probably asking why I did not order the nets to be spread.' How open and vulnerable it looked without them. The nets were usually prepared as the ship was cleared for action, mainly to protect the gun-crews from falling wreckage but also to be joined to the loosely-slung boarding nets, to trap enemy attackers until they could be driven off with pikes and musket fire. Any sign of either would warn the Americans that they were ready to fight.

Likewise, he had told Hudson to keep the marines out of the fighting tops where their bright uniforms would shout the same readiness for action.

Hudson listened to his brief explanation, not knowing whether to find hope in it or to disbelieve it.

Adam said, '*Unity* has all the sea-room in the world. Like us, she depends on surprise. My guess is she will keep to wind'rd and try to cripple us at long range. Then she will attempt to board us.'

Hudson said nothing. He could see the dilemma that confronted the captain. If the Americans were allowed on board there would not be enough men to fight them off: too many were away in *Anemone*'s recently-taken prizes. However, if the captain showed his hand too soon, *Unity*'s massive broadside might dismast them even as she remained safely beyond accurate fire from *Anemone*.

Adam raised his telescope and studied the other ship with complete concentration. She had set more sail and had left her small consort astern. Commodore Beer would not be able to see the convoy as yet, nor would he know it had been ordered to disperse, and *devil take the hindmost*.

He said, 'Full broadside. Double-shotted for good measure. Go to the gun-captains yourself, although most of them will not need to be told.'

He glanced at Lieutenant Vicary by the foremast.

Like the third lieutenant, George Jeffreys, he had barely seen any real action at close quarters. He thought of *Unity*'s guns. They would soon know all about it.

He felt Starr beside him and spread his arms to receive the coat with its gold epaulettes. He had been so proud when he had been posted, just as he had known how pleased Bolitho would be.

It had been fate. *Golden Plover* running herself on the African reef, and all hope given up for his uncle and Catherine. He swallowed hard. Valentine Keen had been reported lost in that wreck as well.

How it haunted him, the night it had happened. Zenoria had come to him to share their grief, and out of that shared grief they had discovered a love they had hidden from one another and from the rest of the world.

He touched his breeches and felt her glove against his leg. Could see her eyes as she had gazed into his when he had reached up to the carriage window at Plymouth.

'All guns loaded, sir!'

He thrust the memories away: they could not help him now.

'Keep the hands out of sight. Just a few idlers gaping on the larboard gangway will suffice. A natural thing, eh? 'Tis not every day we see a true symbol of freedom!'

Joseph Pineo, the old sailing master, nudged one of his three helmsmen, but nobody else moved or spoke.

Adam dragged out his watch and flicked open the

guard. Beyond it he saw one of the young midshipmen taking huge breaths, his eyes watering as he stared at the other ship plunging over the water.

Suppose I am mistaken? That there had been no declaration of war even though he and many others had expected it? Two ships passing, and nothing more?

He said, 'With this puff of extra wind I intend to come about and engage him on the starboard side. He may anticipate it, but he cannot prevent it.' He smiled suddenly. 'We shall soon see if all our drills and exercises have had any value.'

He looked again at his ship, a lingering gaze full of questions, Hudson thought; memories too. Missing faces. Pride and fear, comradeship. He bit his lip. If the worst happened, some of the pressed men might try to surrender. He realised with a start that he was unarmed except for his hanger, which his father had presented to him when he had joined *Anemone*.

'This will serve you well, my boy, as will your fine young captain!' What would his father think now?

He saw the captain raise his glass to study the other ship, to gauge her approach, the moment of embrace.

Adam said, 'I see him, Dick. It is Nathan Beer right enough. Be ready to put the best marksmen aloft. There may not be much time.' Hudson was about to hurry away when something in the captain's voice made him turn back.

'If I fall, fight the ship with everything you have.' He looked up at the White Ensign streaming from the peak. 'We've done so much . . . together.'

As he walked around the upper deck Hudson was struck not by the tension, but by the air of resignation.

222

Anemone was fast. If she could break off contact she might easily lose the Yankee when dusk came. Where was the point in fighting and dying for a handful of poxy merchantmen? Hudson was young, but he had heard that sentiment expressed often enough.

He paused by Vicary, who said quietly, 'She's big.'

'Aye. But Captain Bolitho is just as experienced as this Commodore Beer I keep hearing about.' He clapped him on the arm and felt him jump.

Vicary glanced at the nearest gun-crew as they crouched below the gangway behind their sealed port. 'Are you not afraid?'

Hudson considered it, his eyes never leaving the oncoming pyramid of sails. 'I'm more afraid of *showing* it, Philip.'

Vicary held out his hand, as if they had just met in a street or country lane in England. 'Then I'll not let you down, Richard.' He stared beyond the vibrating shrouds to the empty blue sky. 'Though I fear I'll not see another day.'

Hudson returned to the quarterdeck, his friend's words hanging in his mind like an epitaph.

Adam said to him, 'Pass the word. Just as we discussed it. We will come about and lay her on the starboard tack. Do they all understand?'

'Those who count, sir.'

Surprisingly, Adam grinned, his teeth very white in his face. 'By God, Dick, we shall need everybody, even that oaf Baldwin, stinking of rum in the sick-bay though he might be!'

Hudson loosened his hanger and murmured, 'Good luck, sir.'

Adam licked his lips and said, 'I am as dry as dust!' Then he stooped slightly to stare along the quarterdeck rail, using it like a ruler as *Unity*'s long jibboom appeared around the tightly-packed hammock nettings for the first time.

'*Ready ho! Put the helm down!*'

'Helm's a-lee, sir!'

Even as the ship tilted to the thrust of wind and rudder Adam found time to see one of the marines, kneeling beside the hammocks with his long Brown Bess propped beside him, turn to stare at his captain.

'*Open the ports!*'

As one, the gunport-lids were hoisted on both sides of the ship, the gun-crews already ready at the tackle falls, staring aft for the order.

'*Run out!*'

Like squealing pigs each carriage was hauled smartly to the side, the black muzzles pointing at empty sea and sky while *Anemone* continued to bear round across the wind.

'*Mainsail haul!*'

Adam strode across the tilting deck as the waiting marines swarmed up the shrouds and ratlines to the fighting tops on each mast.

We did it! We did it!

Instead of being on *Anemone*'s quarter, the big frigate was sliding past the bowsprit, her sails in confusion as she prepared to follow suit. She was running up two additional ensigns. Beer had not been completely unprepared.

'*Steady! Hold her!*'

'Steady as she goes, sir! Sou'-west by west!'

Adam stared until his eyes felt raw. '*On the up-roll!*'

Without taking his eyes from *Unity* he could picture each gun-captain looking aft, watching his raised fist, every man with his trigger-line bar-taut.

'*Fire!*'

The ship shook as if she had run aground, as the guns hurled themselves inboard on their tackles and smoke funnelled through each of the starboard ports.

All tension was gone in an instant. Whooping like madmen, the gun-crews threw themselves into the drill over which they had cursed and sweated for months.

'*Stop your vents! Sponge out! Load! Run out!*'

The gun was God. Nothing else mattered, and each man in a crew had learned the hard way.

Arms reached up through the drifting smoke. '*Ready!*'

But Adam was watching the other ship. The range was about a mile and a half, too far for certain accuracy. But he had seen *Unity*'s sails jerking or carrying away as the broadside had hissed over the water and raked her like a deathly wind.

Adam raised his fist. It was working. Three shots every two minutes.

'*Fire!*'

Wreckage splashed around *Unity*'s bows as she continued to come around. Smaller weapons were firing from her forecastle and Adam glanced at the main-course as a black-rimmed hole smacked through the canvas.

Now *Unity* was lying across the starboard quarter

and continuing to turn, gathering speed as her topmen fought to set the royals on her for extra speed. Not that she needed it.

'*Fire!*'

Adam grasped the rail as gun by gun the American began to retaliate. With so many pressed men in the English ships, Beer had probably been surprised by *Anemone*'s agility and confidence.

He winced as he felt the iron smashing into the hull or through the rigging overhead. The boatswain and his crew were running this way and that, marlin spikes and spare cordage already being put to good use. *Unity* still held the advantage. If *Anemone* stood away downwind to obtain more distance, Beer would send a full broadside through her stern. If their positions remained the same it was only a matter of time, gun for gun.

'*Fire!*'

Anemone's one advantage was that, by being downwind, her guns could be elevated to the maximum. Every ball was finding a target; and there were wild cheers as the American's forecastle was blasted into splinters, and one of her bow-chasers was hurled aside on to its crew.

The deck shuddered violently as the quarterdeck nettings were cut to pieces, and scorched and slashed hammocks were flung across screaming marines who were tossed aside like bloody rags.

Adam pulled a seaman to his feet. '*Get to it, lad!*' But the man stared at him emptily as if his mind had completely cracked.

Hudson, hatless, his hanger already drawn, hurried aft. 'Grapeshot, sir!'

'Aye.' Adam wiped his mouth, although it was so dry he could barely swallow. 'He's a confident one not to use his heavier metal at this range!'

The ship lurched again and he saw two guns up-ended, tendrils of blood running across the deck where the crews had been cut down.

'*Stand to!*' The third lieutenant clapped his hands to his chest and fell kicking to the deck. Vicary jumped forward to take his place. '*Fire as you bear!*'

The eighteen-pounders recoiled down the side. Each gun-captain seemed able to ignore the chaos and death, men pulped by incoming shots while they crouched at the guns on the disengaged side.

Adam did not even blink as two marines fell from the maintop to join the crawling, pleading wounded and those who were already beyond aid.

Hudson yelled, '*Get those guns working*, Mr Vicary! Lively now!'

The lieutenant turned and peered aft through the thickening smoke, like a drowning man reaching for a line.

'*Load! Run out!*' He staggered as shots hammered into the lower hull, and more rigging fell on to the gangways to add to the destruction and chaos.

Vicary looked up and stared with disbelief as the American's upper yards and punctured sails rose above the fog of gunfire like a cliff. Hudson retched and turned away as Vicary fell, his fingers clutching what a charge of canister had found and destroyed. There was no face left. Even in this murderous hell Hudson heard his mother's voice. Such an English face. Now, in a split second, he had become nothing.

'Sir! *The Cap'n's hit!*' It was Starr, Adam's loyal coxswain.

'Fetch the surgeon!'

Hudson knelt beside him and gripped his hand. 'Easy, sir! He'll soon be here!'

Adam shook his head, his teeth bared against the pain. 'No – I must stay! *We must fight the ship!*'

Hudson shouted to the sailing master, 'Let her fall off two points!' His brain cringed to the constant crash of shots hitting the hull. But all he could think of was the captain. He saw Starr pulling open the coat with the bright epaulettes, and swallowed as he saw the blood pumping out of Adam's side, covering him, encircling him like something foul and evil.

Another great splintering crash, and the roar of trailing rigging, as the whole of the foremast went over the side taking sails, broken planking and screaming men with it into the sea.

Cunningham bent down and applied a dressing, which within seconds was as bloody as his butcher's apron. He looked at Hudson, his eyes wild and afraid. 'I can do nothing! They're dying like flies down below!' He ducked as more balls ripped overhead or exploded into lethal splinters against one of the guns.

Adam lay quite still, feeling his *Anemone* being torn apart by the unwavering bombardment. His mind kept fading away, and he had to use all his remaining strength to bring it back. There was little pain, just a numbing deadness.

'Fight the ship, Dick!' The effort was too much. 'Oh, dear God, what must I do?'

Hudson stood up, his limbs very loose, unable to

believe he was unmarked amongst so much suffering and death.

He raised his hanger and hesitated. Then with one slash he severed the ensign's halliards, and in the sudden silence that followed he saw the flag running out to the full extent of the line until it floated above the water like a dying bird.

Then there was cheering, deafening, it seemed, from *Anemone*'s bloodied and splintered decks.

Hudson stared at the blade in his hand. *So much for glory*. Nobody would use it to taunt them in defeat. Blindly he flung it over the disengaged side, then knelt down again beside his captain.

Adam said vaguely, 'We held them off, Dick. The convoy should be safe now in the dark.' He gripped Hudson's hand with surprising strength. 'It was . . . our duty.'

Hudson felt the tears stinging his eyes. The sunshine was as bright as before. There was more movement as the great frigate came alongside, and armed seamen swarmed across the deck as *Anemone*'s company threw down their weapons. Hudson watched as the men he had come to know so well accepted defeat. Some were downcast and hostile; others greeted the Americans with something like gratitude.

An American lieutenant called, 'Here he is!'

Hudson saw the massive figure climbing up past the abandoned wheel. Even the sailing master had fallen. Always a quiet man, he had died just as privately.

Nathan Beer looked around at the carnage on the quarterdeck.

'You in charge?'

Hudson nodded, remembering Adam Bolitho's description of this man. 'Yes, sir.'

'Is your captain still alive?' He stood staring down at Adam's pale features for several seconds. 'Take him across, Mr Rooke! Get our surgeon to see him right away.'

To Hudson he said, 'You are now a prisoner of war. There is nothing to be ashamed of. You had no chance.' He watched as Adam was carried away on a grating. 'But you fought like tigers, as I would have expected.' He paused. 'Like father, like son.'

The deck gave a lurch and someone called, 'Better clear the ship, sir! That was an explosion!'

The boarding party were hastily rounding up their prisoners and dragging some of the wounded to the ship alongside.

Starr, the captain's coxswain, walked past. He touched his hat to Commodore Beer, and for only a second, looked at Hudson.

'They'll not take his ship away from him now, sir.'

The deck was tilting over. Starr must have prepared *Anemone* for this all on his own. Now she would never fight under an enemy flag.

And I shall never fight under mine.

As darkness covered the misty horizon, and the *Unity* still lay hove-to to carry out makeshift repairs, *Anemone* drifted clear and began to settle down stern first, the lovely figurehead holding on to her last sunset. How he had wanted it. He thought of Nathan Beer's quiet comment, and did not understand.

Like father, like son.

He looked at his hands as they began to shake uncontrollably.

He was alive. And he was ashamed.

Every moment roused a fresh thrust of agony, pain which defied even the need to breathe, to think. Sound welled and faded, and despite his inner torment Adam Bolitho knew he was in constant danger of losing consciousness, even as his reeling mind told him he would not live if he did.

He was on board the ship which had defeated him, but it was not like that at all. Voices cried and sobbed, it seemed on every side, although somehow he knew the awful din came from elsewhere as if through a great door, muffled and full of anguish like the abyss of hell itself.

The air was still sharp with smoke and dust, and strange lurching figures pushed past, some so near that they brushed against his outflung arm. Once again he tried to move and the pain held him in an iron fist. He heard another voice cry out and knew it was his own.

At the same time he knew he was naked, yet could recall nothing of it, only Hudson holding him in his arms while the battle thundered all about the ship. There was a vague recollection that his coxswain Starr had not been with him.

He screwed up his eyes and tried to clear a part of his mind. The foremast going over the side, taking rigging and spars with it, dragging the ship round like some great sea-anchor and laying open her side to those murderous broadsides.

The ship. What of *Anemone*?

His hearing was returning, or had it ever left him? Distant, patient sounds. Men working with hammers; blocks and their tackles squeaking in that other place where the sea was still blue, the air free of smoke and the smell of charred rigging.

He raised his right hand but was almost too weak to hold it above his nakedness. Even his skin felt clammy. Already that of a corpse. Someone beyond that final door screamed. '*Not my arm!*' Then another scream, which was suddenly cut short. For him the door to hell had closed behind him.

There was a bandage, wet and heavy with blood. A hand reached out and grasped his wrist. Adam was helpless to protest.

'Keep still!' The voice was strained and sharp.

Adam tried to lie flat on his back, to hold the spreading fire in his side at bay.

'He's coming now.' Another said, 'What the hell!'

The dry, stifling air moved slightly and another figure came to the table. The ship's surgeon. When he spoke Adam detected an accent. French.

The man said, 'I do not know your thoughts, Commodore. He is the enemy. He has taken the lives of many of your company. What does it matter?'

As if from far away, Adam recognised the strong voice. Beer, he thought. Nathan Beer. 'What are his chances, Philippe? I'm in no mood for lectures, not today!'

The surgeon gave a sigh. 'It is an iron splinter the size of your thumb. If I try to extract it, he may well die. If I do not, it is a certainty.'

'I want you to save him, Philippe.' There was no response, and he added with sudden bitterness, 'Remember, I saved you from the Terror. Did *I* say, "What does it matter?"' Almost brutally he continued, 'Your parents and your sister, how was it again? Their heads were struck off and paraded on pikes to be jeered at and spat upon. That mob was French, was it not?'

Somebody held a sponge soaked in water against Adam's lips. It was no longer cold or even cool, and it tasted sour. But as he moved his lips against it he thought it was like wine.

The commodore again. 'Was this all he carried?'

The surgeon replied wearily, 'That and his sword.'

Beer sounded surprised. 'A woman's glove. I wonder . . .'

Adam gasped and tried to turn his head.

'M-mine . . .' His head fell back. It was a nightmare. He was dead. Nothing was real but that.

Then he felt Beer's breath against his shoulder. 'Can you hear me, Captain Bolitho?' He gripped Adam's right hand. 'You fought bravely, nobody could deny it. I thought I would beat you into a quick submission, save lives, and with luck seize your ship. But I misjudged you.'

Adam heard his own voice again, faint and hoarse. 'Convoy?'

'You saved it.' He tried to lighten it. '*That* time.' But his voice remained immeasurably sad.

Adam spoke only her name. '*Anemone* . . .'

'She's gone. Nothing could be done to save her.' Somebody was whispering urgently from the other

233

world, and Beer grunted as he got to his feet. 'I am needed.' He rested his big hand on Adam's shoulder. 'But I will return.' Adam did not see the quick glance at the French surgeon. 'Is there anyone . . .?'

He tried to shake his head. 'Zenoria . . . her glove . . . now she is dead.'

He felt neat rum pouring into his mouth, choking him, making his mind reel still further. Through the waves of agony he heard the rasp of metal, then felt the hard hands encircle his wrists and ankles like manacles.

The surgeon watched the leather strap being placed between Adam's teeth, then he held up his hand, and it was removed.

'Were you trying to speak, m'sieur?'

Adam could not focus his eyes, but he heard himself say distinctly, 'I am sorry about your family. A terrible thing . . .' His voice trailed away, and one of the surgeon's assistants said sharply, 'It is *time*.'

But the surgeon was still staring at the enemy captain's pale features, almost relaxed now as he fell into a faint.

He placed the palm of his hand on Adam's body and waited for one of his men to remove the blood-sodden dressing.

Almost to himself he said, 'Thank you. Perhaps there is still hope left for some of us.'

Then, with a nod to the others around the stained table, he forced the probe into the wound, his mind so inured to the agonies he had witnessed in ships and on the field of battle that, even as he worked, he was able to consider the young officer who writhed under his hands, who had moved the formidable Commodore Beer to plead for his life. On the very doorstep of hell, he had still found the humanity to express sympathy for another's suffering.

When he eventually went on deck it was pitch dark, the heavens covered with tiny stars which were reflected only faintly in the dark waters, and as far as the invisible horizon.

Work on repairs and re-rigging had ceased and seamen sprawled about the deck, too exhausted to continue. In the darkness it appeared as if corpses still lay where they had dropped, while the air was still tinged with smoke and the smells of death.

The surgeon, Philippe Avice, was well aware that sailors could perform miracles, and without even going into harbour *Unity*'s men would soon have their ship ready to sail and fight again. Only an experienced eye would be able to see the extent of the English frigate's ferocity.

And the dead? Drifting, falling like leaves into the ocean's deeper darkness, while the wounded waited, enduring their pain and fear, to see what another dawn might offer them.

He found Commodore Beer sitting at his table in the great cabin. Even here, the enemy's iron had left its mark. There was no safe place above the waterline in a ship-of-war. But Beer's favourite portrait of his wife and daughters was back in its place, and a clean shirt lay ready for the morning.

Beer looked up, his eyes hard in the lantern-light.

'Well?'

The surgeon shrugged. 'He is alive. More, I cannot

say.' He took a glass of cognac from Beer's big hand. He sipped it and pursed his lips. 'Very good.'

Beer smiled, his eyes vanishing into the crow's-feet of many years at sea.

'The cognac, Philippe? Or the fact that you have saved the life of an enemy?'

Avice shrugged again. 'It is just that I was reminded of something. Even in war, one should never forget it.'

Beer said, after a pause, 'His uncle would have been proud of him.'

The surgeon raised his eyebrows. 'You 'ave met the famous *amiral* who is said to risk his reputation as much as his life?'

Beer shook his head. *I'm getting too old for this game.*

He glanced at one of the cannons that shared this cabin when the drums beat the hands to quarters. It was still uncovered, the barrel and tackles heavily smoke-stained.

'No, I never have. But I will, as sure as fate.'

His head nodded with exhaustion, and the surgeon slipped away quietly through the replaced screen door.

Beer drifted, thinking of the young frigate captain, and the unknown girl named Zenoria. Next time he wrote to his wife in Newburyport he would tell her about them ... With something like a groan he pulled himself from the chair.

But first, there were the ship's needs to attend to. Damage to assess, his men to be encouraged. Always, the ship must come first.

Captain Adam Bolitho had been ignorant of the declaration of war between the United States and

England. With nothing but instinct and youthful experience, he had fought with a tenacity that might have turned the tables, despite *Unity*'s superior artillery.

He picked up the glove and held it to the light. So small a thing, perhaps a mere gesture, without significance to the woman. But her loss had made Bolitho throw away caution, and prepare to fight his ship to the end.

In his mind's eye Beer could still see the beautiful, bare-breasted figurehead, when *Anemone* had finally given up the fight.

Because her captain had nothing left to live for.

12

Witness

Lieutenant George Avery hesitated by the screen door and knew that the Royal Marine sentry was watching him with an unmoving stare. Above his head he could hear the muffled bark of orders, the sounds of men hurrying to their stations for the last change of tack before entering English Harbour.

He had been wondering what might be waiting for them here, orders, or a new appraisal of American intentions, and the prospect of fresh fruit and the chance of stretching his legs on dry land had pleased him.

That had been before they had met with the convoy, and had received news of *Anemone.*

Against orders, the little brig *Woodpecker* had returned under cover of darkness to the scene of the battle, but had found nothing. The brig's commander, Nicholas Eames, had come aboard *Indomitable* without delay to make his report.

Avery had known that Bolitho was tearing himself apart because of what had happened.

Eames had said, '*Anemone* came about and went

into the attack, Sir Richard. No hesitation, no nothing – you'd have been proud of him!'

'I am.' It was all he had said.

From what the brig's commander had been able to tell them, there had been one main adversary, with perhaps other vessels in company.

'At first, Sir Richard, the gunfire was so heavy and fierce I imagined the enemy was a liner.' He had looked at their faces, Tyacke, Scarlett and his admiral, and had added sadly, 'But *Anemone* could have run rings around one of those beauties, so I knew it must be one of the new Yankee frigates.'

No wreckage, or if there was, it had drifted fast away with the current. And then Eames had described the one small miracle. A survivor, one of the ship's boys. More dead than alive, he had been hauled aboard *Woodpecker*. It was a wonder he had lived.

Avery glanced at the sentry.

The marine tapped the deck with his musket and called, 'Flag-lieutenant, *sir*!'

The survivor had been transferred immediately to the flagship. As Eames had said, 'My brig doesn't have the space for a surgeon!'

Indomitable's surgeon, Philip Beauclerk, had insisted that the youth be allowed to rest in order to recover from the nightmare he had endured. It was doubtful that one so young would ever completely get over it.

'Enter!'

Avery strode into the main cabin, his eyes taking in Bolitho's breakfast tray, scarcely touched, a half-finished letter on his table, an empty glass nearby.

'Captain Tyacke's respects, Sir Richard, and we shall be entering harbour within two hours.'

'I see. Is that *all*?'

Then Bolitho stood up abruptly and said, 'That was uncalled for. I apologise. Abusing you when you cannot answer back is unforgivable.'

Avery was moved by the intensity of his words. He seemed to speak with his whole body, as if he could not bear to be still.

Bolitho said, 'Two hours? Very well. I must speak to this youth. Send Allday – he has a way with youngsters. I have noticed that.' He rubbed his chin, the skin smoothly shaved. 'I have no cause to treat him badly, either. The finest of men, a true friend.'

Ozzard appeared with fresh coffee and said, 'I shall tell him, Sir Richard.'

Bolitho slumped down again and pulled at his shirt as if it was choking him.

'My little crew. What am I without them?'

He began to slip out of his coat but Avery said, 'No, sir. With respect, I think this may be important to the lad. Your rank will not frighten him. He has had enough terror, I imagine.'

Bolitho said, 'You are all surprises, George. Did I choose you, or was it the other way round?'

Avery watched his despair. Needing to help, but unable to ease the way. 'I believe Lady Catherine decided for both of us, sir.'

He saw Bolitho glance quickly at the unfinished letter, and knew he had not yet been able to bring himself to tell her.

Outside the door Allday and the round-shouldered secretary Yovell stared down at the boy who had been snatched from the sea. From death. He was freshly clothed in a chequered shirt and white trousers, the smallest the purser's store could produce.

The boy was very slight, with frightened brown eyes and wood-splinter scars, which had been cleaned by the sick-bay.

Allday said sternly, 'Now, listen to me, my lad. I'll not be saying anything twice. You feel a bit sorry for yourself just now, and that ain't too surprising.'

The boy watched him, as a rabbit would stare at a fox. 'What do they want of me, sir?'

'In this cabin is the finest admiral England's ever had, though precious few says as much! He wants to ask you about what happened. You just tell him, son. As if he was your father.'

He saw Yovell sigh as the boy began to sob.

'Me father's drowned, sir.'

Allday glared at Yovell. 'This is no damned good, is it?'

Yovell put his hand on the boy's shoulder. 'Come with me.' He sounded quite severe, which was almost unknown with him.

'Answer the questions,' Allday said. 'Tell it just as it was. It's important to him, see?'

Ozzard, watching from the door, studied the small figure without expression. To Yovell he said, 'You should have been a school teacher!'

Yovell smiled benignly. 'I was. That, and other pursuits.'

Avery waited for the others to leave and murmured to Allday, 'That was well done.' To the boy he said gently, 'Sit here.'

Bolitho made himself remain very still as the boy sat on a chair directly opposite his table. He looked terrified, barely able to drag his eyes from the gold epaulettes, and obviously overwhelmed by the vastness of an admiral's quarters when compared with a frigate's crowded messdeck.

'What is your name?'

'Whitmarsh, sir.' He hesitated. 'John Whitmarsh.'

'And how old are you, John?'

The boy gaped at him, but his hands had stopped shaking, and his dark eyes were like saucers at being addressed by the admiral.

'Twelve, I think, sir.' He screwed up his face in an effort to concentrate. 'I bin in *Anemone* for eighteen months.'

Bolitho glanced at the piece of paper Yovell had copied out for him.

'And you lost your father?'

'Aye, sir.' He lifted his chin as if with pride at his memory. 'He were a fisherman and got drowned off the Goodwins.' Now he had started he could not stop. 'My uncle took me to Plymouth and volunteered me for *Anemone*, they was recruiting, see.' He hesitated nervously. 'Sir.'

Avery recognised the pain in Bolitho's grey eyes. The boy must have been only about ten when his uncle put him in a King's ship, if uncle he was. It was too common a story these days. Women left to fend for themselves, their men killed in battle or too badly

242

wounded to return home. Or drowned, like this lad's father. This boy had proved an obstacle to someone, and had therefore been removed.

Bolitho said, 'Tell me about the battle. Where were you, what were you doing? Try to remember.'

Again he screwed up his eyes. 'We sighted the enemy when the watches changed. I heard old Mr Daniel the gunner say she were a big Yankee. There was another too, a little one, but the masthead couldn't make her out 'cause of the sea mist. Me an' my friend Billy was at the foremast, sir. The ship was that short of hands that even we was needed at the braces.'

Bolitho asked quietly, 'How old was your friend?'

'Same as me. We come aboard together.'

'I see.' It was clear to him now, as the *Woodpecker*'s commander had described. Adam had believed he must hold off the enemy until it was dark enough for the merchantmen to escape, knowing that, by then, it would be too late for *Anemone*. He said, 'So your ship came about to engage?' He saw the boy nod, his eyes clouding with memories. 'Did you see your captain while all this was happening?'

'Oh yes, sir. He was always about. I went aft with a message an' I heard him tell the first lieutenant to keep the marines hidden and not to rig the nets in case the Yankee guessed what we was doin'.' Then he smiled; it was the nicest thing which had happened. He said, 'Our captain was scared o' *nuthin*'!'

'Go on.'

The boy opened and closed his tar-stained fingers. 'Then the firin' started, sir. We got the first shots off, but the big Yankee found the range and we was hit again an' again! Spars an' riggin' was fallin' all around, and men was dyin', callin' out – there was blood in th'scuppers like I've never seen!'

Voices called overhead and bare feet thudded across the planking. *Indomitable* was changing tack, making for the harbour. But to this boy, it was like the battle being refought.

'The foremast was shot away, an' the whole of the forecastle was covered in riggin' and sails fallin' on us like somethin' terrible!' He turned and looked at Avery for the first time. 'We couldn't move, sir. Men was fightin' to get out, others went over the side, caught like they was in a net. I was held fast. I tried, I tried . . .'

Bolitho held up his hand as Avery began to move forward. 'Did you see the captain?'

'When he fell, sir.' He repeated in a small voice, broken by sobs, 'When he fell.'

Bolitho waited, his muscles bunched like fists. Adam had fallen. And only this boy had survived to describe it.

He stared at him blindly as he continued, 'Then the other ship was hard alongside, sir, the enemy was tramplin' aboard. But our flag had been cut down. We was finished.'

'You are doing very well.' Bolitho glanced despairingly at the flag-lieutenant. 'Did anyone help the captain?'

The boy nodded. 'They carried him to the other ship.' He nodded again. 'I seen 'em.' He looked at Bolitho, remembering where he was, what he was doing. 'Then there was an explosion. We started to sink.'

Bolitho stood up and walked to the stern windows. An explosion, after the colours had been cut down. Somebody unknown, acting as Adam would have done rather than surrender his beloved *Anemone*.

'I can't remember much after that, sir. I called out, but nobody came. There was dead men all around, and even wounded who never reached the upper deck. I held on to Billy, an' together we floated off with some spars when the ship went under.'

Then the tears came and did not stop. He managed to gasp, 'But Billy didn't answer me. He just drifted away. I think he'd been dead all the time!'

Bolitho said abruptly, 'Take him down to the sick-bay and see that he gets a good meal before we anchor.'

Then he changed his mind, and found himself crossing the cabin to the chair, pulling out one of the handkerchiefs Catherine had bought for him. He gave it to the boy.

Avery watched. It was like being under a spell, and he could not speak or interrupt.

Bolitho said, so softly that the boy had to stop his tears to listen, 'Your captain is my nephew. He is very dear to me, as you were to your father. It does not bring back friends, but if it is any help, what you have told me has given me *hope*. Do you understand?'

He nodded, his streaming eyes never leaving Bolitho's face.

Allday padded in silently and shook his head. When the boy looked up at him he said, 'Well, let me tell you, matey, no admiral ever spoke to *me* like that, an' that's no error!' He seized him by the top of his shirt and added, 'We'll go an' take a look at the pantry, eh?'

As the door closed, and Ozzard re-entered with two glasses on a tray, Bolitho sat down on the bench seat as if the deck had been cut from under him.

'That man really is a marvel!'

'I agree, sir.' To himself Avery added, *And so, as it happens, are you*.

Bolitho drank from the glass without tasting it. 'We shall go on deck, George. It is a sight I never tire of.'

Avery asked carefully, 'Where you met Lady Catherine, sir?'

Bolitho looked at him, the life, like hope, returning to his eyes. 'Where I found her, when I thought I had lost her for ever.'

Then he said over his shoulder, 'I am not a fool. I know the odds as well as you do. But he *was* alive, right?'

Avery followed him up to the bright sunshine. *Do not hope too much.* He thought suddenly of Catherine and the endearment he had once overheard. *Dearest of men.*

It was all true. He had just seen him bring a twelve-year-old boy back from the dead. As a man.

Later, with the ship anchored and surrounded by lighters and dockyard boats, Avery sat propped in his hutch-like cabin while he sorted the despatches into coherent order. The courier-brig had not only brought important intelligence for the admiral, but also some mail which seemed to have gone around the world before reaching its proper destination.

There was a tap at the door and Avery opened it with one foot without getting up. It was Allday.

He said, 'Begging your pardon, Mr Avery, but I got a letter.' He held it out, his face baffled and worried.

'Sit down. On that chest, if you like.'

'You don't mind, sir? But I knows you've been busy, what with young Captain Adam and everything.'

'Of course not.' He rather enjoyed it. It was as if he was getting a letter of his own. If there had been someone who cared enough to write.

He said, 'Pour yourself a drink,' and slit open the envelope. It was badly stained. Probably the vessel which had been carrying it had been damaged in the Atlantic gales, the mail transferred to another.

He could see her now. *My dear John, it seems so long since I heard* . . .

Allday waited, perched on the edge of the brass-bound chest. 'What is it, sir? Is something wrong? Tell me, please!'

Avery leaned over and poured a glass of brandy.

He said, 'Congratulations, John Allday.'

Allday was frowning. 'What's happened?'

Avery held out the letter and pushed the glass towards him.

'You've become a father, that is what's happened, man!'

Allday stared blindly at her round handwriting. 'A baby! *She's had a baby.*'

Avery smiled. 'You stay here and enjoy your wet. I'll lay aft to the admiral. I think this news is just what he needs.'

'But – but . . .' Allday waved the letter after him. 'Boy or girl, sir?'

Avery thought of Lady Catherine clambering up *Indomitable*'s side while the sailors had cheered.

He replied simply, 'A little girl. Your wife wants to call her Kate.'

The door closed and then Allday did pick up the brandy.

'Well, I'll be damned!' He grinned at the cabin. 'Well, I'll be *double*-damned!'

Bolitho looked up from his table as Tyacke entered the cabin, his hat tucked beneath his arm.

'With your permission, I'd like to weigh before noon. Mr York insists the wind is about to veer and freshen, although for the life of me I don't know how he can tell.'

Bolitho said, 'I think we shall have to be guided, James. I have no wish to linger here in Antigua.'

Three days since their return, and still no word of *Anemone*'s final moments, apart from the description offered by the boy John Whitmarsh. *Anemone*'s company had been taken prisoner, but there had been no official confirmation. Three days, and he had thought of little else save Adam's fate. If badly wounded, then how badly? If he had survived, would he be exchanged for an American prisoner, if any of equal rank had been taken?

He watched Yovell's pen scratching out the final copy of his orders to the captains of his overstretched squadron.

He had sent off a plea to the Admiralty for another frigate to replace *Anemone*. He suspected there was little chance of getting one. He could almost hear his own words when he had spoken his thoughts aloud to the assembled powers there. The end of the fixed line-of-battle, the coming of age of a faster, more powerful frigate.

Commodore Nathan Beer – and in his heart Bolitho had never doubted it was *Unity* which had been after the Jamaica convoy – had more than proved that. How many more did the Americans have, or intend to build? Apart from *Valkyrie* and *Indomitable*, he had nothing that could stand against them. Determination and skilled seamanship had always been expected to succeed against odds, but the Americans' massive firepower and impressive gunnery had already scattered several local convoys. It had put the Leeward Squadron on the defensive. No war could be won while their strength was divided by fruitless searches and hazy intelligence.

The Americans were obviously intent on attacking Canada, just as the British were determined to increase their military strength by every means available. The Admiralty had sent lists of possible routes and times of arrival of military convoys, all of which would eventually make their landfalls at Halifax. The Americans would know as much of these movements as the British: such activity was impossible to conceal.

It was also known that the Americans were mustering smaller men-of-war for use on the Great Lakes. To find them would be like looking for a needle in the proverbial haystack. Bolitho had used *Zest* and *Reaper* to strengthen Dawes' flotilla out of Halifax. Apart from the local patrols, mostly brigs and commandeered schooners, that left only *Indomitable* and the twenty-six-gun frigate *Attacker* to liaise with the convoy escorts from Jamaica. These convoys had already been reduced to two a month because of the very real threat from the Americans, who had nothing to protect, and to whom every ship was a possible target and prize.

In a moment of frustration and anger Bolitho had exclaimed to Tyacke, 'Our Nel was right, James! The best form of defence *is* attack. So let us find their lair and go for them, and to hell with the risk!'

Tyacke could see the logic of it. If they had to divide their small squadron after each enemy sortie, they would soon be too weak to offer any protection at all.

A week before the attack on *Anemone* they had stopped and questioned a Brazilian trader. Her master had reported sighting a force of American men-of-war, two large frigates and two other smaller vessels, steering south, possibly from Philadelphia. Fearing for his own safety the Brazilian had gone about to retrace his course to the Bermudas.

Two large frigates: could one of them have been the *Unity*? And if so, where were the others?

Bolitho said, 'I am poor company today, James.'

Tyacke regarded him impassively. 'Suppose – I mean, just *suppose* . . .' His fingers played with the tarnished buttons of his faded sea-going coat.

Bolitho said sharply, 'You have more experience of lonely command than any man I know. Speak out – this is the time.'

Tyacke walked to the stern windows and watched a

cutter being warped around the stern, ready to be hoisted aboard. In harbour it was usual to lower all boats, otherwise their seams opened in the relentless heat. At sea, it was sensible to keep them partly filled with water for the same reason.

'Everyone knows about us, sir, more especially about *you*. With Captain Bolitho taken prisoner, and many of his people, wouldn't it seem obvious to the enemy that you would take some action? Direct action?'

Bolitho shrugged. 'It is what I would like.'

Tyacke rubbed his chin. 'And they will expect it. With *Indomitable* gone, what chance would our ships stand?'

Bolitho stared at him. 'You mean that *this* ship will be marked down as the next victim?' He saw it suddenly, his mind clearing. 'That is good sense!' He stood up and leaned over the chart. Yovell continued to write without a pause, except to dip his nib.

'The Bermudas, a likely area for the Americans to gather. No English men-of-war there, they rely on their garrison and the reef.'

Tyacke glanced at the chart curiously. 'Why none of our ships, sir?'

'There is no water there. None. Apart from the seasonal rainfall they have to conserve it as best they can.'

Tyacke gave a reluctant smile. '*That* I didn't know, sir.' It was as close to admiration as he could come.

'Perhaps I am wrong. Perhaps I am presuming too much, to base our strategy on the word of a sailing master who sells fruit for a living!'

He tapped Yovell's plump shoulder. 'I want to send fresh instructions to Captain Dawes in *Valkyrie*. They can go in the schooner *Reynard* when she leaves.'

Tyacke saw the animation and eagerness returning to his tanned features. 'We shall muster a convoy, and the world shall know about it, and *Indomitable* shall sail to meet it.'

'It is not for me to say, but . . .'

'*But?* That word again? And it *is* for you to say what you think. You are my flag-captain, and we must share our views.'

Tyacke watched him warily. 'Views, yes, and I am proud of that trust. But the responsibility lies with you.'

'Don't stop, James. Responsibility is something I am used to.'

Tyacke said, 'Then speak my mind I will, sir.' He stabbed the chart with his finger. 'Here, Halifax.' His finger moved down the coastline. 'Boston, New York, and right here, Philadelphia. If I was the Yankee commander this is exactly the area I would choose, with Philadelphia to run to for repairs or protection if things went wrong.' He raised his eyes to Bolitho. 'But *suppose*, in a manner of speaking, Captain Dawes in his big frigate decided not to act on your instructions without question? If a convoy of soldiers was the real target, and he left it without an escort for the final approach, he might feel that his head was the one on the block, not yours.'

'He is a resourceful captain, James, but you know that.'

Tyacke responded bluntly, 'He is also ambitious,

and the son of an admiral. The two together are dangerous bedfellows.'

'That was outspoken.' He smiled to soften it. 'I like that. But Dawes is acting second-in-command. I have to rely on him.' He paused. 'I have no choice, nor do I have justification to believe otherwise.'

Tyacke looked round sharply as the sentry announced the arrival of the first lieutenant.

'Yes, Mr Scarlett? Cannot it wait?'

Scarlett answered hesitantly, 'The last fresh water is inboard, sir.' He glanced at Bolitho. 'I am sorry for the intrusion, Sir Richard.'

As the door closed Tyacke snapped, '*I* apologise, Sir Richard. I shall have a gentle word with that one!'

He calmed himself. 'Then I shall see that your despatches are put aboard the schooner.'

Indomitable swung lightly to her cable. Perhaps York's prediction was already making itself felt. A shaft of strong sunlight probed through the quarter windows and Tyacke saw Bolitho flinch from it and turn away.

'Can I help, sir?'

Bolitho sat down and pulled out a handkerchief, reminding Tyacke poignantly of the one he had given to the boy. Tyacke turned the chair for him, so that he faced away from the glare.

Bolitho said quietly, 'You know, don't you? Have known ever since you took command as my flag-captain.'

Tyacke met his gaze, equally unflinching. 'Don't blame Avery, sir. He thought he was doing the right thing.'

'For me?'

'And the ship.' He turned aside, as if suddenly conscious of his terrible scars. 'If you will excuse me, sir, I have much to do.'

Bolitho followed him and stopped him by the screen door.

'Do you regret it? Tell me the truth.'

'Well, I didn't do it out of pity, sir.' Surprisingly, he grinned. 'Regret it? I'll speak my mind when we run that damned Yankee to earth!' He was still smiling as he shut the door behind him.

Bolitho touched his eye and waited for the pain, but there was none. He sat again, deeply moved by Tyacke's words, the very strength of his concern. A truly remarkable man.

That night while *Indomitable* thrust her heavy bows into open sea, Bolitho awoke with that same dream still fixed in his mind. Carrick Roads and Pendennis Castle, the ships as clear and familiar as ever. Each one taking in her cable. Where bound? Who manned these phantom ships? There was an additional vessel this time, with the gilded figurehead he knew so well. *Daughter of the Wind*. And when she swung to her cable, he saw that it was Zenoria. Even then, as he fought his way out of the dream, he heard her last scream.

'All right, Sir Richard?' It was Allday, his powerful frame leaning over with the ship.

Bolitho held on to the cot as his feet touched the deck.

'Tell me something, old friend. Do *you* think he is still alive?'

Allday padded after him to the stern windows. The moon was making a ragged silver path on the lively crests. So that was what troubled him, he thought, as much or more than ever. All this time, with officials and officers coming and going with their offers or demands – mostly the latter, no doubt – planning what he should do, placing his ships where they would make the most difference, he had been fretting about Captain Adam. His nephew, but more of a son, a friend, than anyone else really knew.

Then he walked to the sword-rack, and waited for the moonlight to touch the old blade he had proudly buckled or clipped into place before so many fights, so many deeds, which he had shared.

'When we're gone, Sir Richard . . .' He knew Bolitho was watching him in the eerie light, 'An' we can't live for ever, nor have I a mind to . . . this old blade will be *his*. Must be.'

He heard him say quietly, his voice suddenly calm again, 'Aye, old friend. The last of the Bolithos.'

Allday watched him climb into his cot. He seemed to fall asleep instantly.

Allday smiled. The squall was over; the storm still to come.

13

Loneliness

Lady Catherine Somervell rose from the tall leather-backed chair and walked to the window. Down in the street in front of the Admiralty main building, it was raining quite heavily.

She toyed with one of the thick gold ropes that held the curtains, and watched people hurrying for shelter. Heavy, cleansing rain, thinning the traffic, causing steam to rise from the dirty cobbles, refreshing the avenues of trees so richly green on this late summer's day.

She turned and glanced at the empty fireplace, the old paintings of sea-battles. Richard's world. She shook her head, rejecting the antiquated ships. No, more his father's navy. She had learned much merely by listening, by being with him, just as he had shared her London, and, she hoped, learned to enjoy it in a manner he had not found possible before.

She studied herself in a gilded tall looking-glass, imagining nervous sea-officers here, examining their reflections before being summoned to meet whichever admiral would decide their fate.

A plain green gown, the hem and sleeves of which

were spotted with rain even as she had alighted from the carriage. She wore a wide-brimmed hat with a matching green ribbon. She had dressed with care, as she always did, not from vanity or conceit, but out of defiance, and because of Richard. Sixteen months now, and the ache was as cruel as ever.

The room was much as she had expected it would be. Unwelcoming, aloof from the rest of the building, a place of decisions, where men's lives could be changed with the stroke of a pen.

She could imagine him here, as a very young captain, perhaps. Or afterwards, as a flag-officer, when their affair had become common knowledge. The whole world knew about them now. She half smiled, but the Admiralty would not be impressed by her position in his life, or by her rank. If anything happened to Richard, it was ironic that Belinda would be the first to be told. Officially.

Over the months she had kept busy, helping Ferguson, or independently with her own projects. But each day was an eternity, her rides on Tamara her only escape. She had not been near the cliff path and Trystan's Leap since the day of Zenoria's death.

An old servant stood now between the tall double doors. Catherine had not noticed him, nor heard the doors open.

'Sir Graham Bethune will see you now, my lady.'

He bowed slightly as she passed him. She could almost hear him creak.

Sir Graham Bethune strode to meet her. She had resented the fact that he had once been one of Richard's midshipmen in his first command: even though he had explained the complexities governing seniority, it still seemed deeply unfair. Only one rank lower than Richard, and yet he was a lord of admiralty, a power who could help or dismiss as he chose.

But Bethune was not what she had expected. He was slim, energetic, and was wearing a genuine smile to greet her; suddenly and rather unwillingly, she understood why Richard had liked him.

'My dear Lady Somervell, this is indeed an honour. When I heard you were in Chelsea and I received your little note, I could scarce believe my good fortune!'

Catherine sat in the proffered chair and regarded him calmly. He was charming, but he was quite unable to hide his curiosity, and the interest of a man in a beautiful woman.

She said, 'We were deeply concerned at Falmouth to learn of *Anemone*'s loss. I thought that if I came in person you might give me more news – if there is any, Sir Graham?'

'We will take refreshment in a moment, Lady Somervell.' He walked to his desk and rang a small bell. 'Yes, we have indeed received more news, first by telegraph from Portsmouth yesterday, and then confirmed by courier.' He turned and rested his buttocks on the table. 'It is much as I expected. After the sinking, the American frigate *Unity* took what prisoners could be saved from *Anemone*, and because of her own damage was forced to cancel any further attempts on our convoy. It was a brave act on Captain Bolitho's part. It will not go unrewarded.' She put her hand on her breast and saw his glance follow it and linger there for a few seconds.

She said, 'Then he is alive?'

A servant entered with a tray. He did not look at either of them.

Bethune watched the servant opening the bottle with the deftness of one who was called to perform the task often.

'I was told that you enjoy champagne, my lady. I think we have something to celebrate. Don't you agree?'

She waited. Bethune was probably imagining other reasons for her concern.

He said, 'He was badly wounded, but our informants have told us that, thanks to the American commodore, he was well cared for.' He hesitated for the first time. 'We are still uncertain as to the extent of his injury.'

Catherine took the tall glass and felt its coolness through her glove. Word for word, Richard's letter was engraved on her memory: Adam's arrival at English Harbour, and his anguish at the news of Zenoria's death.

It was like some playlet, in which they all had lines to speak. Richard and his dead brother; Adam and Zenoria; and yet to come, Valentine Keen.

Bethune held his glass to the window. 'We have not been told officially what the Americans intend. Captain Bolitho, in the normal course of events, would be exchanged with one of our prisoners. However, as a frigate captain of some stature, with many prizes and successes to his credit, they might decide to keep him, if only in a mood of self-congratulation.'

'Or perhaps to goad his uncle into some reckless action?'

'Has he written to that effect, my lady?'

'You know him, do you not? You should not need to ask me.'

He smiled and refilled her glass. 'True.'

Then he said, 'I hope you will do me the honour of allowing me to escort you to a reception.' He hurried on, as if he already knew that she would refuse. 'Sir Paul Sillitoe, whom I believe you know, wishes to celebrate his new title. He goes to the House of Lords shortly. He will be a powerful adversary there, by God.'

Is a powerful adversary, she thought. 'I cannot be certain, Sir Graham.' She smiled faintly. 'Would not your reputation be a trifle smudged by me?'

He looked away, and for only an instant she saw the freckled midshipman.

It was quickly past. 'I would relish your company, Lady Somervell.'

She said, 'The rain is finished, and here comes the sun. I worship it, despite what it once tried to do to us.'

He nodded gravely. 'The *Golden Plover*, yes, I understand. May I enquire as to your plans for the remainder of the day?'

She faced him, unmoved by the hint in his tone.

'I shall interview a new personal maid, Sir Graham. But first, I must go to St James's.'

'The palace, my lady?'

She held out her gloved hand and felt him lingering over it. Then she laughed. 'No, the wine shop, of course!'

Long after a servant had accompanied her downstairs, Bethune stood staring after her.

His secretary entered and placed some papers on the desk.

260

He said, 'There is bad news, Sir Graham.' He waited patiently for his lord and master to notice him.

Bethune asked, 'Did you see her, man?' He seemed to realise what his secretary had said. 'What news?'

'Not confirmed, Sir Graham, but we have received a despatch concerning our frigate *Guerrière* of thirty-eight guns, which was overwhelmed and captured by the U.S.S. *Constitution* after a fight lasting only two hours.'

Bethune stood up again and walked to his window. 'You are a melancholy fellow, Saunders. You make it sound both trivial and disgraceful in the same breath. Only two hours, you say? I have endured just such a trivial amount of time!' He swung away from the window. 'Believe me, it is like *hell*.'

'As you say, Sir Graham.'

He dismissed the unctuous insincerity, recalling instead Bolitho's voice in this very building, and the disbelief, even amusement in the room when the role of the fixed line-of-battle had been criticised. They might think differently now. A frigate was already reported missing in the Caribbean. With *Anemone* destroyed and now *Guerrière* beaten and captured so easily, some might remember Bolitho's words.

He looked out of the window again, but her carriage had gone.

Then he smiled, picked up Catherine's half-empty glass and put his lips where hers had been.

Aloud he said, 'We shall see!'

By the time Catherine reached Chelsea the sky had cleared, and the houses along the Thames embankment were basking in brilliant sunshine once more. Young Matthew lowered the step and offered his hand to assist her, his eyes everywhere like a watchful terrier.

'I'll put the wine in the house once I've taken care of the horses, m'lady.'

She stopped by the steps and looked at him. 'You hate London, don't you, Matthew?'

He grinned sheepishly. 'Not used to it, m'lady – that's all, I suppose.'

She smiled. 'Only until next week. Then we shall go home to Falmouth.'

Matthew watched her open the front door and sighed. She was doing too much, taking too much on herself. Just like him.

Catherine pushed open the door and stopped dead in the entrance hall. There was a gold-laced hat on the hall table. Like Richard's.

The new girl, Lucy, came bustling from beneath the stairs, wiping her mouth with her hand, flustered by her mistress's unexpected return.

'Sorry, m'lady – I should have been here, ready like.'

Catherine barely heard her. 'Who is here?' It could not be. He would have let her know somehow. If only . . .

Lucy glanced at the hat, unaware of its significance. 'He said you wouldn't mind, m'lady. He said he would leave his card if you didn't come, otherwise he'd wait in the garden.'

She asked, '*Who?*'

Lucy was a decent girl; she had been recommended by Nancy. But another Sophie she was not. Good in the house and as a personal maid, but slow and sometimes maddening in her inability to think for herself.

Catherine brushed past her and walked blindly down the passage to the garden door.

Valentine Keen was standing by the wall in profile to her, only his hand moving as he stroked the neighbour's cat. Unfamiliar in his rear-admiral's uniform, his fair hair bleached almost white from the African sun.

Only when he heard her footstep on the terrace did he turn, and she saw the change in him: deep shadows beneath his eyes, the harsh lines around his mouth which even a smile failed to erase.

She said, 'Dear Val, I'm so glad you waited. I had no idea.' She clasped him in her arms. 'How long have you been back?'

He held her tightly, with affection or desperation; it could have been either.

'A few days ago. I came to Portsmouth. I was told you were in London. I thought, I *must* see her.'

The words seemed to jerk out of him, but she did not interrupt. Who could have told him she was in London?

Arm in arm, they walked around the small garden with the sounds of London beyond the wall.

She said, 'You should be careful of that cat. He uses his claws when you play with him.'

Keen looked at her searchingly. 'Your letter was such a help to me. I wish it had not fallen on your shoulders.' He swallowed hard. 'She was buried in Zennor. How so? You must not mind my asking. I still cannot accept it.'

She said gently, 'There was no proof of suicide, Val.

263

It may have been an accident. The church could not begrudge her a grave in her own parish churchyard.'

'I see.'

Catherine thought of the reluctant curate. The bishop had been signalling his disapproval because it was rumoured that the girl had taken her own life.

'The magistrate was very definite. Her death resulted from misadventure. It is small comfort, I know, but she rests in peace.'

Roxby had been the magistrate, otherwise . . .

'And you were there. I should have known you would be.'

She waited, knowing what was coming next.

He asked, 'Were some of my family at Zennor when she was buried?'

'There were flowers. Do not feel bitter about it. There was grief enough, I expect.'

He did not reply. He was going over it again and again. Trying to understand the reasons, trying to assemble the truth, even if he could never accept it.

He said, 'I loved her so. Even she never knew how much.'

'I think she did, Val.'

'I must go there and see the grave. As soon as I have dealt with things here.' He looked at her, his face drawn, as though grief had made him ill. 'Will you come with me, Catherine? To that church where we were married?'

'Of course. There is no stone yet. That is for you to decide.' She held his arm, not daring to look at him. 'Of course I will come.'

After a time he said, 'You went to the Admiralty. Was there any news of Adam?'

'He is alive and a prisoner of war; it was all they knew. We can only hope.'

She told him what Bethune had said and Keen murmured, 'I expect they know more than they care to make public.' Then he turned and looked at her. 'There is to be a reception for Sir Paul Sillitoe. I was told of it today.'

She forced a smile. 'I know. I was invited to attend.' She thought of Bethune's eyes when he had mentioned it. Perhaps she had imagined what she saw there, but she had never known a man she could trust completely. Except one.

Keen said, 'Then let us go together, Catherine. Nobody could say anything about it, and under the circumstances . . .' He did not continue.

As if someone else had answered, she heard herself say, 'My dear, I would be honoured.' Richard would understand; and he would know that he might need friends like Sillitoe where their power carried real weight.

Keen said suddenly, 'How is Richard?'

'He worries. About me and about Adam, about his men and his duty.' She smiled. 'I would not change him, even if I could.'

The light had dimmed. 'More rain, I think. We had better go inside.'

The housekeeper was waiting ominously by the stairs, and Lucy could be heard sobbing somewhere.

The housekeeper glanced incuriously at Catherine's

hand on the rear-admiral's sleeve. She said, 'Just broke two more cups, m'lady! God, that girl will put me in the poorhouse!' She softened slightly. 'I'll fetch some tea.'

They sat by the window and watched the leaves shiver to the first heavy drops of rain. The cat had disappeared.

Catherine said, 'There was talk of your removal to a house in Plymouth?'

He shrugged. 'No longer. The flag-officer there is expected to have a wife by his side.' With sudden bitterness he added, 'It will be another sea appointment for me. It cannot be soon enough for my liking!'

'Have you seen your father yet?'

He shook his head. 'When I leave you, I shall go. I am sure he will be "working late in the City"!'

She wanted to hold him, like a child, or like Richard, ease his grief, heal his despair. There was no one else.

He said, 'I should have *known*, don't you see? I had so many plans for her, the boy too. I never once asked her what she wanted. She was like you, Catherine, a living, precious creature. She might have been lost in my world. She never told me. I never asked her.'

The housekeeper came in with the tea and departed without a glance or a word.

Keen was saying, 'If I had only been *with* her!' He looked at her sharply. 'She did take her own life, is that not true? Please, I must know the truth.'

'She was not herself, Val.'

He stared down at his hands. 'I knew it. I should have seen the dangers all along.'

She asked quietly, 'Do you remember Cheney, the girl Richard married and lost?'

He hesitated. 'Yes. I remember her.'

'Even though *we* are denied marriage and the acceptance of society – even though marriage may have scarred us – even though such things are impossible, *we* found one another again, Richard and I. Might not good fortune take your hand too, Val, and give you happiness once more?'

He got to his feet and released her hand.

'I must leave now, Catherine. I feel better for speaking with you . . . stronger, in some way.' He did not look at her. 'If there was ever such a good fortune, and things I have seen of late make me doubt it, then I could hope for no more admirable a woman than one like you.'

She walked with him to the door, knowing very well what he had really meant. He was not just attractive and amusing company, in other circumstances; it went much deeper. It would not be difficult to love a man like him.

'I shall ask Matthew to take you.'

He picked up his hat and looked at it, ruefully, she thought.

He said, 'Thank you, but my carriage is waiting in the mews.'

She smiled. 'You did not wish to set the tongues a-wagging by leaving it at my door?'

On the steps he took her hand and kissed it gently. Few passers-by took any notice of them; nor could they or he, she thought, ever guess at her true emotions.

As he turned the corner Catherine stared across the river, remembering those other times. The Vauxhall Pleasure Gardens; laughter through the trees and the dancing lanterns; kisses in the shadows.

She touched her throat. *Dearest of men, come back to me. Soon, soon.*

The tray of tea still lay untouched on the table.

Sir Paul Sillitoe held out his arms so that Guthrie, his valet, could help him into his fine silk coat. As he did so, he glanced at his reflection in the windows. Guthrie brushed his shoulders and nodded with approval. 'Very nice, Sir Paul.'

Sillitoe listened to the sound of music from the wide terrace where the reception would be held. The whole place seemed to be full of flowers; his housekeeper had not spared the purse for this occasion. It was all sheer extravagance. He smiled at his reflection. But he felt elated, light-headed even, an alien sensation for one so habitually controlled.

He could hear carriages already clattering into his large driveway: friends, enemies, people with favours to ask once he had consolidated his position in the Lords.

Power, not popularity, was the key to most challenges, he thought.

He watched the opposite bank of the Thames, the great curve of Chiswick Reach still holding the late sunshine. There would be torches on the terrace, champagne and endless dishes for the guests to sample. More expense. This time he could not take it seriously.

Why had she decided to come? To congratulate him? It was unlikely. For a favour, then, or on some personal mission or intrigue, like the secret she had shared with him even before Bolitho knew it, when she had asked for his help on the death of her hated father in that stinking slum in Whitechapel. Quaker's Passage, that was the name. How could she ever have lived there as a child?

But she was coming. And with Rear-Admiral Valentine Keen, another friend of Bolitho's. Or was he? With his young wife dead – and Sillitoe's agents had insisted that she had taken her own life – might he not look to the lovely Catherine for comfort?

If he held out such hopes, she would soon dissuade him, Sillitoe thought. And if he persisted, his next appointment might well take him back to Africa and beyond.

He patted his stomach. Flat and hard. Unlike so many men he knew, he took care to use his energy in play as well as work. He enjoyed riding and walking; for the latter he usually had his secretary Marlow trotting beside him while he outlined the letters and despatches for the day. It saved time.

Swordsmanship was another of his interests, and he was rarely beaten in mock duels at the academy where he exercised.

And if the need commanded him, he would go to a particular house where he was known to the proprietor and her girls, and where his peccadilloes would be respected.

When he received his title he would have achieved everything he had planned, and would still retain his influence over the Prince Regent when he was eventually crowned King.

A complete life, then? He thought of Catherine Somervell again. Perhaps it still could be.

His valet saw him frown and asked, 'Is something amiss, Sir Paul?'

'I shall go down, Guthrie. It would be churlish not to be present from the beginning.'

As his guests were announced Sillitoe smiled, and said much the same to each one. Not precisely a welcome, but an acknowledgement that they came out of respect. Or fear. The thought gave him immense satisfaction.

His eyes moved restlessly to the great arched entrance, then to the bewigged footmen sweating in their heavy coats as they bustled with trays of glasses, while others stood at the long tables of food, bowing over their charges like priests at an altar loaded with offerings.

Vice-Admiral Sir Graham Bethune and his frail-looking wife. Two or three generals and their ladies, politicians and merchants from the City. Rear-Admiral Keen's father had at first been unable to accept the invitation, pleading a previous engagement. Sillitoe had seen to that.

The footman tapped his staff on the marble floor.

'The Viscountess Somervell!' A pause. 'And Rear-Admiral Valentine Keen!'

The noise of conversation faded away like surf dying on a beach as Sillitoe took her hand, and kissed it.

'It was so gracious of you to come, Lady Catherine.'

She smiled. 'How could I not?'

Sillitoe offered his hand to Keen. 'It is good to have you back at home, sir. Tragic news, of course. My sincere condolences.'

To Catherine he said, 'I will see you again very shortly.' His eyes lingered on the diamond fan at her breast. 'You do me too much honour.'

Catherine and her escort walked out on to the terrace as the conversation buzzed into life once more.

Keen said, 'I am never certain of that man.'

'You are not the first, Val.' She took a goblet from a tray. 'Or the last. It is as well to be wary of him.'

She had not expected to be participating in any social activities during what had been intended as a brief visit to London, and had brought only one suitable evening gown, a particular favourite of Richard's. It was of kingfisher-blue satin, so that her piled hair seemed to reflect in it as if she stood above moving water.

But it was cut very low, and she knew that the sunburns she had suffered in the shipwreck were still visible after nearly four years. So long, she thought, how could the time have passed so quickly? She would not allow herself to dwell on the precious hours and days she had spent with Richard since then, because they could never be relived, could never be had back again.

The torches were lit, and the lights and the river reminded her sharply of the pleasure gardens where she had taken him.

To her surprise she recognised Valentine Keen's father, who had been ushered in without any announcement and presented to Sillitoe. She heard Sillitoe say silkily, 'I am so *grateful* you changed your arrangements.' Neither of them smiled.

Sillitoe glanced up at an overly ornate clock and left his place by the doors.

Then he saw them and came to join them, taking a glass as he passed a footman.

'I have done my part as host, Lady Catherine. Now let me bask in the light which you seem to create wherever you go.' He barely glanced at Keen. 'Your father is here, sir. He craves a word. I think it may be useful if you oblige him.'

Keen made his excuses and left to look for his father. He had said nothing of his relationship with the rest of his family, but he appeared angry at the interruption.

'Was that true, Sir Paul?'

He looked directly at her. 'Of course. But I do see a rift between father and son, which is a pity. Over the girl from Zennor, no doubt.'

'No doubt.' She refused to be drawn.

'Why, Sir Paul!' It was Vice-Admiral Bethune, with his wife. 'May we both offer our congratulations?' But his eyes moved too often to Catherine.

Bethune's wife said, 'A pity Sir Richard cannot be so rewarded for all that he has done for England.'

Sillitoe was, for once, caught off guard.

'I am not certain what . . .'

She said rudely, 'A peerage such as yours, Sir Paul. After all, Lord Nelson was so honoured!'

Bethune said angrily, 'You have no *right*!'

Catherine took another glass of champagne and found a few seconds to thank the footman. She was inwardly burning with anger, but her voice was quite calm.

'If Sir Richard and I were parted, *madam*, he would still not return to his wife, but then, I am certain you know that already.'

Bethune almost dragged his wife away, and Catherine heard him muttering, 'Do you desire to ruin me?'

Sillitoe said, 'I should have prevented it. I know something of that woman's spite.'

Catherine smiled but her heart was still beating furiously. No wonder Bethune had eyes for other women. He surely deserved better.

Sillitoe said abruptly, 'Let me show you something of the house.'

She said, 'Very well, but not for too long. It would be discourteous to my escort.'

He smiled. 'You seem to have a habit of provoking sea-officers, my dear.'

They walked along a colonnade and up a staircase, which was bare of any paintings except one, of a man in dark clothing, a sword with an outdated basket hilt at his hip. Despite the neat Spanish-style beard and the clothing, it could have been her companion.

He was watching her profile, the smooth curve of her breasts, her breathing shown only by the diamond pendant.

'My father.'

She looked at it more closely. It was strange that she knew nothing about this man but his present power, and his confident use of that power. It was as though a door or a locked chest had been opened for the first time.

'What was he like?'

'I barely knew him. My mother was in poor health and he insisted we were in the West Indies as little as possible. I yearned to be with him. Instead I was sent to school, where constant bullying taught me that it was sometimes necessary to hit back.'

She turned her head to change the light on the portrait. Even the same hooded, compelling stare.

The West Indies. He had mentioned his estates in Jamaica and elsewhere. He was obviously very wealthy, but still lacked satisfaction.

She said, 'Was he a man of business, or a courtier like his son?'

He took her arm and guided her to a wide balcony, which overlooked the terrace with its flickering torches and the river beyond.

He gave a harsh laugh. 'He was a slaver. A Black Ivory captain. The best!'

She heard her gown hissing against the balustrade, the din of voices from the terrace. It looked so far away.

'You are not disagreeable to that, Lady Catherine?'

'They were different days.' She thought suddenly of Tyacke, coming to their rescue in his brig *Larne*. 'There will always be slaves, no matter what people promise and pretend.'

He nodded. 'A wise head as well as a beautiful one.'

They reached the end of the balcony and she said, 'I think we must go back.'

'Certainly.' He seemed to be grappling with something. 'I must say, Lady Catherine, that you are quite lovely. I can take care of you – you would want for nothing. There would be no more scandal, no harm done to you by simpering fools like Bethune's wife. Believe me, I would see to that!'

She stared at him. 'Can you see me as your mistress, what it would do to the one and only man I love?'

He gripped her arms. 'As a wife, Lady Catherine. That is what I am asking you. *As a wife.*'

She released herself gently and slipped her arm through his.

'I am sorry, Sir Paul. I thought . . .'

'I can imagine.' He pressed her arm against his side. 'Let me hope?'

'You overwhelm me.' She glanced at his face, but saw only the man in the portrait. 'Once I came to you for aid. I shall not forget. But do not hurt me or Richard if I decline.'

'Ah, your escort is approaching!'

She turned, but Sillitoe seemed quite composed. It was as though she had imagined all of it.

When he had withdrawn, Keen asked suspiciously, 'What happened? I was concerned for you.'

She saw heads turning, mouths whispering behind fans on this humid summer's night. She thought of Sillitoe's words, his cool pride for his father.

'He showed me some of the house. And you?'

'My father had some wild plan for me to leave the navy. He has just signed a deed of contract with the East India Company. Expansion, progress, you know the kind of language he uses.'

Catherine watched him with sudden concern. He had been drinking rather heavily and had lost some of the confidence she had seen in Chelsea.

Keen said, 'He doesn't understand. The navy is my life. My only life, now. The war will not last for ever, but until it ends I shall stand in the line-of-battle as I have been entrusted to do!'

His voice was louder than he had intended. She said gently, 'You speak very much like Richard.'

He rubbed his eyes as if they were hurting him. 'Richard, oh Richard! How I do envy you!'

Sillitoe appeared as if by magic. 'You are leaving, Lady Catherine?' His glance flickered to Keen. 'Are you quite safe?'

She offered her hand and watched him kiss it. Like an onlooker.

'Safe, Sir Paul?' She touched the diamond pendant on her breast. 'I am always that!'

She knew he was still watching them as Matthew brought the carriage smartly around the drive to the steps.

An eventful evening, and a disturbing one. She would write to Richard about it. No secrets. There never would be between them.

Keen leaned against her and she guessed he was falling asleep. The ride from Portsmouth, London and then his father trying to force his plans on him again. Did he have no remorse, no sense of shame that Zenoria had been allowed to throw herself away while in the care of the family?

She watched the trees flitting past in the moonlight and wondered where *Indomitable* lay, what Richard was doing.

She felt Keen's face on her shoulder. Drowsy but

not asleep. She could smell something stronger than champagne; his father's idea, no doubt.

She pressed her head back against the cushions and tried to hold her breath as she felt his lips on her skin, gentle and yet more insistent as he murmured, 'Oh, Catherine!' He pressed his lips on the curve of her breast and kissed her again, his breath hot, desperate.

Catherine clenched her fists and stared into the shadows. His fingers were on her gown, she could feel it moving, her breast rising out of it, to his mouth.

Then his hand fell across her legs, and with great care she moved him back on to his seat.

She rapped on the roof and when Matthew answered she called, 'We shall take the admiral to his father's house.'

'You all right, m'lady?'

She smiled but her heart made it a lie, and re-adjusted the gown.

'I am always safe, Matthew.'

She waited for her breathing to steady. It had been a near thing. The thought shocked and disturbed her.

Was that what loss and loneliness could do?

When they reached the Keen town residence in a quiet, leafy square she watched a footman hurrying down the steps to meet the carriage. Was he always there, night and day, just in case someone arrived?

The idea made her want to laugh. She touched Keen's shoulder and waited for him to recover himself. She knew that if she allowed it, there were more likely to be tears, which she would be unable to stop.

Keen said, 'Shall you come in and meet my father?'

'No. It is late.' She could sense Matthew listening and added, 'I leave for Falmouth shortly.'

He took her arm and peered at her in the darkness. 'I wronged you, dear Catherine! I was beside myself.'

She put her finger on his lips. 'I am not a piece of stone, Val.'

He shook his head. 'You'll never trust me again. I must have been a fool.'

She said, 'I will take you to Zennor. So I must trust you.'

He kissed her on the mouth and she could feel herself tensing, until just as gently he moved away.

Matthew flicked the reins and watched the house slide away into darkness. What would they say in Falmouth if they could see him driving to all these fine houses and places they'd never even heard of?

He thought of the young officer he had just delivered, and relaxed slightly before pushing a heavy cudgel back under his cushion.

Admiral or not, if he had laid a finger on her ladyship he'd not have woken up for a week!

Then, whistling softly between his teeth, he turned the horses' heads once more towards the river.

14

Change of Allegiance

On the morning of September 3rd, 1812, the shadows began to recede, and for the first time in the three months since he had been cut down on *Anemone*'s quarterdeck, Captain Adam Bolitho realised he would live.

The weeks and months had been as vague and as terrifying as a hundred nightmares. People who were only phantoms or perhaps only figments of his imagination seemed to come and go; sharp stabs of agony when he had to bite his lip to prevent himself from crying out; fingers and probes in the depth of his wound like fire, which even drugs could not placate.

In his reeling mind he had tried to keep some sort of record, from the moment he had been carried aboard the big enemy frigate to the ship's eventual arrival at the Delaware River and his journey by coach to Philadelphia.

Apart from *Unity*'s French doctor he had recalled no visitor but for the massive shadow of Commodore Nathan Beer.

And one other. Just before he had been lowered

down by tackle into a cutter alongside, he had found his first lieutenant, Richard Hudson, waiting to say goodbye before he was landed with the other prisoners.

'I wish you well, sir. May God speed your recovery...' he had faltered and had then murmured '... and your release.'

It had been like listening to two strangers, Adam thought. As if he had already died of his wound but was still clinging to the world, unable to accept his non-existence.

He had heard himself, his voice harsh as he gritted his teeth to hold the pain under control, '*I – ordered – you – to – fight – the ship!*'

Hudson had replied hoarsely, 'Our ship was *finished*, sir.'

Adam had felt his strength returning, and his voice was surprisingly steady. '*My* ship! *Anemone* was never yours! *You* struck the colours; *you* surrendered the ship!'

An orderly had murmured something and an armed seaman had touched Hudson's arm to lead him away.

Adam had fallen back on the stretcher, drained by the outburst, his chest heaving from all the blood he had lost, and the total despair which had replaced it.

Hudson had called, 'If we ever meet again...'

It had been as far as he had got. Adam had stared unblinking at the sky.

'As God is my witness, I will kill you if we do, damn your eyes!'

With his strength almost gone, he was still able to realise that the Americans were careful to offer him the best possible treatment. He had overheard a couple of army surgeons discussing his plight when he had rested for two weeks at a military hospital.

'He's got courage, I'll say that for him. Not many could survive in his condition. He must have powerful friends in Heaven.'

Another coach and on to Boston, where he had been taken immediately to a quiet house on the outskirts, guarded by soldiers, but to all appearances a private residence.

Twice a day, a doctor named Derriman visited him to inspect the wound and change the dressings. At first he had said almost nothing, but now after all these weeks a kind of restrained respect, one for the other, had come about. A personal servant had also appeared to break the monotony and emptiness of Adam's life, a Bristol man who had been taken prisoner in that other war, and who had decided to remain in American service on a full seaman's pay and allowances.

His name was Arthur Chimmo and he walked with a heavy limp, having had his foot crushed when a nine-pounder had been overturned on top of him. On this particular day he was unusually excited. 'I've got to shave you nice an' early, Cap'n. Somebody important's comin' to see you!'

Adam waited while Chimmo took his arm and gently swayed him upright on the edge of the bed.

Then slowly and carefully he took the weight on his feet, his muscles bunched against the pain.

It was still there, but when he considered how it had been, the improvement was like a miracle.

Chimmo stood away and watched him while he seated himself in the big chair by the room's only window. Stables hid the road – and everything else for that matter. He had tried to picture it in his mind: Boston Bay, Cape Cod. It might as well be the moon.

Chimmo produced his old-style bowl and razor. He had obviously been chosen because he was as English as Adam, but had been ordered not to discuss matters concerning the outside world. The doctor had told him of a battle between an American frigate, *Constitution*, and the British *Guerrière*: the latter had suffered the same fate as *Anemone*, except that she had been captured and was probably already flying the American flag. At least *Anemone* had been saved from that disgrace. Without knowing how, he was certain that his coxswain Starr had seen to that.

Another piece of news had been the assassination of the British prime minister, Spencer Perceval, in the lobby of the House of Commons. Chimmo had been quite outraged by it, as if his heart still lay firmly in England.

To Adam it had meant very little. Nothing did any more, without his ship, and with only the memory of Zenoria. They would know about *Anemone* by now in England, and in his blackest moments of despair he imagined them all: Catherine, calming the servants at Falmouth, if only to hide her own concern for him; his uncle; John Allday; the formidable Tyacke. He wrestled with another constant thought: Valentine Keen. What might he do? How much did he suspect, if anything?

'There we are, Cap'n.' Chimmo beamed and balanced himself on his wooden stump. 'You looks fair an' brave again!'

He glanced without interest at his reflection. A clean shirt and pressed neckcloth, and a plain blue coat unmarked by rank or other decoration. The face of a man who had come through hell. He knew that he would have died but for the special care he had been given.

It might have ended suddenly weeks ago, when somebody's carelessness had almost cost him his life.

He had been standing by the window, moving his arm back and forth to prevent additional stiffness to his right side and the wound itself. It had been evening, and he had known that the sentries were changing, just as he had known it was their custom to linger near the cook's door for a cup of something. He had often thought that he knew their routine as well as they did themselves.

But he had seen a horse near the stables. Fully equipped and saddled; there was even a sword hanging in its scabbard. It had been absurdly easy. Down some narrow stairs and above what had smelled like a food store. The horse had stared at him with little interest. It had been like a blurred dream. He recalled the tremendous strength he had needed to pull himself up and on to the unfamiliar saddle.

The rest was like mist. Voices yelling, boots hammering across the cobbles while he had slithered helplessly to the ground in an ever-widening pool of blood from his re-opened wound.

Dr Derriman had exclaimed angrily, 'You're a damned fool! They have orders to fire on those stupid enough to try and escape! You would have saved them the trouble! Where the *hell* did you hope to reach, in God's name?'

He had answered quietly, 'The sea, doctor. Just the sea.' Then he had fainted.

The door opened and a lieutenant snapped, 'Is he ready, Chimmo?'

Adam said, '*I* am ready!'

The lieutenant regarded him coldly. 'I am glad I do not serve in your navy, *sir*!'

Adam nodded to Chimmo and retorted, 'I doubt we would have you, *sir*!'

He picked up the stick he had been given and followed the lieutenant along the corridor. He glanced briefly at the small door where his attempted escape had ended within minutes. But suppose . . . ?

Chimmo opened a door and said loudly, 'Cap'n Adam Bolitho, sir!'

It was a bare but strangely beautiful room, with tall windows that looked out on to gardens which must once have been equally appealing. They were now uncared-for and overgrown, the previous owners replaced by the military.

A pale-faced man in dark clothing sat at a desk, fingers pressed together, his eyes deep-set and unmoving.

He said, 'I am Captain Joseph Brice. Be seated.'

Adam said, 'I would rather stand.' There was a log fire in a fine mantelled hearth. Like the one in Falmouth. It was strange to see a fire in September.

Captain Brice said, '*Please* be seated. You have made your point. During your detention I understand that you have made several.'

Adam sat down and winced as the dressing dragged at his side.

'I thought we should meet. I am no stranger to war. I served in the *Trenton* during the War of Independence. As your famous uncle also served. He is back in these waters; so then am I.'

Adam waited. He sensed that the other man was merely the instrument. He looked away. As *Anemone* had been the instrument. But anything was better than staring at the wall or out of the window.

Brice continued in the same unemotional tone.

'You were courageous, and were one of the most successful frigate captains England has ever known. And yet you fought with the *Unity*, and you must have known you had no chance against such a powerful ship. That was not merely brave; it was reckless. Since the fight, many of your faithful and loyal company have signed their allegiance over to the United States – but I expect you saw that as a possible outcome, too.'

'I did what I saw was my duty. Your ship *Unity* was set upon overhauling the small but valuable convoy under my care. The choice of any captain is not always the agreeable one.'

He glanced through the window. Was that the complete truth? Could it be that Hudson had been right in deed as well as appreciation at that time? The convoy had been out of danger when he had cut down the colours. *Anemone* had caused enough damage to the American frigate to prevent a further chase. By fighting on against such odds, many more would have died. Was it any captain's right to make such a brave sacrifice?

Captain Brice nodded slowly. 'I thought I knew you, even though we had never met. I was supposed to put it to you that a rightful and proper command should be offered to you. I shall inform my superiors that it is out of the question.'

'I shall remain in detention, is that what you mean?' It was like feeling a cage closing around him, restricting him until he could barely breathe.

'There is no other solution.'

Adam touched his side. It would have been better to die. Even when he had fallen from the horse in his pathetic attempt to escape, they could have let him die.

Instead they wanted him as another renegade, or as a trophy of battle. He would be unable to walk unhindered in this unknown land; his own reputation had put paid to that.

'After all, your father changed sides during the Revolution, did he not? A good captain to all accounts, although I never met him. Unlike Commodore Beer.'

Adam thought of the massive Nathan Beer, who had visited him in the *Unity*, although he could not remember clearly how many times. It was strange to realise that Beer's home was barely any distance away from this house, near Salem.

Brice watched him curiously. 'You would never give your word under oath as a King's officer that you would accept parole and not attempt to escape?' He paused. 'I can see from your face that you would not: your eyes speak what you believe to be true. Your duty is to fight your country's enemies by any and every means.' He gave a dry cough.

Adam watched him. A sick man, despite his authority and intelligence. Another victim.

'So then must I attend to *my* duty. You will be moved when you are fit enough, and be detained in a safe house. There you will remain until the war is finished. Is there anything I can do for you?'

Adam was about to offer an angry rebuff, but something in the man's voice told him to desist. Brice did not like what he was doing, nor the mission which had been given him by others.

'I would wish to write some letters, Captain Brice.'

'You must realise they will have to be examined, censored if need be?'

Adam nodded.

'To a wife or lover perhaps?'

'There is none.' He met his gaze directly. 'Not any more.'

'Very well. Tell the man Chimmo when you are ready.' He stood up and held out his hands to the fire. In his unemotional tone he explained, 'Fever. The Levant, long, long ago.'

He was still by the fire when the lieutenant of the guard came to escort Adam back to his room.

The true realisation hit him like a fist. *A prisoner of war*. A nobody, who would soon be forgotten or conveniently overlooked.

The lieutenant said, 'Not so much to say now, eh?' He stood aside for Chimmo to collect some cups and added, 'You've had it your own way too long, so accept it!'

Adam regarded him calmly and saw him flinch. 'I

287

shall see that someone spells your name correctly for the grave, mark you that, sir!'

He saw Chimmo staring past the flushed lieutenant, his eyes moving like marbles, back and forth to the room's solitary table.

The door slammed and Adam stood with his back pressed against it until his heartbeat had returned to normal.

A prisoner. He might as well take his own life.

Something caught his attention. The Holy Bible lay on the table, a piece of paper acting as a bookmark. It was the only book in the room and he had certainly not marked a place in it, nor had he even picked it up.

He stared round the room and out of the window to the deserted stable yard where he had lost his chance to ride away at the gallop. As Dr Derriman had asked in anger and amazement, *Where the hell did you hope to reach?*

Adam even thought of kneeling to peer under the bed where he had spent so much of his time.

He walked to the table and opened the much-used Bible.

There was a single sheet of paper, the handwriting scrawled with obvious haste. Adam had seen the same script many times when he had inspected *Anemone*'s daily log.

For a few seconds he felt nothing but despair and disappointment. It was from Richard Hudson, the bloody traitor who had surrendered the ship. He could feel his eyes stinging, and he was about to crumple the letter into a tight ball when something held him

288

motionless like an icy hand. Words stood out through the mist until, with an almost physical effort, he forced himself to read it slowly and carefully.

Do not believe what they say. I heard some officers speaking of you. You are to be moved to a safe place, somewhere on the coast. You will not know where it is but word will be smuggled to the admiral . . .

Adam had to pull his nerves under control. *The admiral.* Hudson was talking of Sir Richard Bolitho.

If I say more, others will suffer.

Adam stared at the last two words. *Forgive me.*

If I say more . . . Adam held the letter to a candle and watched it burn in the empty grate. He did not need to go any further. If his uncle knew where he was and could trust the source he might mount a rescue attempt, no matter how stretched his squadron had become.

He had always treated him like a son. Trusted him. Loved him. Had even held his tongue about his secret, Zenoria.

They wanted to take Richard Bolitho dead or alive. His name alone was the one danger they feared at sea.

He walked to the window and watched the breeze stirring dead leaves around the overgrown, sun-scorched grass.

He thought of the new American frigates, some of which might be right here in the bay.

He rested his forehead against the dusty glass. Aloud he said brokenly, 'Oh God . . . I'm to be the bait . . .'

When Arthur Chimmo came with Adam's midday meal he could barely prevent his hands from shaking.

With one eye on the door he whispered, 'You wouldn't tell 'em what I done, would you, sir? You 'eard what 'appened to your cox'n!'

'Easy, man. I have burned the note. But I *must* know what is happening.'

Adam could hear the officer's boots tapping outside the door. A different lieutenant for the afternoon, one who was usually disinterested, probably glad to have an easy duty away from the war and its risks.

'All I can say is, it were a sailor who brought the message. If anybody finds out . . .' He did not need to finish it.

A sailor. Theirs or ours, he wondered.

It was true that the men involved, including the quivering Chimmo, were risking their lives even by discussing it.

Chimmo had made up his mind, and said very heavily, 'It will be while you're here, Cap'n.' He nodded to emphasise each word. '*While you're here.*'

Adam's mind was working at a feverish pace. No wonder the grave-faced Captain Brice had obviously disapproved. One of the old salt-horse sea-officers. He almost smiled, but the sudden excitement was too much for it. *As my father would have been, had he lived. As my uncle is now.* A man who could still maintain standards and old loyalties despite the endless war and the carnage it brought everywhere in the world.

'I'll see you don't regret this . . .'

Chimmo put down a plate of steaming beef with difficulty and shook his head wildly. 'No, sir, nary a word! I'm 'appy in this country, 'appy as any man with one pin. I'd not want to go back. Beggin' on the streets o' Bristol. What would my old mates think of me, eh?'

Adam touched his fat arm. 'Go your way. I've said and heard nothing.' He looked at his food, his appetite gone. 'I wonder who this man is?'

Chimmo had his fingers on the door. 'He knows *you*, Cap'n.'

Through the door Adam heard the lieutenant complaining, 'Pity you don't pay as much attention to the officers here, Arthur!' Then he laughed. 'Another four hours and I'm off watch!'

Not surprisingly, Chimmo said nothing.

That afternoon the doctor came to make his usual examination. He told Adam he was well satisfied with the wound's progress, but he seemed vaguely troubled.

Eventually Derriman said, 'You'll be told soon enough, so I might as well share the news. You're to leave here tomorrow. You are strong enough to travel, but I hope somebody has made certain that the regular inspections continue, for a while anyway.'

Adam watched him as he put away his bag of instruments.

'Where to?'

The doctor shrugged. 'I'm not trusted to be told, apparently!'

Adam was satisfied that the doctor knew nothing. He was an open sort of man, unused as yet to the demands war would make upon him.

So it was soon. He tried to hold on to the fading glimmer of hope. *Or never.*

But he said, 'Thank you for all you've done, Doctor Derriman. I could easily have gone over the side.'

291

Derriman smiled. 'It was the French surgeon in *Unity* you should thank. A man I'd like to meet, that's for sure.'

They shook hands and Adam said, 'I shall miss our talks.'

Derriman studied him and said, 'So shall I.' Then he was gone.

Chimmo brought some cheap wine, which he had got from the officers' mess.

He moved awkwardly around the room, touching things, peering out of the window.

With a great effort he said, 'Goin' to blow cold tonight, Cap'n. Best keep your clothes close by – too early for fires, the major says. It's all right for him with his fine 'ouse an' mistress to keep 'im warm o' nights!'

Adam stared at him. *It was tonight.* '*Thank* you, Arthur.'

Chimmo watched him worriedly. 'I just 'opes . . .' The door closed.

Adam examined his feelings. Like preparing for battle. The terrible calm while any captain considers the odds on success or failure. *Death.*

Hope, my friend? It is all we can ever have in the end.

He lay on the bed and sipped the wine, watching the square of daylight above the stable roof opposite the room.

The duty lieutenant opened and locked the door without a word, his feet retreating down the stairs where he could be heard talking with one of his guards.

The light faded, and the breeze hissed amongst the

leaves; a light rain pattered against the glass. He had sometimes thought of escaping from the window, but without help he could get nowhere.

Suppose somebody asked for payment? He had nothing; even his watch had gone, probably while he had lain in *Unity*'s sick-bay.

He sat up on the bed and began to pull on his shoes.

He touched his pocket and felt her memory stab his heart like a barb. All he had was her glove.

'Oh, Zenoria, my dearest love, I love thee so. I will never forget . . .'

He stared at the window, barely able to breathe as something tapped softly and then more insistently against it.

Adam slipped the catch and pushed it open. He tensed, expecting the crash of a musket or an outcry in the yard below.

There was a rope dangling from somewhere above the window. He leaned out and peered down where it had vanished into the early darkness.

'Can you climb? Are you able?'

The man was a black shadow, but Adam could tell from the edge in his voice that he was very aware of danger or sudden death.

He whispered, 'I'll manage!'

He swung from the sill, and almost cried out as his wound awakened to torment him.

His guide hissed, '*Faster!* We've no time left!'

His feet reached the cobbles and he would have stumbled but for the man's strong grip. When he looked, the rope had disappeared.

'I've got a cart outside. Keep with me.' He thrust a pistol into Adam's hand. 'If we fail, you'll be on your own, see?'

Adam blundered through a gate, the one he had seen from his window, and out on to the road. He could feel the sweat running down his body, soaking his shirt like a rag, the weakness of the months and days trying to slow him down.

He felt the rain on his lips, and tasted salt in the air.

The sea. Just get me to the sea.

A second man waited by a small horse-drawn cart. He was equally faceless and dark, impatient to go.

He snapped, 'All quiet, John. No alarm!'

Adam pictured the empty room. With luck he might not even be missed until early morning when the soldiers beat up the camp nearby.

He felt his hands shaking badly. He was free. No matter what happened now or what became of him, he was free.

He allowed the man to help him into the back of the cart. A battered hat was jammed on his head and he gasped as a liberal measure of rum was poured over him.

His guide chuckled. 'If we're stopped, you are too drunk to talk.' His voice hardened. 'But have the piece ready!'

'Ready, Tom?'

He turned as Adam asked, 'But why? The risks – what might happen to you—'

He stifled a laugh. 'Why, Captain Bolitho, *sir*! Don't you recognise your old cox'n, John Bankart? What else *could* I do?'

The cart began to move and Adam lay back on a

pile of sacks and bales of straw, believing he was losing his mind.

He no longer knew what to say or think, what to believe or to doubt. A cart on an open road, men risking their necks for his sake. And John Allday's only son, who had once served as his coxswain. It had broken Allday's heart when he had left for America. Adam could remember what he had said about it. *An Englishman you was born, and an Englishman you'll die.* And here they were, somewhere outside Boston, and heading down towards the sea.

He clutched the glove in his pocket.

I'm coming, Zenoria! I promised I would.

He had lost all idea of time, and had to hold on to a wall when they helped him out of the cart.

The man called Tom said, 'What d'you think?'

Then Bankart said, 'In a bad way. Been through the thresher an' no mistake.'

'Suppose the boat's shoved off? Got scared or somethin' – it's one hell of a risk!'

Bankart sounded quite calm. 'I'll stay with him. I owe him that much.'

Adam barely heard him. Just the muffled scrape of oars, fierce whispers, before he was dragged down into a small boat.

The other man called hoarsely, 'Good luck, John, you mad bugger!'

Allday's son moved the battered hat to shield Adam's face from the rain, which was already heavier.

The men at the oars when they spoke to one another used a language he did not recognise. Not Spanish. Probably Portuguese.

He managed to ask, 'Are you really staying with me?'

Bankart grinned, but had it been daylight his sadness would have been very evident.

'Certainly, sir.' He straightened his back. 'As my dad would say, "An' that's no error"!'

Adam pulled the hat away and opened his mouth to the rain.

Free.

15

Trick for Trick

Matthew Scarlett, *Indomitable*'s first lieutenant, ducked his head as he stepped into the wardroom and tossed his hat to one of the mess-boys. Despite the cool northerly wind which had filled the sails well enough for the whole forenoon watch, the air between decks was dank and humid, the Atlantic's warning of what was to come.

Before dusk they would rendezvous with two of the squadron's other frigates, *Zest* and *Reaper*, and ride it out for the night.

He sat down and thought savagely, *For all the bloody good it will do.* The only vessel they had sighted on this bright September day had been the busy schooner *Reynard*, pausing only briefly to exchange despatches before hurrying on to the next point of command.

The mess-boy placed a goblet of red wine before him and waited for instructions.

Scarlett barely heard him and snapped, 'Salt pork again? I'll begin to *look* like a pig very soon!'

He stared aft, as if he could see the captain discussing the latest despatches with the admiral. He swallowed half the tepid wine without even tasting it. Avery the flag-lieutenant would be there too. *Of course.*

Could he speak privately with the captain? After what he had told him when he had taken command at Plymouth, might he be prepared to listen?

The two Royal Marine officers were dozing in their chairs, while Jeremy Laroche, the third lieutenant, sat at the end of the table, idly shuffling and re-shuffling a pack of cards.

Scarlett ignored him. How long would this go on? The Yankees might never break out in strength; even *Anemone*'s loss had been sheer mischance. Had it been dark, nothing might have happened at all.

Laroche called in his affected drawl, 'I say, Matthew, if I can rouse the two *soldiers* here, would you care to make a foursome?' He ruffled the cards and added, 'Chance to even the score, what?'

'Not now.'

'But it'll be *all-hands* before you know it. You *know* what it's been like.'

'I said *not now.* Are you bloody deaf or something?'

He did not see the lieutenant's anger and resentment; all he could think of was the letter which had come with the schooner's mail. Even the sight of his mother's spidery writing had twisted his stomach like a sickness.

It should have been so different. *Could* have been. *Indomitable* had lain at Plymouth undergoing alterations and re-rigging, ready for a role which had not come about in time for the Mauritius campaign. As first lieutenant he had had every hope and promise for promotion, to commander in all probability, on a temporary footing until he could be advanced to captain. Captain of this powerful vessel, a match for any of the crack American newcomers like *Unity* and the rest. The money that went with such a command would be further increased with the prizes he would take or share. A real chance to wipe out the mounting debts that hung over him like a spectre.

His mother was desperate. *They* had threatened her that they would, if necessary, go to the lords of admiralty. But the deeds of the house which her late husband had left her would show an honest attempt at repayment.

The very mention of cards by the unimaginative Laroche had nearly made him vomit.

He knew that he was behaving strangely, but the sudden gusts of rage and his harsh treatment of some of the warrant-officers seemed beyond his ability to contain. On or off watch, in his cot at night or pacing the quarterdeck in all weathers, he was dogged by worry and despair.

Indomitable was not to continue as a private ship, as he and others had expected.

When Sir Richard's flag had broken out at the mainmast truck he had watched his hopes begin to dwindle. It was well known in the fleet that Bolitho often promoted his various flag-lieutenants to command at the end of a commission. For some it had been richly deserved; others, who could say? Scarlett was one of the most senior lieutenants in the squadron, apart from a few of the old hands who had risen from warrant rank and the like.

It was so unfair. But it would not go away. There would be no peace.

Another mess-man faltered by the table. 'Beg pardon, sir.'

Scarlett turned sharply. '*What?*'

'I 'eard a cry from the masthead, sir.'

'Well, so did I, damn it!' He stood up and strode out, snatching his hat as he passed. In fact, he had heard nothing.

Captain du Cann of the Royal Marines opened one eye and looked at Laroche. 'Coming in for a blow, what?'

Laroche was still sulking. 'I hate a bad loser!'

On deck Scarlett adjusted to the hard glare thrown back from the endless, undulating swell of empty ocean. Like molten glass. The emptiness was an illusion. Their last estimated position had been only twenty-five miles south-east of Sandy Hook and New York.

Lieutenant Protheroe, the officer-of-the-watch, studied him warily.

'Lookout reports a small sail to the nor'-east, sir.'

'Who is up there?'

'Crane, sir.'

Scarlett stared up through the shrouds and rigging, at the flapping topsails and topgallants. It was so bright that he could scarcely see the lookout, but from his name he got an immediate picture.

A good, reliable hand, not a man to imagine what he saw. He asked shortly, 'What sort of vessel?'

'I sent up a glass, sir . . .'

'Not what I asked.'

Protheroe swallowed hard. He had always got on very well with the first lieutenant. Or thought he had.

He replied, 'Very small, sir. Topsail schooner, but foreign rig, he thinks Portuguese.'

'Does he indeed.' He took a pace to the rail and stared down at the men working their watch on deck. 'As soon as she sights us she'll be off like a rabbit!'

He saw Isaac York the sailing master, a bundle of charts beneath one arm and his slate-grey hair ruffling in the breeze, pause with his hand above his eyes while he scanned the horizon for the as yet invisible vessel.

York continued his way to the quarterdeck and said, 'I'll tell the Captain, Matthew.'

Scarlett swung round, his eyes ablaze with sudden anger. 'Don't you start . . .'

York stood fast. 'It's *me*, Matthew. Remember?'

'Sorry.' He touched his rough coat. 'So sorry!'

'If you want to talk . . . ?'

He nodded blindly. 'I *know*. I am in hell!'

To Protheroe he added, 'Get aloft, eh? Tell me what you make of her.' To York he said, 'Maybe later I'll be able . . .' But Isaac York had gone below.

York was tall, and had to stoop as he made his way aft towards the marine sentry outside the admiral's quarters.

What had happened to Scarlett, he wondered. A good first lieutenant, one spoken of for promotion. *That was then.*

The sentry tapped on the deck with his musket. 'Master, *sir*!'

Ozzard opened the door and squinted around it, York thought, rather like a suspicious housewife examining a pedlar.

It took a minute for York to accustom his eyes to the comparative gloom of the great cabin, then he made out the comfortable shape of the admiral's secretary, his small round glasses perched on his moist forehead while he awaited the next instruction. Avery, the flag-lieutenant, was standing beside the desk, his body swaying easily to the ship's heavy progress, some papers in his brown hands. And their captain, moving restlessly by a gunport, the reflected sunshine lighting his hideous scars one way, losing them in shadow the next. York remembered how his midshipmen had been terrified of Tyacke when he had first come aboard. Few would even catch his eye. Now, in some strange way, all that had changed. The fear remained, but it was greatly tempered with respect, and perhaps a recognition of his courage.

And of course, Sir Richard Bolitho. Shirt loosened, his legs thrust out while he sat framed against the glistening panorama astern.

York smiled. The midshipmen were not the only ones in awe of admiral and captain.

'Be seated, Mr York. I'll give you the barest details of a despatch I received from Halifax in the schooner *Reynard*.' Bolitho forced a smile. 'Little news of the war, I am afraid, although the Duke of Wellington continues to advance and press upon Napoleon's coat-tails.'

York was as shrewd as he was experienced. There

was tension here. Anxiety in their various stances; no roles for the actors, he thought.

Bolitho watched him, fighting the despair, the sense of helplessness. He continued, 'Word has come from some unknown source that my nephew is recovered from his wound but is to be held captive, isolated like some felon.' He calmed his sudden anger with an effort. 'No chance of exchange, nor a just release because of his wound . . .' He looked directly at the sailing master. 'I need your advice, Mr York.'

Tyacke said hotly, 'It's a trap, sir! That would finish us right enough!'

York waited. It must be bad, for the captain to speak so forcefully to his admiral.

Bolitho showed no sign of irritation. 'Delaware Bay, that is where he is imprisoned. A place named Avon Beach.'

They all watched while York unrolled one of his charts and flattened it on the table.

'Ah, here it is, Sir Richard.'

Bolitho glanced away to the small lacquered box on his desk. A letter from Catherine. How he longed to read it, to share his hopes and fears across the leagues of ocean which held them apart.

York nodded. 'A good choice, if you'll pardon my saying so, Sir Richard. Too shallow for anything but small vessels at that point. Plenty of deep water in the bay, of course. Fine anchorage.'

Bolitho watched York's mind working while the others waited in silence. He turned his eyes back to the small box. Each word in every letter meant so much.

There had been a letter for Allday, too. He would be waiting somewhere, ready to spring out on the flag-lieutenant so he could listen to her voice in Avery's words.

It touched Bolitho deeply that Allday had forced himself to say so little about his new daughter, even though he was bursting with it.

Because of me, and of Kate. He looked at his hands. *And because of Adam.*

York raised his head. 'A landing party, Sir Richard?' His tone hardened. 'Or a rescue attempt, is that what you're proposing?'

Bolitho said quietly, 'Would they really expect me to risk ships and men because of my heart?' He was feeling the locket through his damp shirt, trying to summon her voice. But there was nothing.

Tyacke asked abruptly, 'What was the commotion on deck, Mr York?'

'A small sail to the nor'-east, sir. The first lieutenant is given to ignore it.'

Bolitho looked at him. 'This place, Avon Beach – do you know it?'

'*Of* it, sir. Loyalists were imprisoned there. Now I believe it is derelict.'

They watched him, seeing him creating the prison in his mind. 'It will break his heart.'

Tyacke said, 'It has happened to many good men, Sir Richard.'

'I *know*. It is not honour I seek, nor even yet revenge . . .'

Tyacke frowned as the sentry called, 'First lieutenant, sir!'

'Tell him to wait!' To Bolitho he added, 'I had better

304

go to him.' His expression softened. But for the scars he would have been handsome, Bolitho thought, gentle.

'I meant no offence, Sir Richard. I have too much respect for you, and much more that I'd say naught of in company. I do know your feelings. As your flag-captain . . .' He shrugged. 'You taught me, remember?'

York said uncertainly, 'If you need me, Sir Richard?'

'Thank you, Mr York. We will talk further.' York gathered up his charts and departed.

Bolitho sat with his back against the windows, feeling the warmth through the thick glass, the lift and roll of all of her one thousand, four hundred tons. Men, weapons, and perhaps the will to win. What chance had all these against love?

He looked at his flag-lieutenant. His tawny eyes were very clear from the sea's reflections.

'Well, George? Nothing to say? Your leader taken all aback, and you remain silent?'

'I see someone who is helpless because he cares so much for others. The ships and men who must rely upon him. People he knows, good and bad – they are in his hands.'

Bolitho said nothing, and Avery added, 'A general will say, "Order the 87th to advance." And if they are not enough or are hacked down, he will send in another regiment. He sees no faces, hears no pitiful cries which will never be answered, only flags, pins on a map.'

There was a long silence, and Bolitho could hear Avery's breathing above the other sounds.

'I *know*.'

When he looked up Avery was shocked to see the tears in his eyes.

'I had no right, sir.'

'You of all people had every right.'

They heard Tyacke's voice raised in anger. 'You are *dismissed*, man! Go to your barracks until told otherwise!'

Tyacke's anger seemed to pursue the luckless sentry. 'We are all fighting on the same bloody side, I *hope*!'

Then Scarlett's voice, hoarse and angry. '*Zest* has been sighted, sir!'

'What is the *matter* with you, man? It is near enough to rendezvous. Is that all you had to tell me?'

Avery asked, 'Shall I go and quieten things, sir?'

He stared as Bolitho held up one hand. 'Not yet!'

Tyacke asked sharply, 'What about the lookout and the sighting to the nor'-east?'

'I have set more sail, sir. She will lose us at dusk, so I thought . . .'

Tyacke sounded very calm suddenly, the sharpness of his temper gone like a passing squall. 'Heave to. Signal *Zest* to close on Flag.'

When he re-entered the great cabin he looked quite impassive.

'I apologise for my rough tongue, Sir Richard. I've long since lost the pretty manners of liners!'

Allday entered silently, his eyes questioning the absence of a sentry by the screen door. 'Are you going up, Sir Richard?'

Indomitable rolled heavily as the hands ran to the braces and sheets to shorten sail and bring her up to the wind. On deck there were startled faces every-where, peering at the sea, empty still but for small slivers of sail which appeared to be circling *Indomitable* like sharks while she continued to head upwind.

Bolitho lurched against a stay as the deck tilted over, his shoe sliding on the wet planking.

He saw Tyacke watching, then turning away again as Allday caught his arm.

He took a telescope from Lieutenant Protheroe. Very carefully he raised it to his right eye, hardly daring to breathe as the brightly painted schooner lurched into the lens.

'Have the side manned, Mr Scarlett!' He tried again, afraid that his voice might betray him. 'There is a captain coming aboard, and we shall offer him all honours on this September day!'

He could feel Allday's grasp on his arm, his anxiety.

'What is it, Sir Richard?'

Bolitho looked across the broad quarterdeck where Tyacke was watching his ship respond to canvas and rudder, his coat soaked with flying spray.

Tyacke had guessed. He had known.

Then he handed the telescope to Allday and said quietly, 'See, old friend? There is one other coming aboard today.'

Philip Beauclerk, the surgeon, wiped his strong bony hands with a wet cloth, and said, 'Whoever had cause to attend Captain Bolitho after he was wounded must have been an excellent doctor. I should like to congratulate him, enemy or not.'

Bolitho sat beside the cot which had been rigged in

his own quarters and grasped Adam's hand. He could scarcely believe it, and yet somehow, like Tyacke, he had known. The one and only chance, and it had been theirs to seize.

Adam opened his eyes and studied him, slowly, feature by feature, perhaps to reassure himself that it was not merely another dream, another lost hope.

'Well, Uncle, you cannot rid yourself of me so easily.' He seemed to realise that his hand was clasped firmly, and whispered, 'It was Allday's son. He took a terrible risk.'

'So did you, Adam.'

He smiled, gripping harder as the pain returned. 'I would have been caged, Uncle. He would have been hanged, like poor George Starr. I shall never forget what he did.'

Beauclerk said, 'He is still very weak, Sir Richard. His recent exploits have done little to speed his recovery.'

Adam shook his head. 'Why is it, Uncle, when you are ill, that those who care for you seem to think you are deaf and slightly stupid? They discuss you as if you are only one step from Heaven!'

Bolitho touched his bare shoulder. Even that felt stronger, less feverish.

'You are better already, Adam.'

He tried to force the despatches which *Reynard* had delivered to the back of his mind. The troop convoy had been doubled and would arrive at Halifax within the next two weeks. He had mentioned it to Tyacke while Beauclerk had been examining Adam, and had seen the arguments in Tyacke's eyes.

The Americans had leaked the information about Adam's place of captivity to encourage a rescue attempt, to split the Leeward Squadron when it was most needed. The convoy's size and importance had dwarfed even that.

Would men like Beer really believe that he would make such a reckless and personal foray in the face of such local and forceful opposition? By now they would know of Adam's escape. But it would be impossible for anyone to expect him to have reached *Indomitable*. One favourable card, then.

Bolitho watched Adam's eyes begin to droop, felt the grip of his hand slacken.

'If there is anything I can do for you...' He saw Adam trying to speak and guessed that the surgeon had given him some drug to ease the shock and strain of his escape. 'I never thought you were lost. But I cared very much.'

Adam pulled the crumpled glove from his breeches. 'Keep this for me, Uncle. It is all I have of hers.'

Avery had entered quietly but stood motionless and in silence. The glove, the rumour of suicide, and the young captain's despair told most of the story, and he was deeply moved by what he had seen and heard.

Then Adam said softly, 'A *ship*, Uncle. Please find me a ship.'

Bolitho gazed at him, the words unlocking another old memory. When he had returned from the Great South Sea half dead from fever, and on his recovery had pleaded for a ship, any ship.

'You should be sent home, Adam. You are not yet recovered. What must I do to make you...'

Beauclerk took Adam's hand and put it beneath the sheet. 'He hears nothing, Sir Richard. It is better this way.' His pale eyes were assessing Bolitho curiously. 'He is very strong.'

Bolitho stood up, unwilling to return to the squadron's affairs.

'Call me instantly, if . . .'

Beauclerk gave a small smile. 'When, Sir Richard. *When*.'

Bolitho saw Avery, and said, 'A miracle.'

To Beauclerk he added, 'I meant to tell you, the results of your work in this ship are excellent. I shall see that it goes on your report.'

'As you have seen in my papers, Sir Richard, my service will be terminated at the end of this commission. But there are no regrets either way. I have learned firsthand of the desperate need for improved surgical techniques in the King's ships, and I will do my utmost to make my opinions survive beyond the furnace!'

Bolitho smiled. 'I wish you luck. I am grateful for what you have done in *Indomitable*.'

Beauclerk picked up his bag but lingered to rest a hand on Adam's brow. Then he said quietly, 'In Sir Piers Blachford, I had the finest of tutors.'

Bolitho touched his eye. So he had known all the time, but had said nothing. Loyalty seemed to come in all guises, and he was suddenly glad that Beauclerk had shared the secret.

On deck the sky and the sea were like bronze, the breeze barely strong enough to lift the sails into motion.

Tyacke strode to meet him and wasted no time. 'We made signal contact with *Zest*, Sir Richard. She had a skirmish this morning and suffered small damage when she surprised an enemy brig, well inshore at the time.'

Bolitho saw the reckless Captain Dampier's eager face clearly like a portrait in his mind.

Tyacke was saying, 'I did not disturb you. There is nothing we can do until we meet with the courier brig tomorrow.' He hesitated. 'I am glad about Captain Bolitho, sir. I have much respect for him.'

'*What* damage, James?'

Again the hesitation. In a moment he knew why. 'Very little. A spar or two shot away, but the brig was taken as a prize. Unhappily, Captain Dampier was killed outright by a stray ball. He'll be sorely missed.'

Bolitho paced along the side, deep in thought. Dampier was always one to take risks, to lead his men in person to board an enemy, to walk his deck when all hell was breaking loose around him. A popular captain who had never appreciated that there was always one risk too many.

Bolitho watched the bronze shine on the deep troughs giving way to deeper shadows.

'I shall write to his parents.' It was better not to know men so well. That well. But how could you not, when to lead you must take and hold their confidence despite the pain, the sense of betrayal when they died?

Tyacke said, 'This plan of yours, Sir Richard.'

'You are still against it?'

'I am, sir.' He paused as seamen scampered past to take in the slack of some loose lines.

'Because it might fail? That I might be wrong about the enemy's intentions?'

Tyacke faced him stubbornly. 'Because of *you*, sir.

If the enemy is uncertain of the troop convoy's time of arrival at Halifax, he might attempt an attack in the Caribbean, where he has more chance of success. Either way he can divide our strength, but at least we will have taken all precautions open to us. And this ruse to draw us against Captain Bolitho's proposed prison – I am firmly convinced it would be a trap, to seize or destroy more of our vessels.' He took a deep breath. 'In every case, every action will point to you.'

'You of all people should not be so surprised, James. But I have little or no choice. The Americans will finish us piecemeal if we keep up this unrewarding hit-and-run strategy. We are here to destroy their ships, and to re-open our safe seaways for supplies, and the military for the conflict in Canada. They might still fight on the Lakes, but that will never decide a war.'

They walked a few more paces while the other ships in company seemed to melt into the ocean itself.

Bolitho said, 'Victor or scapegoat, James? The price of admiralty.' Then, 'Send for Yovell. I shall issue the squadron's orders by morning.'

Tyacke watched him stride to the companionway and tried to feel the depth of the man. His energy, his infectious optimism and his black despair. What had restored him? His nephew's incredible escape, aided by a man who had once served as his coxswain? Allday's son. Or was it the letter still unopened in the admiral's little box, Catherine Somervell's words and strength from across an ocean?

He saw Allday by the hammock nettings and asked him how he was.

He saw the tired grin in the shadows.

'I feel at odds with meself, Cap'n. I was flung right over when I saw who it was with Cap'n Adam. Like turning the pages. Friend or father, I'm not sure which. He's not going back to their lot, though, an' that's a blessing.'

Tyacke said, 'Did he tell you what happened?'

Allday stiffened suspiciously. But why not? Captain Tyacke was no enemy. Also, he needed to talk, if only to sort it out for himself, to make some sense of it.

'He couldn't get work, not the kind he quit the navy for, sir. He wanted to fish, or work on the land. Nobody had any use for him.' He gave a bitter laugh. 'Even his wife gave up on him and took to another man's bed. So when he heard about Cap'n Adam he knew what he must do. He'll hang or worse if they catches him.'

Tyacke said, 'Go below. There was a letter from home for you, I believe.'

Allday sighed. 'It makes up for all this, sir.'

Tyacke watched him melt into the gloom and was suddenly filled with envy.

He stared into the darkness, seeing the last of the horizon. Then he touched the weathered quarterdeck rail. Aloud he said, 'We'll fight very soon, my girl. You and me. Never ask the bloody reason, only fight and win!'

Adam Bolitho lay in the gently swaying cot, listening to the groan and shiver of cordage and rudder, the occasional slap of spray against the quarter windows. The cabin was in darkness but for a solitary lantern, and he knew that his uncle was elsewhere expanding upon his instructions to his captains for the courier brig.

It was heavy and close between decks with all hatches and shutters sealed as though against some unseen enemy witness. He was sweating, and the ache in his side felt as if the wound had been re-opened.

It was still hard to accept that he was in *Indomitable*, that he would not be awakened by the one-legged man from Bristol, or the surly lieutenant of the guard.

They would be hunting for him. A needle in a haystack. He prayed that those who had aided his escape would remain safe and unknown.

He listened to the footsteps on deck and pictured the duty watch, the lieutenant and his midshipmen and master's mate, the helmsmen watching the dimly-glowing compass card, their bare feet braced against the tug of the great rudder. Sounds and sensations so familiar and personal that he was even more aware of his sense of bereavement, of not belonging. He heard the scrape of boots and quick murmurs beyond the screen as the marine sentry was relieved. His world, and yet denied to him since *Anemone*'s loss.

A door opened, and he thought he heard Ozzard's sharp voice. Another lantern threw more light around the sleeping-compartment and he saw a small figure with unruly hair and bare feet, treading carefully down the slope of the deck with a tray gripped in his hands like something precious.

Adam forced himself on to his elbow and opened the shutter of his lantern. 'I know you, boy, you're John Whitmarsh. They told me what happened to you.'

The boy stared at him, almost afraid, shocked perhaps to see his captain lying like any wounded seaman.

'Aye, sir. 'Tis me. Mr Ozzard said for me to come to you. I've brought some wine. He said it belonged to some lady, though I didn't understand what he meant, sir.'

Adam reached out and took his arm. There was nothing of him. 'Volunteered' by some relative who found his upkeep and care too inconvenient.

'You survived when so many fell, John Whitmarsh.' He tried to smile. 'Or surrendered!'

'I *tried*, sir.' He did not explain. 'Be you goin' to be all right, sir?'

Adam nodded. 'When I get a ship. I'll be brave enough then.'

He realised that the boy was staring at him, his eyes filling his face. The realisation came starkly to him. The boy had nothing. Even his best friend had been lost.

He asked, 'Will you come as my servant, John, when I get another ship? Will you do that?'

The boy nodded and began to sob quietly. 'I'd be that proud, sir!'

'Can you read?'

'No, sir. But I could learn!'

Adam smiled. 'I shall teach you. Who knows, you may wear the King's coat one day; then I shall be proud of *you*, eh?'

'I dunno what to say, sir!'

Adam sipped the wine. Lady Catherine's. Ozzard would understand. This poor, twelve-year-old youth probably imagined that he was offering him some kind of lifeline. He would never believe that it was the other way round.

The excitement, the emotion, and now the wine were making him drowsy again.

He said, 'On days when we are sad, young John, we can restore ourselves by remembering our old ship, and our lost friends.' His eyes hardened in the flickering lights. 'Our enemies, too, if it pleases you.'

The boy watched until he was asleep and then curled up near by. Without fear, without need. *He was somebody.*

16

The Strength of a Ship

Bolitho walked up to the stern windows of the great cabin and watched the spray soaking the thick glass, hardening like ice rime in the south-westerly wind.

Captain James Tyacke watched him, noting each mood while half his mind clung to the sounds of wind and rigging. His responsibility to his ship.

'You still think I am wrong, James?'

'I'm more worried by the weather, sir. York claims it will remain the same for a few days yet, but I'm not so sure. If the Halifax-bound convoy is caught by wind and heavy seas it could be scattered, and that means they would be without whatever escorts their lordships have seen fit to provide.' He did not hide the contempt in his voice. 'All those men, and horses and guns too. It would be slaughter.'

Bolitho walked to the chart on his table. It was noon, but gloomy enough for sunset.

He tried to picture his extended line of ships, with Captain Dawes' big *Valkyrie* in command, spread along the forty-fifth parallel while the rest of their patrol areas were left undefended. Beer's *Unity* was at

Boston, and the *Baltimore*, another of the new American frigates, had been in Delaware Bay. Waiting for any rescue attempt? It seemed unlikely, although *Zest*'s first lieutenant had reported sighting such a vessel when they had crossed swords with the smart little brig. Every captain would act as he thought fit if challenged, without hope of assistance and support.

Bolitho touched his eye. He had to be right. The convoy of soldiers, now said to be doubled in size, was a prize no commander could ignore.

But if I am wrong . . .

The door opened and Adam entered the cabin. Three days since Allday's son had guided him to safety, and what a difference, except in his eyes. There was tension there, and strain around his mouth which Bolitho had not seen before *Anemone*'s loss.

There was eagerness too, in marked contrast. Almost the midshipman again, or was it only wishful thinking?

'Well, Adam, you *look* the part at least!'

Adam glanced down at his various items of uniform clothing, which had been donated by *Indomitable*'s officers and midshipmen.

Tyacke asked, 'Did the first lieutenant have something to offer?'

Bolitho glanced at him. The sharpness in the question was very evident.

Adam said easily, 'I expect he forgot. All first lieutenants have much to do on the eve of great matters!' He tried to grin, but it did not relieve the intensity in his eyes.

318

Bolitho asked, 'You are so certain of that?'

Impulsively he put his hands on Adam's shoulders. 'I have your commission for you. You will assume command of *Zest* immediately, in case the weather goes against us. But no risks, Adam – you are far from well as yet. Hold the people together and try to keep *Anemone* a kind memory, one that will not incite you to avenge her beyond what you know to be any chance of victory. You are my best frigate captain, so take heed.'

He squeezed his shoulders, and thought of the letter he had sent away in the schooner *Reynard*.

My dearest Kate, I am loath to send him to Zest after what he went through. But he is the best I have, and he needs the command, as I once did.

Tyacke glanced at the salt stains on the leaning windows. He was eager to get it over with. In his heart he knew they all were. Like the last goodbyes; never the proper words when they were most needed.

He said, 'Captain Dampier was a good leader, if a trifle reckless for my taste. But because he is dead he will suddenly become a martyr when anyone speaks of him.' He smiled briefly, as if touched by some memory. 'His company may close ranks, regard you as an intruder, yes?'

Adam nodded, very conscious of the power of this tall figure with the ruined face. 'I understand you.'

'Oh yes, they will curse their new captain and damn his eyes to the full, swear to God he can never hold a slow-match to their old one! But you *are* the captain. Allow nobody to forget it.' He held out his hand. 'And you're taking the boy Whitmarsh with you?' He knew one of the reasons was because the boy had been the last one alive to leave *Anemone*.

But all Adam said was, 'He deserves it.'

A midshipman, his jacket black with spray, peered in at them.

'First lieutenant's respects, sir! Boat's ready alongside!' He fled.

Bolitho said, 'There is one thing more.' He walked to the bulkhead and took down the old family sword. 'Take this. It will be yours by right one day.'

Adam refused it gently, putting it back into his hands. 'We'll not speak of that, Uncle. I shall find another when the need arises.'

They walked out into the passageway between the lines of officers' cabins, hutches which could be ripped down in minutes when the hands dashed to quarters and the drums stopped every man's heartbeat. Figures moved out like shadows: Allday with a handclasp, Yovell, even Ozzard, who rarely showed any emotion at all. And John Bankart, Allday's illegitimate son, unknown for so many years.

Perhaps Adam was thinking of his own upbringing, fatherless as he had then believed, his mother selling herself to feed and educate him.

Bolitho watched as Adam shook Bankart's hand. Never a youth, but now a man of thirty or so.

He heard Adam say, 'Leave the sea, John. It is not for you and never was. I'll never forget what you did for me, nor will your father.' He smiled with genuine warmth. 'Give him time. He is all aback because of you!'

320

The calls trilled and he was down the side, nimbly, and sure-footed despite his wound.

Bolitho shaded his eyes to stare over at *Zest*, showing her copper as she pitched violently in a quarter sea.

Her company were in for a surprise. It would do them good. He watched Adam turn just once to wave from the sternsheets, his borrowed hat pressed between his knees. It would do Adam good as well.

Tyacke had already put the event from his immediate thoughts. 'I shall exercise the guns when the hands have eaten, Sir Richard. This is no time for slackness.'

Bolitho left him and went aft to his cabin. There he took out his unfinished letter and wondered when they would meet with the *Reynard* again, or some other courier who would take it on board.

He sat with the pages spread out on the table and laid her last letter beside them. She had written of the changing colours of Cornwall, of Falmouth. The coming of autumn, and the mists over Pendennis Point.

Each night I lie and await thee, dearest of men. I speak your name, and like that terrible day when they found Zenoria, I feel your hand on mine. Safe, safe, and oh so precious to me. I wrote to you before about Val Keen. He was grieved by his loss. Bolitho had imagined that he had felt her hesitate as she had written it. *But he will get over it, I am certain, and he shall find another.*

There are those who have no such escape . . .

He looked up, annoyed at the interruption, but it was Allday.

Allday said, 'I thought I'd stop them disturbing you, Sir Richard. *Reaper* has just sighted a sail to the east'rd. A brig.'

'One of ours then, old friend.' His eyes moved to the letter. No, he would finish it *afterwards*. Why should that word hold such threat?

Allday said gruffly, 'It's strange to have your own kin aboard. Better he were a stranger – I'd not feel so ill at ease!' His eyes crinkled. 'Still, he was fair tickled when he heard about the baby.'

Bolitho smiled. *Kate.* He hoped it had not saddened his own Kate.

Two hours later, *Indomitable* was near enough to the newcomer to identify her as the brig *Weazel* of fourteen guns.

She had been ordered to patrol as close as was prudent to the southern approaches of Nantucket Sound. As laid down in his original instructions, her commander, a red-faced Devonian named John Mates, had left the sector to find either his admiral in person or one of the chain of vessels that made up this very mixed squadron.

Tyacke brought the news to Bolitho in his cabin.

'From *Weazel*, sir. The U.S.S. *Unity* has put to sea. She slipped out three nights ago.' He spread his strong hands. 'Gone, just like that.' He saw Bolitho's mind working busily on the information, or the lack of it. He added, 'I've repeated the signal to *Reaper* . . .' his blue eyes did not even blink '. . . and *Zest.*'

Bolitho leaned over his chart again. *Not yet. Not yet. Two days more.* How could they know, be certain of anything? This was not warfare as it was expected to be fought. But then, those who made the rules of battle had too often never seen one. This was personal, cold-bloodedly personal. Either Beer must be destroyed, *or*

322

he must kill me. Nothing else would make the vital difference.

Tyacke said quite suddenly, 'I shall give you all I have, sir.'

Bolitho said, looking up at him, 'Then we shall succeed.'

He glanced at the unfinished letter again. *Dearest Kate. Our love is greater even than duty.* Once he might have challenged such a sentiment, but that was in the past.

Tyacke had gone. He was like the strength of *Indomitable* herself, her great keel, her shining batteries of guns: strong enough to control landmen and seasoned sailors like the ship's rigging itself. He smiled. As an old hand who had once trained him had explained every mile of cordage.

'Equal strain on all parts, my young gennleman! That's the *strength* of it!' It certainly described Tyacke better than he knew himself.

On the weather side of the quarterdeck George Avery gripped a stay and watched the majesty of the ocean stretching away on either beam. It was hard to accept, until somebody like York showed you the chart and the pages of calculations, tides, depths and currents, that there was any danger. Land of any kind was beyond the sight of even the most keen-eyed lookout. Only the misty topsails of their two consorts, like linked hands, were visible on the horizons.

He thought of the letters he had read and written for Allday. Vignettes of rural England, small personal comments which he could not fathom, but he could see the true pleasure they gave in the coxswain's eyes.

Bolitho had mentioned Rear-Admiral Keen again when he had received a letter from Lady Catherine. He gave it all a great deal of consideration, intrigued also by the glove, obviously cherished, which was all of his personal possessions that Adam Bolitho had been able to save in his captivity. What was honour when it came to love, no matter how secret the love?

'Is this all you have to do with yourself?'

It was Scarlett, swaying back and forth on his heels as the *Indomitable* thrust through every roller with disdain.

Avery answered calmly, 'I am busy enough. I do not wish to argue, nor do I wish to be insulted.'

He might as well have stayed silent. 'Oh no, not for you, eh! No hard struggle to gain advancement like the rest of us! Privilege, who-you-know, that is *your* navy, sir, but it is not mine!'

'Hold your noise, damn you! The watchkeepers will hear!'

'And that would never do, would it? Because he is a Bolitho he gets a new command, instantly, and I bloody well suggest it will be your turn next!'

'I'll hear no more.' He turned to go but Scarlett's fingers gripped his forearm like claws.

Avery said very quietly, 'Remove your hand, *Mister* Scarlett, or . . .'

'*Or what?*'

'Do not try to provoke me, sir. You can have all the commands on the ocean for all I care. But I tell you this – ' he saw Scarlett flinch under his tawny stare ' – I do not believe you're fit to command anything!'

A midshipman called, 'Captain's coming, sir!' But he dropped his eyes as Scarlett glared past him.

'Hold your noise, Mr Essex, or I'll have you mast-headed, all night if need be!'

He turned back to Avery. When he pondered over it later in his hutch, Avery thought it was like seeing an entirely different person. Scarlett merely said, 'You mustn't be so hasty, man! So quick to burn a fuse, eh?' He even smiled. Like a stranger, and yet they had shared the same mess since Plymouth.

In two days or so they would fight, or so York the sailing master had surmised. Suppose Tyacke should fall? He thought of the momentary wildness in Scarlett's eyes. Something was pulling the man apart. Drink, women, or money? It was usually one of the three. But a madman on the quarterdeck of a King's ship . . . who would carry the blame?

He imagined Bolitho below his feet in the cabin, reading his letters or the leather-bound Shakespeare sonnets which she had given him. The man they all depended on, and yet he was still called to depend upon them. *Us.*

Lieutenant Laroche had the afternoon watch, and was regarding Scarlett very warily as he strode away from the captain.

'Ah, Jeremy, you have the watch. We shall exercise the weather battery this afternoon. But later, in the dogs maybe, do you fancy a game? Good, good – can't bear people who sulk. Bad losers usually!'

Avery saw Laroche staring after him, a look of utter astonishment on his piggy face.

Avery walked to the companionway. *So that was it.*

*

Yovell laid another paper on the table and waited for Bolitho to sign it.

Bolitho said, 'That will have to do. I expect you have done more than enough quill-pushing as well, on my behalf.'

Yovell was peering at him over the top of his gold spectacles. 'You should eat something, Sir Richard. It is not good to fast in the face of danger.'

Bolitho looked up from the table, the ship noises and stresses intruding as his mind cleared. The thrumming of taut stays and shrouds; the creak of the steering-gear beneath the counter; the thousand and one unknown murmurs of a ship at sea. York had been right about the weather: the wind was still strong and gusty, but held steady from the south-west. He tried to see it in his mind's eye: the endless land-mass to the north-west, Cape Cod, then eventually on to Halifax, Nova Scotia.

Yovell had sensed his tension. It was hardly surprising; they had been together a long time.

'It may come to nothing.' Bolitho turned his head to listen as his ear caught the brief sound of a fiddle. The watch below were resting, their last meal of the day cleared away. Did they feel the closeness of danger? Or did nobody care what they thought and felt?

The door opened and Avery stepped into the cabin. 'Sir Richard?'

'I thought you might take a glass with me.'

Avery glanced at Yovell, who shook his head.

'You should eat, Sir Richard.'

Bolitho contained his anger. 'What about you, George? Have *you* eaten?'

326

Avery sat down and watched as Ozzard padded past to fetch the cognac. Bolitho was restless, ill at ease. He replied, 'When I was a prisoner of war I found I could eat everything and anything, sir. A habit that came in very useful.'

Bolitho watched him fondly. Of course, that was why Avery had understood so completely his anguish over Adam. The misery of detention, after the freedom of the sea.

He held up the glass. 'To us, and whenever we are called to prove ourselves.'

He knew Yovell was about to leave, but was lingering by the screen door; just as he knew that anything said here would remain here.

'I think it will be sooner rather than later.' The door closed silently. Yovell would take his Bible to his little office, where he slept and preserved his privacy. A difficult thing to achieve in a ship in the company of two hundred and seventy other souls, from admiral to powder-monkey.

He thought again of his scattered squadron. Suppose he was mistaken, and Beer had decided to act without sentiment and head straight for the convoy? On the other hand far, far astern, the gate to the Caribbean lay wide open and unguarded. Which might tempt him the most? He sipped the cognac and tried not to think of Catherine alone in the old grey house.

Avery said quietly, 'I think that Commodore Beer is much like his opponent, Sir Richard.'

'*Me?* How can that be? I have never met him!'

Avery warmed to his theme. 'It's you he wants. I believe he held *Unity* back because he sincerely

327

believed that you intended a rescue attempt. I also believe that *Zest* was chased by another big frigate. The *Baltimore* was mentioned, I believe.'

He realised with a start that Bolitho was on his feet, moving cat-like about the swaying cabin as he had seen him do so often.

Bolitho said, 'Then we shall fight.' He looked at Avery, searching his face as if to discover someone else. 'You see, George, this will not be like other sea-fights. We have been fighting the French and their allies on and off for twenty years and even before that, out here in these same waters. The English sailor's cheerful contempt for foreigners, the Frogs, the Dons and the Meinheers, has sustained him when all else seemed overwhelmingly against him. This is different, as it was after the American Revolution. It is one thing to stand in the line-of-battle, fighting it out until the enemy's flag comes down. When I was out here at that time, I was young, full of ideals of what I thought the navy should be. I soon learned at close quarters just how different such a conflict can be.' He touched his arm, and Avery knew he had done so without noticing it.

'How so, Sir Richard?'

Bolitho turned on him, his eyes cold, clear grey like the sea at Pendennis.

'Sword in hand, cutting and thrusting all about you, breath gone, your heart filling your mouth, and then you hear them . . .'

Avery waited, a chill on his back, holding him silent.

'The voices, George, *they* are what you remember. Voices from the Shires, the West Country and the Dales, fishermen and ploughmen, farm-workers and weavers. *You hear your own voices* on every side. When we meet the Americans this time it will be the same. They will be fighting for the freedom they wrested from us once before, the freedom of their new country, and they will regard us as the aggressors yet again!'

Avery said, 'Our people will not let you down, sir. I have watched them, heard them. They speak of home, but they seek no other land.' He thought of Allday's letter from that tiny inn at Fallowfield, the contentment and the love which even distance could not break. Men like Allday would not change.

Bolitho clapped his hand on his shoulder. 'We shall have another drink. Then you can tell me what is troubling *you*.'

'It is nothing, sir. Nothing at all.'

Bolitho smiled. 'Methinks he doth protest too much!' He sat down again. 'Scarlett, the first lieutenant, is it not?' Before he could answer, Bolitho said, 'I have watched you too, you know. Ever since the day my Catherine took you to her heart, when you thought I would send you packing. You are loyal, but sensitive, as you showed just now when you mentioned your time as a prisoner-of-war. The unfair court-martial that followed your release has also given you sympathy for others in that position, some of whom deserve nothing but harsh treatment if the people have been placed in jeopardy because of their misjudgement.' He was on his feet again, head turned as a spectre of foam clawed up the quarter windows as if to seize the whole ship. 'If a captain stands his ship into unnecessary danger he can expect to face a court-martial or worse.' He tried

329

to smile. 'And myself? I would probably end up being shot dead on the quarterdeck by Captain du Cann's Royal Marines, like poor Admiral Byng. Half a century ago, perhaps, but still the same navy.' He handed Avery a goblet. 'His vice is gambling, is it not?'

Avery stared at the goblet, overwhelmed by the force of these revelations and his glimpse of Bolitho's true emotion. He dared not think of it as uncertainty.

Bolitho said quietly, 'You forget, George. Like you I have good cause to remember some of my so-called friends, who were quick to remind me of my brother's gambling debts and the price he eventually paid for his folly.'

'I am sorry, sir.'

'I expect Captain Tyacke suspects it; if so, I could feel pity for Scarlett. But he is one of the few experienced lieutenants on board. He has felt the enemy's breath in his face, blade-to-blade, *him or me*: the only code of battle.'

Avery got to his feet. 'Thank you, Sir Richard. For sharing your thoughts and for finding time for my own problems. I promise . . .' Then he shook his head and gave a rueful smile. 'I am sorry. I must not say that. When I first presented myself to you and Lady Catherine at Falmouth you warned me then. You said, "Promise nothing! It is wiser in the long run." '

Bolitho said, 'Send Allday to me.'

'A "wet", sir?'

They grinned like conspirators. The door closed and Bolitho returned to the salt-caked windows.

My little crew. It needed to be stronger than ever now.

Captain James Tyacke walked to the quarterdeck rail and took several deep breaths. Beyond *Indomitable*'s powerful shadow he could see the boiling ridges on every long roller, feel the jubilant chorus of wind through canvas and rigging, a ship responding to chart and rudder. Figures took shape around him as his eyes became used to the unbroken darkness. John Daubeny, the second lieutenant and officer of the first watch, hovered nearby, unsure whether to speak or remain silent.

'Well, Mr Daubeny? I am not a mind-reader!'

'Wind remains steady, sir, sou'westerly, still moderate.'

Tyacke glanced up at the pale squares of canvas, spread like huge wings but barely visible through the spindrift and drifting spray.

The reduced sail plan would suffice until daylight while they sought out their two consorts. And then what? He still thought it unlikely that the enemy would have been expecting Bolitho to fall bait to the tale of Captain Adam's place of captivity. Commodore Beer was an old dog, with more experience than most, and a hard head to protect him against foolhardy schemes.

Daubeny ventured carefully, 'Do you think we shall fight, sir?'

Tyacke smiled grimly. 'As I said, I am no mind-reader. But we shall stand prepared and ready, what say you?'

He guessed that the lieutenant was squinting his eyes as he always did when asked a direct question.

'I think we are prepared, sir.' He hesitated. 'Thanks to you.'

Tyacke frowned. But it was not idle flattery, which he might have expected from Lieutenant Laroche.

He replied, 'I had a lot to learn too. This is a vast change from commanding a brig, with nobody to crowd you and no admiral's flag to fill you with terror!'

The lieutenant laughed. He could never imagine his formidable captain being frightened. Except perhaps when he had found himself on the orlop deck after the Nile, and had seen his own face.

He said, 'I wrote my last letter to my father, sir, and told him of our pride at being Sir Richard's flagship . . .' He flinched as Tyacke seized his arm.

Tyacke said harshly, 'Never speak of a *last letter* to anybody, do you hear me? For it may well be your last, if you dwell on it too much!'

Daubeny swallowed hard. 'Then I shall pray, sir.'

'Aye, do that, although I have more faith in a good surgeon than a prayer book!'

He turned sharply. 'Who is that?' He saw the senior midshipman, Blythe, climbing up from the boat tier where he had been inspecting the lashings.

'Sir?'

'I was going to tell you, Mr Blythe . . .' He hesitated, wondering why he disliked the signals midshipman in spite of the outstanding reports of him from other officers. A confidence as big as his head. *Well, never mind*. He said, 'I have put you in my despatches, to confirm that I am making you acting-lieutenant until your examination.'

Blythe stared at his shadow. 'Thank you very much, sir! That will help considerably!' Even he could hide neither his pleasure nor his surprise. Tyacke rarely spoke with his 'young gentlemen', content to leave it to officers who really knew them.

'I have a question, Mr Blythe.'

The figures standing around them were suddenly quite still, and trying not to appear as if they were eagerly listening. Deane, the other midshipman of the first watch, was paying particular attention in case he was asked the same question when his time came. Navigation or seamanship, gun-drill or boatwork. It would be well to be prepared.

Blythe was standing very upright. Tyacke could almost hear his brain working.

He asked, 'What is the strength of a ship, Mr Blythe? Can you tell me that?'

Blythe was at a loss for words. 'The keel and main timbers, sir?'

Tyacke said curtly, 'I'm taking this midshipman with me, Mr Daubeny. I trust you can manage?'

They walked along the weather gangway, dark shapes jumping aside as they passed. Tyacke climbed down the forward ladder, pausing to study the empty hammock nettings. If Sir Richard was right, there would be blood on the packed nettings very soon.

He examined his feelings. Fear, doubts of his own ability, resignation? No. It was more of an awareness, the tasks of responsibility. Fate might already have decided.

He said, 'Do you go down to the messdecks, Mr Blythe?'

The youth stared at him. 'Sometimes for drills, sir. The bosun's mates can deal with the other matters.'

'Can they indeed? Well, follow me.'

Down another wide ladder, which would be replaced by a less vulnerable rope one if they were called to action. When *Indomitable* had been a two-decker before her conversion, many of the messes had been crammed between the guns on either side. Now they had more space, at least.

There was sudden silence as Tyacke's white breeches appeared on the ladder, and an old seaman bellowed, 'Attention for the Cap'n!' His eyes were popping as if he could scarcely believe it.

Tyacke tucked his hat beneath his arm and snapped to the midshipman, 'Remove your hat, man! You are not called to duty here. And this is *their home*, always remember that!'

Blythe watched almost humbly as Tyacke waved the seamen to reseat themselves on the long benches beside the scrubbed deal tables. The smell of cooking still filled the long messdeck, and Tyacke paused to examine a fine model of a fifth-rate which was being completed, critically watched by the man's messmates.

One said cheekily, ''Tis the only ship Jake 'ere'll ever command, sir!'

Tyacke listened to them laugh, felt their unexpected comradeship, their simple pleasure at what would otherwise be regarded as an intrusion.

He picked out the various faces, knowing the parts of ship where they worked, saw the ditty-boxes in which they kept their small treasures, a few portraits, perhaps, needles and thread, whalebone and canvas for repairs to their sea-going clothing.

He said to Blythe, 'Remember. This is home. All they have is here.'

'We goin' to trounce them Frenchies, sir?' The man fell silent as Tyacke's eyes found him. *Frenchies*. Many of these same men had no idea of where they were, or where bound. Weather, food, security. There were very different values on the messdecks. The smells of packed humanity, bilge and tar, hemp and paint.

He answered, 'We fight the King's enemies, lads. But mostly we keep just the one hand for His Majesty, and the other for ourselves.' He looked around at their intent faces. 'For each other.'

Some stared at the hideous scars, others watched only his eyes. There was laughter, some at the other mess-tables craning to hear or ask what he had said.

A voice called, 'Would you care for a tot, sir?'

'Aye, I'll have one.' It was as if somebody else had spoken as he added, 'Must keep a clear head for tomorrow.'

They watched in utter silence as he drained a tumbler of neat rum. He nodded, catching his breath. 'Nelson's blood, lads!' Then he straightened as much as was possible, no less impressive a figure stooped between the low deckhead beams.

'God bless you, lads.'

They cheered, the din filling the cramped place until Tyacke said, 'Carry on, Mr Blythe!'

Through the Royal Marines' messes, the *barracks* as they insisted on calling them. Neatly piled drums and pipe-clayed belts, stands of Brown Bess muskets and their bayonets, scarlet coats and delighted grins, even a handshake or two from the NCOs.

Tyacke felt the sea air on his face and was thankful it was over. He knew who had taught him the importance and pain of such close intimacy with men you could promote, flog or hang, even in the jaws of death.

A familiar figure lounged against one of the black twenty-four-pounders. Troughton, the one-legged cook who had shared his own horror at the Nile.

'You got 'em, Cap'n! The *Old Indom*'s in the palm of your hand, that she is!'

He was called away and Tyacke was glad. The young, fresh-faced seaman who had been blasted down when the world had exploded around them probably knew better than any, and would see through his disguise if only from memory.

He turned instead to Midshipman Blythe, who was watching him with a mixture of awe and fear.

'Men, Mr Blythe. Ordinary, everyday men – you'd never notice any one of them in a street or working in the fields in England, right?'

Blythe nodded but remained silent.

Tyacke continued relentlessly, 'But they are your answer. They are the strength of a ship. So let them not die to no good purpose.'

He watched the midshipman's shadow melt into the darkness. He might have learned something from it, until the next time.

He thought of the man whose flag flew at the masthead and smiled, embarrassed because of what he had just done.

He touched the tarred rigging and murmured to himself, 'So let's be about it, then!'

17

And For What?

Richard Bolitho peered into the small looking-glass and felt the smoothness of his skin after Allday's careful, unhurried shave. The ship was in total darkness, and with so much low cloud the first light would be late in coming. And yet the ship felt alive. Men moving about, the smell of breakfast still hanging greasily on the damp air.

Suppose I am wrong? He was surprised to see the face in the glass smile back at him. So many times, different ships, other seas and oceans. He knew that he was not wrong. It was not merely the calculations on York's charts, the estimated time of arrival of the convoy at Halifax; it went deeper, so much so. Like the minds of men dedicated to survival but condemned to danger, even death. *So many times.*

Allday knew it too, but had said very little on this chill morning on the great Western Ocean.

Bolitho had touched only briefly on the matter of his son, Bankart.

Allday had hesitated, the keen razor poised in the air. 'I want to *feel* him as my son, Sir Richard. But

337

something stands between us. We're strangers, as we were when I first met him.'

Bolitho touched the locket beneath his shirt. A clean, frilled shirt, one of Ozzard's best. Why was it necessary to do this? Allday had told him that his son had confided that the largest American men-of-war had the pick of the navy's sharpshooters, former backwoodsmen who lived or died by the success of their marksmanship. It was madness, surely, to present an admiral's hat and epaulettes as a ready target, or even a captain's. He had said as much to Tyacke, whose answer had been uncompromising and blunt, like the man.

'I'm proud of this ship, Sir Richard. She's mine, and I know her better than I ever believed possible. And I want our people to *see* me – know I'm with them, even at the worst of times.' He had given one of his attractive smiles. 'I seem to have learned that, too, from somebody not so far away!'

Bolitho rubbed his eye and winced. *But if I have miscalculated, then Beer will have joined his other ships to attack the convoy.* Even *Valkyrie* and her smaller consorts could not withstand such an onslaught.

Ozzard came out of the shadows carrying the heavy dress coat.

Bolitho said, 'If we are called to battle, you will go below.'

'Thank you, Sir Richard.' He hesitated. 'I'll be ready when you need me.'

Bolitho smiled. Poor Ozzard. He always took refuge below the waterline whenever battle was joined, as he had in the old *Hyperion* when she had begun to

338

founder. Allday had even hinted that it had been his intention to remain there and go down with the old ship, as so many had done that day. *How Hyperion Cleared the Way*: the ballad was still ever-popular in sailors' taverns and ale-houses.

Too many ghosts, he thought, ships and men, men and ships. Too many lost, too many lives . . .

There was a tap at the door and Tyacke made his way aft, his single epaulette glinting in the spiralling lantern-light.

'The wind's backed a piece, Sir Richard, more like sou'-west by south. Steady enough, though.' He glanced at the deckhead as if he could see the yards and reefed sails. 'She'll fly when we give her the chance!'

Bolitho tried to clear his mind. 'When we are able, James, signal the frigates to close on us. *Woodpecker* will remain well up to wind'rd.' A lone witness if things went badly wrong.

Tyacke said, 'I was wondering if we should signal *Zest* to change stations with *Reaper*, sir. A captain with a new ship, a ship with a new captain.' He shrugged. 'I'd suggest that *Reaper* would be better placed closer to the enemy.'

So even Tyacke was coming round. He said. 'That is what I intend, James. If I am right . . .'

Tyacke exclaimed, 'You mean that Commodore Beer has anticipated this move, and has outsailed us during the night?'

Bolitho felt the locket again, warm against his skin. 'Wouldn't you? Take the wind-gage if you had the chance? And if we run, we will eventually be caught on a lee shore, yes?'

Tyacke said shortly, 'Sometimes you have me in irons, Sir Richard. But run? Never, while I draw breath!'

He listened to the feet overhead. Recognising every sound, knowing the qualities and the reliability of each man there.

'That was a fine thing you did, James. "The strength of a ship." It is a pity such moments never reach the pages of the *Gazette*.'

'Well, I'm damned if I know how you know, but it gave him something more important than himself to think about.'

Allday entered quietly. 'Horizon's losing its cloak, Sir Richard.' He glanced at the sword-rack. 'Can't see nothing yet.'

Tyacke smiled and left the cabin, saying over his shoulder, 'That son of yours might still change his mind and sign on with us, Allday!'

Allday watched the door close. 'It's no joke, Sir Richard.'

Bolitho touched his arm. 'I know.' It was no time to be thinking of such things. A man could die in a moment of distraction.

He said, 'How do you feel, old friend?'

Allday seemed surprised by the question, then a lazy grin spread over his face and he said, 'We've seen it all afore, Sir Richard.' He shrugged. 'Today or never . . .'

Bolitho nodded. There was a smell of rum in the cabin and again he was moved by Allday's unbreakable faith and loyalty.

'Have another wet, old friend.' He glanced around

the spacious cabin. A place to think, to remember and to hide. In his bones, like Allday, he knew it was almost time.

He went out through the screen door and saw a squad of marines having their weapons checked by Sergeant Chaddock. They did not look up or see him as he passed, so intent were they on their inspection.

It made him feel invisible. Like one of the many ghosts this old ship must have in plenty.

He stooped to peer through an open gunport, the twenty-four-pounder like ice under his fingers. *Not for much longer.*

Very dark, with only a few pale crests breaking away from the lower hull. Just a slight brush-stroke. The eastern horizon.

Oh dear Kate, think of me, of us!

Spray touched his skin, like an awakening, and he thought he heard her voice above the sounds of sea and ship.

Don't leave me!

He rested his forehead on the weapon's black breech and whispered, '*Never!*'

Captain James Tyacke paused outside Isaac York's chart-room and glanced in at the sailing master, who was crowded against his table with his three mates.

York smiled, his sharp eye taking in the dress coat and gleaming epaulette.

'You're about early this day, sir.'

Tyacke glanced over a master's mate's shoulder at the open log, and the date on the first page in York's

341

strong handwriting. *September 12th 1812*, with the time and date of today's estimated position at the head of the column. Their eyes met. York had no doubts, either.

Tyacke nodded at the master's mates. 'Watch well today, gentlemen. You will learn something of your enemy.'

Then he left the small space and walked towards the open deck. Silver, shark-blue, and lingering banks of shadow. Sea and sky. He could feel Scarlett walking closely behind him, could sense his uneasiness. But not fear, that was something at least.

He turned abruptly and said, 'What is wrong, man? I told you when we met, I command Sir Richard's flagship, but I am still *your captain*. Speak out. I nurse the notion that we will be too busy presently!'

Scarlett licked his lips, his eyes so listless that he seemed disinterested, in spite of what the day might bring.

Tyacke was growing impatient. 'In truth I can't help you if you remain dumb, sir. What is it, a woman? Have you fathered a child?'

Scarlett shook his head. 'I wish it were that simple, sir.'

'Money, then?' He saw the bolt strike home. 'Cards?'

Scarlett nodded. 'I am in debt, sir, serious debt!'

Tyacke regarded him without pity. 'Then you are a fool. But we shall speak later. I may be able to help you.' His tone hardened. 'Give of your best today. I am relying on it. *Indomitable* will make this *her day*!'

He strode aft and stared up at the reefed topgallants

and courses, the admiral's flag and masthead pendant whipping out in the wind with the racing grey clouds beyond them.

He could hear the scrape of grindstones as Duff, the gunner, put his men to work sharpening cutlasses and boarding-axes. It could not have been very different before Crécy and Agincourt, he thought. He saw acting-lieutenant Blythe in earnest conversation with Protheroe, the fourth lieutenant. He still wore his midshipman's white patches, but in a King's ship the word would have travelled like wildfire. *Blythe's one of them now!* Tyacke smiled grimly. Or soon would be, if he was prepared to listen for a change.

Allday passed him by, resting a cutlass on his hand to find the right balance. Some of the hands spoke to him but he did not seem to hear.

At the foot of the quarterdeck ladder Allday gripped the handrail while *Indomitable* buried her stem in a long Atlantic roller, hurling spray heavily over the figurehead, the prancing lion with bared claws.

'What are *you* doing here?'

His son, a cutlass thrust through his belt, looked at him and shrugged. 'The boatswain put me with the afterguard.'

Allday tried to make a joke of it. 'Old Sam probably knew you were useless as a topman! Not so many ropes to play with down aft!' He was troubled, all the same. The quarterdeck in any ship was a target for marksmen and swivels; it always had been. The chain of command began and ended here. Many of the Royal Marines served in the afterguard too, their boots and equipment making them useless for work aloft.

Allday folded his arms. 'We may be fighting some of your lot afore long, my lad, so be warned.'

Bankart regarded him sadly. 'I wanted to live in peace, that was all. Cap'n Adam was the first to understand. Why can't you? There always has to be a *flag*, or one *side* or t'other. I hoped to find peace in America.'

Allday said gruffly, 'When we gets home, my son, just remember what it's cost some of us. My wife Unis has already had one man killed aboard the old *Hyperion*, and her brother John lost a leg in the line with the 31st Huntingdonshires. You'll find plenty of good men who've been maimed in Falmouth where Sir Richard's found work for them.'

'And what of you – ' He hesitated. 'Father?'

'I've more'n any man could hope for. Unis, and now my little Kate. They'll both be waiting for me. Now there's you. John,' his eyes crinkled. 'Three Johns all told, eh?'

Bankart smiled, strangely proud of this big man who, for once, was at a loss for words.

They both gazed up at the ragged clouds as the masthead lookout called, '*Reaper* in sight to the sou'-east, sir!'

The frigate must be right in the spreading cloak of silver. The first sighting of the day.

Allday saw Tyacke with Daubeny, who was officer-of-the-watch, conferring together, looking along the upper deck and gangways as more light spilled over the sea's edge like water over a dam.

He heard Daubeny call, 'Aloft with you, Mr Blisset, and take a glass, you idiot!'

The bright-eyed midshipman swarmed up the ratlines like a monkey and Allday murmured, 'Cheeky little bugger, that one! Asked me what the navy was like *in my day*!'

They both fell silent as Blisset's piping voice floated down from the crosstrees.

'Deck there! From *Woodpecker* repeated *Reaper, Sail in sight to the sou'-west*!'

Tyacke called, 'My respects to the admiral, Mr Scarlett, and . . .'

'I heard, Captain Tyacke.' Bolitho waited for the deck to level off and then walked unhurriedly to the quarterdeck rail, where he and Tyacke formally touched hats to one another.

Allday watched. It always unnerved him, even though he knew Sir Richard would never suspect it from his 'oak'.

He turned to speak with his son, but Bankart was already being urged aft by the squat boatswain, Sam Hockenhull.

Allday felt the soreness in his chest come alive like a warning. It never left him completely, nor did it allow him to forget the day he had been cut down by Spanish steel, and Bolitho had been on the point of surrendering to save him.

Always the pain.

Tyacke looked for another midshipman. 'Acknowledge the signal, Mr Arlington.' He turned to Bolitho and waited for the inevitable. Bolitho glanced across the motionless figures, and those who peered up at the lookout's lofty perch as if they expected it to prove a mistake.

He saw Allday looking at him. Remembering, or trying to forget? He smiled, and saw Allday raise one big hand like a private salute.

'When you are ready, Captain Tyacke.'

Tyacke turned on his heel, his mutilated face stark in the first pale rays of silver light.

'Beat to quarters and clear for action, if you please, Mr Scarlett!'

Avery was here too, with the new senior midshipman Carleton, the replacement for Blythe who had taken the first vital step on his ladder of promotion.

Avery said, 'Make to *Reaper*, repeated *Woodpecker*. *Close on Flag.*'

He glanced at Bolitho and saw him smile briefly to the captain. Like a last handshake. He thought of his sister in her shabby clothes, the way she had embraced him on that final day.

The drummers and fifers scrambled into line, dragging their pipe-clayed belts into place, their sticks crossed beneath their noses as they watched their sergeant.

'*Now!*'

The drums rolled and rattled, drowning even the scamper of bare feet as the men ran to obey, to clear the ship from bow to stern, opening her up into two great batteries.

Bolitho watched without expression. Even right aft beneath this deck, there would be nothing to impede the seamen and marines once action was joined. All gone: Catherine's gifts, the green-bound Shakespeare sonnets, the wine-cooler which she had had engraved with the Bolitho crest and family motto, *For My Country's Freedom.*

He could recall his father tracing that same motto with his fingers on the great fireplace in Falmouth ... It would be cold in Cornwall now, the wind off the sea, the anger of breakers beneath the cliffs. Where Zenoria had thrown herself away and had broken Adam's heart ... Everything carried below. A few portraits perhaps, wardroom chairs, a metal box with individual money-pouches, a family watch, a lock of somebody's hair.

'Cleared for action, sir!' Scarlett sounded breathless, although he had not moved from this place.

And Tyacke's laconic comment. 'Nine minutes, Mr Scarlett! They do you proudly, sir!'

Bolitho touched his eye. Praise indeed from Tyacke. Or was it Scarlett's troubles that concerned him more?

'Deck there! Sail in sight to the nor'-west!' Then Midshipman Blisset's reedy voice. ''Tis *Zest*, sir!'

Tyacke smiled. 'I had forgotten all about that shrimp! *Acknowledge*, but tell *Zest* to remain on station.'

Avery saw Bolitho nod to him and he touched the signals midshipman on the arm. He jumped as if he had been hit by a musket-ball.

'Hoist battle ensigns, Mr Carleton!' *How do I feel?* He lifted and dropped the hanger in its scabbard at his hip and saw some of the quarterdeck gun-crews staring at him. *I feel nothing*. Only the need to belong. He glanced at Bolitho, his profile so calm as he watched the horizon for the first sign of the enemy. *To serve this man like no other.*

347

'Deck there! Second sail to the sou'-west! 'Nother man-o'-war, sir!'

Avery expected he might see surprise, even dismay in the profile turned towards him. If there was anything he might recognise, it was relief. He repeated his thoughts in his mind. *Like no other.*

Bolitho stood watching the sea, and his men while they waited for their next orders.

The little *Woodpecker* would give them early warning before scuttling to safety from those great guns. Two ships then, as he had expected. The other one must be *Baltimore*.

'Royal Marines, take station!'

Up the shrouds on either side to their positions in the fighting tops. Marines known to be good shots above the rest; at least three of them, Tyacke had discovered, were once poachers. The rest tramped across the quarterdeck and took up their stations behind the tightly-packed hammock nettings, grim-faced, bayonets fixed, the debonair Captain Cedric du Cann watching them with cold, professional interest, his face almost the colour of his tunic.

Solitary scarlet figures stood at the hatchways, ready to prevent men from running below if their nerve broke or they were driven mad by the sights and sounds around them.

Tyacke called, 'You may cast off the boats, Mr Hockenhull!'

Always a bad moment even for the most experienced seamen, who would know well the additional danger from flying splinters if a longboat were smashed by cannon fire. But as they were lowered and allowed to drift away, many saw them as a last chance of survival if the battle turned against them. Loosely moored together, they would drift with the sea to await recovery by the victors, whoever they might be.

'Rig the nets!'

More men ran to obey, and Allday saw his son hauling on blocks and tackles with his new companions to spread the protective net above the big double-wheel and its four helmsmen.

Just a glance, and he was gone. For a brief second Allday tried to recall Bankart's mother, and was shocked to discover he could remember nothing about her. As if she had never been.

'From *Reaper*, sir. *Enemy in sight to the sou'-west!*'

'Acknowledge and repeat signal to *Zest*.'

Bolitho said suddenly, 'Do your fifers know *Portsmouth Lass*, sergeant?'

The Royal Marine puffed out his cheeks. 'Yessir.' It sounded like *of course*.

'Then so be it!'

Isaac York recorded in his log that on this September morning in 1812, while the *Indomitable* held her same course under reduced canvas, the ship's small drummers and fifers marched and countermarched up and down the crowded gundeck, the familiar tune *Portsmouth Lass* lively enough to set a man's foot tapping, or purse his lips in a silent whistle.

Allday looked at his admiral and smiled gravely.

Bolitho never forgot. Nor would he.

*

Bolitho took a telescope from the rack and walked aft towards the taffrail, his body angling to the deck without conscious effort.

He raised the glass with care, imagining his small force as the morning gull might see it. Sailing in line abreast with *Indomitable* in the centre, the wind lively but steady across the starboard quarter. By and large, as Isaac York would describe it. He steadied the glass once again on the western horizon, still partly in misty shadow compared with the silver knife-edge of the eastern sky.

He tightened his grip on the cool metal, controlling his emotion. The quarterdeck gun-crews were still awaiting orders after clearing for action; some would be watching him, and wondering what this day might cost.

There she was, Beer's *Unity*, with almost every sail set and filled so that she appeared to be leaning forward into the surging spray beneath her beakhead. The huge broad-pendant straight out like painted metal, a picture of naval strength at its best.

Over his shoulder he said, 'Tell Captain Tyacke. Fifteen minutes.' He glanced up to the masthead pendant and felt his injured eye sting in protest.

Avery was ready, the signal already bent on. As they had discussed it for such an eventuality, except that Adam had commanded *Anemone* then. He would be feeling her loss today, with men whose strength he did not know, in a frigate which was very like the one which had been so dear to him. And yet, he would be thinking, so different.

He turned and walked down to the quarterdeck rail and ran his eyes the full length of the ship.

The gun-crews were stripped to the waist despite the wind's bitter edge, their muscled bodies very brown from their service in the Caribbean. Beer could not risk losing them. But he would not expect them to run either.

He tugged out his watch and saw Midshipman Essex observing him with studied concentration.

There must be no mistakes at this stage: Beer had the wind-gage, and that was bad enough.

He felt Allday moving closer, heard his uneven breathing, the old pain probably aroused and reminding him of that other time, and all the rest. *Unity* and *Baltimore* between them probably carried as many guns as a first-rate ship-of-the-line. Together or separately, they would be hard to surprise or vanquish.

He said, 'Mr Avery, general signal. *Alter course, steer north-west by north*!'

As the bright signal flags soared aloft to break out to the wind, he could see Adam's intent face in his mind, and Hamilton of the *Reaper*, and the plump Eames of *Woodpecker* who had defied orders to hunt for survivors.

The topmen were already spread out along the yards, with every spare hand at braces and halliards. The moment of decision had come which could destroy every one of them.

'All acknowledged, sir!' Avery licked his lips to moisten them.

Bolitho looked at Tyacke. '*Execute!*'

351

As the flags darted down again to drop amongst the signal party in colourful disorder, Tyacke shouted, 'Lay her on the larboard tack, Mr York. Steer nor'-west by north, as close as you can!'

With the spokes gleaming in the strange light the big wheel was hauled over, the helmsmen squinting at the masthead pendant and the shaking driver while *Indomitable* continued to swing. He snatched a telescope from a gasping midshipman and rested it on the boy's shoulder as reefs were cast off, and the spreading canvas thundered out from every spar until even the great mainsail yard appeared to be bending like a bow.

From line-abreast to line-ahead, with the little brig lost somewhere beyond *Reaper*.

Tyacke yelled, 'Cast off your breechings! Prepare to load! Full elevation, Mr Scarlett!'

Then, surprisingly, Tyacke removed his hat and slapped it against the nearest breech.

'Come on, my lads! Watch this lady *fly*!'

With almost every sail she could carry filled and hard to the wind, the ship did seem to be bounding over the crests, not away from the enemy this time but on a close-hauled converging tack.

'All guns load!'

Bolitho gripped a stay and watched the half-naked bodies of the gun-crews moving in tight separate teams, the scampering powder-monkeys with their bulky cartridges, each gun-captain stooping to check the training tackles, his heavy gun moving slightly with the breeching rope cast off.

'*Open the ports!*'

352

The gunports on either side were hauled open, as if raised by a single hand. Drills, drills and more drills. Now they were ready, Lieutenant Daubeny by the foremast, his sword across his shoulder while he watched the enemy. Not merely sails any more, but towering and full of menace as they bore down towards the larboard bow.

Heavy artillery roared from elsewhere, and there was something like a sigh as the little *Woodpecker* drifted out of command, her foremast, yards and flapping canvas trailing over the side even as more long-range balls from *Unity* slammed into her hull.

Tyacke drew his sword. 'On the uproll, lads! Lay for the foremast!'

Bolitho gripped his hands together and watched the glittering sword in Tyacke's fist. The *Baltimore* was steering directly for the gap between *Indomitable* and Adam's *Zest* in the van.

The deck tilted slightly, the topsails flapping in protest while the ship came as close as she dared into the wind.

'*Fire!*'

It was like watching an invisible avalanche as it roared across *Baltimore*'s tall side, splintering gangways and timbers alike, upending guns and clawing every sail so that some ripped open, tearing themselves into long ribbons as the wind completed the destruction.

'Signal *Zest*, Mr Avery! *Attack and harry the enemy's rear.*'

Tyacke glanced round. 'He'll need no second order, sir!'

353

'*Stop your vents! Sponge out! Load!*'

Along the deck each grubby gun-captain held up his fist.

'Ready, sir!'

'*Run out!*'

A few flashes burst through the thickening smoke, and Bolitho felt the enemy's iron smash into the lower hull.

Men peered at one another, looking for friends and messmates. Not a single man had fallen and Bolitho heard a ragged cheer: defiance, pride, and the over-whelming madness of a fight at sea.

'*Fire!*'

Allday exclaimed, 'The bugger's mizzen is goin', sir!'

The *Baltimore*'s steering must have been damaged or its helmsmen smashed down in that last broadside. A few guns were still firing, but the timing was gone, the ability to change tack destroyed with it.

Bolitho wiped his face with his sleeve, and saw the long orange tongues spitting through the smoke beyond the big American. Steady and merciless, gun by gun, into the drifting *Baltimore*'s unprotected stern. Bolitho could imagine Adam sighting and firing each gun himself. Remembering what he had lost and could never reclaim.

Scarlett called wildly, '*Reaper*'s struck, sir!' He sounded half mad with disbelief. 'The bastards!'

Bolitho lowered his glass. *Reaper* had been over-whelmed. All but dismasted, her sails like blackened rags, she was falling downwind, her ensign gone, her upper deck like a slaughterhouse. Smashed guns, men and pieces of men, her brave captain, James Hamilton, in a game made for others far younger, killed on the quarterdeck where he had fought his ship to the end. He should have remained in the H.E.I.C. This was not for him. Bolitho looked at his hand on the rail, gripping until it was bloodless. *Not for me either*.

'Run out! Take aim! *Fire!*'

Bolitho coughed as more smoke swirled inboard through the open ports. Acrid, savage, blinding.

Reaper had had no chance. A small sixth-rate of twenty-six guns against Beer's powerful artillery.

He wiped his eyes and saw Avery watching him, surprisingly calm. Distancing himself from the shattered ships and the floundering bodies that marked *Woodpecker*'s sudden end, as he did from many other experiences.

'All reloaded, sir!' Scarlett was staring from Tyacke to his admiral.

A silence had fallen over the ship; even the wind had lulled for the moment. Drifting through smoke as dense as fog, with only the muffled sounds of musket-fire and swivels, and the smells of burning timber. Like the gateway to hell itself.

Then he saw *Unity*'s topgallants, her sky-scrapers, punctured here and there but strangely serene above the smoke and carnage it concealed.

'Stand by, lads!'

Bolitho watched Tyacke's sword, wondering in those few seconds why fate had decided that this vital meeting was to be.

But the sword fell from Tyacke's hand as the smoke exploded in one huge broadside. A world of screaming madness, of falling rigging and razor-edged splinters.

Men dying, or being pounded into bloody gruel even as they stood mesmerised by the enormity of the bombardment.

There were twisting, unreal shapes as the maintop mast thundered down over the side, the corpses of some marines tossed from the nets and into the sea like human flotsam.

Hands pulling him to his feet, although he could not recall having fallen. His hat was gone, and one of his proud epaulettes. There was bright blood on his breeches, but no pain, and he saw Midshipman Deane staring at him from the rail, half his young body pulped into something obscene.

Bolitho heard Avery calling, but it seemed far away, although their faces all but touched.

'Are you hit, sir?'

He gasped, 'I think not.' He dragged out the old sword and saw Allday crouching near by, his cutlass already drawn while he peered half blind into the smoke.

Somebody yelled, *'Repel boarders!* Stand to, marines, face your front!'

Bolitho wiped his face again with his sleeve. There was still order and life in the ship. Axes flashed through the trailing cordage and shattered spars alongside, and he heard the boatswain bellow, 'More men on the forebraces 'ere!'

Tyacke was also on his feet, his coat badly torn by the trailing halliards which had almost clawed him over the side.

But the guns were still loaded, waiting to fire when Tyacke dropped his sword.

'Now!' Bolitho would have fallen but for Allday's

grip on his arm. The deck was slippery and the sweet smell of death was stronger even than the burned powder.

Tyacke stared at him and then waved his blade. '*Open fire!*'

Unity's shadow seemed to tower above them, sails already being brailed up as the Americans lined the gangway and prepared to board the drifting *Indomitable*.

Tyacke's voice seemed to rouse a memory, a discipline which had all but gone. With the hulls barely yards apart the roar of *Indomitable*'s twenty-four-pounders sounded like the climax to a nightmare.

It seemed to give individual strength where before there had been only the raw fury of war. Wild-eyed, the *Indomitable*'s remaining men and the marines from the nettings charged, yelling and cheering, blades clashing and stabbing as they swarmed on to the enemy's deck. Musket and pistol-shots brought down a few of them, and one hot blast of canister cut down Captain du Cann and some of his marines before the frenzied mob overwhelmed the swivel, and hacked the solitary gunner to bloodied rags.

Suddenly there were more cheers, English voices this time, and for one dazed instant Bolitho imagined relief had arrived from the convoy.

But it was *Zest*, grappling the big *Unity* from the opposite side. Adam and his new company were already swarming across the gap.

Allday parried a cutlass to one side and hacked down the man with such a powerful blow that the blade almost severed his neck. But it was too much for him.

The pain seared through his chest, and he could barely see which way he was facing.

Avery was trying to help, and Allday wanted to thank him, to do what he had always done, to stay close to Bolitho.

He tried to shout but it was only a croak. He saw it all as if it were a series of pictures. Scarlett yelling and slashing his way over the blood-red deck, his hanger like molten silver in the misty sunshine. Then the point of a pike, motionless between two struggling seamen: like a snake, Allday thought. Then it stabbed the lieutenant with the speed of light. Scarlett dropped his sword and clung to the pike even as it was dragged from his stomach, his scream silenced as he pitched down beneath the stamping, hacking figures.

He saw Sir Richard fighting a tall American lieutenant, their blades ringing and scraping as each sought the other's weakness. Avery saw it too, and dragged a pistol from beneath his coat.

Tyacke shouted, 'The flag! Cut it down!' He turned and saw another officer running at him with his sword. Almost contemptuously, he waited for the man to falter at his terrible scars and momentarily lose his nerve before he ran him through, as he would have done a slaver.

There was one great deafening cheer which seemed unending, ear-splitting. Men hugging one another, others peering round, cut and dazed, not knowing whether they had won or lost, barely knowing friend from foe.

Then silence, the sounds of battle and suffering held at bay like another enemy.

358

Bolitho went to Allday's assistance and, with Avery, got him to his feet.

Avery said simply, 'He was trying to protect you, sir.'

But Allday was crawling on his knees, his hands and legs soaked with blood, his eyes suddenly desperate and pleading.

'*John!* It's me, John! Don't leave us now!'

Bolitho watched, unable to speak as Allday knelt, and with great gentleness gathered his son's body into his arms.

Bolitho said, 'Here, let me, old friend.' But the eyes that met his were blank, like a total stranger's. He said only, 'Not now, Sir Richard. I just needs a few minutes with him.' He brushed the hair from his son's face, so still now, caught at the moment of impact.

Bolitho felt a hand on his shoulder, and saw that it was Tyacke's.

'*What?*' The enemy had surrendered, but it made no sense. Only Allday's terrible hurt was real.

Tyacke glanced at Allday, on this crowded and fought-over deck, so alone with his grief.

He said abruptly, 'I'm sorry, Sir Richard.' He waited for Bolitho's attention to return to him. 'Commodore Beer is asking for you.' He looked up at the sky, clearing now to lay bare their wounds and damage. If he was surprised to be alive, he did not reveal it. He said, 'He's dying.' Then he picked up a fallen boarding-axe and drove it with furious bitterness into the quarterdeck ladder. '*And for what?*'

Commodore Nathan Beer was propped against the broken compass-box when Bolitho found him, his surgeon and a bandaged lieutenant trying to make him comfortable.

Beer looked up at him. 'I thought we'd meet eventually.' He tried to offer his hand but as if it was too heavy, it fell back into his lap.

Bolitho stooped down and took the hand. 'It had to end in victory. For one of us.' He glanced at the surgeon. 'I must thank you for saving my nephew's life, doctor. Even in war it is necessary to love another.'

The commodore's hand was heavy in his, the life running out of it like sand from a glass.

Then he opened his eyes and said in a strong voice, 'Your nephew – I remember now. There was a lady's glove.'

Bolitho glanced at the French surgeon. 'Cannot anything be done for him?'

The surgeon shook his head, and afterwards Bolitho recalled seeing tears in his eyes.

He gazed into Beer's lined face. A man with an ocean of experience. He thought of Tyacke's bitterness and anger. *And for what?*

'Someone he cared for very much...' But Beer's expression, interested and eager, had become still and unmoving.

Allday was helping him to his feet. 'Set bravely, Sir Richard?'

Bolitho saw Lieutenant Daubeny walk past, the Stars and Stripes draped over one shoulder.

He touched Allday's arm, and then realised that Adam was watching them across the fallen.

'Yes, old friend. It gets harder.' He pointed at

Daubeny. 'Here, lay the flag over the commodore. I'll not part him from it now!'

He climbed slowly across the fallen spars, and on to *Indomitable*'s scarred deck.

Then he turned and grasped Allday's arm. 'Aye, *set bravely*.' He looked at the watching faces. What did they really think? Pride, or was it conceit: the need to win, no matter what?

He touched the locket beneath his stained shirt, which had been clean only hours ago.

Aloud he said quietly, 'I'll never leave you, until life itself is denied me.'

Despite all this carnage, or perhaps because of it, he knew she would hear him.

Epilogue

Lady Catherine Somervell stared at her reflection in the looking-glass and brushed her long dark hair, her eyes critical, as if searching for a fault. *Brush – brush – brush*, automatic and without feeling. It was just another morning, a bitter one too if the frost around the bedroom windows was any gauge.

Just another day. Perhaps a letter would come. In her heart she knew it would not.

In two days' time it would be December; after that did not bear thinking of. *Another year*. Separated from the only man she loved, could ever love.

It had been a hard winter so far. She would ride around the estate and then go to Nancy. Lewis, the King of Cornwall, was ill. He had suffered a stroke, the possibility of which his doctor had warned him often enough in the past.

Catherine had sat with him, reading to him, feeling the frustration and the impatience of the man who, more than most, had lived life to the full. He had muttered, 'No more hunting, no more riding – where's the point of going on?'

She had said, 'There is Nancy to think of, Lewis. *Try*, for her sake.'

She crossed the room now to the tall cheval mirror, the one decorated with carved thistles, a gift from Captain James Bolitho to his Scottish bride. In spite of the cold air which even an early fire in the grate could not dispel, Catherine opened her gown and let it fall over her arms. Again the searching stare, like despair, like fear. She cupped her fine breasts in her hands and pressed them together as he had done so often.

Will he still love me like that? Will he believe me beautiful?

But when, when, when?

The news from North America had been vague and sparse. Reports had criticised the inability of the smaller English frigates to maintain their usual superiority over the new American vessels, which were more powerful and skilfully handled, but that war was a long way from England. The news-sheets were more preoccupied with Wellington's continued success against the French, and the prospect of an overwhelming victory within months.

Catherine dressed herself slowly and with care. It was strange not to have Sophie helping her, starting each day with her uncaring chatter. She would have to find another maid. Perhaps in London, someone in whom she might see herself again.

She opened a drawer and saw Richard's gift lying there. She took it out and carried it to the window. The freezing air took her breath away but she ignored it and opened the velvet box. His last present to her, the fan set with diamonds. When it hung between her breasts she felt both proud and defiant. Together they had defied society, but had won the heart of a nation.

She kissed the pendant and fought against the tears. *I must hold on. It is just another day.* In their simple way the people on the estate, some of them crippled sailors from Richard's own ships, seemed to turn to her, trusting her to look after them with so many of the menfolk at sea or forming squares on Wellington's fields of battle.

She glanced down at the yard. Two horses being groomed, a carter delivering cider for the estate workers, not that there was much to do in this bitter weather.

And beyond, the naked trees, ragged spectres on the headland. Beyond them, the sea would soon show itself as something solid, like water penned in a great dam.

How will he see me when he first comes through those doors? She offered a wistful smile. *More likely he will be worried about how I shall receive him.* He dreaded getting older; even his wounded eye was like a cruel taunt, a sign of the years between them. She sighed and left the room. The dark portraits were all here, watching her pass; the Bolitho faces. She paused on the staircase.

And what of Adam? Would he ever recover?

She saw Bryan Ferguson, the steward, about to leave the house: he had probably been discussing the day's arrangements with his wife Grace, the housekeeper. A man so full of energy and enthusiasm, despite his single arm. He grinned at her and touched his forehead. 'You caught me out, my lady! I was not expecting you this early!'

'*Is* it early?'

Ferguson watched her. So beautiful even with her

rough riding-cloak over her arm. Sad too. The other face that few people ever saw.

She said, 'I'm ready if you are, Bryan. I have no feeling for breakfast.'

He said, 'Don't you let my Grace hear that, my lady – she'll take it badly!'

They walked out into the grey light and turned towards the office where Ferguson kept his estate accounts and records.

She saw his eyes fall to the breast of her gown and the glittering pendant she had hung there almost without realising it.

She said, 'I know you think me foolish to wear it. I might lose it somewhere. It's only . . .' She turned suddenly, her face terribly pale. 'What was *that*?'

Ferguson wished his wife was here. She would know what to do.

He listened as a hollow bang echoed across the headland, and imagined that he felt the ground shake.

He stared as Young Matthew came hurrying from the stable yard. 'Did you hear?' He saw Lady Catherine and touched his hat. 'Beg pardon, m'lady, I didn't know you was here too!'

Another bang. The echo going on and on until lost inland.

She asked, 'A ship in distress?' Her mouth was quite dry and her heart was throbbing with an almost physical pain.

Ferguson took her arm. 'Best you come inside where it's warm.' He shook his head. 'That's no ship, my lady, that's the St Mawes battery.' He tried to control his racing thoughts, hearing nothing but the regular boom of cannon fire.

Young Matthew looked around as other figures emerged into the crisp morning. There was a sudden silence, and she heard herself ask, 'What does it mean, Bryan? Please tell me.'

Grace Ferguson had arrived at last, her plump arms outstretched as Ferguson said hoarsely, 'Seventeen shots, my lady, an admiral's salute. That's what *that* is!'

They all stared at one another with disbelief until Young Matthew exclaimed, 'Well, the port admiral from Plymouth wouldn't warrant that!' He grinned hugely. 'He's come *home*, m'lady! He's *here*!'

Grace Ferguson said, 'You're not riding down there in your state, m'lady!'

Her husband said, 'Matthew, the carriage . . .'

Catherine walked slowly down to the low wall where her roses would bloom again in the spring.

Coming home. It was not possible. But it was.

I must not let him see me like this. She could feel the tears on her cheeks and lips, like salt from the sea.

She said, 'Let us go down, Bryan. I want to watch him come in.'

The horses were stamping and shaking their harness as they were backed into the shafts of the handsome light carriage with the Bolitho crest on the door.

I am here, dearest of men. No more will you come home to an empty house.

The tiny village of Fallowfield on the Helford River was quiet and still, protected from the freezing south-westerly by the hillside and the trees, although the wind had sent even the hardiest fisherman scurrying for harbour.

The little inn with its proud sign, the Old Hyperion, was as always like a haven, used mostly by farm-workers and passing merchants.

In the open doorway, Unis Allday's one-legged brother John stood unmoving in the cold. Years of marching and fighting with his regiment had hardened him against it, and he was more interested in how many customers they would fetch in this day than in the weather.

He had heard Allday's child, Kate, chuckling from the kitchen. A happy little soul, at the moment anyway.

Unis came into the parlour and regarded him thoughtfully. 'I'll fetch you some ale. Tapped it this morning. Just to your taste.' She wiped her scrubbed hands with a towel. 'Quiet, ain't it? Hope we gets more folk in here later on.'

A horse clattered along the narrow road. John saw the glint of buttons, the familiar hat pulled down against the breeze off the sea. One of the Coastguard.

He touched his hat, smiled at the two figures in the doorway and called, 'Did you hear the excitement over yonder at Falmouth? Won't do your trade no good though – there's a King's ship in Carrick Roads so the press are bound to be abroad tonight!' He cantered away, unmoved by the misfortunes of others.

Unis ran out after him, in her apron, something she would never normally do.

'What *ship*, Ned?'

He twisted round in the saddle. 'Frigate! The *Zest*!'

The one-legged ex-soldier put his arm round her shoulders and guided her back into the parlour.

'I know what you were thinking, Unis love, but . . .'

She pulled herself away and stood motionless in the centre of the room, her fingers clasped as if she were in prayer.

'John, remember that letter we had? *Zest*? She be one of Sir Richard's ships!'

She stared around. 'Must change the bed. John, you fetch some of the new bread, tell Annie to keep an eye on young Kate!'

He protested, but to no avail.

She stared past him. 'Through *that door*, my man is going to come this day! As God is my witness, I just knows it!' There were tears too, but she was more excited than anxious.

They had two customers, carpenters working on the little church where Unis and John Allday had been wed.

It would be dark early. He watched his sister worriedly. *Follow the drum, wear the King's coat*, they said. But nobody ever told you about this part of it.

Unis walked into the parlour, her eyes very bright.

'He's coming, John. Like I said. Like he promised.'

Then he heard it for the first time, faint but familiar above the soft moan of wind around the eaves. The steady clip-clop of Bryan Ferguson's pony and trap.

She said quietly, 'Don't go, John. You're part of it.'

There were muffled voices and she whispered, 'Dear God, let it be him!'

The door opened slowly, perhaps even nervously.

And then she was in his powerful grip, her face

368

nuzzling his fine blue jacket with the Bolitho buttons on it. 'Oh, dear John, it's been so long! I've missed you so!'

Her brother, watching, offered, 'No need to look surprised, John. We just heard that the *Zest* was in port!'

Allday stared around, barely able to believe he was here.

'Yes. We was aboard her. Young Captain Adam's in command.' He held her gently as if she might break. 'I've thought so often of this minute.' He thought, too, of the big grey house where he had left Sir Richard with his lady. He must have written to her about his son. That had been almost the worst part.

She had looked at him very calmly and had said, 'He has not really gone, you know. Think of that sometimes.'

And now he was here. He stiffened as the girl Unis had hired to help her came in, with a baby in her arms. He knew by instinct that it was his daughter, although it could have been anyone's. He would not tell Unis about his lost son. Not yet. This was their moment alone.

He took the child carefully. 'She's a mite small.'

Unis said softly, 'The doctor says it's unlikely I'll carry another, John. I know a son might have pleased you better.'

He pressed the child against his body and tried not to relive the scene on that dreadful September morning. Friends and enemies alike, helping and consoling each other when the fighting had stopped and the flag had come down through the smoke.

He replied quietly, 'She's *our Kate*. She'll do me fine.' He hesitated. 'A son can break your heart.'

Unis glanced at her brother but he shook his head. It would keep.

She asked, 'Have you brought somebody with you, John Allday? Left him outside in the cold? What will people think?'

The door opened and Lieutenant George Avery ducked under the low beams.

'A room for a few days, Mrs Allday? I'd be obliged.' He looked around, remembering when they had left here. 'I thought it fairer to leave Sir Richard to enjoy his homecoming.' He was smiling, but she noticed that it did not reach his tawny eyes.

It was a strange feeling. Because of the letters he had written for her man, she seemed to know him well.

Avery was saying, 'Long walks, good food, a chance to think before the next time . . .'

Satisfied, Allday said, 'So you're staying with the *little crew* after all?'

Avery said, 'Was there ever any choice?' He looked around the parlour again, slowly allowing himself to accept the peace and welcome of the place. The child, almost lost in Allday's arms. He would never forget that morning either. Allday carrying his dead son so tenderly across the littered, bloodied deck where so many had fallen; Allday quite alone for those last moments before he lowered his son into the sea alongside and watched him drift away.

Unis exclaimed. 'Drinks for everybody! Now, Mr Avery, what would please you best?'

Like a reply they heard Ferguson's trap clatter away. He had been waiting, just in case.

Richard Bolitho sat by the great fire and held his hands towards the blazing logs.

'When I saw the carriage, Kate . . .' He held out one hand and touched her as she came to him with goblets of brandy. 'I could scarcely believe it.'

She nestled down beside him. 'A toast to my admiral! An admiral of England!'

He stroked her hair, her neck where he had seen the pendant. How could she have known? Really known?

So many memories, to share with her when they walked again. Tyacke's moving farewell when *Indomitable* had entered Halifax with her two American prizes, where repairs, some urgent, would be necessary. Bolitho had clasped his hand for the last time when his flag had been shifted to *Zest*.

Tyacke had said, 'When you need me, Sir Richard, just say the word.'

Together they had looked at the battered prizes, already swarming with men, and Bolitho had said, 'It might be over soon. Once and for all.'

Tyacke had smiled. 'Then I shall return to Africa. I liked it there.'

The long voyage home, soon to be summoned to the Admiralty. He could even find an ironic amusement in that. *Again*.

And Adam's grave pleasure when the guns had thundered out in salute to his new command, and to the man whose flag flew proudly from the mainmast truck.

The formality had been as unexpected as it was moving, after all that had happened. The guns had said it all. Their welcome home to Falmouth's most famous son.

Bolitho looked up at her as she said, 'Bring your drink. I have something to show you.'

Hand in hand they climbed the staircase, past each watching portrait and then to their room.

It was already very dark outside, and Bolitho heard an early fox barking harshly.

She had told him about Roxby. He would ride over and see him, but not yet.

Catherine had covered the portrait with a silk shawl. She smiled, but her eyes hinted at uncertainty.

'Ready?'

It was not as he had expected, or was it? Not in one of her fine shot-silk gowns or riding-habit. She was bare-footed, her hair loose to the wind, wearing the same sailor's shirt and breeches she had worn aboard the *Golden Plover* when it had been smashed on the reef and they had suffered the privations of an open boat until, in all the limitless miles of sea, James Tyacke had found them.

She was watching him anxiously. 'It is the real me. When we were so close, when we needed each other as never before.'

He took her in his arms and faced her towards the cheval-glass.

'I shall never forget, Kate.' He felt her tremble as she watched his hands in the glass, caressing her, undressing her like a stranger, all else forgotten.

She whispered, 'I love you so . . .' The rest was lost as he came to her.

Out in the darkness on the crumbling cliff path, a sleeping gull was suddenly awakened.

But on the wind, it could have been mistaken for a girl's last cry.

THE POWER OF READING

Visit the Random House website and get connected with information on all our books and authors

EXTRACTS from our recently published books and selected backlist titles

COMPETITIONS AND PRIZE DRAWS Win signed books, audiobooks and more

AUTHOR EVENTS Find out which of our authors are on tour and where you can meet them

LATEST NEWS on bestsellers, awards and new publications

MINISITES with exclusive special features dedicated to our authors and their titles

READING GROUPS Reading guides, special features and all the information you need for your reading group

LISTEN to extracts from the latest audiobook publications

WATCH video clips of interviews and readings with our authors

RANDOM HOUSE INFORMATION including advice for writers, job vacancies and all your general queries answered

Come home to Random House

www.randomhouse.co.uk